To Josh
a spectacular
night in Pocatello

Wil Peterson

4·3·15

WILL

PETERSON

CRAWL

ON YOUR BELLY

LIKE A MAN

A Novel of the Modern West

Walrus & Carpenter Books

Pocatello, Idaho

Fiction: Idaho. Falconry. Railroads. Indians. Rivers.
Wildlife. The Occult.

Thanks to Idaho magazine for printing an excerpt.
This book is printed on acid-free paper.

ISBN: 978-1-4675-3503-8

First Edition

Walrus & Carpenter Books
251 North Main
Pocatello, Idaho 83204
Tel: 208-233-0821

In Memoriam

Myrtle Lucille Jensen, RN

And

Willard Marvin Peterson, MD

Somnia vanescumt.
Durat amor.

ONE

In the middle of the night the wind came. Found an angle in the eaves. Commenced to cry like an old steam engine train. Whooooo! Cried like it carried the souls of the dead! Big trees creaked. Kyrie stood a'block, head tucked, one foot up. I admired that discipline. Returned to the sleeping bag. Somebody pounded at the door.

Open the door, Errol!

Who's there!

It's me! Open the damned door!

I did. Billy stood there like when he got back from Nam. But his face was sliced and bleeding now. Wore a checkered bandanna over his head to cover the fact the back of it wasn't there anymore. Held out his hands.

Help me, Errol!

I woke in the empty house. Listened to the wind. It shook the house and trees farther along the street. What had he wanted? I followed the wind across the city and into the desert. Little birds spoke. When I woke again the sun was up. Cars passed. Kyrie flew to the window casement. Cried out.

You'll hunt, sweetheart.

I filled her bathing tray. Carried the papers stained with

chalk to the alley. It had rained. The wind had torn leaves from the trees. Strewn them down the alley. Blossoms and branches. The smell was hot of decay. A drifter approached, bush hat pulled low.

Got a dollar, Bro?

All I have is a card.

That'll work!

It would!

I went inside. Kyrie descended to the bathing tray. Ducked her head, fluffed her wings under the water. Fanned so that water sparkled in the window light. Strutted regally fanning. I loaded the truck. She preened. Turned her head to comb the scapulars. Raised them in sequence to observe their emplacement.

Daylight was burning.

I got the wing out of the cooler. Stripped of feathers so you saw the three finger bones. Held it so she'd step to the glove. She stretched. Cried out. Rowed the air to establish she'd prefer to fly.

You'll fly, sweetheart. Step up now.

She looked around like there were more important things. Hopped diffidently to the glove. Tried to tear the wing from me. I slipped the jesses through her cuffs. Looped the ends around the little finger of the glove. Got the hood Billy found in Pakistan out of my side pocket. Stroked her chest with it. She liked that. Dipped her head to look. I slipped it over so only her beak showed. Tied the drawstring using my teeth. Leashed her to the block using the ten thousand year old Falconer's Knot. Held it a'palm. Folded it between thumb and middle finger.

Knots weren't hard if you memorized the steps. But direction was a function. I'd make what I thought were the right tropes only to see it fall apart. Like when Ginny tried to teach me the Eskimo Roll where the Boise runs past the towers of the University. Tipped the gunwale. I'd get midway. Try to return the way I'd come.

Jesus, Errol! If you was a pup I'd drown you!

It slip knotted. I lowered her so her battle daggers touched the block. Blind she had no further responsibilities. The light lit her breast flecked gold and iron.

I drove to my ex's on the rim rock. Southwest Tudor. Steep gabled roofs with low stucco walls. For two fifty you got the tower between garage and front door. Streets named Prairie Sage and Wildflower. Robbie came out wearing a Capitol High jersey that showed his sculpted shoulders. Stood on one leg with arms crossed.

How you doing, Dad.

Headed east. What're you doing?

Filling applications.

Any bites?

Couple of junior colleges. But the guys tell me that come game time there's nobody in the stands. Not like Borah and Capitol on Friday night.

What about walking on at Boise State?

Quarterbacking? I don't know. At the snap the dudes trying to hurt you get bigger as your friends start running away!

He folded his hands behind his neck. Stretched his back.

I'd like more being hitter.

You could do that.

Lot of work.

I looked away.

Sorry I can't help you more.

Don't worry about it, Dad. You going to spend some time with the old folks?

If I can't get out of it.

Do it for me. Tell them I'm thinking of them.

I will. So who you picking this year? Think LA will get it done?

He grimaced.

The more I'm around basketball the more I think you need guys that'll get in the other guy's pocket. Get there quick and stay there.

Like you.

I had a case of slow from time to time. But San Antonio's got that. And Duncan. Seven feet tall with the upper body of a swimmer. Pulling back water. Pulling down rebounds.

I said, If he hadn't developed a fear of sharks he'd be waiting tables somewhere!

The way it works sometimes.

I looked at the hills above the roofs.

I love you, son. Give my love to Clancy. Tell him I'll call when I get settled.

I will.

I gave him a hug. Turned to go.

Remember, Dad. We rattle before we strike!

That was his great grandfather's line.

TWO

Boise, Idaho in my rear view mirror. The brass bells jingle jangled. Cast off-pitch so you heard them in the wild. Billy got them in Pakistan. Made a sweet music but I didn't use them anymore.

Cloud shadows slipped across Danskin Ridge. Across the desert the Owyhees snowcapped. At Elmore County Line the range all cheat grass or black. Crisscrossed with two tracks. A huge wind devil rose and whirled across Mountain Home Airbase. Airmen looked out after the flight from Iraq.

Oh my Lord! They have returned us there!

Then blister ridges. Feedlots. Another Scenic Detraction: Shoshone Falls. I crossed the canyon at Hansen Bridge. Steel span four hundred feet above the river. Farm trucks made the girders rattle. Far below the Snake divided around a forty foot pillar. The ever running river. At distance and with wind hiding the roar it looked peaceful. I glassed it. Saw the violence. River right made a hole and standing wave fifteen feet high. Left was a curved ledge with reversal. Rushed in huge rockers that turned river right into a whirlpool.

Snake Eyes.

I drove on. Mountains snowcapped on both sides. At American Falls cut back along the Reservoir. White birds bobbed up and down as waves rolled in. White water raged below the Dam. The fishing falls that Western Power ruined when they rebuilt it. Billy saw what had been done. Grew up fishing from those rocks. Drank and talked. How you'd blow that spillway. White caps on the river. Two big boats with hooks out. I wondered how the wind was on the Wapi. Would find out.

Drove toward Big Volcano. I'd flown Kyrie from the rim.

She'd just got adult feathers. Went after harriers she saw working the brush.

I turned west on Not Very Pleasant Road. A vast naked landscape for miles in all directions. Wheeled sprinklers spurted jets of water. Mansions on hilltops. They'd plowed to the asphalt! If you stopped to take a leak? You risked ignition! At the labor camp a dark woman walked to the laundry line. Clothes writhed in the wind. A little boy kicked a soccer ball. At the crossroad I glanced at the Mennonite Cemetery. Rolled up the flank of an old volcano. Wapi Volcano in the distance with her dark lava fields.

There you are, sweetheart.

No fences now. Fire general. Black skeletons of sagebrush. Cheat grass. Skeleton weed. The land skinned but life remained. Horned larks flicked white secondaries. A harrier used a blister ridge as a blind. As the truck crossed it five sage grouse stood on their tails.

Whump! Whump!

Rose like helicopters level to the rock. Shifted to tall gears and hasted away. Flying boxcars! Hooded Kyrie ruffled her shoulders.

Think you're ready, Kyrie?

Wasn't built to kill sage grouse but knew she could. They said too sage grouse didn't fly far. But south of Howe one autumn Schindler watched a flight come like a freight train. Glassed them to Diamond Peak.

The road slanted up a shield volcano. I got out. The wind cold and sweet. Glassed the lava flow. In the distance Craters of the Moon showed green. I let the truck roll to the edge of the flow where a stand of sagebrush held lee of it. Birds in there. When they burned off a country the isolated stands were like holes in a river after the water's been taken.

I crossed between the pillars of Creon's Flow. Saw to the west what Bureau of Livestock Management accomplished. Miles of crested wheat grass. Another blind. I returned to King's Bowl. Broken glass and shell casings glittered at the firepits. Followed the Rift with my eyes as it snaked toward South Grotto.

A cave at South Grotto led to nowhere because its depth exceeded the rope of whoever tried it. Billy had. When he got back from Nam was always out there. Caves general. A lot nobody knew about. The people who found them died. A lot nobody'd ever find. Billy with the cigarette at his lips, the glitter of rope and carabineers over his shoulder. Said when you descended into the upper chamber you heard a deep sighing. As if the earth were breathing.

I put on the coat. Pulled the cage onto the tailgate. The pigeons pressed to the back. Did everything by instinct and well. When the guitarist Romero was in Franco's care a man whispered he should get to the back. Did. Lescanza didn't. Wasn't seen again.

I switched on the telemeter. Checked the signal. Thirty years since I saw him in Twin Falls. Didn't talk about Franco. How America, France and England gave Hitler a free hand. Got the unions under control after all. The confidence it gave the German boys. Flying bombers against undefended towns.

I clipped the transmitter to Kyrie's deck feathers. Too bad there were no pigeons in the Big Desert. Mourning doves nested in the lava and when you surprised them they rose with deck feathers straight down. I'd missed them when we drove in. Wondered how the falcons fared with them. Would have to be very good. Nothing maneuvered like a mourning dove.

I put the unseeled pigeon in my game pocket. Pigeons might be in the cliff at King's Bowl. I could confirm that if I had daylight. No lack in the old buildings of Boise, Twin Falls and Pocatello. I'd seen them in the cliffs at Twin Falls. Impossible to fly a trained bird there. The Snake River Canyon at Twin was the Big Divide as far as a man and a bird were concerned. But if there were terrain for a Peregrine it was the Middle Snake.

Kyrie stepped to the glove. I'd seen Shoshone Falls at flow. Mist jetted where Chinese placered fine gold. Cowboys stood on the rim. Used them for target practice.

I drew the braces with my teeth. Slipped the hood. Her eyes flared. Flashed wings like hammered steel. The sun lit the pillars where the lava had run hissing with fire. Froze jagged and on edge. Impassable. She nipped at the glove. Hungry for the sky. If she went for lava I'd have no recourse. I slipped the jesses. She lifted wrists high. Leapt with deep strokes into the wind.

Spread them. Banked. Looked at me as she went.

On a ledge she looked like a weightlifter with her thin yellow feet and obsidian hooks. Now in the sky was long and thin with sword-like wings. Long deck feathers faired. Like a silver cross. Easy to believe she entered from the sun.

I walked with the pigeon struggling in the game pocket. The wind hissed in the sagebrush.

Hoo! Hoo! Hawk!

Tossed the pigeon. She dropped tail flaps, set wings in V to right herself. Flew downwind. I heard Kyrie's descent out of the clouds at two hundred miles an hour. Streaking like a knife. The splash of feathers as she swung up. But the pigeon rose. Rowed for sky. Kyrie pursued, wings scything so the tips touched. I ran for the telemeter.

Clouds turned blood red. She wasn't in the sky. Sulked along a ridge. I got the seeled pigeon in pocket. Walked up the road. Tossed it. Blind it fluttered and dropped. Kyrie came low over the brush. Her eyes striking fire.

THREE

She turned it on its back. Pinned the wings with her talons. Looked at me with hooked beak down-crusted. The harsh, dark light gone from her eyes. Lustrous now. The anxiety, the anger of the lost kill gone. Just the pleasure of eating. Stiffening her legs to tear strips of muscle. Even her wings--spread to hide the kill-- glowed with it. I sat against a sagebrush with my legs stuck out.

Wapi Volcano lit up in a blaze of red light as the sun went behind Hyndman. I slid on my knees. Got the glove under her. She nipped. I slipped my finger under the sternum. Brought out the heart. She ate it greedily as we walked to the truck, blood splashing her breast.

Heart Eater. Bitch of the World.

I slipped the jesses around the tail gate hinge. Walked with a beer onto the ramp. The west wall of King's Bowl now in shadow. I remembered the falcon that swept into the sky. Showed barred breast, white wings. Hectored me. When I went back ATV's had scarred the rim. Shell casings. King's Bowl: out of the wind, the afternoon sun--looked like a fine place to raise a family.

Now the wind brought evening songs. Slim birds stood atop the lava cones. Throats rippled. The dark came on. The night creatures came out. Their hunger palpable! Clouds turned pale on dark. Then dark against dark. The headlights lit up kangaroo rats skittering. A great horned owl.

It was alright Kyrie missed. We had the whole summer. You had to think what it took to strike at that speed.

Headlights stroked up. Steel walled trailers rattled past. The phosphate factories blazed with lights. Smokestacks licked the night with fire.

Slow For Fog.

FRC was an arc furnace operation that bled the Periodic Table into the wind. Sinklot used sulphuric acid. Dilute sulfuric acid scented the cab with the sting of good paying jobs. Black tanker cars lined the siding. We passed three Superfund Sites into town. The mountain ridge you saw from the desert now rhymed gabled old houses, the French Renaissance High School, the Valentine Building--white enameled with Corinthian pillars. Then we were south of town. A diesel with triadic lights blared. We turned up Mink Creek. Apple trees blossomed whitely. At the National Forest Boundary-Land of Many Abuses--I turned up a side canyon into aspen. They hadn't brought the cows in. I lay on my back in the camper. Swainson's thrushes sang. Their tin whistles slipped the note up with back steps quickening to crescendo. Poor wills piped to each other like signal lights flashing.

I was swimming Redfish Lake. Strange! Because Redfish Lake was icy and deep and I was afraid of it. Huge boulders fell from the cliffs. I swam past them. A huge figure rose out of the water. A giant river otter with red eyes, water streaming down her shoulders. She could drown me. I put up my fists but she took them in her mouth. Her teeth hooked. I couldn't pull away. But she looked at me with such tenderness my fear turned to love.

I woke. Cursed my fear. But her compassion opened a vein in me. The train of my losses followed. I could suffer it no more. Dropped my heels to the road. It is ludicrous to relate: as I stood urinating and looking at the stars tears streamed down my face.

FOUR

I sat on the tailgate. Looked at mountains. Snow lee of the ridges where wind swept. Doug fir with upward pointing branches protected it. Big game bedded. The ravines cut by snow. Mink Creek ran north. The alder and birch hadn't leafed. Birds sang in the tops. Mallards flew. Kyrie cocked her head at crazy angles. Thought about them. Preened meticulously. P-51 pilots sanded the decals off the fuselages.

The call of a train came up the canyon like a harmonica note. Modulated by alternating ridges and ravines. A triple header pulling a mile of red double stacks came out of the Gap. Box cars waited on the high iron. Eighteen terra cotta lions on the Yellowstone Hotel heralded Main Street. Pigeons flew from overhanging cornices. Showed white when they rose; dark when they veered away. I draped my forearms over the wheel.

This might work, Kyrie.

Passed a narrow old building with tattered awning: Michael Angelo's Books. Turned into the parking lot by the Meat Market. Pretty girl at the front desk wore a low cut blouse. Had lace filigree tattooed across the top of her breasts. Sold me a three month membership. In the locker room two silverbacks talked in the hot tub.

Yes. I had a nice little fort.

Where was that?

Khe Sanh. You might have heard about it. I cleared the jungle out a hundred yards in all directions. Strung concertina wire eight feet high at fifty. Buried dynamite packs rigged to trip wire in the event Charlie paid a visit. Positioned M-2's at the four corners of the camp. It was nice fort. It was home.

What's an M-2 fire?

Fifty caliber. The slug weighs 668 grains delivered at three thousand feet per second. You can reach out and touch someone. Or dismantle cinder block houses. Like they have in Iraq.

The old soldier swirled the water languidly with his claw.

The thing about an M-2 is you can set it to single shot. The armature has a screw adjustment for sighting. Choose a target a half mile away. Say the window of a house. The people in there don't know you're in the vicinity. Use the single shot until the slug hits the window. Switch to automatic. Burn the clip. The inside of that house then becomes very uncomfortable for whomever might be in there. Yes. The M-2 is an excellent weapon. Well I've had enough.

A tall, gaunt man with white, close cropped hair and stooped shoulders grabbed the hand rail.

Billy and Dad had that military stoop. I walked with my head high and shoulders back. Had never had to shoot at anybody nor had anybody shot at me. Billy handled an M-2. We were in the Oasis shooting pool. He drilled a solid into the corner. Drew the cue ball back to the center of the table.

Kind of a rush you know. Flying a hundred miles an hour over the trees. Village ahead. We're sending rockets with love. Charlie running in all directions. Captain yelling, Fire! Damn it! Fire! I did. Burned a clip. Saw the figures running around in their black pajamas were mostly women.

You told them you wouldn't do that anymore, Billy.

I did, Errol. But sometimes it doesn't help that much.

Stung the eight ball into the corner.

Rack them.

I shaved. Decided I'd stroll. The ridge above Mink Creek slanted dark blue at the end of the street. Elms stood starkly. The Trinity Church held its cross to the sky. Billy's funeral there. Door locked. Getting hot so I walked. Heard clanking and beeping. When I got to Center Street it wasn't there. A 3200 Cat rocking on its crawler clawed at a huge boulder. The operator had both hands at the controls. Dropped the claw. Tipped the boulder back an inch and the half ton claw slipped. Sparks flew. The boulder rolled back to where the Flood left it ten thousand years ago.

Straw boss chewing on a toothpick. Thinking, Every hour like this I'm a thousand dollars over.

And, Where can I get a guy to work this thing?

And, Should I call the lawyer? Call him now!

The guys leaning on their shovels thinking it too. The operator threw up his hands.

Fuck it!

Lit a cigarette with hands shaking. I looked at the new

pickups at the barricade. 6-B plates. Even in Idaho Falls they should've known better. I didn't want to watch another man's troubles. Walked. The boulders like whales rising. The Victorian buildings looked on vacantly. A freight screeched as it dragged a locked brake over Center Street.

Michael Angelo's opened at eleven. The art deco clock in front of Molinelli's said 9:30. I went into Bernardo's Coffee Shop. He sat behind the counter. Held his thick glasses up in order to read the paperback at his nose.

What can I get you?

Double mocha.

I didn't think he remembered me but he glanced sidelong as he ground the beans.

I see they let Claude Dallas out.

Really.

The movie will be out soon. Don't you think? The sun sets over the West. The boy looks up at his father.

Tell me again, Daddy! How Uncle Claude stood up to the Federal Agents and defended the states rights of Americans everywhere!

Long shot: cowboy riding the range. Overdub: Charlton Heston. The Legend of Claude Dallas. Violins play The Yellow Rose of Texas slow and dirge-like. Camera zoom: the little boy looking up at his father.

Can I have a gun now too, Daddy?

The father puts his hand on his son's shoulder.

Yes, son. It's time.

Bernardo grinned happily. Slid the steaming mocha across the counter.

You like it?

It's a winner, Bernardo.

The last scene? Father and son creep through the woods. Snow on the ground. You see the deer through the trees. Tail twitching nervously. The boy aims. You see the deer through the scope. Hear the beating heart. Boom! The deer falls! Camera zooms in! Blood seeps into the snow. Credits. What d'you think?

Copyright it.

I scanned the paper. Bush with his smirk and airman's

jacket. Hard Work Ahead In Iraq.

Went into the street.

My first job was in Nevada. Talked to ranchers. Asked them to stop using 10-80. Had private landing strips. Coyotes, hawks hung from barbed wire. 10-80 was rough. Cowboys fed it to horses. Gave it time to work. Shot her. Cut her up. Scattered the body parts.10-80 didn't break down! Eagles, hawks that fed on the coyote died too. When the meat was so rancid nothing'd eat it they gave it to the groundwater!

I monitored AUM's in the Humboldt. Robbie and Clancy got death threats on the school bus. Kind of people they were. Big cowboy backed me down. Wide, floppy hat. Flowery shirt. Sprayed on levis. High heels.

Done shot five hundred hawks in my career!

What kind?

Don't matter. Hawks. Eagles. You can see 'em draped on my fence line if you have a mind!

I do.

We got the 10-80 stopped. In Idaho started seeing Prairie falcons in the Pahsimeroi.

Past the neon Greyhound the path followed a suite of parks. At Trapper Park a concrete stream wound among Flood boulders. Cast-bronze crawfish, salamanders, ducks. Cast-bronze moose, bear and coyote prints. Above the stick dam a beaver's tail slapped. An otter raised her head.

I thought it wonderful. But it brought to mind a story an old guy told me.

He farmed the Arkansas Basin above Marsh Creek. Where some Arkansans wandered off the trail in 1846. Like farmers going back to 1607 augmented his income by trapping. Was working his way up the creek. Saw an otter prowling a beaver pond. So mad she didn't see him or care. He guessed the beaver drowned her pups. She dove. Came up fighting.

They were evenly matched. Fought to a depth of ferocity he'd not thought possible. Fought on land and in water. Would retire to gather breath but soon get back to it. In the afternoon she gave it up. Lay down. By the way she looked at him he knew she was dying. Never trapped again.

FIVE

The river ran yellow brown from feedlots. Broke down banks. Entered the concrete channel in a standing wave. Upstream goldfinches flitted. Fox sparrows whistled.

Wheet! Wheet! Chik-chik-chik! Chee-qu'k!

I returned past old houses with gabled roofs, fish scale facades. A starling sang from a power line. Squealing skrakes that varied in pitch and length. Threw in a clanging bell from time to time. Railroad town starling all the way. I got back on Main. Passed tattoo parlors, beauty salons, antique stores. Manikins wearing low cut gowns stared out. A foot and a half section of rail held the door to Michael Angelo's open. A dusty fig tree yearned for the window. Mickey Angel--black hair slicked back, thick glasses, hooked nose--read with his boots up.

Hard at it, Crow?

He turned crankily. Didn't like to be called Crow. Nor distracted when reading. I was backlit. Squatted at his elbow. Put out my hand.

How you doing, Mickey Angel?

He gave me that crooked grin.

Errol! How you doing, old man!

Kicking.

And the kids?

I rapped the corner of my skull.

Doing alright.

Good deal.

He put his hands behind his head.

Thought about you the other day. Don't know why. Time of year maybe. The desert bivouac we said we were going to do. How you doing?

Fish and Game and I parted ways.

Shoot.

Don't give it a thought.

I wondered how you'd do in Boise. Friend of mine did time there. Said you'd be at a party talking to somebody but they'd be looking over your shoulder for somebody more important!

The Art Department here was like that.

Painters are like that, Errol. Looking for perspective.

Right. That dickhead Rojek had everybody paranoid. Who was your friend?

Lionel.

And Lionel was always funny! Remember the story he told that night up Inman? Thought I was going to die! He and his wife were at her office party. She ragging that he was flirting with a coworker?

I don't.

You do. Wouldn't give it up all the way up the elevator and back to the apartment? He was brushing his teeth when he saw her in the mirror with the nickel plated '38. Had to utter those immortal words?

Mickey Angel grinned.

You don't have the guts to use that!

Oh my Lord! Lionel could twist his face like a Tibetan demon. Or drop his jaw and turn white as a sheet. Mickey Angel laughed.

Lucky he didn't pack more heat.

Didn't almost make it as it was. Remember? He was in the Meat Wagon. Blacking out? The EMT was standing on the oxygen! Hah! The ER doctor looked eighteen. Nervous. The big, black nurse berating him because he mislaid the scalpel!

What I remember is drifting off to sleep. Heard this low, guttural growl.

I remembered. I was sinking into a pit. Dark, hooded men drew a bearskin robe over the top of it. Mickey Angel laughed.

It was the growl that woke me. But when you screamed bloody murder? Man! That got everybody clawing for the exits!

I shook my head.

Never had that dream again.

Too bad.

Any of those guys around?

Schindler. And Pavi. But Cliff moved on. Like you. And Billy of course. Never got over that. Guess you haven't.

Billy. Eyes red with rage. Knew I wouldn't fight. Nor forgive. Hated me more for that. Fighting wasn't a big deal to guys like him. Waded in with tails wagging.

Where's Lionel?

Baja. Should be drifting back any day.

I looked at my hands.

Got a favor to ask, Mickey Angel.

What's that.

I need a place to keep my bird. You got that loft back there.

It's pretty cluttered.

I'll clean it up.

How long?

Maybe a month. 'Til I get settled.

He put his hands behind his head.

You got it.

He had parking on the alley. I backed the truck in. Got Kyrie on the glove. Mickey Angel stared at her. It was unfair. He loved animals more than I. Bivouacked in the jungle of Costa Rica to watch bats catch fish with their hands. They saw the fish by echolocation. Nobody knew how they adjusted to the diffraction.

Grab the furniture would you, Mickey Angel?

He did. We climbed the rickety stairs. The loft was cluttered with spinner racks, dismantled bikes, skis. When I backed her hallux to the block she screamed. Fanned. With her plumed hood looked evil.

She don't look too happy.

She'll abide.

The window opened to the alley. Was translucent with spider webs. Swung outward so she would have cool night air. We went back between the wall and stall shelves. Books stacked to the ceiling. I saw him cart them in. His powerful shoulders, short spindly legs. The race he came from. Short, wiry men that rowed relentlessly with legs folded. Tossed me a key. I leaned against a shelf.

I was hoping I could do something about those pigeons.

I like pigeons.

I do too, Mickey Angel. But it would help me out. If I could trap a couple from time to time.

He closed his eyes.

Check it every morning.

He picked up his book. I went out to the truck. Heard

meadowlark. Saw starling with throat feathers puffed. His mate flew to him with a stick in her beak. Then to a rafter of the Trinity Church. I walked over. The male flew to the roof. Stropped his beak. Churred unhappily. I shook my head. It was her mistake not mine.

SIX

I rented a mailbox at the Renaissance Revival Post Office. Crossed the street to the cartoon Molly painted on plaster. Steam engine at Pocatello Junction. Indians on painted horses. Spearing salmon. Freighters with oxen headed to Montana. Wooly mammoths and saber toothed cats. The plaster flaked from the brick. I guessed it wasn't worth saving. Drove past Felony Flats. Stumble bums in the doorways smoking cigarettes. A young woman wearing too much makeup stared with eyes full of tears into the street.

Put yourself into the gentle arms of the State.

The right-hand lane swung over the tracks. I slowed at the top to look at Big Volcano. The Navy proved sixteen inch guns at it in 1944. Said it looked like Iwo Shima. I bought plywood and polyurethane sheeting. On the way back herring gulls swarmed the waste area between the Oregon and Montana lines. Keened and made a racket. It was tidal flat to them except there were no waves coming in. I glassed the gray streaked juveniles as they cavorted in the wind. Didn't get adult plumage until the third year so the adults didn't drive them away.

I fixed up Kyrie's loft. Walked down Main. It turned cold. Powerfully turning cumulus clouds came over Kinport. Debris flew down the cross streets. I stepped into the telephone booth at Midley's. Took a deep breath.

Yes, Mother. I'll be over.

Drove past the golf courses. Golfers raced their golf carts.

I made money caddying for World War Two dudes. If play slowed they played seven card rummy. Told stories. I loved them. Guessed we needed a union. Wedge Lane accessed Spanish style duplexes with red tile roofs. Black Max beat his furry paws at the window. My mother put out her cigarette as she got up. Gave me that look indistinguishable between love and anguish that women can summon.

We've missed you so much!

I've missed you too, Mama.

Max flew about my feet, snuffling for air. Flopped on his back so I could scratch his belly. Squirmed and beat the air with his paws. Looked at me with eyes slightly mad with happiness.

Max! How you doing, Buddy!

He did a flip. Was on his feet rushing around the room. Grabbed a toy. Ran. Slipped under the coffee table where he taunted me with his shining, black eyes. I got on my belly. Tried to get it from him. He beat his paws on the carpet. Backed to the other side. I chased him. My mother complained.

Go see your father, Errol! He's waiting for you!

I turned. The old man stared at me. His head so big his frail shoulders hardly able to support it. Shuffled toward me. Halted. Big, brown eyes magnified by the glasses.

It's your son, Ben! Give him a hug!

I stepped toward him. Lifted my arm. It was a mistake.

It's your son, Ben! It's Errol! Give him a hug!

He recovered.

I know that, Honey. You got a cigarette?

He sat by the window. The photo on the wall showed a Navy Officer seated knees akimbo. Big guy with coffee black eyes, broad shoulders. Leaned toward the camera like he'd fight it if given half a chance. Other photos: Billy in full dress uniform with sad eyes. Grandpa in old age astride his paint Comanche. It was hot. The weight of the past heavy. Brocaded sofa and chairs. Carved oak armoire with cut crystal bowls. Mother got them in Butte. Clocks she inherited from her aunts ticked in odd, asynchrony. Dad sat straight with hands folded in his lap looking at nothing. Mama handed him a cigarette.

I said, I'll have one too.

You don't smoke.

Maybe I'll start.

Don't be funny.

Could we sit on the patio then?

It's too cold.

I'll get him a sweater.

Dad growled, the cigarette dangling from his lips.

I don't need a sweater.

I got water from the tap. It was good water but had the taste of furniture. Found the vodka. We went out on the patio. You saw lava cliffs through bare trees. The last golf carts of the day went by. Men in pastel clothes got out. Meticulously chose their weapons. Whacked the ball. Got back in the golf carts. Dad puffed at the cigarette. Glanced at me. A fox squirrel hopped onto the terra cotta planter. Stood on her hind legs looking with interest at the bird feeder. Mama came out.

Shoo! Get out of here!

The squirrel looked at her. Whipped her beautiful red tail. Mama opened the sliding glass door.

Squirrel, Max! Squirrel!

He rushed out barking. Chased the squirrel into the next yard. Pranced back proudly. I sipped the vodka.

Nice operation.

Dad nodded.

We got him on retainer.

On Chink's Peak shadows curled like vines up the ravines.

So you getting out, Dad?

Max and I do a tour around the block once a day.

You got to get out. You know what you told me. That the legs are the first to go with a fighter.

My fight is over.

Can't quit, Dad.

Don't tell me what I can't do.

I finished the drink. Mom went inside. He watched her go.

And it's been cold. The wind blowing and this and that.

He looked at me for the first time.

Where are you now?

Boise.

And your wife?

We divorced five years ago.

He puffed at the cigarette. The ash the length of it. He stroked the crusted skin of his temples. His hands seemed surprised by the change but his touch was so soft he hadn't broken it.

What are you doing now?

I'm with Fish and Game.

His hands were mottled but the fingertips soft. All he'd done with them was touch people. Set the left like a strut. Tapped middle knuckle with the index and ring finger of the right. Felt the resistance of flesh to steel. I watched him open a fat rancher's inner thigh in a stroke! Tied the femoral, sewed up, went out the door! Did the first open transfusion surgery in Northeast Montana. Was ready when they sent him to Okinawa. A Marine on the beach said he watched the Zekes slip through the flak.

A train came out of the yards pulling a mile of double stacks. The hogger leaned on the horn for Black Rock. The old man stroked his temple. The ash of his cigarette in a perfect curve. Mom came out.

Ben! Your cigarette!

He reached to cup it with his hand. The ash broke. Splashed. He brushed it to the carpet as she fussed.

Take your father for a walk, Errol! It would be good for both of you!

She got his blue overcoat. Helped him with it.

I'll get your hat.

I don't need a hat!

It's pretty cold, Dad.

He growled.

This would be a peach orchard in Montana.

Max saw the leash. Ran from antique chairs with lion feet to armoire with women's faces. Finally allowed himself to be captured. Lay on his back snuffling with a crazy look in his eyes. Mother handed me the leash.

I'll be back in an hour. Don't leave. I have to talk to you.

Take your time, Mama.

It was in fact an old apple orchard. Trees along the street in blossom. A dark cloud came over the mountain. Blossoms swirled and eddied in the wind. Dad turned up his collar. Still had the cigarette butt in his mouth. Hadn't shaved. His jowls grizzled, his mouth grim. Max lunged. I unleashed him.

Can't lose the dog!

I'll watch him like a hawk.

Max scampered over the trim lawns. Sniffed trees. Kicked up grass. As he pranced his feathery ears and tail danced.

You been following the Cubs, Dad?

He kept his eye on Max.

I saw them play the first game of the '38 Series. Dad and Charles came to visit and we went. They had runners at first and third. No outs. Crossetti made that double play at third. Yanks in four.

We arrived at Bannock Highway. The old man hunched. Cigarette butt in his teeth.

Are we going back now?

Let's just cross and go up the road. Maybe look at the old house.

The old house?

He looked back.

Then we'll go back?

I promise.

I leashed Max. Cars approaching from a quarter mile saw the old man. Slowed. Time slowed. I saw where deer came through the juniper. The wind was roughing up the highlands. Smelled sweet. Cars gunned engines. Dad looked back.

I've got to get back.

We just got started, Dad.

Things I have to do. Papers to take care of. When you have property there are always things you have to take care of.

The Montana farm?

He looked at me closely. Then away.

We're leaving any day. Got to have the papers ready. For when we get there.

We returned across Bannock Highway. Max scampered. Blossoms held by a leashed moon snaked ahead of us. I liked walking slow. Wished I'd known before.

What's that song, Dad? I'll Be Seeing You?

Lady Day.

He raised a withered hand. Sung it word for word at perfect pitch.

Nice, Dad.

We returned to the house and the interpreted past. Max

licked his paws under the coffee table. I leafed through a book on Corsairs. Gull wings in heavy seas. Wind whistled. The brass clock from the Montana House gonged. Went there every summer. Dad smoked that cigar. Zoomed the big DeSoto down and up the thousand ravines. Talked about the giants that lived those days. The traveling salesman that could drop a fly into a cuspidor across the street. The Sioux with broad shoulders and spindly legs that played with Sousa. Hit high C above C on a trumpet suspended by a string from the ceiling. Killed in one of those ravines. Dad swore the Sioux at a certain level of drunkenness and velocity veered from bridges. Or Sandeleki who played Legion Ball for Butte. The sound was louder when he connected and the ball went over faster than anything he'd seen. Sandeleki, whose blood ran out at Tarawa.

The DeSoto dove and swooped. I cried.

Let me out, Daddy!

I left more breakfasts along Highway 13 than Mother Theresa.

Clocks tolled. I looked at photos.

Look all you want, Errol.

Clancy and Robbie when they were little. I rubbed dust from the frame. Saw a sticker on the back of the armoire. My sister's name. Went through rooms. Everything tagged. Fern stand, piano, dining room table, chandelier. My ex's name. Had they gotten together or my sister decided ex parte? I poured a double. Sat on the patio. Chink's Peak dark. The glass door slid open.

You found it I see.

Yes. Thank you.

It's too cold out here! Come inside.

She put on Rachmaninoff's Third. The shine on the dining room table so high it reflected the chandelier. She sat in a high backed chair. Lit a cigarette. Rachmaninoff was good for the Snake Country. Got the distances right. Gave you the feeling not of places you'd never get to but the ache of knowing that. Mama had that.

I'm so glad you're back!

I am too, Mama.

She shook her head. Started to cry.

I just don't know how much more I can take!

I'm sorry.

And the boys? How are they?
They're fine.
I know we weren't there for you, Errol, but your father--
Let's not talk about it.
All right. We won't.
She turned the ash.
You haven't written me off have you, Errol?
I wouldn't do that.
But you seem so cold.
I don't mean to be.
It's when you married you seemed to abandon us!
I didn't mean to.
And when you divorced it wasn't like we abandoned you!
I know that.
I had to keep the lines open. You understand that.
I do.
We didn't do it to hurt you.
Let's not talk about it.
You haven't written me off then?
Did you hear me, Mama?
Don't be angry with me, Errol!
She started to cry again.
I just don't know how much more I can take!
What do you want me to do?
There was nothing anybody could ever do. He was a big, tough guy that made a lot of money. She'd wait up for me.
Her mother ruined him!
What did she mean?
Divorce him.
And then where would we be? I know your father! He'd drink himself to death just to spite us!
We'd be alright.
You don't know, Errol. What it takes!
She got her revenge. Sold the house. Now he walked at night. Lost. Stood staring out the window. She lit a cigarette.
I'm looking at assisted living. You could help with that.
I could.
I stood up. She gave me that tragic look.

You don't have to go so soon!

I have to check on Kyrie.

She whimpered.

It's like I've been trapped my whole life.

I'm sorry, Mama.

Stay awhile! We haven't talked about anything fun!

We've got time. I'll be around.

She looked at me with eyes brimming.

Where are you staying?

A bit of here and there.

You could stay here!

Clocks ticked in the rooms.

I can't sleep here, Mama. Chronophobia.

I'll turn them off!

I wrote Michael Angelo's number down.

Get in touch with me here. I love you. Don't worry.

She got up.

Come for dinner tomorrow. I'll make a casserole. You always loved that.

I'll call. I promise.

How long are you here?

I don't know. Few things I have to take care of.

I always loved you, Errol. And I took good care of you.

I know that, Mama.

Errol?

I looked back. She picked up the cigarette.

Don't get hooked up with no squaw? Can you do that for me?

I laughed. Outside wind whined in the power lines. I thought of my old man. The money he'd made. I'd spent a lot. His cronies at the Bannock Hotel. The tentative way they reached for the check. How my mother hated them! And where were they now? I saw the old people in the rest home. I was three when he took me there. They had the sunken eyes and wasted limbs of the dead. Reached out to me not with hunger but kindly. I ran. Had brought no blood to drip in their mouths.

SEVEN

Snowflakes danced in the headlights. I pulled a ski cap on. Crawled in the sleeping bag. Wind whistled. Cars strummed the cattle guard. Woke to birds singing in the snow. On the road to town cars slid. Fog poured through the Gap with reversal. The crest had an inward curve that was translucent. A train snaked out. Whoo! Whoo! People shoveled snow from cars. In Old Town pigeons kited. Fanned tail feathers. A snowdrift curved in front of Michael Angelo's. At the Meat Market Bush did his soft shoe. Buy that car! Take out that second mortgage! Let us do our job! Sophocles spit over his left shoulder. A silver-coiffed, muscular pretty boy explained Shock and Awe.

A beautiful operation! Just a textbook operation!

The lady newscaster getting wet as she interviewed him. I gave the weights an extra jolt. In the locker room big guys talking.

Thought you'd've died over in Nampa by now.

Derailment east of there. Whole system shut down.'Til they investigate anyway.

Why? It's Operator Error!

He was a sturdy guy with powerful shoulders and big belly. Went to the pool. The old ladies did water aerobics. Boom box rocked, You Ain't Nothing But A Hound Dog! Raised their hands. Shouted in unison. The railroader was in the steam room looking at his feet.

I said, So does snow affect the trains?

No. Trains are too heavy.

I thought steam engines carried sand.

Steam don't have the torque a diesel has. A steam engine could pull more freight but took longer to get rolling. Was a engine on the Pennsylvania Line that pulled two hundred coal cars at thirty five miles an hour. Even a diesel can't pull a train from a standing stop. Back them up to get the slack in. That's the banging you hear.

How much slack in a train?

With sliding sill six feet at a coupler. A hundred car train has six hundred feet.

What d'you call slack when it's compressed?

Slack in. Slack out.

He turned the cold water spigot.

A good hogger can feel the train behind him. If he don't? That's when you crack the whip. Boys at the back don't like that. Don't like that Big Time. That's why most hoggers are big guys. Don't have to be big to drive a train but you got to be able to handle yourself.

Why's that?

It's not as bad now because you don't have the caboose. In the old days the conductor could go right through the end wall. Wood stoves back there too. Lot of men hurt that way. Dad wasn't sorry to see the end of the caboose. The union screamed but he didn't say nothing. After a rough ride you'd climb down from the cab. See the crew coming down the track. You know?

He grabbed the cold water hose.

Wasn't all that funny. But you were talking about the weight of those trains. Was a guy a few years back that fell asleep on the track at the Black Cliffs.

Where's that?

Cheyenne Crossing. Railroaders have names for all the track. WP put up signs with numbers on them but we still use the old names. The Sand Track is where the old Sand Shop was. Ice Track where the Ice House was. They still call the siding at Center Street the Chippy Tracks. Where the whore house was. Those walls were torn down a hundred years ago.

It was a city block with a ten foot wall on 1st Avenue. The hard side because it was lee of the steam engines. Soot and cinders blackened the curtains. Girls in their shifts stood at the windows looking at the yards. Laudanum and whisky bottles dug out of privies the only evidence they existed. Vials of mercury to treat syphilis. Now mercury in Silver Creek. Rich guys from Sun Valley luring mercury-laced trout.

Or he might've been red lighted. But the train come by and took his legs off. Like that!

He snapped his fingers.

Yard man heard him screaming. We come running. Loaded him in the wheel man's truck and took him to Bannock Regional. He done fine. Well I don't know how good he done but he healed up. Signed the release papers. UP gave him fifty bucks and put him on a Greyhound.

Didn't bleed to death?

The weight and heat of those wheels sealed the arteries as it clove them.

Even in the steam room I felt the rumble of freight rolling through. Boom. Boom. A hundred tons hitting the Lander Street seam.

Another funny thing about track? The rail you see stacked along the Main Line? WP gets top dollar for it. Seems like there's nothing like railroad track to make razor blades. Train rolled steel. Tear up good track for cash. An old story. Like when the City Council took dime on the dollar earnest money for the Naval Ordnance Plant. The so-called company took the overhead cranes and lathes in the middle of the night and went their merry way.

I remembered the night Billy and I went in through a window. Biggest guns in the North America rifled there during World War Two. Didn't want sharp curves freighting eighty foot guns. Billy heard ghosts fell from the overhead rails. I slithered sixty feet above the floor with my arms wrapped around the girder. Billy traipsed with arms out like a demented angel.

I said, You seeing any game?

Killed a moose on the Green River Run last week.

Didn't hit the horn?

Horns don't do nothing. The bull sees you coming? Just puts his rack down. Lay on the horn? Make him madder. Gets bigger and bigger. You're thinking if he raises that rack he's coming through the window!

He pounded his fist.

Wham! Snapped his head clean off. Got up. Stood at the side of the track. But its head wasn't there no more. The neck gushing blood to the heart beat.

I thought it'd happen more in the fall.

No. Spring. Young males moving out. Establishing territory. Lying on the horn just makes them madder. Gets old.

Cars kill more don't you think?

Trains. Trains take out whole herds. Mulies. Elk. Prairie goats. If they cross in a line in front you might kill one or two. But if they're lying on the track? The train takes out the herd. Why you don't want to get flanked. Double the money. We killed a herd of elk last month on the Green River. Twenty below. The train come on them before they could get to their feet.

He splashed himself with cold water.

A buddy of mine was headed west past Lamb Weston. Come over the hill. Saw a quarter mile of track covered with the tan and white of prairie goats. It's February so all the females have twins inside. Count the twins? Five hundred goats on that track. You know? He's riding ten thousand tons at sixty miles an hour. Hit the horn. Leaned back. Body parts spraying the windshield.

He shook his head.

The stink of death all that summer. Bobby didn't know it though. Completed the run. Walked into the Station and tossed his keys. Didn't say a word and never come back. But it's easy to drive a train. You know?

EIGHT

The mountains were white. Rainspouts gushed into the alley. Drummers set up bass and snare drums in front of the High School. The brick façade a fine amplifier. Boom! Chick-a-boom! A raptor screeched from the parapet. Skreek! Skreek! Kyrie hectored me. Flew to the ledge. I fed her wing soaked in water. Climbed onto the roof. The trap held two pigeons. They'd spent a bad night. Tried to fly against the bars.

I got needle and thread from the possible bag. Slipped the black nylon over the smaller pigeon. It was arbitrary. Had no way of knowing which flew stronger. Gave her chloroform. Stitched the eyelids shut. The gate of the trap swung in but not out. They had to pull it to get out. Didn't get that. Easy to enter but hard to get out.

I walked down Main past tattoo parlors, antique stores, limited care facilities. A big fat girl wearing war paint and low cut blouse sauntered past. I hoped she was on her medication. Lefty's sign said, Bacon and Eggs, $3.99. I sat at the counter, my legs blocking the adjacent stool.

Coffee?

No thanks. I know what I want though. If you got that

special.

She clipped the order above the window. The cook stood at the flat grill. White paper hat, military tattoos. Sign on the wall. Undercooked Food Can Be Hazardous To Your Health. We Shoot Every Third Salesman: The Second Just Left. Lost? Keep Going: You're Making Good Time. In Case Of Nuclear Attack Hide Behind Toilet: Nobody's Hit There Yet. I liked a place I could read things. Went back to the counter. An old guy sat next to me.

What can I get you, George?

Glass of hot water.

You want a toothpick with that?

I looked at her through dark glasses. She'd gotten heavy but had nice shoulders and hips. Curled her hair and painted her lips. George tapped the spoon.

Why don't you just do your job?

How 'bout I kick your butt? That make you feel better?

Two homeboys by the window looked at menus.

You been out fishin'?

No. Been at the City of Rocks. Workin' at my sister's place.

What you doing down there?

Puttin' in head gates. It's all granite and sand so the run off carved holes around the head gates. We went in and poured new ones. Then had to spend a month in court talking to lawyers. County said we done it without a permit.

For the creek water?

We own the water. And not a drop leaves the property you can bet on it. No. They just went and made it a historic district. So even though we had the head gates in we had to go and act like we was sorry.

They didn't do nothin'?

'Course not.

Where's the land?

Fifteen hundred acres between City of Rocks and Castle Rocks. Grazing rights to BLM land on three sides. Lot of sagebrush. Used to be anyways.

He laughed jovially.

They wouldn't let us burn it you know? So we diverted the

creek and drowned it. How you kill sagebrush. You drown it. Used to be good deer hunting there. Counted twelve hundred a few years back. This year there was maybe thirty.

What happened to them?

Lions got 'em. Pinheads at ISU got a grant to pay the hunters not to hunt them. Wanted to do a study or some such thing. Now you got lions in every canyon and no deer. And don't be telling me coyotes don't kill deer. I seen 'em. I seen coyotes run deer so ragged they just fall.

He took a mouthful of hash browns.

But I talked to the Bishop. He's Minority Whip you know. He said ISU will be a tech school in a few years if he got anything to say about it.

The cook rang the bell. The waitress didn't jump. Leaned with her butt out reading the paper.

Order, Janelle! Damn it!

She got the plate languidly from the window. Slid it in front of me.

He don't want a bell. Point of fact? What he really wants is a cattle prod.

Her eyes warmed.

Ketchup or Tabasco?

Both please.

The guy doing the listening said, Well if you change your mind I'm going down to the Narrows tomorrow.

Oneida?

Might be the last year. Talking about putting in a dam. Would be a shame. The last free running section.

I hope they do! Would be good for the small mouth bass!

Deer got to have somewhere to cross.

Deer can swim a reservoir. I seen 'em.

I thought of the City of Rocks. The way Ginny's body looked up there. I didn't like to climb but liked to handle rope. The City had granite towers like drift stone. Vultures roosted in the alcoves. At dawn they turned slowly with wings outstretched to warm them in the sun. The unhurried way they did that made them look like priests in a dance. After awhile you looked again. They were circling in the sky.

Ginny loved the City because it was easy on her hands. It was soft and smooth yet gave purchase. If you got in trouble it had joints you could slip into. The rock itself had a sweet energy. She said when the sun warmed them and you were clinging full length? It was like laying full length against your lover.

NINE

The snow bank vanished into the gutter. Two pigeons on the lintel regarded me with red orange eyes. Their iridescent throats oscillated green to purple as they fidgeted to keep me in focus. Then the male thrust into the air. The female followed. Flew to the cornice of the Petersen Building. It was pressed tin. A bracket had fallen away. That's what they flew inside.

Mickey Angel--white plastic sacks like giant spider sacs at his feet--had books stacked on both sides. A cigar box filled with bookmarks set on the desk. I pulled up a chair.

Delta Airlines Boarding Pass: Salt Lake to Denver. Union Pacific Schedule, 1955. Santa Anita betting stub; Race Number 6, April, 1965.

Oh, the ladies in their pretty dresses! The shiny new cars with big fins!

Trojan condom still in wrapper. Bookmark, Golden Unicorn, Newport, Oregon. Pioneer League ticket stub: Idaho Falls Electric vs. Pocatello Braves, 1959.

Billy and I at Halliwell Park. Waiting for balls to come arcing through the klieg lights.

Newspaper clipping. Obituary. Tear stain? Facsimile of a Sal Maglie bubble gum card. Nordstrom's clothing tag: Size large, Color black. Lab work order: blood test. CAT scan report.

The relentless assault of death upon the imperative to read.

Brown Hotel, Denver, Colorado, note sheet. X-ray film of ghostly knee joint; arthritis. Exam question regarding Flaubert's A Simple Heart. Aspen leaf. Guidebook to the Tetons?

Ill disciplined Mickey Angel--scientist that he was--had destroyed context.

Itinerary of Etruscan tombs at Herculaneum; marginalia: 78

aureus, 2 dinars, 147 gold Roman. Egyptian tarot card: 8 of cups, kelches, coupes, copas: a woman praying by a date palm tree. Or looking for her contact lens? Small copper Cross.

All the dead. All the dreams. All the lost. I held the betting stub from Santa Anita. Saw the horses come around the bend with hooves pounding.

Mickey Angel spit shined covers. Wet dog-eared corners with a fingertip. Filed fore edges with an emery board. Blew puffs of dust. Stacked them so corners fit. That explained the books stacked in nonconformity in the aisles. Geology, literature, car repair one atop the other. Somebody rapped at the window. Patrick Miskowitz leaned in the doorway. Mr. Collision. Wolf blue eyes. Blonde pony tail. Cross beam across the chest. Red T shirt: Workers Of The World Unite. Smirked with his big paw at the doorframe.

What a touching scene! If I only had a camera!

What's up, Misko.

I'd tell you, Bat Man. But you might want to come look for yourself.

I'm busy, Misko.

Get out of the chair or I'll drag you out!

You and who else.

That seemed funny. Mickey Angel maybe 150. But had eighty of it in the guns. I'd seen him turn Misko. At a party. Told him he didn't want to listen to Utah Phillips anymore. Misko towered over him.

What happens when a Dago makes a little money!

Got the Mickey Angel bad look.

Whatever, Bat Man. Put on Billy Idol if you want!

Now we followed him outside. He reached for a pack of smokes. Gazed meaningfully into the sky.

Take a good look, Bat Man. They're looking for you.

In the high blue sky of a spring day four dark crosses turned round and round. Thermals spiraled up from the train yard. The vultures sailed without a wing beat. Mickey Angel smiled. He loved birds as much as I did. Misko sent a jet of smoke into the air.

I think they just saw you, Bat Man.

Why is that, Misko.

I saw Johanna in the Office last night. Dressed to kill and looking for you.

She's going to look a long time.

What a tough guy!

Mickey Angel put his palm out. Misko glanced out of the corner of his eye.

What?

Give, Misko.

You ever buy, Bat Man? Smokes are five bucks a pack!

Don't whine.

Misko handed over the pack. I watched the vultures. They drifted wings locked toward the Gap. Misko shook his head.

I could learn a lot from you, Bat Man. Just couldn't be that cold.

How's that.

The way you work her. Don't have it myself. The blood you Dago's got.

Talk, Misko.

Misko was gleeful.

She saw you at the Free Clinic Dinner. You didn't even look at her. Walked past like she wasn't even there.

I didn't see her.

Cold. Very cold.

I didn't see her, Misko.

She started to cry. With all you'd been to each other! Her pretty mascara running. You should call her.

It's over.

But she loves you! She loves her little bat man. Not everybody gets that. I tried to console her. Put my arm around her. But she said you were the only one!

Forget it, Misko.

Misko tossed the cigarette in the street.

Just a spat between lovers. You'll be together by Memorial Day.

Where? Massacre Rocks?

You're a funny man, Bat Man! But still. I wouldn't be sitting with my back to the window. Last I heard she was frequenting Doc's Gun Barn.

Mickey Angel glanced up Main. It was one way with cars parked on both sides. Misko caught it.

Hee! Hee! She was looking at those cute little 22's. The kind you slip in a purse.

She doesn't like guns. Won't have them in the house.

Times change, Bat Man. Yes. Love walked in wearing a low cut blouse and carrying a Saturday Night Special! Where you keep that shotgun?

In the back.

What you want for it?

Not for sale.

You don't hunt.

Mickey Angel tossed the cigarette like the taste was bitter.

No. But it's cold.

How cold?

Dad gave me it in 1968.

Misko guffawed.

Oh yeah? What'd he use if for?

It was new.

Right. Trust a Dago to give away a new gun! Well I got to go. Stay away from windows, Mickey Angel!

He walked. It was a nice day. We followed. Waited for the light at Center Street. Box car flashed sequentially across the top of the Underpass. Burlington Northern, Union Pacific, Wisconsin Central. The Thunk-a-thunk of a hundred tons hitting the bridge. Box cars, cattle cars, flat cars with spines. Names fading on sun blistered sides: Rio Grande and Santa Fe, Great Northern, Norfolk Southern, Green Bay and Western. Rail Rock, Route Box, Super Shock Control. The loud bray warned the yard men. The light changed. Misko didn't walk.

You heard anything from Roxie?

What're you talking about, Misko!

I asked whether you'd seen her!

How would I know?

You're always up Mink Creek. She comes in the store. Tell me! What's the big deal?

No. I haven't.

That's all I wanted to know. You'll tell me right?

You've got her number!

I can't talk to her on the phone. I have to see her in person.

Whatever, Misko.

Thank you!

He reached toward his shirt pocket.

It's the dogs I miss. Used to take them up the hill. She said it wasn't good for them but they loved it.

Mickey Angel said, They're nice dogs.

Misko stretched his shoulders, paws clenched. Glanced into the sky. The vultures had gone.

Maybe you're right, Bat Man. Maybe it wasn't you they were looking for. Maybe it was something in those cars.

This would be the season.

He glanced at me.

Yes it would.

He descended to the Underpass. We went back to the store. Mickey Angel stacked books in his left arm. Started plugging them along the wall shelf.

I said, Who's Roxie?

She moved to town a couple of years ago. Nice gal. Just got a few bad habits.

Like.

Not for me to say.

Pretty?

Oh yeah. Let's say Roxie don't lack men to walk her dogs.

I picked up Caesar's Conquest of Gaul. Where he killed every man, woman and child in the town of Bourges.

Need some help?

No thanks. Got to be able to find them.

What does she do?

Takes people apart.

I mean for money.

He flashed that crooked grin. Light shone into the store in dusty motes. Lit up the varicolored spines of books in the tall bookshelves. A big old guy in coveralls came out.

Couldn't help overhearing. Was a rather marvelous dog at LaGrande in the old days. Car man had her.

What was a car man?

Kept the rolling stock in shape. Wheels. Brake lines. All the stops along the Main Line had them. Burley. Glenns Ferry. Nampa. Men that could do just about anything in terms of repairing a steam engine. Build it from the wheels up if they had to. But the car man at LaGrande had a dog of a different order. Could find leaks in the brake line by the steam escaping.

What was she?

One of those mongrels sheep men brought into the country. Back when sheep were run from Challis to Chico. It's important to keep in mind the kind of weather a car man might find himself in. Blizzard. High winds. Torrential rain. But it wouldn't do to have the brakes go out on the Blue Mountain Grade. The dog ran along the train and nipped at steam she saw escaping. Made it easy for that car man.

One day he took the westbound for Portland. Had a heart attack on the line. Never came back. Day and night the dog met the eastbound train. Lay with her head between her paws an hour before Arrival. Had the schedule in her head. Finally they let her sleep by the tracks because she'd take the door down if they forgot to let her out. When the diesels came in she kind of went around the bend. The way the air brakes crackled. Wore her teeth out biting at them. Kind of sad.

Happens that way.

A clackety-clack came down the sidewalk. The old railroader cocked his ear.

That a horse?

Skateboarder.

Thought it was a horse.

The skateboarder wearing dreadlocks and combat boots hopped off the board. Came in the store.

Funny thing about the sound those air brakes make when you bleed them.

Why do they bleed them?

That's what stops the train. Pressure on the brake shoes. To get it going again you have to bleed the lines. That's the screeching you hear. A guy dragging in a couple of cars with wheels locked. So you'd be at the Granger siding. Waiting for the eastbound. See a flicker of white in the sagebrush. Prairie goats with ears twitching.

Couldn't resist the sound of brake lines popping.

Mickey Angel grinned his bat grin.

I love pronghorns.

I did too. They were lovely and childlike with big black eyes and horns like a sign. Would run with their black and orange racing stripes along the truck. When the skate boarder handed Mickey Angel a paperback the old railroader saw the title.

Tommyknockers?

Cheap thriller, Elroy.

The kid got on his board, kicked his boot, swung it forward for balance. Elroy slapped his book against his thigh.

I just saw the title. Took me back to the time I was riding circuit for the Feds. A Cornish brakeman took me home for dinner.

Cornish?

UP brought them in by the hundreds to do the hard rock work. When that ended they drifted up to Butte or stayed on. This Jack had a house on the Main Line in Wyoming. Six daughters and they all sang. It was like the angels singing. They sang as they cooked or darned or polished pots. If one began a song the others would take it up. They sang as many parts as there were singers. It was like being in heaven. After dinner the old man took me up to his prospect. Trimmed the lamp and lit it. Took a sandwich out of his pocket and laid it on a rock.

What you doing there, Jack?

It's for the Tommyknocker!

The Tommyknocker would hide your hammer when you were a mile deep. You'd put it down just a moment before! Could not be found! Or they'd blow out your lamp. Irksome little devils! But if a rockslide were coming? You'd hear this pinging above you. The Tommyknockers hammering with their little, silver hammers! From the moment you heard that pinging? You were advised to throw down everything you had and run.

What town was that?

One of those old railroad towns that are ghost towns now. Perfect for Cousin Jack. He could work the railroad and work his mine. They say it gets in your blood. It got in mine. Before I went out on the Line I'd get my maps out. It kept me out of the bars. One time out of Ely I was down in a hole. The quiet. The dripping of

water in the darkness. Heard a ping-pinging. But saw color so I
kept digging. The pinging became insistent. The hair at the back of
my neck stood up. I was at the entrance when it collapsed. Blew
me into the tailings. Had a few bruises but otherwise was none the
worse for wear.

Mickey Angel grinned.

The Tommyknocker.

And the conclusion of my career as a prospector.

Elroy was a sweet old guy. I knew when blocks sheared
against each other the crystal geometry set up harmonics. He knew
it too. Kyrie hectored me from the loft.

TEN

She bent her head to let me scratch her nape. My mother trained us
to scratch her between spine and scapula. Even Dad had to. My ex
and Ginny would ask. Seemed a female thing. We drove past
Felony Flats. At Midleys got red onions, potatoes, jalapenos. It was
a nice store. Just didn't want to go there on Halloween. At the meat
counter a gal in paint-on jeans loaded prime cuts into her cart. I
worked my way to get a look. She was cute but twitchy. I got a leg
of lamb. Case of Budweiser. At the checkout she paid with a State
of Idaho credit card. Felt me looking at her. Scratched her nape
with a fingernail.

Little hawk! Feeding your babies all that meat?

Desert camouflaged personnel vehicles lined the siding by
the gun factory. Black cows along the Snake where it came out of
the north. Horses with foals in the fields. We turned on Coffee
Point Road. After awhile high power pylons marched across the
desert. Shadow in the crossbar. I glassed the eagle before she flew.
Dark as she rose but blazed gold when she turned from the sun.
Then a dart streaked! A falcon counted coup! The golden eagle
turned talons up but the falcon was on his way!

Now sheep in multitudes. Herders sat in the shade of the
trailer. Watched me go by. Horses stood saddled with tails
whisking. Farther an ewe stretched her head out on the road. Eyes
open. Sides heaving. Dying was hard.

I turned up a ridge where lava had belched fire. Set Kyrie atop the truck. She turned her eyes upward to pierce the sky. Raised her tail. Sent a jet of chalk over the truck. Lifted wrists high and was off.

The lava rock blazed with red and green. Skulls of small mammals in the crevices. The ruined nest of a ferruginous hawk. Raptors perched here a million years. I saw prints of mice and gophers but the ferros had moved on. Kyrie was heaven kissing. I stood with my head bent back. Out of the corner of my eye saw a plume of dust. A man got out of a pickup. Walked toward me smoking a cigar.

You seen a dog?

I haven't.

Had her running behind the truck last night. Until she went her merry way.

Female?

How'd you know!

I looked where he came from. There was a lot of it. Ridges one behind the other like the waves of the ocean. He caught my look.

I'll find her. Hire a plane if I have to.

Bent his head back.

At least you're flying her right.

You fly?

Some. We were out at Rock Lake. You been there? The stockmen impounded the spring melt with rock. Ducks see it on their way north. I'll scope them from a mile or so. Let Krishna get sky. Then walk in to bump them up. They see me but don't see her. Most of the time I don't see her. She's moving so fast. But you see what she's doing to them. They start looking around when they hear the sizzle. Start dumping their wing loading.

You don't see her?

Just the ducks. What she's doing to them.

What d'you fly?

Pair of Black shaheens right now.

He looked up.

Look like she's not coming down for awhile.

He was right. Two Swainsons out of Argentina were

circling with a thermal. Maybe five hundred feet up. The sun shone through their secondaries. I smiled.

She's got time. What kind of dog you got?

English pointer. Never runs away. Must of picked up a scent and got turned around.

Not hard out here.

The lava flowed in troughs and crests. Compasses got distracted. Landmarks changed. The ridge you had your eye on had another in its place. Men stood atop them. When you got closer they became piles of rock. The falconer puffed on the cigar.

I can't understand it. She never runs away.

She's a bitch right?

Right. Don't matter how long a man thinks on something or how hard he works at it. A woman's going to find a way to make it take more time and burn more money! You going to serve her soon?

The Swainson's had moved on.

I'll let her fly awhile.

Right.

He was a courteous man. Parked on the road. Flicked the ash of the cigar.

Well. Got to find that dog.

I'll keep my eye out.

Fish and Game said they would.

What are they up to?

Counting leks.

I looked at the country. It rose like shields streaked with snow leeward. The last refuge of the sage grouse.

Shaheens take grouse?

The bitch will take anything she's got a mind to.

I looked skyward.

Stop by for dinner.

What you having?

Lamb.

I can't eat sheep.

It's rib loin.

Don't matter. My old man and I chased sheep all over this country. Can't stand the stink of them. To this day I can't go near a

Basque trailer.

I've slept in them. They're pretty comfortable.

No. No matter how hard you scrub you can't get the stink out. Why I started smoking these damn cigars! See you down the road.

It was a vile cigar. He descended to the road. Puffs of smoke trailing blue behind him like the far mountains.

Probably wasn't just the smell of sheep. Was the father. Hemingway mentioned that. The mechanism that drove the adolescent away. I thought of them living in that trailer. The father giving orders. The stink of sheep. Above it the blue sky and the prairie falcons. Their clean killing. I read how he learned to trap them.

He watched them arrive at fences before sunrise to wait for gophers to come out. Kept the sun at their backs. Dropped and glided. The gophers didn't know what hit them.

He set netting in the middle of the night baited with sparrows. Falcons can't resist flutterers. Couldn't see the netting unless the wind were blowing. Swooped with hooks open. Like ourselves saw what they wanted to see.

I was glad he left. After a blinding stoop Kyrie missed. Crackled with speed but braked early. I didn't want to think she'd lost her nerve. Knew she'd have a cripple served. We took a side track toward Big Volcano. I weathered Kyrie. Made a rock bed for the dutch oven. Sagebrush bark blazed. I loved the smell. Ground pepper and salt on the loin. After it sizzled turned it. Sliced veggies on top. Poured in beer. Closed the lid. The juices dripped onto the meat. It was a wonderful way to cook.

Birds perched atop the lava. The baroque whistles of meadowlarks. The buzzing runs of Brewer's blackbirds interwoven like a string quartet. No finer company than wild birds.

At midnight song dogs started. Yipped and cried. As I slipped into dream understood their song. They sang of the cyanide and long range guns of man. But they would fight to hold the part of earth God gave them. Sang too of their love for each other. How they would take care of each other no matter what was brought against them. It was a bitter and defiant chorus I heard that night.

Sometime in the night it ceased. I slipped out of the camper shell. The Scorpion dipped her tail under Bannock Peak. The east sky lightened. I wrapped the sleeping bag around me. Sat in the camp chair. Birds spoke. The sagebrush winnowed as if the wind were blowing but there was no wind. It was the hens scurrying here and there. As light strengthened I saw the bucks had established.

They had ruffs around their throats like Italian tenors. Strutted, tail fans straight up. Bowed to the ladies. Then arched their backs. Filled the yellow air sacs at their breasts. Hopped. Sent packets of notes into the air that popped like bubbles. It drove the hens wild. They raced back and forth.

They called it sage grouse booming but it was more like the ringing of bells. As the desert birds piped a background chorus the bucks strutted. Scraped the air sacs with their wingtips. Esquarado! Hopped and sang. It wasn't singing. It was ventriloquy. The notes opened in the air like blossoms. Then the sun lit the stage. The dance increased in frenzy. I lost all sense of scale. Sagebrush behind the strutting tenors looked like great, shaggy trees!

I got out the notebook. Counted five bucks. Twelve hens slipped here and there. Years back I monitored a lek on the Little Wood. Counted a hundred and twenty. This little band now held the rituals of life.

The sun rose. The hens slipped back into the sagebrush. The bucks stayed a little longer. One left a garland of notes in the sky. Then he too was gone. Larks whistled. Blackbirds buzzed.

What you saw before you was a mudhole with no other meaning than that.

ELEVEN

Big Volcano sent its shadow west. I headed east. Wended my way among lava rock until I came to a fence. Black Angus milled at the trough. Calves lying in the dust. Got to their feet when I slipped the wire loop. Neotropical birds floated in the trough. Two bluebirds. A warbler coated with bacterial scum. A yellow breasted chat. I stood there thinking whether to give them a decent burial when I heard the growl of diesel truck. Brand new 350 came over the ridge. Hit the brakes so as to lift a cloud of dust. Cowboy got out.

Pulled his belt up under his gut. Hat pulled low over his eyes.

H'ep you with somethin'?

That was a lie. He didn't want to help me. I leaned against the trough.

Checking things out.

You're checking things out.

That's right.

He ducked his head. Looked at my truck then back. Narrowed his eyes.

You look kind of strange.

That hurt. He had low pig eyes. His nose almost met his chin like in Appalachia or Saudi Arabia. Inbreeding wasn't all bad; but you had to have good stock.

What'd you mean by strange?

He moved close. Used to dealing with cows. If you stood your ground it confused them. I did. He was. Looked away. The bluebird license plate on my rig.

I mean like I ain't seen you around here a'fore.

It was funny. Cowboys in Idaho talked more Southern than Southerners. Like they'd learned it in a movie. I grinned.

Just checking things out.

Looks good don't it.

I looked at the trampled seep that had been a slough. The grouse that used to come for the water and insects.

You're a prince.

He looked hard at me under his hat. I kept my arms folded. Turned to the water trough.

Like the trough here.

He pursed his mouth.

Birds.

That's right. They've been traveling for two maybe three thousand miles. Crossing desert when they see this water. But they don't understand it's not a natural thing. No rocks or branches. Don't understand that if they land in it they won't be able to get out.

His neck turning red. I knew why. U.S. Government plates.

So what you do is weld a strip of sheet metal at the water line. If the birds get waterlogged they can crawl out. Some folks float a two by eight. That's better than nothing.

He drew the corners of his mouth down.

I'll talk to the boss.

I'd appreciate it.

Close them gates.

Yes sir.

He walked. I couldn't let him go so easy.

What office you out of?

What you talking about?

I nodded at the plates. He sneered.

Just work for them part time. Got a ranch out in Pingree.

BLM?

Right.

Range improvements?

You got it. Close them gates.

I did. Opened and closed five as we traveled. Saw young stands of sagebrush here and there but not enough to hide. Turned south on 39. Stopped at Betty's Café. Big trucks with manure crusted fenders. Bumper stickers. Wolves: Smoke A Pack A Day. Thou Shalt Not Steal: The Government Hates the Competition. Farmers Feed the World. They turned in their bulky overalls. Stared at me when I walked in. Wore greasy John Deere ball caps. Turned back to their coffee. I sat by the window. Looked at boarded up windows. An old guy turned to me.

What brings you to Aberdeen?

The café turned quiet. Like when you crossed a field of Black angus. Some stopped chewing.

Sage grouse.

See any?

A few.

Where'd you go?

Coffee Point Road.

Used to see 'em by the thousands. You'd come over the top of a hill. See 'em on the road and both sides too doing their fandango. We'd pull out the shotguns, rifles. Whatever we had in the truck. Let 'em have it. Funny. Don't see that many around anymore.

Funny thing.

The old man turned back to his coffee. The café got loud. A lot of them had land by the Reservoir. Dumped potato refuse atop the sloughs. Cheaper than the landfill. Witch's brew. Ducks nested below. You either located the violation by boat or got a Federal Order. Fish and Game looked the other way. As I got up to leave the old guy grinned.

You have a nice day!

Thanks. But I got other plans.

That it were true. Shiny flanked mares stood with foals in the fields. Calves born in winter. Pelicans floated above Tilden Bridge. Kids with bare shoulders slid rafts into the River. I watched it uncoil its bright, shiny scales. At the Meat Market I shadow boxed with five pound weights. Phantoms streaked across the sky of Iraq. The locker room was crowded. A Mexican and a black sat on the bench.

Where you been, LaRoy? Haven't seen you around.

LaRoy took off his socks.

Florida.

What you doing there?

Working on my tan.

The white guys laughed. Didn't look white. Getting out of the hot tub looked orange.

Yeah right, LaRoy! Something you got to work on. Like us Mexicans.

Think I was born this way, Cruz? Think that's how I got this big dick?

It's not your dick is so big, LaRoy. It's your hands are so small!

The white guys laughed but dried off fast. LaRoy built like a bull. Strode regally toward the toilets.

Got something for you, Cruz. Something for your lunch. Coming right up.

La Roy!

Toilet door slammed. As I stood at the mirror shaving the room turned white. It so startled me I turned. The white guys had pulled their white angel long johns on simultaneously! Cruz whined.

Jesus, La Roy! Even a scratch back wouldn't talk like that!

I turned to him.

Thought you were wetback.

He looked up.

No. Scratch back. You get that coming under the fence.

I went outside. LaRoy was legendary. Yard man for WP. Threw a party one long summer day. Booze, broads and barbecue. Motown pulsed at a two hundred decibels. 'S Hurry Down! Was a stone soul picnic until the redneck crashed it.

You gonna turn that music down, boy?

Next thing he was flying. Backwards over the fence he built himself with his Craftsman table saw. LaRoy threw a two hundred pound redneck in a twenty foot arc over a seven foot fence. Two engineers from Sinklot spent the evening arguing the math. Finally agreed. It was a marvelous thing.

I carried Kyrie into the loft. Out the window saw two Indians come down the alley. A slim little woman wore a golf hat and backpack. Limped. Waved her hands as she talked. Mickey Angel had lain a cedar slab from the Clearwater District by the back door. She decided she would sit on that. The big guy with long black braids stood.

You didn't see many lame street Indians. They kept on the move. Didn't look in dumpsters like whites. Had the look of people with somewhere to go. To the Snake to fish or to Nevada to visit relatives. Started out in the willows by Kraft Hill. Walked up to the stores on Pocatello Creek. The little Indian lady got one gram of protein and a hundred and fifty carbs in that Miller Lite. Pocatello was a long, stretched out town but there was always a Quik Stop close by.

I worked construction with a guy who lived on Miller Lite. Drank it on site. Didn't wear a shirt. Nobody cared because he outworked everybody. Had the body of a god. Drank at night because it helped him sleep. I went out the back door. The big Indian grinned.

How you doin,' buddy?

Beautiful day.

Nice morning!

The woman looked up at me.

This your store?

I have business here.

Mm. We was up at Binco this morning. Now we're working our way back.

Fort Hall?

She shrugged.

Who knows?

I saw the campaign pin his hat.

Where'd you train?

Fort Puke.

Where's that?

Louisiana.

Nice.

No. Not nice. To hot down there, man. Too many bugs. I like it better up here.

What did they make you?

What d'you mean?

What did they make you into?

They made me crazy! What d'you think!

He was big and funny. I didn't think he was Shoshone.

You must be Sioux.

He grimaced like he smelled stink.

I'm Blackfoot, man! She's Cayuse. Cayuse women never shut up!

She nodded. Sipped her beer.

There was three Blackfoot tribes. The Blood lived in the mountains. The Piegan lived in the foothills between the mountains and the river. The best country for horses. You could go down to the river in the morning and up into the hills when it got hot. And the Gros Ventres. They lived on the plain. When the Gros Ventres won a fight they cut off the heads of their enemies. Stuck them on poles and danced around with them.

She waggled the Miller Lite can.

After the dance they would plant the poles with the human heads on them at the edge of the village. When the Blood won a fight they cut off the head and arms and legs. That's what they danced around with. Body parts. But the Piegan were the worst. They dismembered their enemies with great care. Cut the meat from the bones and gave it to the dogs. The Piegan had happy dogs.

Then they threw the bones in the river. The enemy could not put himself together again to return to the Upper Country. That's how the Piegan got the best land for horses and for hunting. They were the worst. The Piegan.

She took a sip of her Miller Lite. Nodded at her friend.

That's what he is. A Piegan.

The big guy grinned happily.

I said goodby to them. Hoped they stayed together. Merlin Lady screeched. I glassed her skulking at the rampart of the High School. The starlings in formation. Were aware of her. Fear a geological force. When the wolves came to Yellowstone riparian zones improved because elk stayed together when they went to water. People were like that. I misguided treks into the Wapi. Told people to stay together. If the wind were blowing you could lose somebody thirty yards away. They invariably scattered to follow the designs the lava made. Until Captain Fang shook his castanet.

Snake!

Everybody single file now. A tight, little tribe that resembled a snake as it traveled over the landscape.

TWELVE

I had late breakfast at Lefty's. When I got to Mickey Angel's the geologist Eichorn had the red recliner. Wore a wide brimmed hat, limestone shirt and slate green pants. Slumped at the angle of repose.

If it isn't Feral Errol.

How you doing, Ike.

Can't complain. You give up Farming and Grazing?

Yes sir.

Good buyout?

Enough.

I liked Eichorn but didn't sit. Turned card racks. Had a bad dream. Was sitting by the fireplace in the old house. Saw Clancy in the fire. He wasn't trying to get out. I pulled him from the flames but realized the pain he would feel when the oxygen hit his wounds would be more than he could bear. Mickey Angel had nice cards.

Sandstone cliff with moon. Black and white sea breaking on rocks.
Eichorn shifted.

Well I best be going.

Buy you a beer later.

I got plans. Roxie wants me to do some mud work.

Mickey Angel tossed the book.

What're you talking about, Ike! That'll drive Misko crazy!

Not a long trip.

He was just talking about how he's going to make up with
her!

Eichorn stared into the distance. Like he were looking at a
landform twenty miles away.

He's a got a gear stripped if he thinks Roxie is going to take
him back.

That doesn't mean you have to get in the middle!

Just doing her bathroom, man.

He's the best friend you got, Ike.

I'm doing her tile, man. That's it. She's out of my league.

The doorframe rattled. Mickey Angel started pushing books
flush to the wall.

So why risk it!

Stuffing coke up her nose isn't going to work for long with
a babe like Roxie.

Shut up, Ike!

Eichorn slapped his gloves on his thigh. I opened a falconry
book.

> In falcons the female is larger
> than the male. The female is called
> the peregrine, the male the tercel.
> Scientists theorize this sexual dimorphism
> allows the brooding pair to exploit
> a wider range of prey. This is true
> world wide except the Saudi Arabian
> peninsula where the male is larger
> and more powerful.

Now there's a rig you don't see often, said Eichorn. Ugliest
truck ever made. Fifty Four Dodge. See the handle on the side of
the hood? Opened from the side. V-8. They took the running

boards off. Too bad.

Mickey Angel shook his head.

Sad day for pulp fiction when they did that. Detective Joe could jump on the running board. Stick the gat through the window. And look at that!

A pink Cadillac with big fins pulled up in front of the Round Up Room. Pigeons courted among the letters of the neon sign. It looked like an illuminated manuscript. Eichorn pulled down the corners of his mouth.

1955. Was a time every rancher and rock scraper in Nevada had one. I was at eight thousand feet in the Rubies when I heard the low growl of a V-8. Old Caddy. The guy just walked it up the washouts. Had a long stroke so they had lots of torque. You could take them anywhere. Sleep in the back seat.

You saw old cars with original paint all the time in Pocatello because it was infested with machinists and mechanics. Did the work themselves. Eichorn nodded.

Nevada was crawling with guys in Caddies chasing the Grail. Had it good too. Salmon came up Salmon Falls Creek. You could do a little prospecting. Gamble, get drunk and laid in Wells if that was your inclination.

The Nevada Hat Trick!

Eichorn slapped his gloves.

Those bars and whorehouses in Nevada got a lot of stories to tell, man. Like the prospect they called the Holy Cross.

I thought it was a mine.

Must I need remind you guys? A tunnel is a prospect until it pays! So Desert Rat was kicking around the foot of a butte near Contact. Found color. High grade too. Got a partner. Sent a tunnel straight in. Nothing. Got more money. Drove that tunnel near all the way through that butte.

Opened a window?

Could've. The vein had to be there. They got more money. Went midway and cut a tunnel to the right. Nothing. Another year. More money. Headed a third tunnel to the left. When they got done? They'd spent a million post World War Two dollars and all they had was the biggest cross in the world.

Crazy.

Years later he was an old man having a drink in Cactus Pete's. Talking about that gold. How it had to be there! A kid just out of school tipped his hat back.

I'll go out there with you, old man.

Drove south on 93. Took a two track through the sagebrush. Kicked around for awhile. Got back on 93 and took a two track up the other side of the valley. Up to where the pinyon pine commenced. Could see the butte across the valley with the mountain range behind it.

See that mountain range, old man? That's where your gold is.

The butte broke off that range maybe a quarter billion years ago. Slud the ten miles to where it stood now.

I said, Wasn't even a North America then.

No.

Eichorn curled his chin.

Lot more money made in the practice of mining than's ever took out of the ground.

How's that?

Like the Iguana Mine. Butte, Montana. One of the deepest and widest veins in the history of silver. The Fuggenheims got hold of it. Paying real good. Stock going through the roof. Miners' wives buying dresses on Galena Street. Houses going up in the nicer parts of town. Everybody knew the vein would pay forever. Silver is used for everything, man. From the fillings in your teeth to photography. Dentists and shopkeepers all over America buying stock in the Iguana Mine. When shares hit $80 the Fuggenheims bought the appropriate geologist, a couple of government inspectors, the newspaper publisher. Word went out the Iguana Mine was played out!

The Fuggenheims did their part. Began quietly selling off stock. Rockslide in no time. Shares fell to 17 cents! Miners told to go home. The mine boarded up. Gates locked under twenty four hour guard. Nobody stopped to ask what they were guarding. No more pretty dresses. Nor food for the kids. Stores on Galena boarded up. But the bars? They were going good. A cold and bitter wind blew down the streets of Butte that winter.

The Fuggenheims started quietly buying up stock. Shares

they sold for $80 they bought back for 17 cents! Pretty soon they got it all. The geologist decided he'd take another look at the maps. Now there's rumor of another strike. By summer shares are up to $40. And the Fuggenheims quite willing to sell.

Cold.

Very cold.

How often did they turn that?

Between 1893 and 1905? Twice. Had to have the journalists on the payroll. And police to keep track of the journalists. Or a miner talking too loud. Like now. Well I best be moving. Got some tile work to do.

Say Hi to the dogs.

Eichorn wrinkled his nose.

Those dogs, man. One thing Indians did right.

What's that?

Ate their dogs.

He left. Mickey Angel stood up.

I'd like to go up the street if you wouldn't mind watching the till.

How do I know what to charge?

Make it up.

I liked the view. Pigeons preened in the Coffee Shop sign. Liked the C, P and O for nesting. Skirts carried packages to the Renaissance Revival Post Office. A purple DeSoto with swept back fins pulled up. A scrawny little guy with a wispy beard and cape pulled an old doctor's satchel out of the back seat.

Where's Michael?

He'll be back.

I returned to the book but the little man kept his eyes on me. Stepped past. Turn the satchel upside down on the desk so it spilled crystals. Ran his fingers through them so the smoky scepters, the amethysts with splayed points sparkled.

You can't believe the scene down there! Very heavy energy!

Where was that?

New Mexico.

He held up a double shafted crystal.

You know what this is don't you? Double Scepter. Very

powerful.

He wore a floppy purple hat. Long, stringy dark hair and crescent moon earrings. Held up a crystal so it showed pinkish sparkle. Trace of manganese.

Nothing like the one that found me in Taos though.

What was that?

The Master Scepter!

He looked far away.

I couldn't believe how powerful it was! My informants took me to a woman in Albuquerque. She was very depressed. The Dark Lord had hold of her. Nobody could get through. I gave her the Master Scepter. Told her to hold it and if not that to keep it by her body. When we came back later that night she was flying around the apartment with the vacuum cleaner. The boom box going full blast. She was really high, man. Her eyes shone with The Light! The work of the Master Scepter. Had to destroy it though.

He ran his fingers through the crystals, humming to himself.

You had to destroy it?

It had fallen into the wrong hands. Found something more powerful though.

He nodded toward the back of the store. I followed. He jumped out from a bookshelf wearing a head band with three huge crystals. Superman's parents wore headbands like that on Krypton. Was it the Past or the Future? Or a parallel universe? I was stunned.

What does that do for you?

I am able to read minds!

Oh my god! Why would you want to do that!

He glared at me.

There are evil forces at play in the world!

He was right about that. I went back to the desk. He removed the headband. Handed me a smoky crystal.

Your spectral body is weak. Keep this close to your body.

Thank you.

You have a lot of dark energy in you. Be careful.

I will.

He raked the crystal hoard into the satchel. Handed me a

sceptered crystal.

Give this to Michael. Tell him Lawrence stopped by.

He got in his Crystal Mobile with his cape flying. Roared off in cloud of smoke. I gave Mickey Angel the crystal. He put his feet up.

Good old Lawrence.

Quite the piece of work.

Wouldn't be quick to make judgments, Errol. One day you're a kid trapping fish up Rapid Creek. The next Uncle Sam has handed you a uniform. Put money in your pocket to take girls to the movie. All you got to do is climb down tunnels they got in Vietnam. Because you're just the right size. They tell you how tough you are. But it's dark down there. You can't hear them. But they can hear you.

He picked up a book.

Tunnel Rats I knew if they made it back just faded into the background noise. Lawrence is still around. The other thing, Errol? You noticed how Vietnam Vets pack?

And he reads minds.

Mickey Angel grinned.

That too.

The old brick buildings leaned toward the Gap. At Bernardo's a long haired guy wearing camo and two feet of lens on his shoulder turned.

Bernardo tells me you were with Fish and Game.

That's correct.

What do you think about Stanger retiring?

Doesn't mean anything.

Come on! There's got to be something you can tell me!

I scanned headlines. Detonations in Baghdad.

There's always a guy they can bring in to do a job. You just got to figure out what they want done.

What do you mean?

How about, Have you noticed Stanger has the mouth of a sucker? You want to print that?

He grinned.

You sound like you got some venom in you!

I tossed the paper.

I do. I've seen what happens to people who lack it.

THIRTEEN

I drove up Gibson Jack. Trophy houses on the ridge. Balsam poplar along the Creek with tassels backlit. It was my favorite fragrance. Gibson Jack spilled slate gray over a concrete dam. A tall blonde climbed out of the exclosure with specimen bottles in each hand. I swung the gate for her.

What are you monitoring?

Phosphorus. Nitrates. TOC's.

TOC's?

Trace organic compounds.

Right. You with EPA?

It's my Master's project.

Could you get the dam torn out?

She snapped the lock on the gate.

It's not a perfect world.

She was right about that. Wore tight jeans and high heeled boots. As she walked to the truck I tried to get her to swap ends.

You thought about mercury?

I have enough to worry about.

I climbed. Snow on the ridges. Towhees whistled. Drink your tea! Ravens honked. Flashed silver black out from the tall fir. Chokecherry unfolded red buds. Somebody pull-started a two stroke engine. Whup-whup-whup! Ruffed grouse. Beating wings downward for love.

Billy was lying on the deck of a junk in the early morning with a girl beside him when he heard that sound. Fishermen starting up their outboards. The sound of grouse back in Idaho. It was more than he could bear. Looked at that 45 different for the first time. A woman shouted.

Slow down, Socks!

A pretty woman in shorts descended the trail holding the leash of a very big dog. Socks had the body of lion. Would go where she wanted.

Don't pet her! She's been rolling in horse poop!

Socks was friendly. Looked at me with big, brown eyes. I riffled her ears. The woman narrowed her eyes. Tugged at the leash. Off they went. I stopped at the bridge. Watched the water spill with silver filigrees around a red boulder. Sparrows sang.

Konk! Wheet-wheet. Chit-chit-chit!

I knew the north fork infested with blue and thimble berry. Took the south. Climbed into winter. Saw where moose descended through the snow. Snow covered the trail. I cut through aspen. They bent this way and that like dancers. A chickaree warned. I smelled camp smoke but it didn't register. Entered the camp before I knew it. Wisp of blue smoke from the fire. One-man tent. Hand-axe, head angled in a log. A deep voice.

Looking for someone?

All I saw were aspen and deadfall.

Just passing through.

An older man wearing a knit ski cap and airman's jacket stepped from his blind. The automatic pistol gleamed.

And you don't call? You don't write? You don't send flowers?

Sorry.

Of course you are! But do me a favor? Lay your pack on the ground if you would? Thank you. Now I must ask your permission to search you. Would that be alright?

He patted me down. Went through the backpack. Slipped the automatic in the holster. Smiled.

You understand I have no option.

Whatever.

You're angry! I'm sorry! Is there some way I could make reparation? A drink perhaps?

Make it two.

He bowed sardonically.

At your service.

I sat on a fallen log that had dead leaves on the branches. Chickaree chattered. My heart slowed. Heard other songs. The Wank! Wank! of a nuthatch. My assailant brought out a steel flask. Poured mine into a steel cup. Raised his.

Vive La Guerre!

Vive La Guerre.

It was fine rum. Highly flammable. He kept his eyes on me as he drank.

In the coastal mountains of California it's too late if you

stumble into the wrong place. Booby traps. The kind that take off hands.

This is Idaho.

It is. Care for another? Call me Gerald. And you?

Errol Husky. What's your last?

Durkson.

Norwegian?

My lineage is strand of tangled barbed wire stretched across the centuries. My ancestry is stained with the blood and smoke of war.

Scottish?

Let's say a dark people arrived at an island long ago. Killed the men and bedded the women. Stood on the shingle daring their kinfolk to take them back. You think that's funny.

I do.

The tent contained his belongings. Outside just the axe and a box of Arm and Hammer.

It's a nice camp, Gerald. What's the baking soda for?

Toothpaste. It tastes alright and balances the ph in your stomach. Commercial toothpaste is a no-no.

Why is that?

Imagine you're traveling in the jungle but don't want certain people to know you're there. And if they do? Who you are. They might be very good at tracking human beings. They might arrive at the place where you spat toothpaste. When they put it to their noses? It spells Gringo! That information might be of use to them.

Where did you sleep?

He nodded upward.

A sling?

Of course. They are lightweight and comfortable. You pass the place you've chosen to spend the night. To a river if one is available. Wade down a ways and double back. Whoever is following you will pass right under.

Wouldn't look in the trees.

Not unless you farted. Or cried out in some strange dream.

What are the dangerous countries?

In South America? Colombia of course. Very bad. Bolivia?

Not too bad.

I heard Peru was bad.

No. For the most part you meet very nice people in Peru. Chile, though? Not so good.

Chile? Why Chile?

His eyes flickered for an instant.

One might have a history there.

Right.

I stood up.

Thanks for the drink, Gerald.

All is forgiven.

Todos es perdonado.

He bowed with palms out.

I got on the trail. The sun at my back. Spring beauties and yellow bells at snow's edge. The little valley widened into red birch and willow. I heard women talking. Thought it strange they were out this late. Saw the dark long ears of Mama Moose above the willows. Her yearling fed close by. She spoke to it and they fled. Should've had Gibson Jack to themselves this time of evening. I thought of Gerald on the ridge. How in Spanish the words for loss and forgiveness are so close.

On Lundborg Pond ducks settled in for the night. Greenheads quacked and swam in interlocking patterns that wove like water itself. Golden eyes with white bellies reflected across the water. At the Wagon Wheel I ordered a beer at the bar. Watched Bryant wheel, fake a drive then lean back to rise and shoot. Desmond had a hand in his eyes. Unkind iron. Took the outlet pass. Flew down the lane. It looked like Robbie made the right call. Bartender Lady had a wing of tinted hair over one eye. Low cut blouse. Gave me a cigarette.

I went out on the deck. The river ran beyond. Freight engines huffed like draft horses. A young woman smoked a cigar, bracelets glittering. Birds sang. Then it started to get light. The full moon rose over Chink's Peak. Banged like a gong.

Look at that!

She turned. The lady on the trail. She'd let her hair down. Put on a suede jacket. Gold earrings.

ER is going to be busy.

I'd heard that.

It's true. Kitchen knives. Kids falling off cliffs.

Critters get stirred up.

They do. I was in Yellowstone last night. The bison bunched up along the Madison. The wolves howled. All night long the sound of big animals moving in the moonlight and the wolves howling.

We don't know a lot about them. Starting to.

What do you do?

I was with Fish and Game.

And now?

I'm in transition.

Those are tricky.

She tapped the ash on her cigar. Tried the shot glass but it was empty.

I'm having another. You want one?

Please.

As she moved past I got a look at her flanks in the tight levis. Her perfume stayed. The moon shone through the trees. Big trees with tassels and white trunks. Box cars crashed. The concatenation ran Gapward. God throwing loose change. Wisps of cloud brightened as they passed the moon. You felt its pull. The big trees drawn toward it. The lady handed me a whisky on the rocks. Sat regally.

To the wolves.

To the wolves.

What are we drinking?

Jamesons.

My brother drank only Bushmills. It was one of the disciplines he imposed on himself.

That's Presbyterian Irish. There are bars in Philadelphia you wouldn't order that unless you had an exit strategy.

What were you doing there?

Contract work.

Where'd you stay in Yellowstone? The Lodge?

Right. I was with the Science Institute. We had a front row seat to the Lamar Pack.

Too bad about the Lamar coyotes.

Yeah. Wolves are hell on coyotes.

She sat with her back to the moon. It illuminated her red blonde hair like a halo. She lit the cigar.

The grad student with us spent three years at the Lamar Den. Was there when the pups arrived. As soon as Mom and Dad left the ravens showed up. Knew the pups would disobey orders and come out.

Being the reason for the coyote program.

Right. The ravens would swoop and nip their tails. When the pups whirled to defend themselves the ravens hopped out of range and laughed! By summer's end the pups came out to play whenever they arrived. By the second year the pups were working members of the pack. Now the ravens stayed in the air. Hovered up and down and made as if to fly away. Veered back to see if the wolves were getting it. They did. Followed when the ravens flew. The grad student found the wolves at an elk carcass. The ravens hopping around the perimeter complaining. Whenever they got too close the wolves bared their teeth. But when they were sated the ravens moved in.

I said, You can hear the ravens say, You can do a lot with a wolf if he's caught young!

She tapped the ash of her cigar.

It was probably the little bitches.

Did he say?

He didn't.

The moon was so close I could see the lava plain. In the pattern of light and dark saw a woman with her mouth open giving God an earful.

I said, I once saw vultures flapping above a hillside. When I got there the coyote at the carcass. Don't know which got there first. The vultures waited until they thought coyote was getting sated then drop on him. If he was still hungry he'd snap. But if he was full he'd move off 'til he was ready again. Like you said. That push and pull.

The lady winnowed her hand like a stream meander.

What's the Law?

Plot it on the X and Y. X: hunger. Y: fear. Time: constant. If all else fails? Hierarchy of Needs.

I didn't know Fish and Game read Maslov.

I shrugged.

Nothing like divorce to widen your reading.

She reached for the cigar.

So how do you sit for hours on end just watching something?

They make you. So I got a Yellowstone story. I was at Colter's Bar when a guy sat down. Said he'd been photographing the backcountry.

Was a photographer or took pictures?

Can't tell you. He was wearing a safari jacket. Said he camped by a lake he'd never been to before. In the morning saw prints by the water. They went into the water. Big ones with turned in claws. They weren't there the night before. He got up before light. Heard Griz come through the trees. Smelled him. Knew Griz smelled him too.

The lady grinned. Tapped her cigar.

Wasn't sure how the game would turn.

Griz stood to look around. Then entered the lake. A loud whooshing as he went down. Came up a minute later with a full grown elk in his claws! Can you imagine! Lolled around in the water tearing out big chunks of meat. Then took it down again. Returned to shore. Shook himself like a dog!

You think it's true?

Doesn't matter.

I thought your were a scientist!

Scientists freak out when you tell them animals think and feel and plan. Makes it hard to keep them in cages and cut them up. That story.

She got a funny look in her eye. Sat with her back very straight.

The bear would've had to secure the carcass in twenty feet of water!

No problem. I watched a Mama grizzly carry an elk cow in her mouth across the Madison and up a hundred yards of scree.

Did he get photographs?

No.

Just a fairy tale then. Did he tell you where it was?

No. Said he'd never go back there. Kind of why I believed him.

Even though he wore a safari jacket.

Photographers are different, darling.

She finished her whisky.

Would you go there? If you knew where it was?

No.

Why not?

A lot of reasons.

Name one.

How about, The thought of running into a full grown grizzly bear scares the shit out of me?

She snorted when she laughed. Nothing prettier than a woman laughing truly. She tossed back her drink. Looked at her Rolex. Stood and put out her hand.

Early day tomorrow.

I stood.

What's your name?

Roxanne.

She was looking in my eyes when she said it. If I'd been prepared I could've stayed the blind.

I said, Maybe I'll see you again.

She shouldered her purse.

You never know.

Her perfume stayed in the air. I watched the moon. It was high in the poplars. The river hissed past the levee. Freight cars boomed. The moon was cold. Reflected all the loneliness in the world even as it drew it out of you. But didn't draw it out in a good way. Just made you feel it more. Rolled like a silver dollar above the Gap and stayed above Kinney Creek. Woke coyotes. One cried at the top of the canyon. Sounded like she was coming down. I crawled out of the camper. Saw her flicking in and out of the trees. My spine went cold. She had the eyes and fangs of a rattlesnake. The whispery body and tail of a coyote. Looked at me like I'd shot her mate. Put her forefoot out. Showed her fangs. Then shook her head, turned tail and disappeared.

I thought how beautiful she was. How if she bit you you hoped you died quick.

FOURTEEN

The moon was like an orange. I followed it up Trail Creek. Saw the plain with its lava scars. Thought how the moon was like an empty woman when overhead. But give her a little rouge? Set her over Mount Hyndman? Greatest thing going. Drove back through Pocatello. Yellow school buses at stop signs. Women all dressed up in Japanese cars with cell phones at their ears. When I stepped out of the shower at the Meat Market Cruz looked up.

Sounded like you were having sex in there, dude. Bad sex.

There any bad sex, Cruz?

You don't know? Guess you didn't grow up in no labor camp.

Where was that?

Aberdeen. No day care. Young mothers working in the fields. Drifters coming in off the tracks. You dig?

I guessed I did. Toweled off.

It's the cold water finish, Cruz. A Swedish girl taught me.

You just bragging.

I was. Summer at Goteborg. Stood amid wind twisted pines above the sea. Snow geese streamed along the cliffs. Their rhythmic honking, the whistling of wings like a vast chorale that ranged from the booming of surf to the cries of fairy terns. Yvette pointed at the sky. Out of the upper cloud hood a tiny dart streaked sea ward. Bent a corner. The duck was falling seaward when a second falcon bound to it. Carried it to the cliff.

Yvette thought of us that way. I leaned against the truck. The moon and memory tag team style. Women in iridescent body suits arrived. Sparrows fluttered in the arbor by the Church. Didn't want me there. The sign at Lefty's said, New Waitress. New Attitude. It was. A plump Mexican lady took my order. The eggs came out over easy. I sent them back. The cook hollered at her.

I shouted, My mistake! It was my mistake!

At the store Mickey Angel paid bills. Invoices scattered at his feet.

Morning, Mickey Angel.

He glanced at me.

You Ok?

Leaking a little oil.

You're too young for that.

That would be transmission fluid!

He grinned. Wrote a check. Enveloped it.

Your bird's been asking for you.

I'll feed her.

Good deal.

I got a zip lock out of the truck. Went into the alley. Ma and Pa starling perched on the power line preening each other. Saw me lean the ladder against the Church wall. Stropped the wire with their beaks. Churred unhappily. The chicks huddled under the flashing. I slipped one into the ziplock. It felt no pain. Kyrie crushed its skull. Brains dripped down the sides of her beak. I cleaned her. Went back through the stacks. Misko growled.

You seen the pumpkin headed Mormon?

Not today.

You see him? Tell him I'm going to put his head in a vice. Turn it until his eyes pop out!

Why would you want to do that, Misko!

He was at Roxy's last night. I saw his truck in the driveway.

Did you call ahead?

I told you. She won't talk to me.

You sure it was his truck?

Like we haven't bounced all over Idaho and Nevada in that truck!

Mickey Angel tossed the checkbook.

He's doing her bathroom. That's it!

It doesn't matter. If he's up there I can't talk to her.

She won't talk to you! You said that!

She will. I just need to talk to her in person. Make her understand.

Understand what, Misko?

That I love her. That I love her like nobody ever will.

Mickey Angel put his face in his hands. Misko paced. Picked up a book. Looked at it. Threw it.

After further deliberation I'm not going to put his head in a vise. I'm going to put his dick in it. Squeeze it until his head pops! Pumpkin headed Mormon!

Forget it, Misko! We've got that trip to the Craters!

I'm not going. Smoky wants to run the Murtaugh that weekend.

We've planned that trip for a year!

Misko stretched his shoulders. Flexed biceps.

Not a bad idea though, Mickey Angel. Get Pumpkin Head out on the lava. Stuff him head down in one of those crevasses. Or wait until July. Drop him off with a jar of peanut butter.

Mickey Angel hid a grin. Misko saw it. Seemed happier.

I got to go. Got an appointment at the Office with the Pumpkin Head.

He stood at the door. Pulled a cigarette pack out of his front pocket.

That's the concept. Put his dick in a vise until his head pops. I'm looking forward to it. Say hi to Captain Fang.

If I see him.

Oh you will. You two have a special relationship.

Because I'm always in the lead.

Don't forget Benadryl. Nor the tourniquet. But why be arbitrary, Mickey Angel? Cyanide when the pain gets bad!

That's passe, Misko. Use a tourniquet you could lose a hand.

The old railroader appeared from behind the stacks.

There's a lot that's passe, Michael. We stopped at Glenns Ferry a few years back. A ranch couple from the outer district lay by the track like the day they were married. Nobody knew how they got nipped or why they waited to come to town. Probably didn't want to spend the money. But you know how a hand looks when it's been envenomed? All swollen purple and black? That's how their faces looked.

Yeesh!

So a tourniquet might not be all that bad if that's all you had. Another time I was standing where the Main Line crosses the lava beds. Remember it still. The sun setting quietly over the desert. Birds singing. As I admired the view I felt this pinging on my boots. Looked down on a nest of baby rattlesnakes.

Oh my god!

I was wearing high topped boots so no harm intended. But the sight of that yellow venom running down them? Made me feel kind of queasy.

Misko tossed the cigarette.

Get rid of the tennis shoes, Mickey Angel!

The old railroader watched him go.

Sorry to run off your clientele.

He was going anyway. So tell me, Elroy. How many cylinders in one of those engines?

Sixteen on a bank.

Two banks?

Right. Thirty two cylinders. Six thousand horsepower. One point eight to the trailer ton. That's to the east. You do the math. Sell me this book will you, Michael?

I heard a rumor they're taking the hump yard out. That true?

If a rumor's bad it usually is.

Town's going to be awfully quiet.

The Hump Yard was by the University. Boxcars were backed up, switched, let down the grade with brakes locked. Made a wonderful sound. A high, loud, wavering screech at irrational intervals like a deranged violinist. Every few years an adjunct professor of English wrote a whale song poem. But if the brakeman set brake hard on the light cars or light on the heavy? That didn't work so good.

Elroy slapped his thigh with the book.

WP always trying to save a dollar. Makes management look good. We'd be repairing track and see a white collar guy sneaking around the weeds. Trying to clip a paycheck. They offered to move me up a couple of times. But I saw the kind of people I'd be working with. Don't worry, Michael. Pocatello is a One Spot Shop. If an engine breaks down on the Line they have to take it to the

nearest shop. That's the Law. Right now it says you have to have a
One Spot Shop every thousand miles. But if they changed it to
fifteen hundred? All you'd hear was the whistle coming through.

Elroy left. I turned a spinner rack.

So Roxy don't want Misko no more?

She cut bait.

Looks like he kept the hook.

Got a cigarette, Errol?

Don't use them.

He picked up an invoice.

They were big time for awhile.

A little Indian in a long black coat came up the street. Had a
cigarette in one hand and Styrofoam cup in the other. Had lost a
wheel and was dragging an axle. Smoke from his cigarette scrolled
like a priest's censer. He spit on it. Put it in his pocket. Came in.
His voice had been scraped with rusty knife.

Borrow a dollar?

You owe me for last time.

I paid you.

Mickey Angel shook his head.

No.

Pay you two. Monday then.

Mickey Angel handed him a dollar from the cash box. The
Indian put it in an inside pocket.

Two dollars. Then we're even. Right?

He hobbled out.

I said, That boy packs a fragrance.

Mickey Angel put his feet up.

Have him show you his arms sometime. He's an artist.
Does pictures of his girlfriends.

Portraits?

Full body. Without clothes. Except he does it the old
fashioned way. I told him I'd pay him for one done on paper but he
said he only does it for love.

Smart guy.

Beat him out of a dollar now and then. To keep up
tradition.

Shouldn't joke, Mickey Angel. I was in Salmon for a public

hearing. Cowboy hats. Stink of cow shit. A Sho Ban did his song and dance. How if we kill all our animal brothers the world will die. A ranch wife got in his face.

You're a conquered race! We conquered you! Why don't you just shut up!

Like they did such a great job at Whitebird Hill.

You been reading your Idaho history, Mickey Angel. That's good. See how Lapwai won another State Championship? Don't want to mention that when you stop in Grangeville!

I handed him Sand County Almanac.

Not much defense. But they can take it down the wings!

I leaned the ladder against the roof. Nez Perce liked cavalry. The ranchers at Grangeville talked the Army into going down to Whitebird. Not a bad idea but putting the citizens on the flank was.

I let the pigeons out of the trap. Pigeons at adjacent firewalls rose in whirling bands. Had a good life. Ledges on the old buildings. Grain the hoppers spilled on the tracks. Main Street was better than a cliff in every way.

I drove south. A cliff band highlighted the south gate of the Gap. Six hundred million year old rock harder than the strata above and below. Didn't look much from the road but presented a problem when Billy and I got there. He snaked up a chimney. An overhang stopped him. He reached with his left hand. Pulled himself over.

I walked up Kinney Creek. Little bright eyed birds peered at me. Flew from juniper to chokecherry. A black lab bounded up. Dashed into the chokecherries where an old man lurked with a long pole and hook.

Hey, old man! You molesting the wildlife?

He peered out at me.

Errol! You're a sight for sore eyes!

He had binoculars in a harness on his chest or I'd've hugged him. Went back to checking nesting boxes he'd put up the year before. Jabbed the hook to pull out debris.

Damned fox squirrels! Jam the nesting holes!

They don't use them?

No. Just make sure nothing else can.

There used to be a fish farm on the Portneuf where it entered the Snake. Great blue herons came to fish. The farmer handed out shotgun shells to anybody who'd shoot them. Schindler hauled in a beat up trailer house. In five years trapped and banded eleven hundred herons. Banded herons were rarely trapped. Death seemed the only lesson from which they couldn't learn.

I asked, What are the little birds with the crests?

Topknots? Juniper titmouse. Tough little birds. Stay all winter.

What do they eat?

Juniper berries! Peel the cover off. Crack the casing by holding it in their beaks and whacking it on a rock. Whack! Whack! Tough little guys.

Feed on insects in the spring don't you think?

Nobody knows much about Juniper titmice. Just they need Utah juniper.

I went up the road. Plucked a berry from an overhanging branch. Peeled off the casing. Rolled it around in my mouth. Schindler was right. The Juniper titmouse was a tough, little bird.

Indian Peak rose with twin buttresses at the head of the creek. Snow bones lee. White blossoms on the hawthorn along the creek. Cows trimmed them underneath. Black hawthorn had thorns the length of your little finger. Were the last to stand on overgrazed creeks. Ruffed grouse roosted in them. Songbirds. Hawks didn't venture into those thorns. On my left ravines at intervals had shed the snow pack. One late winter I saw all the mule deer of Bannock County there. Looked like a river flowing as they moved toward the ridge.

I passed the Game Exclosure. The sign explained how little overgrazing affected the land. Hadn't put it around the creek. Another blind. At the fork of Kinney Creek I ascended the north buttress. White and Pink phlox. Monkey flowers. The Fort Hall Landfill below. Cars glittering on I-25. Above me brightly colored flags fluttered in the wind. Somebody set a pole in the tailings of an old prospect. Strung it with prayer flags. Orange, blue and green they rippled and snapped. Distributed prayers to the wind.

I sat on the tailings. Looked at the valley. A magnificent procession of white clouds sailed over. The Snake River Plain flat as a promise. Wolf Jaw Mountains white. Wild birds spoke to each other. Did they forgive? And if they did what was the nature of their forgiveness?

FIFTEEN

I got daffodils for Mom at Albertsons. Light came into her eyes. She put them in a vase on the dining room table.

The rest of my days I'll not forget the blood. Hadn't turned my back for a second! You got the dime in that rocking horse and climbed on. How you howled! The howling and the blood. I'd never seen a little boy so mad! The manager came running. White in the face. The bakery girl gave you daffodils. That shut you up. You just stared at her with those daffodils clutched in your bloody little fist. Wouldn't give them up. Held them as Ben stitched you up. Remember?

I remember you telling me.

I wonder what happened to that girl. Her mother was a strange one! Would walk by the house and smile but I never got a word out of her. The girl would come over and listen to records with Chrissy.

I remembered that. I watched from the door. The girls sat on the floor with their legs akimbo in the short plaid skirts. Listened to Elvis or the Marcels. Silhouettes On The Shade. A Summer Place. Chrissy was ringleader. They worked on a Navaho sand painting for a week until it was finished. Thunder beings in yellow, turquoise and black. What strange energies had she brought into the house? Mom was a Navy wife. Sang show tunes from South Pacific or Windjammer.

I put my arm around her waist.

Haven't heard you sing in a long time, Mama.

No reason to.

You're a sweet singer.

She finished slicing the tomatoes and red onions for the salad.

Nothing to sing about.

The daffodils hadn't lasted long. I found the vodka in the

upper cupboard. She dried her hands.

Go see your father. He's waiting for you

He sat on the patio. Stared fixedly down the sixteenth fairway.

How you doing, Dad?

He glanced at me. Wouldn't make a sudden move if I didn't. I sat so I could look too. A triple header came out of the Black Cliffs pulling a mile of camouflaged jeeps and field artillery. The Black Thunderbird of Southern Pacific painted on the face of the lead engine. I sipped the vodka.

Another rough start for the White Sox, Dad. Talk about the Cubs. The White Sox are the ones with the curse.

A spark in his flat, black eyes.

I saw Risberg play. And Happy Felsh. When they played for Scobey. The Swede could play any position. I saw him catch a shot barehanded down the line at third and throw it underhand to first.

The old man flicked an underhand throw.

Whit! Like that! A bullet! The Swede scared everybody. Shoeless Joe was scared of him. He pitched too.

What year was that?

1921. I was five years old. The rains came after seven years of drought. Scobey shipped more hard kernel wheat than any town in the world. Money because it keeps. Only grow it dry land. Irrigated wheat is soft. Dad took me out to the fields. It flowed like gold. Combines stalled. Roughnecks standing around. Straw boss a big guy from Missouri with a smile and a cloudy eye. Dad only five eight but from the lumber camps. Wore steel toed boots. I still see him with his head back arguing with the big guy. The rough necks gathered around. I was scared. Then straw boss was on the ground. Dad was putting the boots to him. The roughnecks didn't look so tough now. Dad tossed a wad of greenbacks.

Take him to town.

The old man raised a right fist and a left.

That's all it took.

The camouflaged train went into the Gap. You felt it gain momentum in order to make the grade at Portneuf Canyon. The hogger leaned on the horn for Black Rock Crossing. A flock of geese rose barking into the air. Dad grinned. Leaned forward on his shrunken forearms.

Straw boss came in the store the next week.

You were there?

I worked from the time I was seven years old. Why my back is bad. Straw boss came in with his arm taped to his chest.

Just wanted you to know, Mr. Husky. The one you gave me here?

He pointed to his chin.

That was pretty good. But the ones you gave me here. And here?

He pointed to his ribs.

Those were bona fide.

The old man smiled.

Bona fide.

Mom brought the casserole. Plank potatoes covered with cheese, onions and jabaneros. She looked up as she put it on the table.

There are your friends, Ben.

Two sand hill cranes stepped tall and stately down the fairway. The old man tried to get to his feet.

I'll get something, Ben.

She returned with a plate of prosciutto. He took it. Hobbled out to them. Bowed by years of standing over an operating table his protocol was perfect to approach cranes. They trumpeted. Bowed in return. Ate out of his hands. When there was no more stepped back. Raised their great wings in unison and fanned. Turned and walked away down the fairway.

Come and eat, Ben. Your dinner is getting cold.

He looked down the fairway. The shadows of trees lengthened across it. He looked like a sullen and willful child that knows it will not get its way. Shuffled back to the table with his head bowed. I held the chair so he could grip it in order to sit down. He cast me a black look. I made conversation.

Did you see the armor go by? They were camouflaged like desert rattlesnakes.

Mom brightened.

The insignia for the 116th is the rattlesnake. Orange on

purple field. I saw it at the dry cleaners.

Too bad camouflage is no defense against IEDs.

Let's not talk about it, Errol.

Dad looked up.

Every generation needs a war under its belt.

Right. Put a hundred thousand GI's in the middle of a billion crazy Moslems.

He narrowed his eyes.

I fought. Billy fought. You think you can have what you want without killing for it. You had somebody else kill for you.

It had been a good blind. Our eyes met. My mother pleaded.

Don't Ben. Please.

Her voice coming down the corridors of time. The table with goblets of red wine and the chandelier glittering above. The pheasant fragrant with wild rice we'd taken from the ditch banks of Southern Idaho and the hand made dinner rolls just out of the oven.

Don't Ben. Please!

Billy stood up. Threw his napkin.

Go to hell, Dad!

The old man's eyes had that dark, cold fire. I found Billy standing outside under the tree. Smoking. His hands shaking. Love an irrational equation. Splintered as it refracted your view of it.

Sit down, Errol. For me.

I did. The old man already feeding. His head bowed because it hurt to raise his arm. I drank the vodka. Looked at the tulips blooming in the corner of the yard. Chink's Peak faded. Mars gleamed like a fiery jewel.

The garden looks nice, Mama.

She lit a cigarette.

Winter never quit this year. It froze hard the twenty fifth. Burned the primroses.

They'll come back.

Spring came late but summer always arrived hot with cool nights. You just had to wait.

You remember that 50 caliber Billy sent back, Mama?

Dad glanced over.

Sold it for drugs.

Mom narrowed her eyes at him.

He sold it when he bought the fish store. Remember? The old building at the corner of Lander and Main?

It was the year Billy was happy. Blue Betas with long, flowery tails. Tiny sharks with wise, old eyes. The peaceful sound of pumps and flowing seaweed.

Do you remember who he sold it to?

I remember when it arrived. Special Delivery from Manila. It took me an hour to open. Covered with packing tape. The parts were oiled and bedded in an army blanket. How they shone! I took them in my hands and smelled them! How I cried! He was coming for Christmas so I decided I'd surprise him. Got all dressed up. Jimmy Whitworth from down the street carried it to the car. I drove to the Marine Corps Recruiter in the Bannock Hotel.

She picked up a cigarette. Smiled happily.

I'll never forget the look on that young man's face! I had on my best suit and my hair done up. Could still turn heads back then. Told him I wanted to surprise my son who was a Marine and was in Vietnam.

Oh, My Lord, Mrs. Husky! Please don't tell anybody you showed this to me! It could get your son twenty years at Leavenworth!

She laughed happily.

I promised. Hid it from your father. Didn't tell anybody.

Dad glowered.

Billy was a screw up. Why are you asking about the gun?

The Taliban are paying top dollar for Fehrmachts. They say they're the best. The Austrians are playing games so State has blocked their sale here.

The Browning fifty caliber machine gun is the best gun made.

Must be. They're going for twenty grand.

I stood up. Kissed my mother. She pleaded.

You could stay longer!

I've got to get back.

The old man looked away. I patted him on the shoulder. Scratched Black Max around the ears. He looked sad too.

SIXTEEN

Three iron workers stood outside the Office smoking.

Wouldn't go in there if I was you! Lot of roughnecks in there!

Looks like the trouble is out here.

No. They get bigger as you go in.

They did. Mr. Collision at the bar. A bigger guy with a pony tail next to him. Juke box tooting Papa Was A Rolling Stone. Slender black dude doing the step and glissade. The barmaid came over. Shimmed into a white blouse and levis.

What'll you have?

What you got on tap?

She arched her back to look.

Bud. Bud Lite. Miller Lite. Amber Bock.

I'll have a Bud, please.

I liked Pocatello. With its faults there were a few blacks around. Some in Boise and Idaho Falls but that was it for the State of Idaho. The Secesh left their beloved South for here because there weren't so many blacks they couldn't drive out and the rest they could keep out. I was talking to a farmer in Soda. Gave me a big smile.

Consanto wanted to bring in some Negroes a few years back. We told them, That's not going to work around here.

So proud of himself. Fascism with a smile. I sat next to Misko. He watched the Saturday game in St. Louis.

Hey what's up.

East Center is hopping.

Not like it used to be. Right, Smoky?

The big guy shook his head.

Tamale vendors. Flim flam men. Holy roller preachers. Dice games on the curb. Blanket Indians with their backs to the wall watching it all.

You're not that old.

Hell I'm not.

It was that way in the Sixties?

Into the Sixties. You bet.

You grew up in Pocatello?

Right on this street.

The bar filled up. Cigarette smoke. Perfumed women with shining lip gloss. The black guy by the juke box danced with a couple of mud sharks. Everybody talked loud but Smoky was easy to hear.

Us kids got an education. We'd go by the Shanghai. Pol Lu standing in the doorway smoking a cigarette.

Hey Pol Lu! What's a matter? You got no grasshopper to eat?

We'd cackle and run. Thought we were real comedians. One day he waved us over.

You know I fresh out. You bring me some I give you a penny a piece.

Handed us a gallon jar. Should've seen our raggedy asses fly! Crawled into the Yard. Tumbleweeds. Abandoned equipment. Went back to Pol Lu like conquering heroes.

You want money or food?

Food, Pol Lu! But don't give us none of them grasshoppers!

Smoky laughed.

We ate like kings. Every time we asked if he needed grasshoppers he never said no. Old Pol Lu. Don't know what he did with those grasshoppers.

He pushed his glass toward the bartender. Lit a cigarette. Spouted smoke.

Then I got a job at the Pocatello House. That was a kick.

Where was that?

Corner of the next block. Through that mirror and down fifty yards.

It was a nice mirror with different colored bottles. The barmaid added effect. Smoky blew out a stream of smoke.

Had money in my pocket for the first time. Even though I wasn't near old enough we'd go across the street to the Wyoming. That was the Indian bar back then. After it got dark we'd slip into the alley. Watch the Indians do it standing up. The squaws would shout.

Get out of here, you little dicks!

We'd laugh and hoot. They'd pull down their skirts and

chase us into the bar. We'd have another drink. Try to catch them at it again. The town was hopping then. All along Center Street. Tamale salesmen. Grifters doing their flim flam. Preachers shouting about the End Times.

Any tunnels under here?

You bet. This was Reservation in the early days. Couldn't sell liquor in any event. So the shops on this side of the tracks were legit at street level. The big money was made in the blinds underneath. There were tunnels between work stations under the Yard. That big stack out west? That was the vent for the whole system. Nobody knows how many tunnels there are under Pocatello. They say the Chinese dug an escape route to the River.

Misko said, You don't know any of this, Bird Man?

No.

That's right. You were the rich kid on the hill.

A tiny, older lady bumped into me. Malay. Had on a pink T shirt and Dodgers cap.

We go now!

Her husband was grey haired. His hat with gold braid said NAVY. Held up his empty glass.

Just one more, Honey.

Her eyes slitted. She shouted above the roar of the bar.

I your Boom Boom Girl, Sailor! I suckee! I fuckee! I sit on face! What you want, Sailor Boy!

The old guy grinned. Took her sedately by the arm. They went out the door like Philemon and Baucis. There was a whoop! The women by the juke box dirty danced. Smoke wreathed around them. Colored lights strobed. The blonde crouched like a lioness sticking out her butt. The brunette placed her V against her. They moved in time, earrings and bangles gleaming.

Looks like the moon is full.

Past.

It's out there somewhere.

The two women entwined their thighs. Lip gloss shone. A skinny guy holding a drink tried menage a trois but they pushed him away. He regained his dignity. Juke box blared Heard It Through The Grapevine. He leaned against Misko. Sang a verse in his ear. Misko growled.

Sit down!

He did. Appraised me with the arrogance of a drunken ferret.

You're cute!

Thanks.

Behave, Timmy. Or I'll take a baseball bat to you.

I asked, So what do you do, Timmy?

Name, rank and serial number. That's all you get.

Misko twirled his index finger.

He rides that black whirly bird you see flying over town.

Pilot?

Fuck no. I'm the guy that returns you to this pathetic level of existence. I'm the guy that packs the good stuff. So you better watch it, Big Boy! You wake up and see me grinning at you? Your ass is mine!

He took a slug of tequila so it ran down his chin. Bad sign. Aztecs drank tequila.

I got drugs that will turn you to stone. You won't remember a thing. Just that people laugh the way you sang like Shirley Temple!

Misko shrugged.

But he doesn't share. If he did we'd show him respect. Call him Doctor.

You fucker!

You fuck her. You brought her.

That's my line!

He tried to tweak Misko's nipple but Mr. Collision was ready. Gave him an elbow that sent him flying. He slid his shot glass onto the bar.

You're harsh, Misko.

He made the rotary sign to the bartender. Tilted his head back. Narrowed his eyes.

Let me tell you about Nurcuron.

You heard how much water is going over Milner?

Four thousand.

Still want to go.

I'm getting to that! Barkeep!

He banged his shot glass on the bar.

Crawl On Your Belly Like A Man

So we got a call from the Superstitions. A guy walking along the Reservoir decided to take a little sunbath. Was asleep when the Boy Scouts arrived. Thought it'd be fun to throw rocks at him. Boy Scouts are like that. They were having so much they didn't stop when he started running around screaming. By the time we got there he had head trauma. Running around like a chicken with its head cut off. Campers weren't happy. Where he didn't have tattoos he had rings. Where he didn't have rings he had spikes with chains. I hit him with a triple load of Nurcuron. Didn't want him waking up. Helicopters are squirrelly. Anything can take them down. One summer we picked up a stiff in the Superstitions. It was ripe. I talked the pilot into letting me hang it from the struts. Coming down the canyon it started swinging. Copter going one way, stiff the other. Pilot screaming.

Cut that rope!

Search and Rescue was just going to have to go find him again.

Bad Luck Mountains.

So I got Mr. Metallica on ice.

How long does it last?

I'm getting to that. Nurcuron completely immobilizes you. It's like you're dead. You have to keep closing their eyes because they dry out. The nurse on duty cleaned him up. He had rings in his dick so they chimed when he walked. Spikes. Needles. Chains. Eyelids, nipples, testicles, lips. Nurses have a funny sense of humor. That's how they are. Pretty soon every doctor, nurse, and candy striper in the hospital is taking the tour. Did they uncover him for educational purposes? Was there speculation as to the use of those chains? I can't tell you.

Not by you of course.

Let's just say morale was high. Next day I went to see how he was doing. Still couldn't move. Had the tube up his nose but glared at me. Motioned at the note pad with his head. Wrote in capital letters: I HEARD EVERYTHING!

Oh my God! My career crashed before my eyes!

He saw you?

His ocular muscles were immobilized. All he could see was the ceiling. Maybe he got used to my voice. Something I said.

You, Timmy?

Nurcuron freezes motor synapses but leaves you awake. Fentonel blocks the memory synapses. If you can't remember pain you can't experience it.

Misko said, They gave me Fentonel when I tore my knee. I remember going in and then the pain when they woke me up.

Because you don't remember does that mean you have no memory?

Too deep for me, Timmy.

Let me tell you then. A little Chicana staggered in one night. Ready to deliver. I gave her Fentonel to stop the screaming. When I woke her asked if she'd felt any pain.

No, Senor.

During the delivery she hadn't stopped screaming.

SEVENTEEN

Max the barkeep slid the pitcher. Tim spilled greenbacks out of his pockets.

So how you doing, Max.

Max was a young, tough guy. Built like a bull.

Got a little headache.

What's your pain threshold?

Max sorted greenbacks.

I can't tell you.

Tim leaned toward him.

Your pain threshold, Max. Like would it hurt if I shoved my fist up your ass!

Max looked at Misko and me. We looked glum.

Get out of here, Tim!

He'll shut up, Max. I promise. If he doesn't I'll stuff him in the dumpster.

Tim gestured at the pile of greenbacks.

Take it. Take it all. I don't want it.

Barmaids were vying for Max's attention. He shook his head. Turned his back. Misko lit a cigarette.

So you must've run into a few snake bites in Arizona.

Snakes too. Rednecks like to show how smart they are by bringing in the rattler. We're screaming.

Get it out of here! We know it's a rattlesnake bite for Christ's sake!

He looked thoughtful.

I hate snakes. If I see a snake--any snake--I start to shriek. The fear has contracted my trachea so I can't breathe. I shriek.

Misko blew out a stream of smoke. Smoke hung in strata of grey and blue where shadows moved.

How d'you treat it?

Tim stared into space.

People get bit on the hand because they're either rock climbing or drunk and playing with it. As the swelling goes up the arm you mark it with a line.

With what?

A Marks-a-lot. As long as the swelling proceeds we hit them with antivenin. If the venom hits the heart they're cooked. We hook them up to every med known to man. Some docs slice the arm to relieve edema. Let me explain it to you this way. The venom is a complex of enzymes. Some cause bleeding. Some cause coagulation. So you're bleeding internally and throwing clots too! It's marvelous. To compensate for the bleeding your heart beats faster. It's either stroke or heart attack. Whichever comes first.

Ever lose anybody?

Once. Two rednecks brought a guy in. They'd been in the desert drinking and shooting snakes. The guy showed them how tough he was by using one for a lariat. Got him on the neck. They'd heard electric shock counteracted rattlesnake venom so--

Homeopathic rednecks!

Tim pointed his trigger finger at me.

Bang! They hooked him up with jumper cables to the truck battery. We don't know what stopped his heart. Venom or electric shock.

Smoky listened in.

I had a dog that got nipped. Poking around a coyote hole on Chink's. Didn't do him no good. Couldn't control his bladder after that. Spent the rest of his life pretty much ashamed of himself.

Who dug those holes?

Think there might be a reason they call it Chink's Peak, Errol?

There's gold up there?

Showalter says there's Pleistocene stream gravels interbedded with old rock. I don't know. If a Chinaman found gold it went back to China.

Timmy said, What is it about dogs? Can't resist a rattler no matter how often they're nipped.

It's hard wired. Couldn't be allowing snakes around if you had pups in dens.

Misko snorted.

It's a matter of honor, Bird Man!

He turned to a little gray haired dude wearing suede cowboy hat, suede vest and lizard skin boots.

Jasper! Just the man we want to see! What's worse? Woman or snakebite?

You left out lightning, Misko. But you're right. They are similar.

Misko grinned.

Because with all your money I don't see a babe on your arm.

All in all I'd say a woman's worse. Hit twice by lightning was enough for me.

Mickey Angel wandered over.

Worse than snake bite?

Oh yeah. It's not like you're bending a corner at Albertson's with a six pack and see a snake coming at you!

Misko threw his head back and roared.

Told you! Best brakeman on the line!

I said, I knew a field man got hit by lightning. Confirmed bachelor. Always had a joke. Next thing we know he quit drinking, got married, stopped telling jokes.

Jasper shook his head.

It's a bad thing. Grandpa had a 160 acres up Teton Basin. Back when you plowed with horses. Had them in the field. Wasn't looking or didn't care a dark front was coming in fast. Now I'm here to tell you. You don't get lightning here in Pocatello in a real sense. Teton Basin is like the all time lightning capital.

Tim nodded.

We life-flighted a guy out of there last summer. Was on the Grand when a storm came out of nowhere. He looked at his hands. The electricity was flowing between his fingertips! Rocks falling from nowhere. Lightning bolts were blasting them from the cliff! Like which is going to take more? The Snake or the Grand?

Jasper agreed.

They are brothers. So the sky got dark. The wind whipped through the trees. Grandpa ain't paying attention. You know sometimes how a front will strike an arc a mile ahead?

Jasper raised his arms like a preacher.

Boom! Lightning hit the traces. The plow lit up. Killed the horses. When Grandma got there saw her beloved horses stone dead. Still smoking! Grandpa flat on his back. Eyes open. Not seeing nothing.

Eyes fixed and dilated, said Tim.

They got him back to the house. Laid him on the bed. He lay there one, two, three days. On the fourth opened his eyes. Grandma clasped her hands.

Hallelujah! It's a miracle!

Gave Testimony that Sunday. How she saw the Spirit come in the night and touch his forehead.

Thank the Lord! Thank the Lord!

Everybody in the congregation on their feet and chanting.

Thank the Lord! Thank the Lord!

A girl got up.

Brother LaBoyd! I have Testimony!

Come up, darling Jessica. Come up and give Testimony!

I saw three young men come down the road from Driggs that evening. Handsome and righteous young men they were! Discoursed as they walked. Turned and smiled at me. Then they went down the road until I could see them no more!

The Three Nephites! Thank you, Jessica! Thank you for your Testimony. Hallelujah!

Misko growled.

Hallelujah. Hit me again, Max.

Jasper shook his head.

True story! That day on? Everybody in the Basin knew a

lightning storm was coming by the way Grandpa staggered in from the fields. Took to his bed. Lay there three days and nights like he was dead. I'll have my usual, Max. Light on the vodka, por favor. Yes. Two marriages is enough for one lifetime.

I drifted. My mother came from the Basin. Her Aunt Cynthia killed that way. Had a milk pail in each hand when it happened. They took the kids out to see where she died. The pails still there where she dropped them. Her shoes too. The lightning had split them.

Oh! Cynthia was the prettiest of the girls! She could still see her coming down the pasture with the pails in her hands!

SEVENTEEN

Mickey Angel said, We were out at Old Juniper Kapuka. Cold and rainy. Snakes were so cold they wouldn't even rattle! We'd locate them when we stepped on them!

They were too cold to strike.

Easy for you to say. Gresham got nipped last year.

Don't know him.

He was tenure track in Economics at ISU. The markets kind of volatile in '87? Channel 6 wanted him to talk about it on camera. El Presidente called.

We don't want you to do that, Dr. Gresham. Business leaders are concerned the impact your interview would have on local business.

What if I do?

I'll fire you.

You can't.

Famous last words. Heard later it was Demetrius Papalos. Couldn't read English but was on the State Board. Made his chops taking photos of anti war demonstrators. So Harvey moved to Challis. Became a gunslinger in Federal Court for the Tribes. Zuniland called.

You be here Saturday morning.

His beautiful raven haired daughter sashayed with her boyfriend into town. Wanted to do a river.

He got Zuniland on the line.

Can't make it.

You better!

They were rolling down the Snake at Hells Canyon. Harvey scouting ahead in the canoe, the kids following in the raft.

He had a canoe in Hells Canyon?

I'm telling you, man. Harvey is a stud. Second day he pulled onto the rocks. Was sitting there eating an apple when he saw a gust come upriver. Before he knew it the canoe was in the river. He was scrambling. The canoe went through a rapid and into an eddy. Just as he got to it another gust came up. Took it back into the current. It was like a dream where this was going to keep happening! He was climbing through a strainer when he felt the sting. Saw the rattler ready for reprise.

Eeek!

He limped along. Finally caught up to the canoe. Three days of big water ahead.

Didn't get a lot of sleep I guess.

No. Had marijuana though. That helped.

You listening, Timmy?

Seemed to have slipped it but a week later had a heart attack.

Misko drained his glass.

Those Zuni's have a real sense of humor. He ever talk to them about it?

They just laughed.

Hey Bridge! How much water going over Milner?

A bearded guy in a ball cap shouted.

Three thousand! But they say when American Falls tops out they're going to open the gates!

Misko and Mickey Angel went down bar. Tim slipped out the door. Juke box played I Call Your Name. The babes danced toward me. Bangles shining from earlobes and wrists. The blonde put her arm around me swaying her head side to side. Pressed her breast against me. I felt the buzz. Her friend moved her head side to side so the hoop earrings swung in synchrony. Looked me in the eyes. Fish whose sexual accoutrement become enhanced in breeding season. Put her beautiful tanned hands around my neck.

Slipped onto my thigh. Slid her V to my hip joint. Whispered in my ear.

Do you like this?

I do.

She arched. Slid back toward my knee with her arms still around my neck. Slid toward me again. Eyes, day-glow lips half open. The brunette whispered in my ear.

You want to take us someplace?

All of us?

Yes. We like to watch.

The woman riding my thigh slid up against me. Put her hand on my chest. Stared into my eyes.

She likes to watch me and I like to watch her.

I glanced at the rock blazing on her hand.

What about your husbands?

The woman riding my thigh wrinkled her nose.

Fuck them.

She slid reluctantly off. Her friend withdrew her arm from my neck. They drifted back to the juke box. It flashed and throbbed. The black guy poured in quarters. Sugar Pie Honey. Did the side slip moon walk. Mickey Angel, cowboy hat pulled low, sat with his back to the wall. Bridger shook his head.

No way, Crow. When I turn in my keys I'm getting far as geographically possible from the WP.

WP's been good to you, Bridge.

I just bought land New Mexico way. No water or electricity. But you can't hear a train from nowhere.

Tell Errol the wetback story.

Bridger glanced suspiciously at me.

We're at the Opal Siding. Got a call there was a delay. Freight coming our way had the main track but was stopped anyway. We could see it up there. Headlights blazing.

What's the problem?

Couple of wetbacks.

What the big deal about that?

The train coming your way is pulling fifty hoppers of Hanford dirt. Ten flats of TNT. But for safety's sake? They alternated a few empty box cars. What the Mexicans crawled into.

Thinking it their lucky day!

When was this?

Last year. Wouldn't do to have terrorists detonate that train as it rolled through Salt Lake City. So we hung out on the cat track. Looked at that train. Wondered how far you'd want to be in the event it detonated.

Mickey Angel said, Not in the Blue Book, Bridge?

I said, What's the Blue Book?

Rules and Regulations. And it's written in blood! For example I could never figure why they made you halt at a siding at least a quarter mile from the switch. No exceptions. Then I saw it. Big Time. The freight coming our way was going sixty when it hit the jammed switch. High sided. Heavy laws of physics in play now. Like how far is that double header going to ride the port wheels before box cars fly. And did. Three hundred ton diesels swapped ends. Box cars tumbling. Heart Attack City. Then they just piled up fifty yards ahead! Smoke and fire! Somebody screaming. Thought it was somebody in the wreck but it was me! Started running. Thought I'd save who might be left alive but there wasn't.

Bridger tossed the whisky down.

My Lord In Heaven! My heart has never been the same! But that's the Blue Book. So yeah! When me and Unruly Julie fly south like a couple snow hens? It's going to be fifty miles from the nearest track.

Horns don't carry that far?

Not on the coldest, clearest winter night.

What was the funniest thing you saw?

Funniest thing? Had to be when the cowboy hijacked the Amtrak the other side of Lava. The conductor come up.

A cowboy in the dining car says he's hijacking the train.

He what?

He's got a knife and wants to go to Fairfield.

You can't hijack a train, Parley!

I explained that to him. What rails are and how trains run on them. But it's not getting through. He's drunk. He's got a knife. The people in the dining car are not happy.

Earl Sprague was Dispatch.

We been hijacked, Earl!

You can't hijack a train!

We explained that, Earl.

We're rolling past Robbers Roost. Calling our buddies.

Can't make that poker game. We been hijacked.

We got to the station in Pocatello. Cops took him away.
Didn't even make the Journal.

You wonder where he is now.

Idaho State Legislature.

Bridger stood up. Mickey Angel put out his hand.

You got a lot of friends here, Bridge.

He winked.

And some of 'em I haven't even used yet!

The high drift passed. Juke box silent. Fragments of
conversation.

Now, Dan. Your brother always loved you.

When he could get something from me.

You want another, Mickey Angel?

He had his hat pulled over his eyes.

No. Going to sit here until I can walk. Well I can walk but
I'm not sure I can stay on the sidewalk. Cops hate that.

Think you and Johanna will get back together?

She'll keep me on the hook.

Why?

You can tell me about women let me know. Got a letter
from her yesterday. Her pretty handwriting. My heart doing flips.
Said she'd gone into a deep meditation. Saw me on the deck of a
ship with my sword at my side. It was my ship. She was my slave.
I'd used her badly even though I loved her. She hated me for that.
Realized she'd come into this world once more to absolve herself
of that hate.

Doesn't seem to be working, Mickey Angel.

No. Funny she'd say that though. I love the sea. Love to
look at it. Buy any books I can about it. Look at the pictures.
Sailing ships too. But never went out on it. Never got on a boat to
deep water. Had my chances too.

EIGHTEEN

I drove to my parent's house. Lombardy poplar along the road. The house with yellow shutters. Mom came out on the porch. I heard Robbie crying. Found him under the dining room table. Sobbing because he'd been abandoned. I lifted him with my left arm. He put his arms around my neck. Clancy held the tiny warrior they'd been fighting over. Raised his arms.

Up! Up!

I knelt to swoop him in my right arm. Stood with them hugging my neck. They glared at each other. Little falcons! The love I felt for them was more than I could bear. Woke in the back of the truck. Box cars rumbled like boulders crashing in avalanche. Fiery snakes crawled at the edge of my vision. I leaned against the truck. An engine came out of the northwest with headlights blazing. Looked like a big yellow mastiff with black muzzle. The thump of wheels at the Underpass. I drove under the tracks. Saw the V of the canyon above West Center. Took an ibuprofen. The old soldier hunched in the steam room.

I said, You were airborne infantry, right?

Yes sir. 101st.

When you dropped in some Godforsaken place? How'd you find your way?

Before Global Positioning? Had to have a map. A good one. And two men. Hard to do alone. Selected a landmark. Headed toward it. The man in front held the compass. Tried to hold a straight line.

Hard to do in the mountains.

Very. The second counted steps. If you had another he counted too. At the landmark you wrote distance and direction. Chose another landmark. If your map were reliable you'd know where you were after two or three entries.

Had to keep counting.

Keep walking. Keep counting.

The steam swirled. Talk made me feel better. Figures slipped into the pool. The old soldier reached for the cold water.

A propos of record keeping there's an interesting story if you'd care to hear.

I do.

A private was captured at the encirclement at Chosen. It happened a lot. Intelligence told you there were no Chinese in the vicinity. You'd be marching down a road and see the ridges crawling with them. They marched him to Hungnam. Kept him in solitary. As the months passed he heard through the grapevine--

Morse code?

Of course. He heard of the deaths of men by torture or execution. Began to make a list because nobody would know what happened to them. Whether they died on the march or in prison or deserted. He wrote on the back of soup can labels. Envelopes. Whatever he could steal. One day the guards tossed his cell and found it. Beat him for three days. Bruises he'd received one day were given special attention the next. He gave no information. Had buried a copy in the yard. At the Ceasefire gave it to the attending officer who filed it under Lost. When he returned to the States began a career as hobo, drug addict, dishwasher, drunk.

He'd given up the only thing of value to him.

That's correct. Thirty years passed. One day in Alexandria a young clerk was going through files. Found it. When they tracked him down he was a bum on the streets of St. Louis. Gave him the Navy Cross and a new suit of clothes.

Stiffs sat smoking on the retaining wall by the High School parking lot. Kids walked to school. The sun lit up the Cross atop Trinity Church. I had a mocha at Bernardo's. Read papers. Walked along the river. When I got to Michael Angelo's he was lying on his back. I leaned against the door frame.

You look a little off color, Mickey Angel.

I feel off color.

Embalming fluid might help.

Got any?

Formaldehyde. In the truck.

No thanks. Prefer not to be preserved in this condition.

Hah! Rough crowd last night.

You left before the fun started. Ike wandered in. Misko had to be restrained.

Stay the fuck away from her, man!

I'm doing her bathroom, Misko! That's it!

Smoky chipped in.

Helping her with her eccentric coupling, Ike? How to adjust the ball and cock? Haw! Haw!

No blood lost?

No. Had to hand it to Ike though. Stood his ground. Misko feinted like he was going to strike but Ike didn't budge.

Bad idea. Jeopardize your watering hole for a woman.

Ike's not interested in Roxie.

Give me a break, Mickey Angel. Everybody's interested in Roxie. Watching her walk in a room gets you interested.

Don't want to talk about it, Errol.

I turned a spinner rack.

How'd she and Misko link up?

Here. Misko talked about the Lower Salmon. Big holes you can fish. Roxie likes the Big Outdoors. We went to Lionel's. Miles and Santana maxed out on the boom box. Misko and Roxie on the sofa when he started shouting at her.

Shouting?

Misko's a big guy. You noticed that? Roxie started crying. Went to the bathroom. When she came back? Took him by the hand and they left. Any doubts I might have had about the role of male dominance in female sexual arousal were pretty much dispelled.

What'd he tell her?

The Railroad Strike of 1923. When the men on the rolling stock broke rank. Left the machinists high and dry. The Republicans couldn't've done it without Main Street. Misko's grandma did laundry for the Station Master's wife. The old man stroked out at fifty.

Roxy was crying?

She's got that patina, Errol! If you went to her bedroom in Ohio? You'd see the four poster bed, the satin coverlet. Beatles posters on the wall. Mama keeping it nice for when she visits. Misko went right at her. She was nodding her head.

I know! I know!

You'll never know! What it does to a family! When they make you crawl for the least crumb!

Those pretty, green eyes filled with tears. When she came

back from the bathroom looked down at him. He looked up at her. And they left!

Mickey Angel lay with his eyes closed.

He says when they broke the Strike it moved the Italians and Irish out and the Mormon kids from the outlying farms in. That true?

I didn't say Grandma and Grandad drifted up from Raft River that year. Got a job as brakeman when you halted a train by running atop the cars to turn the wheel brake. When he lost his leg in Georgetown Canyon had the down payment for the Laidlaw acreage. Mickey Angel didn't know. In Southern Idaho there was a Mormon behind every woodpile.

I drove up Mink Creek. Birches leafing out. Sat on the tailgate to pull on the waders. Birds sang. Here I am! Here! I got ruler and thermometer. The creek ran high. Pulled at my ankles. Where it widened to a pool I took measurements. Eleven inches. 41 degrees. Plucked stones. A couple of mayfly larva with their big shiny eyes and six grasping legs. That was it. West Fork was closed to cattle but the East and South Fork were pounded. What saved West Fork was that it was the water supply for Pocatello in the early days. The pipe still crossed the scree above. I waded up the riffle to another pool. Silt sucked at my boots. Decided I would set traps when the water went down. Goldfinches flitted among the branches. Mists of insects drifted here and there. They could say Mink Creek was a fishery but without clean gravels it was just another blind.

I drove up East Fork. Walked between cows to the creek. No birch, wild roses, currants or chokecherries. Just grass and cow pies. The creek ran fast like a ditch. Got back in the truck. Passed road cuts colored red, yellow and green. Pulled over at a switch back for a view of the Wolf Jaws. Foreshortening shimmed the plain to a strip of gray.

The old guys looked at those peaks. Didn't savvy how much lava intervened. Headed toward the only water on the map at Big Butte. Root Hog Spring. Not a spring. A seep. As in, Root, Hog, or die!

A man traveling toward Big Butte saw a figure staggering in the heat waves. Something big and red sticking out of its mouth.

The horseman wondered about that. When he got closer saw it was the man's tongue! Would be unable to tell him then or anytime thereafter how he arrived at that place.

At Justice Park sub alpine fir sheltered deep snow. I glassed the chant rock for chalk. Saw none. When I got back Mickey Angel was talking to an old guy with hooded eyes and close-cropped grey hair. A sleeveless T shirt showed off his powerful shoulders. He bowed.

We meet again.

I could only nod.

He turned to Mickey Angel.

Look. I have some business across the street. I was hoping you'd watch my jacket for me. Would that be alright?

He left the jacket under the chair. I watched him cross the street. The finish on the goat skin airman's jacket sand blasted soft as cashmere! It was folded over a canvas pack with a pistol and six magazines of twelve rounds. I replaced it. Handed Mickey Angel a beer.

I said, Where'd you find this guy?

He wandered in a couple of weeks ago.

He's got enough heat in there to hold off half of Pocatello's Finest!

He buys books.

So you go for the phony English accent?

No. Can't place it though. Funny thing about accents. A few years ago a kid came in looking for a guide to the City of Rocks. Something in his voice.

Where you from?

San Diego.

Where were you born?

San Diego.

You lived there your whole life? What about your parents?

My father is from North Carolina. My mother is Viennese.

I'd heard that uvular turn of the vowel.

I said, Got it with his mother's milk.

Maybe. Wagner told me a great story.

Who's he?

Smarter than you or me will ever be, Errol. Never worked a

day in his life. Grew up in American Falls with a Mennonite kid from Desert Entry. The kid spoke German at home but perfect English at school. Wagner swears you couldn't hear the slightest shade of German. Just an American farm kid. When he enrolled at ISU it came to the attention of the CIA. It seems the kid's family came from a region of East Germany with a strong dialect. They offered him the moon.

He took it?

Nope.

Smart guy.

He took Spanish at ISU because he liked languages. The professor was a Spanish émigré. The second semester assigned La Luna y La Caballero to be committed to memory. The kid recited it perfectly. The professor turned white. Walked out. Was unable to return.

I don't get it, Mickey Angel.

In pre war Madrid there were always students from Germany hanging out at the cafes. Talking and laughing. Several were his friends.

I still don't get it.

Mickey Angel twirled the empty bottle.

The kid recited La Luna y La Caballero with a German accent.

NINETEEN

Gerald crossed the street. Looked side to side with the unhurried wariness of a rattlesnake. Glanced at his jacket. At me.

Have you noticed all the mass shootings in America have taken place where guns are not allowed?

What do you pack?

He drew the pistol out. Admired it as if for the first time.

Nine millimeter Glock.

Mickey Angel leaned over.

That little gun shoots a nine millimeter?

With hydro shock. The slug is engineered to create hydraulic suction as it traverses the wound channel. It doesn't matter where the individual is hit. Organic activity in the vicinity of the wound ceases. He will be in shock in a matter of seconds.

He returned it to the pack.

Herr Glock wanted a light gun that could deliver payload with neither recoil nor interval between flash and bang. In this he succeeded. He told them he was looking at polymers. They told him he was crazy.

A pretty woman lurked in the tall shelves. Set a stack of books on the desk.

This is a dangerous place.

Mickey Angel grinned. Gerald admired her backside.

What book is that?

Mickey Angel said, Mutant Message Down Under. I loved the part where they let ants crawl over them. Into their eyes and ears so they had glossy skin and could hear really well.

Gerald smiled.

There are variations of that method.

The woman gave him a stern glance. Departed. He raised his eyebrows wistfully.

Rump reader radar. They all have it. We had entered Cambodia and made contact with all the local chiefs. Sat around the table eating. The head man wrinkled his nose.

Man! You guys are really lousy!

We were. Had waited in the jungle for three weeks so nobody would know we were there. Had picked up all the local varieties. They made us take off our clothes. The only uncomfortable part was the instrument they inserted in the urethra. Other than that it wasn't too bad. The plug inserted in the anus as well. They covered our eyes with a gooey salve and gave us hollow stems to breathe with. We lay with our clothes beside us between two huge ant mounds. Soon we were completely covered. I can assure you my friends: for two hours I had no other thought than the thousands of ants crawling over, under and into every crevice of my body. It was not an experience that is soon forgotten. I had achieved that state of complete attention so admired in religious circles as red ants stimulated every nerve ending in my body. After awhile they drifted away. Returned satiated to their loved ones. We were left clean as the day we were born.

Babes in the wood, I said.

He gave me a hooded look.

Our clothes were clean as well. Other methods would have killed the lice but the egg packets in our clothes would have remained.

Mickey Angel asked, What other methods did you use?

Vaseline. In the jungle you use it everywhere. On cuts. As a general rule all over your body. Anything to keep the jungle out. For example you cover a cotton ball dipped in alcohol with Vaseline and insert it with a Q-tip into your urethra. This keeps out the tiny fishes that inhabit the rivers of South America. Should you attempt to cross a river? They will try to migrate to the Holy Land of your bladder.

Yeow!

Oh it's not so bad when they go up. It's when they panic and flare their spiny fins to return that it can be rather unpleasant! For the same reason you take a cotton ball treated in the same manner and insert it up your rectum. Essential for keeping out the lovely fauna of those rivers. As a bonus you use it as a fire starter. It burns forever.

Mickey Angel looked at the clock.

We're going to the First National if you want a drink, Gerald. I'm buying.

Where is that?

On the corner by the Underpass.

Do they have food?

Cathy will cook you a burger.

Agreed.

He draped the jacket over his forearm. As he left I saw words tattooed on his calves.

Marche o meurt.

Good advice. We went into the street. Waited for traffic to pass. A Jeep Grand Cherokee screeched to a halt. A beautiful dark woman jumped out with hair flying. Skirt swirling. Mickey Angel back pedaled. She pounded his chest with her fists.

Why haven't you called!

Blood red lipstick and fingernails.

What are you trying to do to me!

I haven't had time, Johanna.

You have time to hang out with your drunken friends! You bastard! You son of a bitch!

She turned on me. Big brown eyes, pupils oscillating.

Who are you!

I back pedaled. Cars honked. Tires screeched. She turned back to Mickey Angel.

It doesn't matter! Just another shill! Using you for what you have! Don't you see how you hurt me! Don't you see how it hurts me to see you drinking yourself to bits! When all I ever wanted to do was love you!

I'm not drinking myself to bits, Johanna.

You bastard! Ruining myself for you! My job! My reputation!

Her shoulders sank. She wept. Tears cut through eyeliner and rouge. She was a sweet looking babe. Was shaking. I felt sorry for her. Cars honked. A jerk yelled.

Get the fuck out of the road, lady!

She stared at Mickey Angel with her mouth half open. A little falcon left out in the rain.

I love you! Don't you understand! I gave you my body and my soul and look how you treat me!

It's not something I want, Johanna.

Then do something! Show me you love me! Show me anything!

He looked at the traffic jammed all the way back to the Yellowstone Hotel.

I'll call you. I promise. I love you.

She slumped. Wiped her eyes. Stared at her hand as if surprised to see the black and red.

You don't love me, Michael. Why don't you just say it.

I won't.

The honking was general. A siren approached. She shook her head as if coming to her senses.

Of course.

He took her by the arm. Got her in the Jeep. Nodded as he listened. Shut the door. She backed up. Put pedal to metal so the tires smoked. The siren closed. He stood with hands in pockets looking at the pavement.

We can do this some other time, Mickey Angel.

No.

He pulled his hand out. Looked at the coins as if there were a message there.

I said, Nice to be loved.

He looked at me like the guy in the docket trying to remember how he got there. We passed the Paris Building with spikes atop the façade. Freight cars crossed Center Street. Two Mexicans lay on the Railroad Dispensary lawn on their way to somewhere. The rolling stock went Thump Ka-thump! Old cars with sun warped sides. Chicago Northwest. Wisconsin Central. Marinette, Tomahawk and Western. Cattle cars, gondola cars, box cars with side doors open. Colorful graffiti scrolled. Scripts you could never read.

TWENTY

Stained glass above the door to the First National used to be above the bar at the Bannock. I used to study it as I waited for Dad to tell one more war story. Studied it now. At the window a pretty woman smoked and read. Mickey Angel held the door.

You coming?

Stained glass above the bar. The drunks looked like dingy saints with the smoke from their cigarettes scrolling up. I heard a whistle.

Errol! Over here!

The woman by the window had her thumb and index finger still at her mouth.

Rachel! I didn't expect to see you!

I know! I swore I'd never come back! Karmic vortex I guess. Sit down!

Mickey Angel still pale.

I heard it was the Karmic Debt Center.

I said, Everybody has a variation. The Curse of Chief Pocatello. Magnetic Anomaly in the Gap. You can't get out. Or keep coming back 'til you've worked out some deep, dark debt.

Rachel laughed happily.

That's even worse!

The barmaid had rhinestone eyeliner, narrow cat eyes that glowed green like pools of Prestone. Wore painted-on leopard skin lycra.

Not only that! You'll get sucked in to help somebody work out theirs!

Oh my gosh, Tina! Who said that?

She nodded at the bar.

A social worker. Sat on that barstool every night.

Somebody else there now. On the stage a muscular guy with a ring glittering in his ear set up microphones.

Chief Pocatello? asked Rachel

I said, They buried him with his horses in a spring above American Falls. When they built the dam it flooded his grave. So he leads lost souls here. They think it's a job interview or classes at ISU. It's an illusion.

Rachel gave Mickey Angel her best smile.

How'd you get here?

Graduate School.

In what?

Biology.

I said, Mickey Angel studied bats.

Bats! I love bats! What happened?

My advisor got in a fight with the Chair. I was in Costa Rica. When I got back he was gone. My data had vanished.

I raised a toast.

Number 357 in the category, How I Got Left High And Dry In Pocatello.

What are others?

You're driving to the Coast. Your car breaks down. It's a hold up to fix it. The job you get to pay for it doesn't pay enough. You think, Next year. Next year never comes. But it's pretty.

Rachel wrinkled her nose.

It's an ugly town. But it's got nice light.

Cold nine months of the year. The wind blew dirt from the rail yards. Flowers froze in June. Neighbors informed if you smoked pot or strolled the street with a beer. But it had nice light.

Rachel shone hers on Mickey Angel.

Where're you from?

Wisconsin.

Wisconsin? I'm from Wisconsin! What part?

Milwaukee.

I knew that accent! I got my degree at Marquette. What's your name?

Michael.

I know! Your last name!

Cronisteri.

Rachel clapped her hand to her mouth.

Oh my gosh! Errol! Didn't you know? He's from the biggest Mafia family in Milwaukee! They helped kill Kennedy!

He hunched. Flicked dark, unhappy eyes. I patted him on the back.

Think of him as the Bad Seed.

She laughed.

I bet you have your rosary.

I do.

Which bats did you study?

In Costa Rica? Fishing bats. Here I did a survey at RML. Where the money came from.

I said, Back home in Milwaukee he saw ISU advertising a fellowship in bat biology. It seemed they found his data and the money was still there!

Imagine that.

He came back. Showed them the letter from his lawyer. Stopped at the Round Up Room. Saw the For Rent sign across the street. The rest is history.

Rachel pointed her trigger finger.

You came back too! What bats at RML?

Big browns. Townsend's big eared. Small footed myotis. A lot of them out there.

What's a myotis?

They have the wing membrane all the way to the tail. It's paradise for them out there. They have the lava tubes to roost in. All that open country. No pesticides, no ATV's, no bubbleheads. If you trespass? A jeep with a mounted M-2 comes at you. Marines jump out with orders to kill. Can't arrest you but they can shoot you.

Why is that?

Armed Forces have no civilian authority.

So no redneck survivalists from Blackfoot. No crazed ranchers.

Mickey Angel said, Just radioactive waste dumps and an ambulance that will be hot another million years.

Why is that?

They had a big bang.

When?

1955. Back when they hauled radioactive slag into the desert and buried it with a backhoe.

Ok. What was the big bang?

A tech at RB1 pulled a rod out. They found him impaled on the ceiling sixty feet above with his hands still locked around it. His best friend at the far door like he was trying to get out.

Oh really?

You got it. The wife had called a couple hours earlier to tell him not to come home.

I knew a guy that worked at Hanford. He watched an engineer in a white lab coat set two tiny globes of plutonium in the jaw of a vise and turn the screw until they spat. Dancing With The Dragon. One day he turned it a little too far.

Rachel rolled her head like she were awakening.

And the ambulance?

They headed for Idaho Falls with the two guys in it. The guard at the gate swept it with the Geiger counter.

I don't think so, boys.

So it's buried out there. Because it's too hot for anywhere.

Mickey Angel raised his eyes and palms to the ceiling.

Encrypted, so to speak.

A rap at the window. Gerald looked in. We waved. He came in, the jacket over his forearm, scanning the bar. Took Rachel's hand. Kissed it. Looked deep into her eyes.

Enchanted, my lady.

She shivered with pleasure.

Myself as well!

He sat back to the wall. The drunks hunched over drinks.
The guitarist tuned his guitar. Rachel pulled a cigarette out of her
purse. Mickey Angel told Gerald he'd been reading about the Fall
of Singapore. How hard the English had been on poor Percy.
Gerald flicked the chrome lighter.

His defense was juvenile. But you must remember the
General had commercial interests on the island that might have
limited his options.

It was a lovely lighter. Had a red monogram I couldn't
catch.

I didn't know that.

It's an old colonial tradition not mentioned in the history
books. The commanding general always got his cut. Mining.
Agriculture. For instance can you name the Military Governor of
the Philippines before the war? Douglas MacArthur. The reason he
had to return was he had too much money invested not to!

He lit his cigarette.

Can I see your lighter, Gerald?

He scowled at me. Put it back in his pocket.

Have you never been to Singapore, Michael? Above the
harbor stands a granite obelisk five stories high. On it are engraved
the names and nationalities of the individuals that died in the
Defense. British. Australian. Indian. Malay...Vietnamese.

He took a deep sensual drag of the cigarette.

Percy ordered the heavy cruiser Bonham with its sixteen
inch guns scuttled in the harbor. The soldiers told to fight on. As
they awaited the Japanese the oil dumps behind them were ignited.
Not good for morale. A hundred thousand surrendered to thirty.

You must read everything!

Actually, my lady, I got this from personal experience.
After the War the Admiralty sent in a salvage crew. The Bonham
was there but the guns were gone! Four sixteen inch guns eighty
feet long! Where had they gone? It was a mystery. But they showed
up eventually. Can you guess where?

Dien Bien Phu?

Sixteen inch guns, Michael.

The musician strummed chords. Harmonic waves swept
through the bar.

A ridge overlooked the DMZ. As there was some ambiguity who controlled it we as an elite force were ordered to secure it. This would be good not only for morale but strategically as well. Are you following me?

Totally, Gerald!

Intelligence which in Vietnam was a magnificent oxymoron informed us resistance would be negligible. Nor was artillery present. 312 of us made the assault. At the summit we had a hundred. The ridge was limestone lifted from an ancient sea. Sixteen inch shells cut shards of rock from the cliffs that cut men in two! We saw the puffs of smoke across the valley. Imagine our pleasure when the B-29's arrived. Turned that ridge into flame. But that night as we bedded down heard distant thunder. What could it be? Then the shriek of sixteen inch shells coming in.

He snubbed out the cigarette.

We made other sleeping arrangements. But I can tell you. The memory of that descent through the night with the screams of men being cut in two was not easily forgotten.

The Viet Minh had dug six tunnels by hand a quarter mile into the mountain. Lined them with railroad track. Nobody tried to find out where the guns of the Bonham had gone. We found out. It was like a novel where characters appear, disappear and reappear when you least expect it!

Rachel put her hand on his forearm.

How did you get over it?

It is the art of war. I had a friend who fought with the Resistance in Greece. He was captured because of information supplied to the Germans by a man of the village. My friend--shall we call him Odysseus? Was delivered to the S.S. Every day they took one thing more from him. Would inform him of the method they would use the following day so he would have the night to think about it.

But he didn't turn. He knew they wouldn't kill him because of what he knew. This knowledge kept him alive.

Gerald lit another cigarette.

I asked him how he endured without losing his mind. He said he knew there was that possibility. That if the hate took over it would destroy him. So he taught himself to love that hate. To love it with complete devotion. This he accomplished.

Rachel had tears in her eyes. I wanted a cigarette.

Even when the Brits kept the collaborators in power?

Gerald looked at me. The cobra raised its head. Slipped back into the dark. He smiled.

Love is eternal is it not?

TWENTY ONE

I looked at the flowing curves of the river running high but clear. I saw the interweaving currents. A dog swam from the depths. I had her by the leash. She pawed at the current but when she got close gave up. Or didn't want to leave.

It was dark when I drove into town. Tall lights shone on the railroad yard. I went on the roof. Half moon over the Bannock Range. In the trap two pigeons. One to fly. One to die. Flew against the bars. I sat at the parapet above Main. Heard clatter of wings. Two pigeons settled in front of Bernardo's. Then one flew across the street. The other fluttered wildly above the sidewalk. A shadow emerged from the doorway. Reeled in the pigeon by looping the line over his elbow. The little Indian in the long black coat returned to the shadows. After a moment flung head and wings into the gutter. Lit a cigarette and hobbled down Main.

I slid the cage under the firewall. Watched a bat fly in the alley as the sky lightened. It flew like a butterfly. I descended to the truck. Dreamed. When my boots hit the sidewalk saw American flags unfurled along Main. Street Indians in black came down the alley laughing. Crows on power lines cawed at them.

I remembered the story of the boy that went to the land of Centipede. His brothers and sisters had gone there and not returned. He snared a little bird for dinner. She looked him in the eye.

If you spare me I'll tell you how to enter the land of Centipede. If you don't he'll kill you.

Talk, little bird.

You'll see him when you cross the mountain. He'll shake his robe and lay it on the ground. Don't sit on it. Sit on the ground.

He'll try to get his arms under yours. Don't let him. Choose the game you want to play. Don't play the Hand Game. Choose Football. You'll beat him in the end. You'll go to a dark place where it's always night. The Indians lost their ball there and the game. After that he burned them. These two eggs will go with you. Centipede won't see them. One is Gopher. The other is Owl. Owl will blink so it is light. Gopher will dig a hole that Centipede will lose his ball in. He'll try to pay you in hearts and hands. Don't take them. Take him by the arms and burn him up! There is only one of your people left. He is so burned he turned into a crow.

The crows rocked on the power lines, puffing out throat feathers. The street Indians went their way. I drove to Deseret Industries. Across the street a bear-like old man loomed in a field of iris. None had bloomed. He had a metal folding chair as a crutch. Held a shovel in the other. Started stabbing the earth with the shovel. Cricket chirped. Finches sang in apple trees. It was a noisy garden. He didn't use pesticides. Used the shovel. I stood at the fence.

Cold weather slowed them?

He looked at me like an old, rheumy eyed bear.

It's backed them up some.

People must be looking forward to the next couple of weeks.

He nodded.

Might be my last year though. Twenty years is enough.

How'd you get so many?

I started with a few. Then people brought them. As people died and this and that. Kind of got out of hand.

All year the guy worked for two weeks of bloom. Mickey Angel drove up in his metal mustang. Waited at the door of Deseret Industries. The B minor Mass ended. I crossed the street. A portly old guy wearing a Navy hat and red suspenders stood next. A grizzled dude wearing a beret with combat pin sidled up.

Look at the people waiting to get at dead people's things!

The man with red suspenders grinned.

Look at you! You're here too!

Mickey Angel turned to him.

So Lou. How'd they make ice in the old days?

In the Ice House!

How did you make it and get it in cars?

You poured water into the ice cans. Ran NO2 around it. That's how you made ice. We made the best ice in the country because we had good water back then. Pocatello always had good water. Then they put the dump at Fort Hall Mine.

How'd you carry the blocks?

With a picaroon.

What's a picaroon?

You don't know nothing. A picaroon is a big pair of tongs. You'd hook the block and swing it on your knee down the plank. Hundred pound blocks. In the old days every town had an ice house. You had a layer of ice then straw then ice again all the way to the ceiling. Bear Lake was a big ice producer. Shipped it out of Montpelier.

They ever find copper at Fort Hall Mine?

Not enough to pay. Who's your friend?

Errol.

What's his last name?

Husky.

I thought you looked familiar. Spitting image of your old man. Taller though. How's he doing?

Hanging in there.

Lou shook his head. Laughed.

Never forget as long as I live. Was up Whiskey Mike's drowning a worm at the railroad crossing. One of those blue and gold days. A big sedan come up the road fast. Big guy in a blue suit got out. Your dad. Had on a pair of hundred dollar Italian loafers. I waited for him to change but he just grabbed the rod and slipped down the bank. I couldn't believe it! Didn't even look at me. Worked his way up the river making little sidearm casts. I just sat my butt down and laughed. Those Italian loafers? Cost more than I made in a month! Your dad. He's was something else.

Mickey Angel shrugged.

Soft leather shoes would be good on river gravel if you thought about.

Sure! My wife Stella worked in Surgery twenty years. Swore your dad hung the moon. They'd brought in a young woman to work on her female parts. She started to bleed. Blood pressure fell to nothing! Stella looked at Dr. Gordon. Sweat pouring off his forehead.

Call Dr. Husky.

Your Dad took one look.

Help me turn her over.

He went through her lower back with shears. Strong as a bull your Dad. Found the artery. Saved her bacon. Saved everybody's. Nobody like your old man!

No.

I looked at the apricot tree in blossom across the street. Wondered what happened the day he went fishing at Whisky Mike's.

Looks like the apricots slipped the frost.

The Nam Vet looked over his shoulder.

I hate apricots. Every time somebody opened a can we got whacked.

Mickey Angel turned.

What tank did they use in Vietnam?

The Patton.

I was reading that the Sherman couldn't match up to a Tiger but Patton liked them because they went forever.

Men were expendable.

I read they laid concrete across the front.

75mm went right through a Sherman. Both sides if hit broadside. Which was good. The shell didn't ricochet. Funny story about Sherman's. I was living by a run down section of LA. Crack houses. Places the local talent took their clients.

Where the Okies lived before they moved up.

Right. The City hired a guy to level it. Urban Renewal. He come with a Sherman Tank! Bush hog welded to the front. I sat on the porch with a beer and watched this Sherman go through shanty town! He'd drop the rear end into a basement every once in awhile. Have to call a Cat. But other than that leveled a square mile of LA in three weeks!

With a Sherman Tank!

The Vet grinned.

How we kept the gonorrhea rate down in Vietnam. Behind

you, Lou.

The manager opened the door. Mickey grabbed a basket. Flew down the aisle. I found a cut glass vase for a dollar. Lou looked at figurines.

You were in the Pacific, right?

Yes sir.

Mechanic?

Gunner on DDB.

What was that?

Dauntless Dive Bomber.

Fifty caliber?

You bet. The Browning Machine Gun was the best gun made.

I saw him shooting into the sky with his back to the pilot. Flying through flak. Hoping they caught the hook on the way back.

How'd you do it?

Had to have your fangs out.

Thank you, Lou.

Mickey Angel went through a stack checking for water damage, cigarette smoke. I saw a hardcover For Whom The Bells Toll on the rack for $2. Showed it to him. He shook his head.

Book club. No jacket. If it had I might've got it.

Dust jacket's that important?

He grinned.

Errol? A book without a dust jacket is like a red head without black nylons.

TWENTY TWO

Memorial Day. Meat Market closed. I made coffee on the Coleman. Bathed in Mink Creek. Put on a clean shirt. Stopped at a Queen Anne house for sale on Garfield. Tulips in bloom under the bay window. Put them in the vase. Down the street the Stanrod Mansion stood with its two towers, mansard roof and widow's walk. Leaded windows. Hand carved stairwell and bookcases. Stanrod wrote the water law for the Idaho Constitution. Ruined the fisheries of Idaho forever. The History of Idaho 1912 said, Judge

Stanrod never let money get in the way of principle. They gave him a bank too in case he ran out.

The Brady Chapel stood with its gabled roof, pointed arches, stained glass windows. Cars glided past the gravestones. The apartment I shared at ISU was down the road. Memorial Day came hard on Finals. We invited all the girls we knew. Festooned the apartment with flowers. Spicer was Botany so no lack of double entendre. Burnett, Pharmacy. Slipped the Archive lock. Donated a bottle of tincture of opium. We made cigarettes with it. That's all I remember.

Fox squirrels came down the trees headfirst looking for handouts. I looked for vultures. At the end of the lane my mother stood in a long wool coat. Crows cawed. Ragged clouds swept over. It always rained for Memorial Day. Cyclonic systems over the Pacific turned clockwise as the North tilted sunward. Linked storms swept over Idaho bringing snow mixed with rain. Had nothing to do with sorrow or regret. My mother turned.

I didn't think you'd be here.

Hi, Mama.

Gave her a hug. Set the tulips by the headstone. It was polished granite with crossed swords. She had placed red roses.

I still see him coming in the door with his bat and mitt and his big grin. Like it's yesterday. It's all yesterday now isn't it?

I looked at the clouds going over the tops of the trees. Didn't want to talk. Hoped we didn't have to. She knelt in the long coat.

I didn't know what you fought about. Guess I should have asked. When he came by that day? Said you'd turned your back on him? Thought you'd get over it. But you never get over anything do you, Errol?

She arranged the roses.

What could he have done to you? He loved you so much!

The wind came now. The tops of the trees started moving. Creaking.

Did he tell you how cold you were? Did that make you mad? How you punished people?

I don't try to do that, Mama.

But you're so good at it! You don't fight or call names. You just leave. If you knew how that hurts!

She traced the letters--William Stenham Husky--carved in granite.

I don't know where you got that. When you and your father had that fight you left for a year! You were trying to hurt him but you hurt me! Thinking of you every day. Not knowing where you were!

She shrugged.

Don't worry, Errol. I'm not going to cry. Don't have any tears left anyway.

She put her gloved hand to the headstone. Got to her feet. Beautifully dressed with her silk blouse ruffled at the throat. Long suede skirt and suede boots. That morning she had looked at the clouds. Gray, dark, fast moving. Thought, What should I wear? Would the wind blow the flowers over? Would they freeze in the night? I tried to breathe.

I'm sorry, Mama.

You will be.

We stood by the grave. I'd received my blessing. She squeezed my elbow.

Well. I can't leave your father any longer.

She bowed to set the vase closer to the headstone. I walked her to the car.

TWENTY THREE

It snowed in the night. Wolf Jaw mountains etched white against blue. I warmed a nestling in warm water. When I opened the door the light lit up Kyrie's eyes wild with anger. She looked haggard. Gaped. Threw her wings up.

We're going out today, Sweetheart. I promise.

Was beginning to hate me. Hated herself because she knew my mediation would succeed. I held the little corpse with its head falling to the side until she took it.

Old globes atop the tall dusty bookshelves. Mickey Angel in profile with his feet up. A big guy wearing a fisherman's hat and a long ponytail leaned against the wall. Khaki pants. Black work boots. Caleb. Fish Man for the Tribes.

Errol? You know Caleb?

Sure enough. How you guys doing, Caleb?

He stuck his tongue to the side of his mouth like a chaw of tobacco.

Trying to spend a little of the 300 million BPA has.

Where you been?

Little Salmon.

I heard there's snow pack.

And with the cold it's holding. Going to be a lot of water coming down. Right now fishing's pretty good.

Where the salmon going to be?

When I figure that out I'll tell you.

He was the voodoo fish man. Figured the size of the run and where it was going to be. Then the big guys set the season. Salmon used to go everywhere. Now just here and there. Nobody knew how Caleb figured it out.

Right now fishermen elbow to elbow from Riggins to the

Swiftwater Inn.

Steelhead? How they doing?

Like always. White dudes in Gore tex jackets making perfect casts with their thousand dollar rods. When they reel in? Nothing on the hook. Down the river Cayuse Claude has a rock to himself because he stinks so bad. Greasy shirt and pants. Gut stained tennis shoes. He's reeling 'em in!

Why is that?

You white dudes like to analyze things. The perfect fly for the hatch. Like there's a hatch du jour or something. Or read the river. Some say it's the head of the riffle where the water swells before it heads through the rocks. I'm not saying that's wrong. All I'm saying is the more I'm around rivers and fish the more I think it's that fish hate the smell of human beings! You sit in a nice warm room in your Eddie Bauer shirt tying flies with nice, clean hands? You're not going to catch fish! I'll smell this horrible stink coming up the river. Thinking, Has some redneck dumped sewage in the river? Then I see Cayuse Claude on his favorite rock. Catching fish! And you know why? He don't smell human! Hasn't washed for months. Has plunged his hands in fish guts and wiped his pants with them. It's rotting on him! When he handles a hook or ties a line? There ain't no taint of human on it! It stinks of dead, rotting fish. And the fish love it! Don't stand a chance! All those white dudes that showered in the morning so their wives will sleep with them? Put on clean clothes? They're changing flies with the cloud pattern and it just don't matter!

I sense a blind, Caleb.

What d'you mean?

Some analytical work.

Right. When they built John Day Dam they put fish ladders up both sides.

He made the sign of jacking off with his left hand.

Stood and watched as the salmon refused to go up. Nose to the bottom step then turn and mill around. Big Alcoa Plant. Could be a factor. So they set up a study where they sluiced various chemicals past the fish. We're talking one part per billion! Three things salmon hate:

He raised a thumb.

Fluoride. It was leaching into the dead water from the aluminum plant.

Two? Bear claws. Essence of Bear Claw dissolved in water at one part per billion.

Three? Human beings. Salmon hate the smell of human beings!

So it ain't no mystery salmon find their way three thousand miles to the stream they grew up in. Creeks like Herd Creek high in the East Fork Mountains. The flesh is torn and hanging from their bones. As they shoulder aside cobbles for the redd more flesh is torn away. They drop their seed and die. Their flesh sinks into the gravels where it rots and ferments. The smolt swim around and feed in the smell of their parent's rotting flesh. Eat the insects that feed on that flesh. The smell of that creek is them! And the sedge and mint that grow along it. Like a perfume in their spirit. And no matter long how long they are in the sea they remember it.

Caleb shook his head.

We're like that too though we don't want nobody to know. The smell of home you never forget. The wildflowers and rocks the rains bring from the cliffs. The smell of your dead. It ain't no mystery they fight so hard to get back. Fly up those falls. Find the pools they were born in. It ain't no mystery. The crime is we won't let them!

He slipped the shades over his eyes. Plucked a title from the rock climbing shelf. Just as I asked where he was headed Gerald darkened the door. Nodded at the street. Mickey Angel followed. Caleb watched them.

Watershed inventory in the Frank Church.

He pumped his fist above his crotch.

Plucking rocks.

How's Snorkel Bob?

Same old Bob. Swears it's his last year. Like every year.

When you going?

End of June. Getting cards now to send to loved ones. In case the cowboys get out asses.

You could behave.

I could. Nice thing about the Tribes though. Little more play in the line.

I got the sign for jacking off, Caleb. But what's the tongue in the side of your mouth?

You don't know that one, Errol? All the time you did with Fish and Game? That's the Government's dick in your mouth!

Caleb!

I turned a spinner rack. Devil's Bedstead with blue gentian and monkey flowers like the Fourth of July.

I wouldn't mind tagging along if you needed a hand.

He looked at me a second short of too long.

You don't mind counting bugs? Sure thing. We'll be camped on Iron Creek in a fortnight.

He slapped his thigh with his hat. Stood up.

I best be off. Bring your tent.

I sleep in the truck.

Big mosquitoes up there, Errol.

Nothing like Gray's Lake, Caleb. All that marshland? They stand flat footed to hump a dog!

Caleb threw his head back and laughed.

TWENTY FOUR

Mickey Angel got his wallet out of the cash box.

You going anywhere? Gerald wants me to run an errand.

I pulled Schweibert's Nymphs out of the lawyer's bookcase. Looked at May and damsel flies. The larva like dragons with powerful claws and long tails. Stout little predators that became fliers with diaphanous wings. Mickey Angel came back.

Thanks, Errol.

You could've stayed longer.

Good duty isn't it.

What'd Gerald have you do?

Deposit a check.

Why would he have you do that?

Said he doesn't want his ex to know he's in Pocatello.

His ex.

That's what he said.

He settled into his chair. I read and dozed among the stacks.

When I woke shadows lined straight across the street. I let the pigeons fill up on corn. Drove South Bannock to where it swung above the vast Church Farm. Tax man wept when he looked at it. Main Line at the far side and Mink Creek to the right. Trophy houses beyond that. I slung the telemeter. Followed a wheel line to the wood line. Now had a half mile of young wheat to the Black Cliffs in the distance. Hoped the pigeon would go for them. Knew she would. Try to get home like everybody else.

Kyrie bobbed. Looked around. Became the wind. Rang up lazily until she was so high she could see the Tetons. The Snake slithered to the Reservoir. The pigeon took a moment to right herself. Headed homeward. Kyrie streaked like a dark knife. Wrists cowled. Shock waves shearing. The pigeon tried to juke but was late.

I ran. The down floated in the wheat spears. I knelt to pick them up. Out of the corner of my eye saw a figure approach. A huge man in overalls. I stood.

How you doing?

He kept coming.

Stop there please!

You're on Church land and you're telling me--

The falcon doesn't know it's Church land, sir.

He looked at Kyrie. She looked at him as if to kill. Her shoulders hunched, wings spread.

He said, What is it?

Peregrine falcon.

Don't look as big as I'd expect.

She flies big.

She does. I was watching from the house. Couldn't figure what you was up to. Walking onto Church land in broad daylight. Got the binoculars.

He was a big man. Three hundred pounds. Coveralls with straps over the shoulders that served his paunch. Left his shoulders free. Had on slippers like he'd settled in for the evening.

Had a chicken hawk when I was a kid.

What kind?

Kind that kills chickens. She'd fly to the top of the elm and call. I'd take her scraps. She'd drop out of the tree and eat out of my hand.

Nice.

One day she didn't show up.

I looked a Kyrie feeding. She looked up at me with a shard of meat sticking out the side of her beak. Her breast blood-stained.

Went out every evening but she never showed. Guess I was more attached to her than I thought.

They have a hard life.

My mother--God bless her! There isn't a day goes by I wouldn't give everything I had to have her back! She told me if I loved that hawk it'd be waiting for me in heaven.

Critters go to heaven?

If that's what you want. I did pastoral work when I was Bishop. I'd go see an old couple that had a little dog that sat on their lap. Couldn't see but could bark. Made a general nuisance of herself. One day the old guy said, When me and Geraldine go to Heaven will Moxie be waiting?

Oh I think so, Harold. If that's what you pray for.

That's good. Because I don't know if we'd want to go there if Moxie weren't there.

He looked at Kyrie.

I thought she'd just swing up a ways. Come down when you brought the pigeon. But she kept going. Couldn't follow her even with the glasses.

Most work that way.

So you just let her fly? More dangerous isn't it?

No. They're less vulnerable from above. I had a friend was an up-and-down guy. The falcon was watching the dog in the brush when an eagle took her. Nobody had seen it. She hadn't seen it either.

He said, Wouldn't want to lose her that way.

No. Lost them every other way.

Well, he said. I best be going. You're not planning on flying her here anymore dare I say?

No. Thank you.

He turned and walked. I was happy. Smart to stack the deck. Gave her a flat field. Knelt to pick them up. Curved my finger under the sternum. Brought out the heart.

I drove Mink Creek to West Fork. Wind rippled the aspen. Put on the pack. Across the creek scraggly juniper twisted out of rock. Kestrels cried. Flew from the top of a Doug Fir that stood creek-side.

Keely! Keely! Keely!

They had a nice prospect. From the fir could swoop on the hatches. See mice descend to water. Didn't want me there. Turquoise dragonflies flitted at a muddy pond. Tiny houses with gabled roofs stood along the beaver ponds. The beaver were gone. At Elk Meadows Road a black angus fed on wildflowers. Flushed up the road. I was following his big butt when I heard bicycle brakes. A bare-chested man on a unicycle! Wore his hair in a pony tail, black tights and striped black and white stockings. Bounced along beside me.

I said, why don't you slip past him on the right?

He looked at the half ton of haunch and horn.

I don't think so!

We followed Bully up the road. Only in Pocatello, I thought, could you herd cows with a clown on a unicycle!

If Ferdinand'd get his fat butt out of the way!

Ferdinand looked back. Bawled at me. Every time I abused him he did that. I started to like him. At the top of the canyon he drifted into the meadow. The unicyclist went on through the field of yellow balsamroot.

I turned back. Stratocumulus piled up high. Willows silvered along the creek. A cyclist ascended the trail. Simultaneous to that a mama moose pulled herself out of the pond. Crashed through the aspen. The cyclist didn't see it. Passed me. A second cyclist halted.

Errol! What the hell!

Pavi!

Water walker. I clapped him on the back.

I'm just glad your buddy scared her up. Don't know what the effect would've been on me.

Last time I rode with your brother we ran into a bull moose. He lowered his rack. We discussed the effect a thirty pound mountain bike would have in the event he charged.

Where was that?

Coming down Box Canyon. Ten years now. Can you believe it?

Can't.

Well I best get on the gears. Steve'll be looking for me.

How far you going?

Monument Gulch.

I was headed that way. A little too hung over. Feeling better now though.

Pavi grinned.

The Moose Cure!

The trail was rocky and eroded. So even though storm clouds piled up on Scout. Even though willows whispered along the creek I watched my boots. Saw the chunk of obsidian the size of a man's heart. Tossed it in my hand.

Pressure-flaked the facets gleamed! How long had it lain beneath slope of the hill? This was the old road into Arbon Valley. An Indian could've dropped it as late as 1910. The smart guys at ISU could measure the attrition on the crystal lattice with an electron microscope. Date it.

Dark blue thunderclouds towered over Scout. Thousand foot high cliffs rose one above the other. A broad wing came up the ridge. Used it as a blind. Flapped like a harrier but looked bigger. I lifted the obsidian.

Brother!

His eyes flashed red. A lightning bolt split the cloudbank. Quivered. Pain seared my arm and heart. I fell to my knees, the obsidian in my fist. Thunder boomed. The hawk dipped a wing. Slipped over the ridge.

TWENTY FIVE

Thunder came with rain. Washed the trail away. In the morning I drove Highway 50 to Reno. Along 20 three ranches occupied Pine Creek. Heard a clattering roar. A helicopter took off for Carson City. I passed the Maynard Dixon Mountains. The playas curved high as the summits. Old mountains. Man at the desk said, We'll keep you in mind. I returned on I-80. Tin can settlements with minimum wage clerks at the fast food stations. After cow-skinned Nevada the Pocatello hills looked positively furry. Mickey Angel with his boots up.

Your lucky day, Errol. Rachel invited us to a barbecue.

I got a twelve pack at Albertsons. Returned. An old man with wispy hair and mottled hands was talking to Mickey Angel. His fingertips in a pointed arch.

The Kwakiutl are good but the Inuit are better. It's an established fact canoeists get better the closer you get to the Circle.

Why is that?

You ever swum in freezing water? Canoes are deadly. I once went on a canoe trip that lasted six feet! We were on the Bottoms. One of those creeks that feed into the Snake. Spent an hour packing guns and bow and arrow. Everything we were going to need.

Why bow and arrow?

We were going to shoot carp in case we got bored. The wind was blowing. As we pushed off a gust came up and blew us into some thorn trees. As we leaned away from those the canoe lowsided. Guns. Bow and arrow. Whiskey. Spent the rest of the day drying out twenty thousand dollars worth of guns. That's how I learned the first thing you do when you get a canoe is take out the seats. You see men standing? That's safer because at least your feet are below water line.

Mickey Angel grinned.

Women and canoes. Want to be on your knees.

That's right. You probably never heard of Pulling. Taught physics at ISU. Best around when it came to a canoe. He was eighty when he taught me and I was forty two. Would spot me sixty yards in an eighty yard sprint and beat me by five!

Using the J-stroke?

No. You see a man holding the oar with the thumb of his top hand? Doesn't know what he's doing. The thumb should be straight up so you can return the paddle along the gunwale. An Indian's paddle never leaves the water. With the J-stroke the paddle is the rudder at the end of the stroke.

So half the stroke is drag.

Right. A good canoeist steers with his knees. Pulling

spent summers in Alaska to make money for school. Got a job in the bow of a freight canoe. That was when the freight of the North was carried by canoe. Some of them eighty feet long.

He looked back through the shelves.

As long as this building. Six years the Indians watched him labor in the bow of that canoe! On the seventh a Blood came up to him.

You don't know how to paddle, man.

And they taught him.

Mickey Angel laughed.

Indians! We're headed to a barbecue, Carl. If you'd care to come. Might get a game going.

The old gambler got slowly to his feet.

No. But thanks.

Afraid we'll take your money?

No. I'm retired.

Mickey Angel switched off the lights. I thought about the Indians. How they juked the paddle the same as the recovery stroke of a bird's wing. Happened too fast for man to see. We learned it from high speed photography. I wondered if an Indian watched birds so long he dreamed it. How to paddle a canoe.

We walked past the Romanesque Legion Hall with red tile roof and terra cotta trim. Three inch guns with iron rimmed wooden wheels aimed over Memorial Park. Four inch Navy AA gun with gunner's seat totally exposed. At the corner of Wyeth an old man swept the walk under a giant tree that spread its branches over the street. Hadn't leafed. Mickey Angel looked up at it.

What kind of tree is that?

The old man stopped sweeping.

English walnut.

When does it leaf out?

After the last frost.

Should be safe now. It's the first of June.

It's getting ready.

Up the street the trees were in full leaf. Rachel knelt in her garden.

How does it know?

It knows. It's an old tree. It don't listen to nobody.

Mickey Angel looked admiringly into the branches.

My mother used to cook walnuts in red wine.

Squirrels get these.

I saw one on the roof waving its bushy tail.

Be good practice with an air rifle. Keep your eye in shape.

No. Gives the cats something to do. Keeps them out of trouble. They sit at the window and watch the squirrels.

Squirrels are good eating.

You know it! I grew up eating squirrel. Squirrel and chub.

Where was that?

North Fork Trinity River.

That would be Texas?

That would.

Not much on a squirrel.

You fried up the hind legs.

How did you skin them?

Make a cut around the ankles. Nail 'em head-down to the barn wall. Give a tug. The pelt come right off. Know what I really liked though? The brains. Fried in lard with salt and pepper.

Mickey Angel nodded.

Fat and salt. Nothing better. We're going up to Abner's if you'd care to drop by. You know Abner?

Oh sure. I know Abner.

Rachel squatted in her garden. Hand-watered pepper and tomato plants. Gave us her Fourth of July smile.

Abner's in back. I'll be right there.

We went along the side of the house. A giant wolf dog howled. Ambled up. Abner crouched at a blazing fire pit. Lean, wiry, with a blonde pony tail. T-shirt had the Fish with four legs. Acanthostega. Held an iron rod to the fire with tongs.

Shut up, Makalu! Or you're going in the pen!

Mickey Angel scratched Makalu's ears.

Why so hard on Makalu?

Abner picked up the ball-peen hammer. Drew out the rod. Hammered the faintly glowing end. Was going to take a lot of hammering.

We went up the bench this morning. He took off. I called. I trudged. I called. He's gone. Climbed around all afternoon like an idiot. Found him hunkered down on a deer carcass some redneck gut shot last fall. Held my nose as I tried to pull him away. He snarled. Bared his fangs.

Makalu! Not you!

Makalu looked at Mickey Angel with his big grey eyes. Howled piteously. Abner thrust the rod back into the fire.

Man's Best Friend. He's thinking, This carcass will last me a week! So back off, old man! I don't need you!

Imagine the taste of that finely cured venison!

Abner shot Makalu a dark look. Makalu sighed. Lay down to lick his paws. Whiff of Essence of Rotted Meat. A young guy wearing a wide brimmed fisherman's hat reclined out of range of the flying cinders.

Might want to leave him out tonight.

Abner wiped his eyes. Pulled the rod out of the fire.

Right. So he can howl all night and stir up hatred among the neighbors!

Abner was finding out how long it took to make a spear point without a bellows. I admired the first-hand knowledge he was getting. Would get. Rachel came out.

Abner! You haven't started the grill?

He lay the rod in the fire like he weren't letting it off so easy. Introduced us to River Man.

This is Terence. We call him Hoodoo. He's going to take us down the Murtaugh.

Mickey Angel said, I always wanted to do that.

Sunday morning. 5 AM.

Going to be any water?

Call Reclamation.

Mickey Angel cracked a beer.

I can wait. Can't be that hard at low water.

Hoodoo shook his head.

No. The Snake is very technical. Even at low water you got to know the routes. Ledges. Every one with an undercut hole. All you see is the line. The water going over smooth. Maybe a little spray. But it's a big river. That line is two hundred yards wide! One route glides. The other goes straight down. You don't want that. Get the raft sandwiched around you.

Best jump free.

If you can. Big whirlies. You're going round and round in very cold water. Lot of folks die that way. Think it's summer. They've been walking around in the hot Southern Idaho sun. But that water's come down fast from the Tetons. They're in it. And they can't get out.

Whoo!

Hoodoo tipped back his PBR.

The Snake is very unforgiving. Unrunnable at high water. Raft. Catamaran. Whatever. You can take a kayak for short runs if you're good. At average flow? Got to know the routes. Just got to. The hydraulics are so huge! Like Pair O' Dice. Only one way through and you got to hit it.

How you do that?

Use the Garage.

Where's Pair O' Dice? asked Mickey Angel.

You can see it from the Hansen Bridge. The river divides around a pillar. Right glides into a hole so if you miss the Garage you might make it. Left is suicide. A twenty foot ledge. You see the haystack pulsing river right? You got to get to that pillar. Pull with all you got. That's the garage. The strongest guy grabs the rock. Then you shoot the line between the falls.

I said, No eddy line when I saw it.

You saw it?

May 1st. The left hand flow was turning the right inward and into the north bank. Big whirly. Ridge of water six feet high.

What I'm saying. But it's the only way to run Pair O' Dice.

I heard it called Let's Make A Deal.

No. Snake Eyes at high water. I've seen folks make it if they hit it right. Most of the time you're swimming. That's a big hole, man! I saw a twenty foot raft with six bully boys go through the rinse cycle for ten minutes before they came out! Swept into the chute. Were at the top of the wave whooping like cowboys because they thought they made it. Then the reversal took over. I was standing on the bank. It looked like great, foamy claws were clawing at that raft. Now they're digging for their lives! But it's too late. I heard a loud growling roar! The Snake held that twenty foot raft straight up into the air and just swallowed it! Oh my Lord! I don't know how long it was before it popped out and we got hold of it! Good thing too. Those boys were in no shape to do anything. Young, tough men. Reason they survived.

I watched the sky turn pink over the volcano. Nothing better than talking about rivers around a fire. A train called mournfully as it came off the Plain.

Hoo! Hoo!

TWENTY SIX

Abner brought the steaks. Cheap grad student cuts marinated three days. They spattered on the grill as the fat sizzled in the embers. Hoodoo reached for another beer.

Like the guy from Salt Lake that decided to run the Milner at 60K. Big catamaran. Camera crew. Girlfriend watching from the shore. Everything on the table.

Eek!

The Snake will get you. What is the rule of life, Michael?

Wear a life jacket on the Snake.

Rachel came out fresh and pretty.

Or fly into Salt Lake with a wind advisory. I almost cried last time. What is it about Salt Lake?

Hoodoo said, The wind sweeps up the Front. Sets up huge back eddies. You hit those holes? Bad. Look at those 747's. All thrust. They just drop. I talked to a guy was flying to Hawaii. They were cruising between thunder bumpers at fifty thousand feet. Hit a hole. Fell nine miles in twenty seconds!

Oh my Lord!

There are rules you can disobey from time to time but some you must never. A guy that knew better was wading along the bank at Eagle Rock. Then his friends don't see him no more. And the Snake don't give up his dead. You know why, don't you? Mighty carp!

He kicked the embers with his steel boot.

Every few years they bring in underwater welders to work on the turbines.

Why do they need welders?

The water wears them out. They weld a line along the leading edge.

Sand?

No. Rotation of the blade against the water sets up microscopic vortices. Microscopic bubbles form along the leading edge. As they burst it wears the blade away.

Crazy!

Idaho Power brings guys in from all over the country. Big, tough guys. Paid big money. But some won't go back down. For any amount. Big fish bumping against them in the dark.

Hah!

But the real reason is the weird lamination of basalt, rhyolite and welded ash. Lava tubes too. I was canoeing up from Massacre Rocks at low water? Saw a gleam of wave. When I got there the river was coming under a lava bridge! Portaged to where it went under. Didn't want to be going down there!

Rachel stood up to get the casserole. Makalu woofed at her.

Bad dog, Makalu!

He put his nose between his paws. Looked miserable. Hoodoo twirled the beer can.

Sometimes it doesn't matter what you do. I knew a bully boy from Twin. Two ninety easy. All his buddies that size. Heard the Snake was running high. Sunday was Mother's Day but they told their wives it would be a fast run. They'd be back for dinner. Stood at the put in and looked at it. It had a low rumbling sound. Hissed as it swept the rocks.

Sure you want to do this?

Rex said, We can always get out at Turkey Shoot. I know a guy that farms by there. If it's too big we'll call the women. They'll come get us.

Won't be happy.

No.

Rex said the reason they decided to do it was that it was such a gorgeous day! The Snake just sparkled. Cliffs fancied up with currant bushes in blossom. Meadowlarks singing. Eighty degrees and sunshine! So they put in. Were rolling along at a nice clip. Laying on their backs drinking beer.

This is going to be the fastest trip ever, dude!

Blew past Turkey Shoot. Cliffs now dark and vertical. Looking ahead they saw white caps. Felt the chill before it hit. Wasn't eighty degrees no more. Tumbleweeds flew left to right over the top of the canyon. Nevada Low with the Queen of Spades in her garter. Temperature dropped forty degrees in fifteen minutes. Now they're digging to keep in the main current. The wind was lifting the prow of the raft and shoving it into the eddies. Huge boiling back eddies! The only thing that was funny? Seeing those homeboys scrambling to get away from the side the Snake was sucking at.

The raft was losing buoyancy because of temperature drop.

Right. They'd inflated it in full sun. So they pulled over to the rocks. Wet and freezing. The only way out? Crawl the five miles back to Turkey Shoot.

Three thousand dollar raft.

Right. And having made five major errors why stop now? It was Rex's raft.

Let's ride a few more miles. If Pair O' Dice looks too rough we'll pull out.

So they did. The wind whipped water off the white caps. Threw it freezing in their faces. Lander lost feeling in his hands. First sign of hypothermia. And then the wind went down! The Snake just rocked them along. They started talking about how they were going to do Pair O' Dice!

Lander can't climb out, man. Let's see what it looks like.

They heard the roar before they came around the bend. The wind brought the news. Big time. They saw the haystack.

Shore! Shore!

Poled for all they were worth but were in the gut of the current.

Abner speared shards of meat dripping with fat and spices.

Time to eat, boys. Grab your plates.

Hoodoo took a bite. The juice dripped down his chin.

Rex tried to keep the prow downriver.

Wait 'til we hit the rim!

They did. The raft floated an instant then dove. Swooped down and up the twenty foot wave. They dug with all they had. But a huge wave banged them from the side. Turned them. The screaming you hear might be you or it might be the river. Your body is being twisted in every direction. Then it's over. Darkness. No dreams. No memory. Then Rex saw a light. Swam toward it. Clawed into a back eddy. It was running twenty miles an hour back along the bank! Crawled onto a rock. Lander popped out a minute later. Waving his arms and screaming like the day he was born!

Rachel gave Abner the look.

You're not going, Abner. No way.

Thanks, Hoodoo.

Rex pulled him to shore. The other guys were on the far bank.

The boat! Did you see the boat?

No!

Just then the raft just popped out like a cork. They watched it go rocking and rolling toward Let's Make A Deal.

What's the one after that?

Duck Blind. Well named too.

Did they get it back?

Oh sure. But Rex don't run the Snake no more. Don't know what it said to him but he was able to remember quite clearly. Think about the hydraulics! To hold a thirty foot raft at rinse cycle for that long!

How'd they get out?

They separated to find a route. Left Lander by the river. He was in shock. They watched farm trucks roll by on the bridge! At twilight Clark saw a trail in the cliff. If it faded he'd shot his wad. But he told himself if somebody put that much work into it it had to go somewhere. Dark came. Somewhere in the night he arrived at the rim. Saw the all night service station shining like the gates of heaven!

Who cut the trail?

Could've been anybody. People been in that canyon for twenty thousand years. ISU found corn cobs they dated at six. It was a nice set up if you knew how to work it. South facing garden. River at your door. Deer coming down the canyon. Fish. Ducks. You might've thought you were living next to God.

The air got cool as it turned dark. I finished my steak. Gave a piece to Makalu. The old man came up from down the street.

Stood in the firelight with a beer in his hand. Said this'd be the year he fished Wildhorse Creek. I loved Wildhorse. Saw it run sparkling out of the twelve thousand footers. Abner grinned.

We'll take your motor home, Don. You fish. I'll climb.

It's a deal.

The old man talked about fly fishing with his beer and his big belly. I thought about how cobbles moved. How you didn't want to lie to yourself any more than you had to. But then again?

What do you do, Abner?

Microbiology.

Stream analysis?

Too messy. I like things I can control. Right now I'm working with ferro bacteria. Bacteria that breathe iron the way we breathe oxygen. We've shown that if you damp down the available iron the bacteria will send out filaments to share it. We've gotten gorgeous photos that look like the lattices of crystals.

Using isotope tracer?

Right. The other thing we're doing is isolating E coli DNA. See if we can make it produce insulin.

Gene splicing. How do they get it now?

Horses. Thousands and thousands of horses.

The two dogs crawled up to his feet. Looked reverently up at him. He tossed pieces of meat. It had been dark. Now it was light. I went to the side of the house. The full moon banged like a gong.

Look at that!

Rachel came over.

Oh my gosh! I could feel it. I just didn't know it was up!

What does it feel like?

Sometimes it's really strong. Like she's yanking at my uterus. Sometimes she speaks.

I thought about Ginny on Railroad Ridge.

She's spoken to me.

No. She doesn't speak in words. It's like she's a tuning fork. When she rises I feel the humming in my womb. One night I was in my garden. The asparagus and Brussel sprouts all penisy. Like they were growing towards her. I felt it in my womb. That I was like them! I sank to my knees!

The men listened by the fire. The cicadas chittered. Not in full chorus like late summer. Isolated singers. The old man spoke.

That was your chance, Abner.

Yeah right.

He tossed the last chunk to Makalu.

The neighbors would've loved it.

We laughed. Rachel wrinkled her nose. Went to her garden. Reappeared later with a beautiful woman on her arm. Lucy had dark, shining hair, wore a squash blossom turquoise at her throat. A powerfully built young man hung back talking on a cell phone.

Who's your boyfriend, Lucy?

Demetrius. He has an olive grove in Crete. Isn't that romantic!

Demetrius snapped the cell phone shut but stood back. I went over.

Were you speaking Russian?

He looked indignant.

I am Greek!

It sounded Russian.

I speak five languages: Russian, Bulgarian, Serbian, Italian and English!

How did you learn Serbian?

I was in Serbia seven years.

Mickey Angel! This guy speaks Italian and has an olive grove in Crete!

Demetrius hooded his eyebrows.

Who tell you that?

Your girlfriend.

He gave her a dark look. I didn't like him at all now. I liked her. She was the star of the show. Necklace, eyes, lips glittered in the firelight. I introduced Demetrius.

Mickey Angel is cooking lamb next week. You should come by. Show him how to do it.

Demetrius raised his chin.

Nobody cook lamb like a Greek. I cook the best lamb there is.

What do you use?

For lamb you must have olive oil, garlic and rosemary.

Only the best olive oil. And a little lemon.

Mickey Angel swayed slightly. Stared at Demetrius through his thick glasses.

He's right about that.

They were the same height but Demetrius had him by fifty pounds and twenty years. I was enjoying the standoff.

We'll have a contest. Who can cook the best lamb. I'll work the grill. All you guys have to do is cook. We need a Basque though. To make it fair. Know any Basquos, Mickey Angel?

Sebby.

We'll invite him.

Demetrius stared at Mickey Angel.

How you cook lamb?

Garlic. Olive oil. Tarragon and basil. That's all I'm telling you.

Actually I don't think either of you can cook lamb like a Basque.

When we do this?

I'm going on the river this weekend. We'll do it the next. You'll be in town?

I be in town.

What brings you to Pocatello?

My great uncle.

Who's that?

He gave me his aggressive look.

Constantine Papalos.

The realtor?

Is correct.

I've heard a lot about him.

The look got darker. I smiled. Told everybody they were invited to the cook off at Mickey Angel's. Demetrius made himself at home. As well as knowing five languages he was an expert in Mediterranean politics. With his short, thick head, his gleaming black eyes, his massive shoulders he looked like a small bull by the fire. I thought of Orion Kolometes whose father yoked him to the plow.

I can see you grew up in your olive grove.

Why is that?

Your build. You look like you've worked the land.

He flexed pectorals involuntarily. Grinned.

You must be joking. That's what Albanians are for. I am a weight lifter!

Rachel leaned toward him.

You said you were in Serbia. What were you doing there?

Business.

It must have been very hard for you.

No. It was not that bad. A lot of what happened was exaggerated by the press.

Really.

Of course. Like the Jews. They get too much mileage out of what happened during the War. Everyone suffered you know!

I stood up.

Right. Well it's been fun, Rachel. Thank you

Rachel looked up with her beautiful eyes. In shock at what Demetrius said.

You can't go!

I could. Hadn't brought him. Gave her a hug. Mickey Angel said he was going too. We descended the street. Cicadas purred. Here and there came the tap of a tiny snare drum. The moon shone. Lorca's moon bled white. Kept her face to the Earth so she saw everything. I felt sorry for her.

What d'you think Demetrius was doing in Serbia?

Don't know. Don't want to know.

You think he was dealing? He said he spoke Russian.

The Russians have plenty of thugs of their own. They don't need a Greek. He's probably a school teacher.

We passed the guns at Memorial Hall. Walked toward the lights of Main. He staggered slightly.

These guys aren't hard to understand. They talk like that because there aren't Jews in Europe anymore. They come over here and talk like that because they forget there are Jews still alive! Jews everywhere in America.

Quite the babe he was with.

Lucy? Yes. She's a doll. You've noticed though haven't you, Errol? How butterflies are attracted to shit?

I laughed.

Hard to believe though. The past happened.

We ask these questions, Errol. Why there is such cruelty in the world. As we ourselves lie dying and in pain we ask these questions. But nobody is watching.

He stood under the streetlight. Terra cotta Cups of Knowledge atop the High School.

We're out here wagging our tails.

TWENTY SEVEN

I left him at his apartment. Walked toward the streetlamps of Old Town. The moon reflected in the windows. Names of lawyers in gold lettering now in Mount Moriah. I passed the blind columns of the Franklin Building. At the second floor windows girls danced in ballet tights. In the Twenties the Ku Klux Klan pranced in their billowing sheets. At the Bistro the Guinness sign shone red as woman's lipstick. I sat at the bar. Watched a West Coast game. Mariners and White Sox. Mist drifted past klieg lights. Nice to live in a town with baseball. Never had to be alone. A woman slipped silkily onto the stool beside me. Expensive perfume. Johanna. Lustrous hair piled up. Tight black dress. Big brown eyes and silver prayer bracelet on her wrist.

How are you Johanna?

Ok.

She lied.

Can I buy you a drink?

You can.

I told the bartender I'd have a pilsner. She sipped a red.

And you? How are you doing?

I'm doing Ok.

You're sure about that?

I'm watching a game. A pretty woman just bought me a drink. Sure. It's Ok.

You're living in a truck. Your kids are in Boise. You're hanging out with a bunch of drunks in Pocatello, Idaho.

It's a nice town. It's got nice light.

You don't think your kids need you?

They're at the age they don't need the old man that much. In the wild they try and kill him.

Really, Errol?

I'm in transition, Johanna. That's it.

Scamming Michael for a place to keep your hawk.

Falcon.

Falcon. Keeping him entertained with the rest of your drunken friends. While he loses the best thing he ever had.

She tossed down the wine.

And when he's broke down or in jail you'll go your merry way.

He told me all y'all do is fight.

I saw the white squall approach but wasn't married or sleeping with her. She bit her lip.

You're sitting here drunk and alone in a bar in the middle of the week and tell me what a fight is? You don't even know what a fight is! When a woman fights for what she needs! You know the difference between a good woman and a bad, Errol? A good woman drains the hot grease from the skillet before she throws it!

The bartender laughed. She wrinkled her nose. Cocked her head.

What do you want out of a woman, Errol? Somebody to lie down when you want to screw. Feed you when you're hungry?

Barkeep.

I nodded at her glass. When he poured she took a sip.

Did you ever do anything with your wife that you hated but she liked? Tell me.

Johanna didn't need to throw things. Sipped her merlot.

I was with an old man today. He's dying. You know what he wanted to talk about? Getting laid. You believe that? Nothing about his kids that don't want to see him. Or his ex wives that won't talk to him. His drinking buddies are in the graveyard. And he acted like he didn't care. Does he care, Errol? That he turned his back on the people that loved him?

She turned in her chair like she was leaving. I patted her shoulder.

What else did he talk about?

How he killed ravens.

How did he do that?

She shut her eyes.

Come on, Johanna. How did he do it?

He was at a gold dredge on Great Slave Lake. It was winter. He was alone. Kept thinking about killing himself. Didn't know why. Kept looking at his guns. Gray. Cold. The only things moving were ravens. The only sound their calling. He came to an agreement with the man that owned the field next door. Built a blind in the trees. Went out in the middle of the night and spread ketchup on the snow. At first light they arrived. One. Two Then the whole flock. He waited until they settled.

Crazy.

He said he owed the ravens a lot. They got him through a tough winter.

He used ketchup?

She squinted at me.

He'd let the site cool off. But when he went back? They'd be back.

I said, Had too much hunger to remember.

She said, A lot of us are like that.

I wanted to talk but she was on her way. Turned.

Michael has something none of you have right now. But it won't last. Would you tell him that?

Her perfume, the glass of merlot stayed. I decided I'd finish it with the pilsner as a chaser. It had the bitter taste of her lipstick. I remembered walking Slate Mountain. Aspen yellow in the ravines. Heard laughter. Ravens surfing the ridge like a band of gypsies. Pecked at tail feathers. Side slipped. Fell rockward before kiting up.

It would be easy to kill ravens if you had no laughter in your life.

All night long the trains keened, clanged and whistled like a band of Shoshones blowing their eagle bone whistles. I ended up on the East Side. Naked with my sleeping bag wrapped around me. I turned the corner to the Underpass. My mother reclined atop the retaining wall. Had turned to stone but turned her head.

Don't go down there, Errol!

Blue and amber lights flashed. I knew Billy was there.

The stone woman wept.

It was my fault!

I left her to grieve. Raised my arms to catch an updraft. Kited through telephone and high power wires. Railroad tracks shone like ribbons. The back door to Michael Angelo's was ajar. I saw Kyrie hanging with the jesses around her neck. Heard the train come with a soft and mournful call. It wavered as it flowed along the hills.

TWENTY EIGHT

Took Lost Trail Pass to Missoula. No luck. Headed back. Looked at the keeled ridges smooth as driftstone. Big horns on the road. At nightfall camped where the Salmon turned west. Departed as stars faded. At sunrise the Diamond Lady's mantilla turned pink. Birch Creek danced. I passed three canyons to the cave where the Sorcerer stood with arms outstretched. Five moons arced between the points of his horns. By afternoon saw the stacks of Pocatello. At the Meat Market Cruz stared at his feet. Gold bling around his neck. I dressed down.

Looking a little down, Cruz.

You got that right.

Why's that?

Every Sunday I put ten in the jar. Get down on my knees and thank the Lord for everything he's given me. Then put in another ten and beg forgiveness for what I had to do to get it!

I laughed. Outside thunderclouds rose above the Blackfoot River. Wheels stacked on flat cars gleamed like crescent moons. I fed Kyrie. Poured her bath.

Use the phone, Mickey Angel?

Twenty seconds.

I'll take it outside.

That would be best.

He tossed me a dog chewed book, Merle's Door.

Used to be the only dog chewed books that came in were training books. Now it's anything with a dog on the cover.

I said, Some bitch is sending Mama pictures!

I took the phone into the street.

Glen? This is Husky.

Yeah.

I was hoping you were off today. Like to come out and talk if I could.

I'll be leaving for the field at six. Click.

That was Obermayr. But I had told him he flew birds like a disc jockey. Alcohol a contributing factor. Got the furniture. Kyrie saw them, her wings throwing sparks.

I won't lie to you, Sweetheart.

We drove through Fort Hall. The Mission Church with its old trees and gravestones. Highway 91 the oldest track in the country. Linked the horse trade of the Rio Grande to the Missouri. Now only Indians thought ghosts traveled it. Only Mexicans decorated it. The Snake piled against the piers of Tilden Bridge. I stopped at the other side to look at it. Had never tried Kyrie on a big river. Too many complications. Kept going. Turned on a gravel road with manorial house at the end. Obermayr in his officer's camo, knee high black boots.

Letting her ride in the cab, huh? What can I do for you?

I turned away. Took in the house that had the finest collection of falcon art in the West. The weathering sheds leeward.

Thought you might want to take on Kyrie.

I don't board birds.

I'm not asking you to. I'm giving her.

Didn't say, She's a finer bird than anything you got. Didn't have to. A new look came into his eyes.

Take her out.

I slipped the leash. Drew her out.

Take off her hood.

She looked everywhere at once. House, sky, the sheds with falcons dark at the blocks. What in Obermayr was free of anything but love of falcons took over. Stroked her wings, shoulder joints, breast. But when he gauged her weight via her pubic bone she got him. He shook his hand.

She's a little heavy.

She likes to fly a little heavy.

He drew the purse strings of his mouth.

This is your lucky day. I lost a gyr last winter.

How.

Eagle.

We went to the sheds. Cedar walls. Joinery trim and varnished. Gravel clean and raked. The falcons called out angrily when they saw Kyrie. Threw out their wings.

Hope she doesn't stir things up too much.

He grunted.

I've handled birds a long time. Made mistakes. The thing is not to make two in a row.

Unlatched the door. Nodded to me.

We'll leave her leashed and hooded.

I leashed her. Stroked her nape. Turned and walked. Heard the latch click. Across the field a back hoe drudged. Obermayr followed my gaze.

Used to be a slough there. One of the reasons I bought this place.

I drove. At the Snake walked onto the bridge. The current side saddled. Undercurrents boiled up. Sucked backward into the ongoing flow. A mallard fanned tail. Set feet and splashed. Hard to find anything more beautiful than the Snake. Indians owned the springs so as long as they survived the Snake would run. The roof of the Superintendent's house on Agency Street caved in. You'd've thought the Tribal Council would level it. Sentimental, I guessed. Tin can trailers along C street. A pack of scrawny Rez dogs skipped up. Their lucky day. Had strips of meat I'd saved for Kyrie. Held it with the back of my hand out so they wouldn't nip me. Pawed at my legs as I shut the gate. It was different on the Rez. A gringo told me about the boy with the big smile at Fort Hall School.

My Dad and my Uncles dragged a man behind a horse yesterday!

He still alive?

The little boy grimaced.

No. He didn't look so good.

Thought it the boy's imagination 'til a few months later. Saw on the front page they found a Fort Hall man on bail for child molestation out by the lava flows.

Willy Jack's tin can blistered by the sun. Frayed by the wind. Desert wildflowers bloomed. He opened the door. Big round head, black braids, big smile.

Hey, Old Man!

My fingertips sunk into his shoulders he was so fat.

Getting big, Willy Jack. One of these days a squaw is going to hang you from barbed wire like a rock chuck!

They already tried. Call it Willy Jack grease. They like it! What you doing in Indian town?

Taking time off.

Drove your ass out, huh? Come on in!

Marine Corps banner above the sofa. Black and white photos by Wrensted of Sho Ban men dressed in the Spanish style: beaded vests, silver trimmed horsemen's gauntlets. The four hundred years Shoshone traded with Spanish. When the Snake Country was Quivira!

I was hoping you'd guide me to the petroglyph field, Willy Jack. The one with the Sorcerer.

I showed you already.

I know, Willy Jack. But remember? I went back the next week and couldn't find it?

Always in a hurry, Errol.

I know.

And maybe the Man don't want you around.

It's a possibility.

And you white guys aren't that quick.

I agree, Willy Jack. I was thinking we'd go out tomorrow. Take my rig. Have dinner.

He bent to look out the window. Dogs yipped.

Why we got so much trouble out here. Too much white blood. The more a Indian gets the stupider he gets.

He got a couple of Cokes out of the fridge. Handed one to me.

We laugh about it. When great grandfather surrendered to Bernard in 1877 they took us to the prison at Vancouver. Hung twenty of our young men. Soldiers got into the women. A lot of our women come back with half white kids. When I go up there the

Yakimas joke with me.

They hung a lot of you guys up here, Willy Jack! And fucked your women!

Could we go outside, Willy Jack.

Sure thing, Errol.

The dogs jumped with their paws on the fence.

Willy Jack looked at them.

Where our troubles come from. Too much white blood.

I know.

You don't, Errol. I keep telling you that.

You going to take me out there or not, Willy Jack!

Always in a hurry, Errol.

I pushed the dogs aside.

I'll be at Oliver's at noon.

Took I-15 back. The sun threw differential shadow past the volcano because it stood out of line with the mountains. Jagged whipsawed ravines. Got a six pack of Bridgeport at the Grapevine. A portly, white haired man talked with Mickey Angel. I handed each one.

To Lily.

The professor spoke like an Oxford don.

I'll go along with that. But whom might Lily be?

Lily Langtry. The Swedish Nightingale. Sang one night in a town on the Pecos nobody knows the name because Roy Bean renamed it Langtry in her honor.

To Lily then. A propos of nothing? Do you know why the Roman consul disowned his daughter the day they set foot in Paris?

No.

She had the Gaul to get married!

That's funny, Leonard. But I don't know how many people will get it.

Maybe this one then. Why did the Eleusian priestess stop by the pharmacy on Fifth? She had to get her Rite Aid!

He laughed. Had the silver mustaches of a cat.

These are all originals you know.

Mickey Angel grinned.

We're on our way to the Office, Leonard. If you'd like to

join us.

No. Thank you though. I have to spend a couple of hours with Thucydides. A cup of espresso is therefore in order.

He glanced at the vacant windows of the old hotel.

No matter how dedicated my Mormon colleagues are I have to feel sorry for them.

Why is that?

Coffee is unavailable to them.

For reading Thucydides?

He shook his head. Narrowed his eyes and mouth.

No. It's more than that. A day will come when you arrive in Venice. It will be a cold, gray day with the wind bringing rain off the Adriatic. You will have come a long way to see Venice and it is too cold and rainy to walk. The rain sluices down the windows where beautiful women once looked out. The wind moans along the balustrades. Venice is then a vast mausoleum of dreams, lost desire and beautiful books. The one thing you can do? The only thing of any consequence? Is to sit at the window of an old café. Look up at the windows of the old palaces with the rain whispering down them. And sip very slowly as if all eternity were yours a dark and very bitter espresso.

TWENTY NINE

Sometimes Canada geese made no sound as they flew. Sometimes no trains crossed the Overpass. You saw the buildings of East Center. The neon guitar above the door. Shadows at the bar. Pretty ladies with cigarettes pluming. Misko limped over with a Bud in one hand, Jameson's in the other.

You seen the pumpkin headed Mormon?

Mickey Angel shook his head. It was like being underwater at Lunch Counter. Magic Sam had both hands on the juke box. It was turned up full blast. Aretha shouted, What you want! Wailed glissandos like no creature on earth. Saxophones laid out harmonic cascades. Big tough guys in turquoise suits high stepped and swung the horns.

You seen him? Tell him I'm going to put his pumpkin head

in a vise and turn it real slow!

Mickey Angel got in his face.

You're turning into a jerk, Misko! Nobody wants that!

Misko began to lament. Mickey Angel nodded like a priest. I looked for the bartender. By the time I got a pitcher he had a table by the pool tables. Players strutted. Bent to line up shots. The colored spheres rearranged in infinite patterns. A skinny guy spent a lot of time around the table while the others racked. I nodded at him.

See that guy, Mickey Angel? How his right shoulder hangs lower than his left whether he's walking or sitting down? That's a bad sign.

We'd drunk half the pitcher when Gerald approached with his jacket over his arm. Sat with his back to the wall. Mickey Angel went to get a glass.

You be in town long, Gerald?

He scanned the crowd.

Long enough to establish communications. Then I'm headed north.

Yellowstone?

Greyhound doesn't go to Yellowstone. You're surprised?

Not many travel by bus these days.

You're wrong. A lot of people do. And if you showed the driver a Grover Cleveland there might be no record.

Mickey Angel poured. Gerald slipped his jacket under the chair.

From Vegas it's a direct route. I was climbing with a friend in Red Rocks. Talk about geological unconformity! From Red Rocks you see the stalagmite nightmare of Vegas. My friend had to dance that night. Driving back took the wrong exit. We were not in a good part of town. An ambulance screamed. She turned into an apartment complex to turn around. A white kid with dreadlocks we learned later was Monkey Boy leaned at the gate drinking a Malt Liquor 800. I was awake now. Saw the lookout atop the roof with an assault rifle. A second at the corner. The turn signal going tic-tic. A girl staggered toward us. Maybe fifteen. Red vinyl mini skirt. Black vinyl boots up to her crotch. She was an assistant crack whore. You know what that is don't you? She does what the first-class crack whore won't do. Had the clumsy knee high step you saw in the whores of Southeast Asia. Black syphilis.

Black syphilis?

The genera of spyrochete that prefers as its home the frontal lobe of the human brain. She was crying. Blood streamed down her face from a scalp wound where someone had pulled out a chunk of her hair. I was thinking that the ambulance that pulled in behind us thereby cutting off our escape was coming for her. But no! Lying half on the curb and half in the gutter was a big black man staring at the sky. A pool of blood widened beneath him. Tic-tic. We got turned around. The medics pulled out equipment. The lights flashed. When we got to the gate Monkey Boy decided to run in front of the car. The lookouts shouted.

Run, Monkey Boy! Run!

His quadruple large gym shorts fell to his ankles and when he tripped with dreadlocks flying the quart of Malt Liquor 800 shattered beneath him. Got up, hands and forearms bloody, crying, Mama! But she was engaged elsewhere. The turn signal stopped ticking as we turned onto the thoroughfare. Ah, Las Vegas! What happens here stays here!

He took a long draft of beer. Mickey Angel stared at him.

Thank you, Gerald. I was depressed when I came in? But now I'm feeling much better!

Gerald smiled. A light of pleasure lit up his eyes. He drew out the chrome lighter.

Just giving you a feeling of the New West, Michael. In the event you don't find it in the novels of Barbara Kingsolver.

He spun the wheel of the lighter. Lit his cigarette. It had an ignitions system like an old wheel lock gun. I almost caught the monogram before he slipped it in his pocket.

Borrow your lighter, Gerald?

You want a cigarette? I'll give you one.

Thank you.

He covered the monogram as he lit my cigarette. Leaned back. Blew a stream of smoke into the rafters. Mr. Collision came over.

Roxie been in?

No, Misko. I told you.

You'll tell me. Right?

I promise.

He towered over us.

That white belly. Fish belly white. Bush red as a Budweiser sign. Eyes like sagebrush after rain.

Gerald looked up at him.

Very poetic.

You don't know poetic until you see her climb the Big Horn Crags wearing no underwear. I saw God that day.

Mickey Angel raised his glass.

The Burning Bush!

I laughed. The nicotine had lit up my arteries. I blew out a plume of smoke. Looked admiringly at the scag.

So round. So firm. So fully packed! Tell me again, Misko. What a trailer weighs? Fully loaded?

Bulk head flat with spines? A hundred tons. Got to keep your eye on them. Worse in the old days. A mile of train with a hundred yards of compressed slack could jimmy a hand brake. Slip through the din of the yard. Wouldn't be much left of you. Thousands killed that way. WP decided the men at the Chicago Yard were beating up the rolling stock. So they devised a system called poling. Dangerous as hell. Forged coupler of soft steel. Nipple the size of your fist. Shunted the car from the siding with an iron pole. Think about it. The torque on that pole. They lost a man a day in Walltown before somebody decided maybe it's not that good an idea!

Misko tossed back the Jameson's.

Men were cheap. Will be again. But you were talking about engines. A few years back WP leased fifty engines to the Federal Railroad of Mexico. Got 'em back two years later. We were making a train on the slope by Black Cliffs. Fired it up. Nothing. Backed it up. More heat. Nothing. Took it to the shop. The chili chokers had switched engines! Management just wrote if off.

The Mexican Exchange!

Might been more than Mexicans involved, Mickey Angel.

So is it that hard to drive a train, Misko?

No, Bird Man. You got a mile of cars behind you. Ten thousand tons. Half going one way, half the other.

How's that?

Six feet of slack at a coupler. A hundred cars. That's six hundred feet of slack. You come to a hill and don't have speed? Five thousand tons slip backwards. Bump it and you've cracked the whip.

He looked at his empty shot glass.

My first memory of that shack on Shoshone Avenue? The clunk-a-clunk as the engineer let out slack in order to get rolling. Couldn't pull ten thousand tons from a standing stop. Diesels hold rail better but engine to engine? Steams pulled twice the freight. Especially after they invented the sliding sill. Slack taken out more gradually. Less stress on the coupler.

How does diesel hold the rail better?

Pistons turn the drive wheel. Rotary force applied directly to the rail. Look at the old steam engines. That long horizontal drive rod.

Made great music though.

Mickey Angel pumped his forearms.

Tchoo! Tchoo-tchoo-tchoo. Tchoo! Tchoo-tchoo-cchoo!

Misko grinned.

You'd've been proud of me, Mickey Angel. The other day I used my higher powers to control the forces of nature. We were headed west with a hundred empty cars. A new kid at the controls. Just as we got rolling the signal lights to the horizon turned red. Electrical glitch but nothing you can do. Run one and you're through. You know that desert through Minidoka? Just an endless succession of ridge backs? As soon as the kid got rolling the light ahead turned red. He was showing the strain. I got behind the controls. Saw thunderclouds to the north.

See those clouds, son? Soon as I get this train rolling thunder and lightning are going to be general. We'll see what happens to those signal lights!

Misko raised his huge hand.

As God is my witness!

The pool shark behind him turned to look.

Soon as I got that train rolling? The desert lit up like Fenway on Saturday night. Those red lights turned green to the horizon!

Able to do that often, Misko?

One other time. Headed east out of Nampa. The range bleached alkali white. We're staring down the track into the sun. Carlos shook his head.

Five hours of misery, Misko.

No, Carlos. See that cloud above Danskin Mountain? It's coming out of South Fork. Going to get bigger and bigger until it shields us all the way to Glenns Ferry.

And it did! We had shade all the way to Pocatello.

Mickey Angel handed me a twenty.

You fly. I'll buy.

I did. Max was busy. By the time I got back Misko was gone. Gerald was talking urgently to Mickey Angel. Didn't know I was there!

Flames tall as men raced through the trees. We ran. I heard automatic fire across the ridge. Knew we had none. A man shouted.

Where is the doctor? Someone go back for the doctor!

But my father wouldn't leave the cave. We'd been there three months. There was typhus. Children died. Were dying. He wouldn't leave them. Had entered the place where living and dead walk together.

Gerald's eyes shut hard.

I could not understand his abandonment. Or why I had not gone back! And which betrayal was more crucial!

You were a little kid, Gerald.

He leaned back with a sigh. Had the shades on. His haggard face lit luridly by the neon sign.

So I learned quite early. The force of our love is exceeded by the force that will destroy it. That is how the world is made and what I have become.

I sat down. He gave me a big smile.

I'm going to teach you a song, Errol. Would you like that?

Of course, Gerald.

It's not very long. You understand I'm teaching you these things in the event I have to leave suddenly and you no longer have my counsel. Are you ready?

Ready, Gerald.

He pounded the table with his fist. Sang in a deep bass. The beer glasses danced.

Vive la mort! Vive la guerre. Vive le mercenaire! Try it!

We did. It was a good song and easy to remember. I tried harmony.

Vive la mort! Vive la guerre! Vive le mercenaire!

I poured another round but Gerald stood up. Slung the jacket over his forearm.

No, my friends. It's time for me to go. I have enjoyed your company. But in a little while I'll have only one regret left me. That I'm old. That my knees creak. That I no longer march on a hard road under a cold moon with men I love. Goodbye.

It sounded corny but that's what he said. We shook hands. As he left a drunk staggered into him. Gerald lowered his head. A darker, denser thing than the shadows around him. Then he was gone.

Mickey Angel and I had a full pitcher. Had to drink it. I went out to the Underpass. A dwarf staggered at the other end backlit by the streetlight. Leaned against the wall. It was a Mexican girl holding her fully pregnant belly with one hand, the wall with the other. Portneuf Medical Center quite distant.

THIRTY

The morning sky was tranquil. Tall clouds stepped over the mountains. I went to Mickey Angel's. An old guy talked, head held high as if used to lecturing.

All the sailing ships of the Nineteenth Century are gone. It's true. In 1910 the insurance companies got together and raised the premiums on wooden ships regardless of history. Put them out of business.

The freight not the ships.

Of course. They sailed them onto spits of land. Lashed them to posts. Let wind and wave do what they would. Ships that had taken ten thousand years to build!

How do you know this, Henry?

I saw it. When I was in the Coast Guard. There was a yacht

available to non coms if the officers weren't using it. I waited for a nice weekend. Sailed down the coast. Came to an estuary where the hulls of sailing ships rose out of the sand like the skeletons of giant fish.

Horrible.

It's the American Way. Same with the old steam engines. Another time I went north. Came to a glen running down to the surf. It was filled with old steam engines. I thought a hurricane had left them but heard booming from the bluff. Saw puffs of smoke. Realized they had a switching yard up there. Had just pushed the old engines over the cliff.

They cut them up here for scrap in World War II.

All of them?

There's a two-four-two at Ross Park. So how late did the clippers run?

Clipper ships carried goods between San Francisco and Alaska into the Thirties. Canned goods up. Fish and lumber down. Nothing fancy.

Mickey Angel turned to me.

How you feeling, Errol.

I feel the infinite compassion of Buddha. Forgiveness too. Working on that.

Henry flicked a speck from his neatly pressed trousers.

I've found that forgiveness is easier if you hit back hard right away. When I got the call in 1965 they advised me to enlist. I did. Asked where I was going.

Vietnam.

I told them I couldn't do that. We only fought Germans in my family. Well I'll see you around.

He left. Mickey Angel turned to me.

Before I forget. Your friend in Pingree called. Said come get your bird.

I drove up Center Street. Stayed on I-15. Saw out left the Three Buttes. No wonder the Navy liked to shoot at them. Looked like islands. At Tilden boats slipped onto the river. Glen came out the front door in camo and jack boots. Nodded. I got glove and jesses. Kyrie was leashed but unhooded. Bated. He unlatched the gate. Didn't look at me. Kept hands clenched as he stepped back.

The mew adjacent empty. Kyrie fixed me with her black, implacable eyes.

Has she eaten?

He spoke heart in throat.

Had them a'block in the yard. Careless.

I'm sorry, Glen.

It was my fault.

I'm sorry.

He looked at me under his hat.

You want me to say it again?

I knelt with the gray corpse in glove.

Step up, Kyrie. Eat.

You better hood her.

I will. Step up, Kyrie.

I was looking in her eyes. Instead of stepping to the glove she bated, wings beating. The leash threw her backward. Hallux caught me under the eye. She flung backwards whipping her wings. I grabbed her with both hands. Blood splashed her nape as I unclipped the leash. Held her with one hand. Stanched the gash with the other. Heard Glen say he had bandages in the house. I didn't look back. Leashed her in the cab.

She watched the road, ditch banks, fields. Hungry, mad, filled with blood lust. At Tilden Bridge saw dark shapes atop the cottonwoods. The sheen of the gliding Snake. I pulled off the road.

If you get on the glove you'll fly, Kyrie.

She did. Fanned but didn't bate. Blood spattered my boots as we descended the embankment. The Snake coiled, uncoiled, hissed as it swept along the bank. Mallard flews. Settled in a back eddy.

Come back, Sweetheart.

She leapt. With one high wing beat caught the breeze. Was soon among clouds. If she drifted east I would never find her. The Snake glittered bright and shining but was dark, cold and coiling. Egrets stepped along a gravel bar. Willows waved. I heard teal calling then saw them coming from the Reservoir. Hadn't seen her ascent. Didn't get the meaning of that sound. If they dropped to water now they'd be safe. Didn't until she flashed among them. Her left wingtip touched water then zoomed to embrace a hen and with that momentum carry her to the willows.

Thunderclouds trailed rain over the mountains. Mickey Angel heard me stumbling around.

Jesus Christ!

Don't look too good huh?

Something the cat drug in.

Was a big cat. You got a beer?

You need more than that. What is it?

Green teal. Cut a slice if you want. Nothing better than green teal.

I wrapped what remained in the fridge. Looked at my face in the mirror. Washed and taped it. Mickey Angel stood by.

Let me look at it.

Just look.

You need stitches. I can see the fascia.

Needle and thread in the truck.

Why d'you have those?

I lied.

Replace feathers.

There's a Doc in the Box on Yellowstone. I'll drive you.

No insurance. You can do it, Mickey Angel. It's not that hard.

I'll call Solomon.

I drove past Caldwell Park. Kids swung on swings. A little man in a gray suit stood at the door by the alley. Bowed sardonically. Had a long, horse face and bulging gray eyes. Wore black cowboy boots. The breeze splayed his thinning hair.

How did this happen?

My falcon hit me.

Female? How did I know. I'm on my third marriage. With each one I get poorer and end up in a more god forsaken town. Your health good?

I don't have any choice.

Most people don't. Your health is good?

Yes.

Give me your arm.

He wrapped the tourniquet around my bicep. Pumped it.

Very good. Are you on medication?

No.

Drug allergy?

Tetracycline kills me.

He got towels and a bottle of antiseptic. Peered at me through thick glasses. I smelled bourbon.

This is going to hurt. Close your eyes. I don't want to see you cry.

He broke the crust I'd protected. Probed the wound while he swabbed it.

The wound is ragged. Damage to the ocularis. Not too deep though. I suggest you go to Emergency. Have them call Dr. Armistead.

I don't want him working on me.

You know him?

Just superstitious.

It's your face! Your eye might have a sinister droop.

Give it character. Shall we, Doctor?

As he filled the syringe I saw the dark bags under his eyes. Wondered what else he was using. Like the old man.

How do you know Mickey Angel?

He cocked his head.

Say it again. A tank commander has the cannon to his left. I'm deaf there.

Mickey Angel. How do you know him?

I like books about cars and dinosaurs. Fast cars and big dinosaurs. Especially those that lived at sea. This is going to sting.

He hit the perimeter of the wound with the needle. My eye sagged. I moved my mouth.

How did you get to Pocatello?

I was at a hospital in Ohio. There were Indians there. Brahmins. Spoke that subcontinent English everyone finds so charming. Unfortunately for me it was against their religion to treat Untouchables.

Lot of those out there.

You got it. But when my blood pressure shot up when I heard them laughing in the Doctor's Lounge? After an especially bloody situation? And the pleasure it would give me to bring my Hechler-Koch to work?

That's IDF.

How did you know? Yes. I was in the Sinai in '74. Alright. Here is your Father's Day present. Tell me if it hurts.

It did. I felt the tug as he drew it through. Tears started. Tears and antiseptic ran down my face. He talked.

I was on the tarmac. A Texas flyboy came up.

Y'all American. Why y'all fighting for Israelis?

Y'all from Texas. Why y'all flying this equipment in?

My grandfather escaped Stalin in the Thirties. Jewish doctors were bad for the health of the apparatchik. He didn't take away their licenses. He killed them. Everybody says what a bad guy Sharon was. But he saw the gap at Mile 124. It was all over after that. Women crawled toward us with palms up. We sent them to the rear. Some had their clitoris cut off. Vaginas sewn shut. We counted the dead. They had been stripped by the Faithful. Bloated and black with flies.

A thunderclap hit. The building shook. Boomed like box cars clashing. The stink of bourbon. The dead covered with flies. I was getting sick.

How'd you cross?

We brought up pontoons. The farm had bunkers we didn't know about. It took a lot of work to kill the soldiers there.

How did you bring up the pontoons?

With Pattons. Forty of them.

You were in a Patton?

God forbid. A Centurion! The best tank made. Had a Rolls Royce engine. We called Pattons Ronsonols. The way they lit up.

He tied the last knot. Swabbed antiseptic.

It was easy to separate the Nubians from the Egyptians without getting close. The size of their schlongs.

Solomon had a nifty bedside manner. Put his hand behind my shoulder. Pushed me up.

You're going to have a nice scar.

Sometimes that's all you get.

If you're lucky.

He got samples out of the cabinet.

Take them all. If the eye gets infected you're fucked. Here's some Vicodin. That's all you get. Can you walk?

He escorted me to the back door.

Michael told you about Dr. Armistead? Forget about it. He just likes people to know what he's worth.

I will.

You've heard the saying? Your friends can do a lot for you but your enemies can do a lot more?

I hadn't. Thunder crashed. Rain danced on the sidewalk. I walked to the truck in the rain. It felt wonderful and cool.

THIRTY ONE

The Vicodin worked. I didn't move for twelve hours. Herring gulls perched on lampposts. Swept over the high school parking lot with long pointed wings. A fat bellied cowboy lounged in the hot tub. Had ten acres, a couple of horses and a pension from the Highway Department.

My buddy was just up North Fork. They was driving up the road and seen four dead deer under the cliff. Wolves had run 'em. They seen their tracks all around. Just run 'em over the cliff.

The right side of my face throbbed. I tossed the bandage. Looked at my face in the mirror.

Now Dalton don't have no trouble with wolves. Keeps 'em cleaned out to Fish Creek Summit.

How's he do that?

His men carry guns. Heh! Heh! Fish and Game boys? Seem to be always in a other part of the country!

They laughed. I was confused. Only knew Fish Creek Summit east of Lava.

Yep! Them wolves just chased them 'til they run over the cliff. They ought to take every wolf lover and--

I turned.

You shit kickers ruin the range. Ruin the streams. Have your elk every fall like it's your divine right! And I have to listen to your shit?

His eyes opened wide. Stared up at a naked man with a livid wound under one eye. I slammed the door to the shower so it bounced. Slammed it again. When I came out felt better. They

didn't. At Midley's filled the cooler with Budweiser. Drove up
Arthur into the sun. They laid the Oregon Short Line 45 degrees to
Base Line. President streets parallel. I thought the sun would shoot
the crossing streets at solstice. It never did. In the Carnegie Library
pored over Drylands by Philip Hyde. Took a table by the window
at Oliver's. Sparrows swarmed. The waitress took my order then
filled bird feeders. They swarmed to it. One held place by hanging
upside down like a parrot. The waitress took my plate away. Kids
in orange vests mowed the jail lawn. Willy Jack slid into the seat
across from me.

How you doing, Old Man? Thought you'd wait for me.

I thought about it.

With all I done for you. What happened to your face?

Kyrie nicked me.

Must've been mad. You fooling around?

He ordered biscuits and gravy with bacon and ham on the
side.

Females got it hard wired. I got a uncle is married to a
Basquo. She grew up in the sheep camps. White blouse. Gold
crucifix at her throat. Knew how to use the knife though.

I nodded. In the spring when they cut the jacks the boys ran
around grinning with testicles between their teeth. Willy Jack
talked.

Uncle Brice? Hard to handle on a ordinary day. Korea
didn't help none. Come home twice with his head kicked in. Steel
plate installed to hold the brains in. Maria could deal with that. But
one night he run into Luanna Parrish at McDermotts? Stayed too
long. Why he neglected to shower I can't tell you. But woke to see
Maria straddling him. No Kama Sutra. She'd clipped one nut and
was commencing on the other. He didn't ask for change. Put that
Ford 150 through a dozen flashing yellow lights to Bannock
Regional. Holding that nut like they do when the center's shooting
the game free throws.

The waitress brought his plate. Got his full attention.

They still together?

Oh yeah. He just don't stay long at McDermott's. Nobody
makes jokes. Like Jake the barkeep says, With half a brain and one
nut he's still twice the man you find in Pocatello these days.

Willy Jack ate slowly and leisurely.

That's going to kill you, Willy Jack.

Everybody dies, Errol. Did you know that?

I leaned back. Stretched my legs. Across Fifth a hawk slipped into a tree on the jail lawn.

Look at that! Sharp shin, Willy Jack! Second tree from the corner!

Willy Jack was so fat he could barely turn. Gravy dribbled down the corner of his mouth. The hawk sailed across Fifth into the trees of the University District.

How'd you see him?

Keep your eyes moving.

He finished. The waitress took his plate with one hand. Tried to pour coffee with the other. I put my hand over the cup. He looked hurt.

I was only a half hour late!

It was an hour. Wasn't it Ma'am?

Over an hour.

I handed her a twenty. Slid out of the booth.

So we're flying.

You're harsh, Errol.

Sparrows whirred from bush to busy. Didn't have much of a life but stayed interested. We passed the lava wall at Ross Park. Climbers like spiders. Willy Jack looked at them.

You seen the panel at Cheyenne Crossing?

The bear paws and dancing men?

Know what it means?

They killed a griz there. Everybody hoo-rawing.

No. Bear is Medicine Spirit. In spring everybody was weak from the winter. Eyes, noses running. They saw bear out there on the hillside digging roots. She didn't feel so hot either but knew where the good herbs were. Those bear paws? That meant a medicine man found her spirit in that place. It's holy.

Not anymore I guess.

No. A lot of angry spirits there now.

We drove through the Gap. Turned the corner. Saw Oxford Peak yonder. Marsh Creek ran past feedlots. Juniper twisted atop the lava cliffs. The cliffs became more broken. Willy Jack pointed out an esplanade.

That's where we're going.

I parked at the gate to Indian Rocks. Shouldered the pack. It had been a fine State Park. The legends as to its demise were many. Murders. Wrecks on the freeway even though it ran straight toward Oxford Peak. A vortex centered on the petroglyph boulders. State Senator wanted the grazing rights. The Visitor's Center looked cursed with fire blackened walls. The boulders abided. Ten thousand years gave them a blue brown patina the artists nicked to make the design. Wolfman danced with his pointed ears and long snaky tail. Caphead man burst the boundary of the fourth dimension.

Must've been getting high around here, Willy Jack!

Water table was higher. Algal reefs impounded the Portneuf because it never froze. They called it Falls River for the way the water glittered over the dams. Moose. Elk. Bison. Perfect for mushrooms.

Lightning and rain etched along the upper rim of a boulder. Like a hand turned down with fingers spread. Or the way the afternoon sun lights up secondary ridges. Salamanders with long bodies, arms and legs. Knobbed fingers to hold on to rocks in the turbulence. We followed a cow track. Came to a cliff.

The village was down there. That low place? A pond. I helped excavate the village. We got to the level the people occupied when the whites arrived and the funding ran out. They had it pretty good. Lot of fish. Crayfish. Game coming to water. In all of Shoshone land this was the land we asked for. Then the Utah Northern blew the algal reefs. The springs dried up.

We descended the cliff. Followed a cow trail to a basalt monolith that stood above Marsh Creek. Two figures danced with arms raised side by side. The man had deer horns and swollen genitals. The woman gave birth as she danced. The baby headfirst with arms straight out.

How old is it, Willy Jack?

Two thousand years? The etching is dim. Takes time to do that.

Marsh Creek glittered. We descended to it. Whistling marmots warmed their bellies on the rocks. Squaw current bloomed. Juniper smelled like gin. We climbed a boulder flow up to the bench. Willy Jack like a bear in blue overalls. Sat back. Wiped his brow with a red handkerchief. Above his head the etching of slim animal with long tail. A real weasel scampered in the corner of my eye. When I looked she was gone. A cloud crossed the sun. Cold seeped from the crevasses. Willy Jack looked vaguely sinister.

The old ones let their dead down here.

Now I saw images of the dead everywhere. Two men stabbed a third. A man fell headfirst off a cliff. Two figures with heads cut off. Willy Jack murmured.

This is a place of the Dead. Weasels, skunks, mice were the intermediaries. What was left sluiced to Marsh Creek.

That's the meaning of the weasel?

I don't know. Maybe a medicine man needed help to go down there. To find out something of importance to the people.

The cloud passed. The sun was hot but the cold still seeped. I didn't like the hot and cold. Stood up. Wanted to get out of those rocks. Willy Jack looked around.

We lived in the spirit world the way fish live in water.

I started toward a grove of juniper.

I just know that when I go I don't want a lot of tears.

He scanned the rim rock.

Don't worry, Errol. There was enough of that when you was around.

I crawled in the shade of a juniper. Pulled out the water bottle. Looked at the cliff. It was pleated as columns split off. Juniper twisted like images of the wind. Willy Jack looked down at me.

How you feeling?

I don't know. We haven't been out that long. It's not that hot.

Heavy action here, Errol. Nobody knows how deep the caverns go. What's been done and unforgotten.

How did you come here?

BLM hired me to do an inventory. Everything down to the faintest scratch mark.

He let a handful of dust sift through his fingers.

I spent a lot of time here. For a couple years that's all I did. It became an obsession. I hunted down informants that knew of other sites. Went all over Southern Idaho. One by one they began to die off.

How many were there?

Three. One a Vietnam Vet. The others artists. Like me they were obsessed. Obsessions are funny. The more you are involved with them the more insistent they become. They were drawn to these sites for reasons unknown to them. For example I don't know why you're here.

What did they die of?

Brain cancer. All three.

You're not making me feel any better, Willy Jack.

We picked our way through the rocks. Magpies squawked. The sun headed to Scout Mountain.

We don't know the intention of the people who carved these designs. What power they were able to acquire. An old woman watched a sorcerer walk into a lightning storm. He went to the place the lightning struck. Smoked and dreamed. Etched the rock while it had the odor of lightning.

The cliff hemmed us. Thirty foot blind columns. Willy Jack poked around.

The women who have been to these sites don't seem to be affected.

Men must carry resistance.

Maybe.

The landscape had a sculptured look. The only erosive features what the Flood made. Juniper twisted out of rock. The wind came up.

Over here!

A boulder lay flat to the ground half hidden by a sagebrush. A sorcerer balanced a skeleton in his right hand and a shield in the other. Lines coiled up inside his torso like entwined snakes. A purse swung from his left elbow.

That's his puja. His power pack.

It's more fantastic than I remembered.

The skeleton had curving deer horns and swollen genitals. Had undergone death because his ribs were hollow. The shield was ornamented with diamond lozenges. Below his big feet two figures joined the dance. The first had a star for a head with twelve flaring rays. The second had horns and a long tail that was cut off when the boulder split.

Crazy how hip he was! How long do you think it took?

With quartzite? Try it sometime. To chip away the field to bring the diamonds into relief took years.

You see that diamond design in Ireland. Wish I packed a camera.

Why I like you, Errol. In some ways you're like a Indian.

He drifted away. I stared at the cliff in order to triangulate. I hoisted the pack. We climbed over columns with sides cut so clean you saw where they fit the cliff. Was jumping one when I saw the diamond pattern. Captain Fang looked over his shoulder. I was suddenly atop another boulder. Doing the Rattlesnake Fandango.

Snake, Willy Jack! Snake!

His big head appeared.

What?

Didn't you see him?

A rattlesnake?

The biggest I've seen!

Sure it was a rattlesnake?

I almost stepped on him! Jesus Christ!

Was it a really big one?

You heard me!

I was wondering where he was.

Him? Is this a den? God damn it, Willy Jack! How many are there?

Don't take the Lord's name in vain, Errol.

Now I saw every detail. Lichen like sunbursts. Moss waiting for rain. Tiny wildflowers in the cracks. Listened for the rasp of scales on rock. Swallows squeaked as they swooped above Marsh Creek. After awhile Willy Jack sat with a spray of gold currant at his elbow.

Wanted to show you this.

The lava separating as it cooled sequentially left a shallow cave. On the wall pictographs: two figures lying side by side. I crawled in where it was cool. Lay on my side to look at them.

Rolled on my back. Birds sang. Then an owl hovered with her great soft wings. Looked in my eyes. I was sinking. A hand grabbed my shoulder. The owl vanished. I flew toward the light and it hurt.

Leave me alone, Willy Jack!

Get up, Errol.

Just let me lie awhile.

This is a man's grave, Errol. Get up.

I let my head fall to the side. Saw cars across the valley. Lichen on the rock above. They took a long time to grow. A millimeter a year. I rolled out.

He had a nice view.

He did.

We looked at Marsh Creek silver in the sun. Horses swished their long tails.

Might be playing a little close to the edge, Errol.

Sleeping in a truck ain't that great.

Stay at my place.

No. I'm in transition. That's all.

Transitions can kill you. What you learn in basketball. The transition game.

I didn't know you played.

Why? 'Cause I'm so fat? Us Indians love basketball. Like to take it down the wings. You seen the movies. Horses. Flaming arrows. Forget that half court stuff. Hit 'em on the flanks. Don't want to stop in Grangeville around tournament time. The way Lapwai handles 'em.

Run up the score? That's bad, Willy Jack.

No. You can never have too many points. Like my cousin Ronnie Bronco. Poured 'em through so fast and from so far away the zebras had to stop the games. The spin stripped the net! Maybe it was because they weren't even touching iron. Would've damped the energy somewhat. Ronnie Bronco. He'd light it up. Fake a pass to him and he'd shoot.

I got beer and sandwiches. Watched clouds come over Old Tom. Willy Jack talked.

His old man was in the Philippines when the Japs overran it. Sixteen when he enlisted. The nuns at St. Ignatius had got on his nerves.

I thought he was Fort Hall.

Indians always moving around, man. My Dad was born in a field in Texas! Old Bronco escaped the Death March. Hooked up with a girl on the cumulo granite. Had a kid with her. But somebody in the tribe betrayed him. He was in a Jap ship headed for the tin mines when a US war fish hit it. Was in the water. Grabbed a spar. In the light of the flames saw a Jap soldier go down once. Come up. Go down again. One thing a Indian can do is swim. He got hold of the Jap from behind like they teach you and hauled him onto the spar. And you know? That Jap ended up guarding him in the tin mine. Treated him worse than the other prisoners.

Maybe it was because he looked Japanese.

No. The Jap lost face. Bronco caused it. The other thing he told me was that one night the Japs brought his cellmate back from the mine. Dumped him on the floor. A stope failed and crushed his leg. They cut if off. Just threw him on the floor. It was winter. All he had was a blanket. Bronco knew he was going to die by the way he curled up in the fetal position. Kept a death watch. In the early morning the ghost rose from his body. Looked down. Shook his head with pity and walked away.

Bronco must've been dreaming.

You think, Errol?

A haze--summer hatch--drifted over Marsh Creek. I looked at the back of my hands. A big horn sheep drifted up. We returned along the Portneuf where you saw traces of algal reefs. Left Willy Jack at his truck. Returned past Lower Ross Park. Poor wills called. Dark came down. I dreamed of animals that lived in this country. Watched as God assembled their bones in the sky. Told myself to concentrate and remember because in the morning I would be unable.

THIRTY TWO

Wind whipped the Coleman flame. I sat on the tailgate. Watched the trees. Birds not singing. Ragged clouds raced. At the Meat

Market two shadows talked in the steam room.

Where you think you'll go?

I heard there's work in Salt Lake. Ten dollars and up.

Falliburton's starting up again in Wyoming. Might look them up.

Been there. Done that. Too many drive-by's for my blood in Rock Springs.

The big guy sluiced himself with cold water.

Sheriff sold good rock though. Strictly high grade.

Right! Lot of unsolved murders back then in Rock Springs.

But the good times might be heading back. If Falliburton comes to town.

The little guy shrugged.

Not for me.

Lot of houses going up in the Boise area.

No. Always a Mexican on the corner that'll hang dry rock for five an hour. Nothing plumb. Corners crooked. Just tape and paint.

A young gal with bleached blonde hair and big brown eyes hopped in. Perched beside me for a moment then hopped out. I watched her preen by the pool.

Say what you will about Mexicans. The women improve the view.

Oh hell. I'm Mexican. Indian too! Mexicans kicked my ass because I was Indian and the Indians because I was Mex!

The big guy turned the cold water tap.

That was me growing up Bohunk in Butte. Fight every corner. Jumped mine shafts for kicks. Always ready for the next big lift. Rock Springs was perfect for that. Now I'm just a mellow fellow from Pocatello.

Boom box played Johnny B. Goode. The old ladies whooped. Raised waves. In the locker room two silver backs talked in the hot tub.

Here comes the Whistler!

Just like the radio show!

I tossed the razor on the wash basin.

There a show called The Whistler?

You bet.

Thirties?

Forties. You heard the Whistler coming and knew the trouble would start.

He solved crimes?

Just stuck his nose where it didn't belong. Always trouble when the Whistler came around. You remember that, Charlie? You get the Whistler out in Idaho?

Oh sure! Soon as I got a younger brother big enough to climb into the tree and hold the antenna. Until then I was in the tree!

What was the antenna doing in the tree?

He doesn't know much does he, Larry?

With the interference of the branches why didn't you put it on the roof?

It was on the roof. You ran it to the nearest tree.

The antenna?

Was a wire antenna. Copper wire with insulation at each end. The crystal picked up broad band, narrow band. Short wave, long wave. Had to have a little brother though. To adjust the wire. You'd be listening to Jack Benny. Signal'd fizzle.

To the right, Jerry! No! Now to the left! Perfect! Stay right there!

The silver backs laughed happily.

It was good to have a little brother. So the wind gone down?

It's whipping pretty good.

Nothing like the Robin Wind, said Charlie.

What's that?

Robin is at the bottom of Garden Creek Gap. Wind blows there.

Venturi effect.

Right. Growing up we had a pole in the front yard with a tow chain hanging from it. In the spring we'd look out the window to see if it was any use going out. If the wind lifted that chain gentle like it was a woman's skirt? We might get some plowing done. But if it stood straight out? Didn't pay.

I laughed. Turned toward the showers.

Hold on, son! You haven't heard about the Robin Wind!

When the wind ripped the links off that chain? Then you had a
Robin Wind!

Outside metal signs squeaked. Trees spangled. I looked at
the terra cotta dolphins holding shields atop Poky High.

Pweep! Pweep! Ch-ch-ch-ch!

A male merlin dropped to a terra cotta rainspout in the wall.
Fidgeted.

Skrreek! Skreek!

His common law wife screamed at him from the roof. He
cast off with sharp tipped wings. Headed for the hills. The wind
moaned in the doorway of Michael Angelo's Books. Mickey Angel
looked up from his book.

Caleb called.

What'd he say?

He'll be at the Office tonight.

Good deal.

An aging weightlifter wearing a tweed jacket with leather
elbow patches came in.

Top of the morning, Michael!

Mickey Angel didn't raise his eyes.

What's up, Kerry.

Checking on you liberals.

I'm not a liberal, Kerry. I'm a radical. If you crowd me I'll
cap you. You dig?

Kerry laughed. Sat down.

So. You think there'll be war with Iran?

You?

The drumbeat is there. A propos I have an anecdote that
you as a dealer in books will appreciate. I have a friend that was
one in Teheran.

CIA?

In Iran book dealer is an oxymoron. He sent me a cartoon
of two merchants. One a seller of candy the other of books. The
bookseller is gaunt and hungry. The candy seller is fat and happy.
His shop is full of people. When the Islamic Guard came to power
things turned quite well for him. Can you guess?

Mickey Angel shrugged.

Kerry said, Books with pictures of naked, beautiful women

became quite dangerous to have. He was able to buy illustrated editions of the Rubaiyat for a song. The Hanson History of Art with the Greek statues and the paintings by Titian? What he bought for a dollar he sold for hundreds on the black market.

I shook my head. It was true. Booklovers could not bear their destruction. The wind howled. Kerry smiled.

Right out the Arabian Nights, don't you think?

Chalk up another for the CIA.

How do you arrive at that, Michael?

Eisenhower and British Petroleum took out Mossadegh with the help of the fundamentalist clerics. Mossadegh wanted girls to go to school. The Shah was cheaper. You know that, Kerry! So don't act stupid!

He stacked books in his left arm. Started plugging them in the wall shelf. Kerry flicked lint from his trousers. Mickey Angel picked up an ice cream chair. Threw it feet first against a bookshelf so it stuck. I back pedaled. The professor departed. Mickey Angel put his boots up.

I don't think he's coming back, Mickey Angel.

He grabbed a book.

Never buys anything.

Something clanked on the roof. The wind tearing roofing. Flashing. He threw the book down.

Look. I got a package to mail. You mind watching the till?

I took his chair. Thought about the Shah. His inbred nose meeting his chin. His beautiful long sable coats he wore in Sun Valley. The Valleyites so thrilled to have a king on their mountain! Farriman had a marker in. You knew that. Awnings rippled. Light flashed. I thought it a cop car but was a steel sign twisting in the sun. The phone rang.

Michael?

This is Errol, Johanna.

What are you doing there? Are you boyfriends too?

I don't know we are, Johanna.

You Scandinavian types! Sitting around ornamenting your penises with Celtic knot-work!

I laughed. She slammed a cabinet door.

Give him a message for me will you? Tell him it's over!

He'll never see me again! I have a three foot rattlesnake tacked to my wall to remember him by!

Sure it's a rattler?

Want to see it? Come on up! I'm looking at it right now!

How did you get a rattlesnake?

The dogs were barking at the corner of the retaining wall. I thought I'd left the sprinkler on because I heard this Chit-chit-chit! A huge rattlesnake. Coiled. Ready to kill my dogs!

It must have liked the warmth of the wall.

Thank you for your analysis, Errol. But I'm not interested. Tell Michael to send his weird, snaky energy somewhere else. I don't need it! I have a life and dogs I love! I don't need him sending his snaky energy to kill them!

I don't see how Michael figures in this, Johanna.

You don't? You don't feel it? How he's always traipsing around in the desert! Instead of taking care of the woman who loves him!

Michael is terrified of snakes, Johanna.

He has reason to be! I can't talk anymore! I'm so upset I'm shaking! It's over. It's finished. Will you tell him that for me?

You don't want him to call you?

I never want to see him again. I don't need it. What he does to me. I have a three foot rattlesnake tacked to my wall to remind me. I'm looking at it right now. And they're not beautiful. They're ugly!

What did you do with the head?

I cut it off.

You want to dispose of it carefully, Johanna. The fangs still have venom.

Good! Tell Michael to lock his Jeep at night!

She hung up. I put the phone down. Thought it judicious I didn't tell her she shouldn't have killed it. Wanted a cigarette and a drink. It was true. What men and women did to each other was like snake bite. Tristan and Iseult died on the same day by their own hand because of their love for each other. Shakespeare would give them a potion to forget their pain and remember the pleasure of each other's arms. But there was no potion. Mickey Angel should just crawl. Mexicans did. I remembered hooded penitents crawling on the Day of the Dead. Whipping themselves with knotted ropes.

Virgen Preciosa! Tenga mercia!

Had walked for days without food or water. Dusty faces streaked with tears.

Virgen! Intercessa paranos!

The knotted ropes danced on their backs. Had forgotten the hymns the Jesuits taught. At the Church Atonticlico staggered to their feet to pour tears and pesos into bowls carved in the stone pillars. Christ stood in his parrot feather skirt, his back crisscrossed with blood. Conquistadors astride horses looked on.

Mickey Angel returned. I was going to tell him about Johanna but a woman in a tight skirt and high heels walked past.

How'd you like that swinging on your porch, Mickey Angel?

She's coming in!

It was Roxie. Tied her hair in a bun. Wore a silvery jacket, short skirt and black nylons. Perfume to exceed sixty miles an hour. Glanced at us.

If you shut up I might buy something.

We did. I picked up a book, my hands shaking. Down the aisle she knelt in her tight skirt. The lame Indian came down the street in his heavy long coat. Styrofoam cup in one hand, cigarette in the other. The smoke described intricate trigonometric equations. Spit on his finger to put it out.

Here's two dollars. We're even now right?

Right.

You got a dictionary? I need a dictionary.

I got lots of them, Louie.

He came back with a thick paperback.

That got all the words?

All of them. Two bucks.

Louie got greenbacks out of an inside pocket. Lot of pockets in that coat.

How do you cook pigeon, Louie? I asked.

Grill it. Marinate in olive oil. Pepper and salt. A little lemon juice.

On a grill?

Cut off the wings. Split the back so it lays flat.

Sounds like you're a chef. You like squab?

His eyes deep and black.

Hard to get squab.

I glanced out the window. Awnings rippling in the wind.

I'll get you one, Louie.

He turned to Mickey Angel.

We're even now. Right?

Hobbled out.

You wonder what he has in those pockets.

You do.

Roxie came up with a stack of books against her bosom. Set them on the desk. Waved the air with both hands.

Quite the clientele you have, Michael.

It's taken time to build up.

I leaned against the wall shelf. She turned to me.

Why are you wearing dark glasses? I can't tell what you're looking at!

Mickey Angel grinned.

Oh you know what he's looking at!

She turned her back. He tallied. Put them spine down in white plastic sacks.

Nice buys, Roxie. One twenty. You getting out this weekend?

She wrote that big check like it was nothing. Let it float on the desk.

The girls and I are going to Challis Hot Springs.

She picked up the sacks. When she turned let our eyes meet. That perfume stayed like a calling card.

Nice sale, Mickey Angel.

He sat happily with his hand behind his head.

I love Roxie.

I didn't tell him about Johanna. Outside the wind licked the last snow bones from Scout. Maple and chokecherry foamed up City Creek. I drove where the river entered its concrete channel. Mud sucked at my boots as I took readings. The channel ran with barbed wire two miles to Sacajawea Park. I drove there. People walked their dogs. Mallard and hybrid gabbled along the bank. A shadow floated. The broad wing kited then banked and flew with lazy wing beats toward the volcano. His mate keened from a huge old willow. I took samples. Slogged out. Two scruffy kids jumped from a low limb.

Hey mister! What you doing?

Checking the water.

You a fisherman?

I am.

Us too. You can't believe the fish we caught the other day! It was this big!

Nice. What was it?

A trout!

Good deal! How'd you cook it.

They grimaced.

Mom made us throw it away!

You'll catch more.

They scrambled into the tree. I thought of the kids in Ohio they couldn't keep out of the rivers. Flippers in the second generation. Billy and me with buckets over the handlebars riding to Hiline Canal. The farmers treated it to get rid of the rushes. Dead frogs floated. We cried. An old man sat in the shade of a thorn olive. Blossoms heavy with perfume. The black dog bounded up.

Dr. Schindler!

Hey old man!

You see the hawk?

Right on!

I thought he was ferruginous he was so big.

No. No ferros around here. Swainson's. Mama's got a nest in the willow over there. You can hear her now. Ki! Ki! Ki! Come from Argentina to do their fandango.

Think they'll make it?

Why not? Plenty to eat. Gophers on the hillside. Squirrels in the trees.

I noticed them acting a little circumspect.

It's a new regime!

Think there were peregrine in the Middle Snake?

Peregrine need cliffs.

I mean the canyon between Milner and Twin Falls.

Oh yeah. Michael told me he saw a peregrine climbing at

Massacre Rocks.

I thought they liked clean water.

They like ducks, man! Ducks!

Right! Got to keep your priorities in order!

Driving back across town I thought of the Portneuf when old men fished it. Girls in bathing suits lounged along the banks. Feedlot Aristocracy refused to spend a few dollars more. Nobody made them. Biological Science Building stood at the west boundary of ISU. It was Saturday so I was able to park on Carter. Carried my pack up the air conditioned stairwell. Lab door open. A pretty girl in lab smock turned. The girl at Gibson Jack. I smiled.

Abner said he'd meet me here.

I unpacked specimen bottles. Scanned the beautiful machines. Microscopes. Centrifuges. Digital weight scales.

Could you lend me an agar plate? Abner must be delayed.

She tossed her hair.

What are you doing?

Stream analysis. E coli concentrations.

How are you going to do that?

Count.

That went out twenty years ago. You place it in reagent and scan it with the spectroscope. Spectral bloom will give the count.

It was peaceful. The hum of coolers and convection columns. Radiometric scanners. She hooked spectrometer to computer. The screen flashed big numbers.

The Portneuf right?

How did you know?

Every first year microbiology student wants to do a pathogenic survey of the Portneuf. We tell them to find something else.

So how hot is it?

Let's say if you wanted to construct a system for producing E coli? It would be that concrete channel on a hot summer day.

The beautiful cowgirl in tight jeans under her lab smock returned to work. I carried my bottles out under the tall old pines. The Army Corps of Engineers and the feedlot aristocracy made perfect partners. Not often a government agency and the private sector were this successful. I tossed the bottles. Kids and dogs.

THIRTY THREE

Treetops swayed but the truck was hot. At the Office Caleb sat with a pretty Indian lady. Shades on the brim of his fisherman hat. Steel toed boot across one knee.

Elvira? This be Errol. He's a good guy.

Thank you, Caleb.

I ordered a Bud Lite. Elvira had big almond shaped brown eyes. Long wolf nose. Black hair glistened in the neon lights.

Where you from, Elvira?

Window Rock.

What brings you here?

A job.

Caleb grinned.

You know how it is. Things get too hot down Navaho way they come to Fort Hall. 'Til things cool down.

Elvira gave him an elbow.

Watch it, fella.

Looked like Elvira could heat things up. Caleb grimaced like a little kid.

So you going into the Salmon with us? What you going to do with the bird?

Take her with.

You're crazy.

Don't have a choice. Isn't that the meaning of freedom?

Elvira wrinkled her nose.

Not the kind I want.

Think about it, Elvira. Those salmon have only one thing to do and they do it.

She looked at me. Women like pronghorns had only three weaknesses. I kept moving.

So where do the Navaho come from?

They came out of the earth.

Anthropologists say you're Athabascan. The last to cross the bridge.

We've always been here. When the spirits of the lower world decided it was time they made us. Told us to climb into the upper world.

I thought Anasazi were the old people.

Beer had spilled on the table. She drew designs with a fingertip.

The Anasazi came out of Mexico. They enslaved the Navaho through terror. Forced us to built their towns and bring them tribute of food and turquoise.

They were Aztec then?

She looked at me with appreciation.

Yes! They were cannibals! We lived in terror of them. Then our medicine men got together and summoned a cataclysm. The Anasazi were crushed beneath the stone palaces we built for them!

They were all killed?

We don't remember. But even your honky anthropologists find decorated pots in the ground. At a certain level they are shattered!

How did the Medicine Men do it?

With crystals! They brought the crystals together and had a vision. Their vision brought the cataclysm.

I got the barmaid's eye. Made the rotary sign for another round.

You said the Anasazi were cannibals. How do you know that?

It was terror of the worst kind! They lived in castles at Chaco and Mesa Verde that we built for them. Once a year they ordered the People to come to a big ceremony. If you didn't come they searched you out and killed you. At the ceremony the priests decided which family would die. They killed them and dismembered them. Cooked them in a big pot while they danced to the sun. Then they ate those people! Went to the hogan of that family and defecated there!

Wow.

She leaned forward with her eyes wide open.

You think I'm making this up? Your honky anthropologists find pots with human bones in them. The bones rounded at the ends as if they had gone round and round in a boiling pot!

I looked at Caleb. He shrugged. The barmaid brought another round.

When else did the Medicine Men get together?

When the Utes and the Mormons got together.

She jabbed Caleb with an elbow.

What was his name? The gun maker for the Mormons?

Browning.

Browning. Brigham Young traded guns to the Utes. The Utes came down to Navaho land to settle scores.

Caleb tipped back his beer.

And acquire a few ladies on the way.

Beautiful Navaho girls! But the Medicine Men saw them coming.

How did they see them?

With crystals, man! Aren't you paying attention? The Medicine Men saw them come over Black Mesa. Had the warriors waiting at Forest Lake. It was late winter. We attacked as they foundered on their horses in the deep snow!

Her eyes glowed with pleasure.

They killed every one. That was the first time the Navaho saved the Union.

How's that?

The Battle of Marieta Pass would have been different if the Utes had destroyed the Navaho.

Caleb shrugged.

That's true. The Utes and Jeff Davis' boys liked trade in boys and girls.

What was the second time, Elvira?

The Navaho code talkers of World War Two!

Elvira left to check on her daughter. The bar got noisier and smokier. Venturi effect as smoke flowed out the door. The Mormons passed a law in 1855 outlawing slaves. As to the Anasazi I didn't know. Was patrolling Down County. Saw a commotion at the top of a ravine. Two gold eagles. Ravens hovering. When I got there the eagles flew. Lucky they headed downhill because their bellies were so full they skimmed the brush. The deer carcass nicked as if by knives. If the Anasazi did sky burials I didn't know. Wouldn't explain wearing at the ends of the bones. Diesels coughed. Mournful cry as a freight turned onto the straight past Kraft Hill. No matter how far your thoughts took you a train brought you back. Misko sat with his paw around a Jameson's.

How's Bird Man?

So Misko. What was the most powerful steam engine train?

The Big Boy on the Pennsylvania Line. Pulled a hundred sixty coal cars at thirty miles an hour from the coal fields of LeHigh to the mills of Pittsburgh.

Diesels have more tractive power.

Right. Why you had the Sand Shop.

He turned in this chair.

Well looky there.

Billy's second wife Gretchen strolled in. Hoggers at the bar turned their heads. She wore a ruffled blouse and short tight skirt. Misko turned back.

Didn't give us the big hello, Bird Man.

No.

Always leading her boy astray. The wreck at American Falls in '49 what you're talking about. Steam engine lost traction. Stalled in drifting snow. They put flares at the top of the hill but guessed fog rolled in from the Snake. Or the eastbound engineer had a heart attack. Hoped that anyway. The guys in the westbound saw the lights coming. Were in the borrow pit when the cars started flying.

Misko tossed the Jameson's down.

Had to get those steam engines out of the system.

What did they call the old steam engines?

The Iron Horse? I don't know.

You're Irish Jew, Misko. Not Indian. You can come up with something better than that!

It's high on my list, Bird Man.

He went up to the bar. The juke box lit up. Started throbbing. Lit up Gretchen's face. Looking East. Jackson Browne. Always had a Hammond and two slide guitars to back him up. Brass feathering steel at two thousand volts whined like ten miles of rail. I enjoyed the buzz and Jackson's nasal croon. Had to visit the restroom though. Gretchen at the juke box. Had a vodka tonic and a stack of quarters on the console. On my way back she turned.

Errol. What a surprise.

Hi, Gretchen.

Her smile had a sly curl.

What are you doing back?

Taking time off.

Me too. The Department is sending me to the book binding school at Milan. It will be fun because Billy and I went there. We took the train to Lake Como and stayed at the hotel where Hemingway met the Count in the afternoons for billiards and champagne. Remember? How he said he thought it an excellent custom?

Right.

The table was still there. As we played we could see the lake through the window.

I loved Gretchen. With her high German reserve was a wonderful hostess. Talked well not only about what she knew but what Billy taught her.

Who's Chair now?

Ariel. Isn't that a hoot? Billy called her the Duck.

Wicked Billy. Ariel got stout in middle age. Walked with high heeled shoes pointed out.

That's funny!

Gretchen smiled brightly.

Yes. We had names for everyone.

Her eyes locked into mine. Had a glitter. Which way would I go? Would I take the hook? Either way she won.

Really?

She cocked her head. Eyes flickered.

It was one of our games.

She looked away with an ironic smile. Picked up her drink. She was telling the truth. Billy had a name for her too.

I'll call you, Gretchen. Maybe we'll shoot a game.

I'd like that, Errol.

She turned to the juke box. Looked at her beautiful hands as they selected songs. She'd won the game but it hadn't lasted very long. Caught me lying three times in a couple of minutes which isn't bad. The game would remain something she and Billy had. That she didn't have to share with anybody. It was too bad because the names were funny. A lot she made up herself. She punched the number for Operator. Maybe one day she would. It would be like a tapestry where players paid to get glimpses but only she would see the whole. Something would be risked. She wondered if anyone would. It was unfair. Wasn't the price she'd paid.

Snake bit I sat by the door. Freight cars clashed. Misko swaggered.

Ready for a fishing trip, Bird Man?

Where we going?

You'll find out. Won't need your waders.

We went out on the street. Old buildings starkly lit. Got into his 88. Rolled under the tracks and north on Main. He touched the brakes at cross streets. Lander, Fremont, Bridger.

I didn't know you were in Iraq, Misko.

116th. How'd you guess?

The way you drive. What was it like?

What can I say, Bird Man. Ragheads stink. Lie to gain the least advantage. Hate Jews. What can I say?

Bikes glittered in front of Louie's Lounge. Misko nodded.

Cowboy coke hangout.

They don't like the Hi de Ho?

No. Meth heads like ambience. Coors on tap and Ponderosa reruns don't make it. You know why Pocatello is the meth capital of the Rockies, right? Phosphorus. We handle thousands of tons of it. Wear masks and stuff but I've looked down and seen my boots aflame.

Not phosphorescence?

Elemental phosphorus, Bird Man. Hitting the sweet night air.

How's it shipped?

Phos cars have plugs in the belly. The phosphorous is piped in from above and covered with a foot of water. When it gets to its destination they unscrew the plugs and it pours like sand.

What do they use it for?

Fertilizer. But a lot goes to the military. Nothing like elemental phosphorous to make bombs or something groovy like napalm. One of the reasons they put FBI headquarter here. Keep track of the weapons-grade phosphorous.

A pearly cloud boiled up by the point of the mountain. He

swung the 88 along the high iron by Sinklot. Fat bellied black tanker cars full as ticks with sulfuric acid. The factory blazed with lights. Lights strung along seven story cat walks. Stacks screamed fire. Misko turned north into a parking lot with barbecue grills and horseshoe pits. Hooked his arm over the seat.

One night they neglected to tighten one of the plugs. The guy on the Hump saw the fire flowing like a river up through town.

Crazy!

Meth heads got up from watching NASCAR. Staggered toward the yards with their arms straight out like zombies!

I laughed. Smelled the dilute sulfuric acid. Misko got out. Hitched up his pants.

Takes a lot of match heads to make a little meth. Time not even a welfare boyfriend wants to spend.

We crossed the park to the wood line. The river ran. Canada geese barked from the far field. A double header rattled out of town with a hundred empty flat cars. Then the bray of a quatro loaded to the gills with double stacked flat cars from China thundered. The factory exhaust pipes screamed. Misko put his finger to his lips as if anybody could hear us. A milky blue settling pond surrounded by chain link and barbed wire smoked under the moon. A dark, skinny figure crept along the bank. Misko slipped a key into the lock. The gleaner bent to his task didn't see us. Misko lit a cigarette.

Hey Phos Man!

The figure jerked. Crouched and faced us.

How you doing?

Oh we're just fine!

We had the factory lights at our back. Phos Man wore camouflage hat and jacket. Eyes glittered. He smiled showing bad teeth.

H'ep you with something?

You can, Phos Man. That bottle you just slipped in your pocket? Put it on that rock and we'll be on our way.

You ain't cops!

Militia.

Which one!

Misko elbowed me.

I'd be happy to pursue this subject at a later date, Phos Man. But for now? Hand over the bottle. You don't want me holding you face down in that pond. You don't.

Flicked his cigarette so it sent sparks over the pond. Phos Man twitched like a rabid opossum. Pulled the canister out of his pocket with shaking hands.

Thank you, Phos Man.

Misko locked the gate. A freight left town jingle jangling. The owl flew from the trees. Set the geese to barking.

What if he'd had a gun, Misko?

Not likely. Hee! Hee! H'ep you with something?

What're you going to do with it?

Trade it.

You don't use it do you, Misko?

He gave his circus clown grin.

Everybody needs a kick now and then, Bird Man. Trim the drag.

We took Garrett Way. Huge yellow back hoes, cranes towered into the sky.

Look at it this way, Bird Man. I'm keeping it out of the noses of fifteen year old girls. You dig?

Revelers stood in front of the Odyssey and Lizard. Extra large divas in pancake makeup, jittery dresses and high heels smoked in front of Charly's. In the Office juke box throbbed Can't Get Enough! Misko handed me a long-necked Budweiser.

Thanks for the assist, Bird Man. Militia! Hee-hee! That was good!

He wandered off. A pretty Indian girl had joined Caleb and Elvira. Let out a Shoshone war cry.

Ki-yee-ay-ay-aiee!

THIRTY FOUR

Caleb leaned back with a big grin. Elvira laughed. Indian girl tilted her head back. They whooped along. At the juke box Leon boogalooed with a pretty mud shark. I leaned toward Indian Girl.

That's red tail.

Caleb leaned across the table. Started with a K at the back of his throat. Became a short frequency ululation. Released with lips tight and wide.

Ki-yee-ay-ay-ay-aiee!

It wasn't the high whistle you heard when they were in the sky.

How you know that, White Boy!

He's Fish and Game.

I'm a scientist.

Whoo-eeee! That's real impressive!

Thank you. What do you do?

Fight fires.

Wildland?

Right, White Boy.

She had on red lipstick and black eye shadow. Glistening black hair tied in a pony tail. White T shirt, khaki work pants and black, steel-toed boots. Caleb sipped his beer.

We call her the Ant. She can carry anything anywhere. Her real name is Suzy.

She raised her arm. Flexed her bicep. I was impressed.

You like to fight fires?

She wrinkled her nose.

You crazy? And what brings you to this beat up old railroad town?

Resting up. Like you.

They say you white boys got to come back here. Karmic debt collection or some such.

What's that?

A place you go 'til you pay some deep, dark debt. What's yours?

I'll tell you when I know you better. If I thought you really cared.

'Course I do! If it's one thing we Indians know you got to take care of your ghosts. Right, Elvira?

Elvira was emphatic.

You got to know what they want. The other thing is they might not like you. Even if you're pretty.

Especially if you're pretty. Like Water Babies. They hate pretty boys.

I sipped my beer.

I've heard about them. That they lived in the Bottoms. Never believed it though. Maybe if you took me out there.

Suzy pulled the corners of her mouth down.

I won't go there. No way. I don't like it in the daytime. One night my boyfriend made me go out there. I could hear them. They cry.

Elvira put her arms around herself. Shivered.

Whoooooo!

Raised a Snakebite. Tossed it down. Pushed a shot glass toward me. I shook my head.

I heard when the People were starving they took the babies to the river rather than watch them starve.

Happened more than that. Mama told me about a girl that had three kids by a man. He started playing around. When she found out she went crazy. Drowned those kids in the spring where he went to drink. That night The Spirit came to her. Told her her kids had been turned into Water Babies. Had the eyes and teeth of cats. Long fingernails for claws. The cry something between the cry of a baby and the scream of a cat. Hungered for the blood of men.

Elvira shook her head.

Even in my grandmother's day if a girl got pregnant the women would get together and talk. If they thought the man was no good? They'd gather around the newborn and look at it. Lot of times they just put it in the river.

Best be careful, Caleb!

He grimaced. Elvira gave him a kiss.

Caleb is a good man. My great grandfather? Sold my great aunt to an old man. He was bad. Hit her. She came back home after a big fight. Pregnant. When the time come the women told everybody the baby was stillborn.

Caleb raised his shot glass.

To the Snake.

I downed the shot Elvira had offered me.

I don't think I want to go out there anymore.

That's smart, white boy. A lot goes on you don't want to know about. Jerry Livingston heard a racket in the field one night? Saw a pack of dogs playing with a cat. Skipping around by the light of the moon. Tossing it in the air. When he shot at them a man stood up. Hissed at him holding his shoulder and ran away.

Whooo!

Did he check the hospitals the next day?

Suzy shrugged.

Lot of stuff out there you want to stay away from. Two days before? Lucretia Two Eagles was driving to work. Saw a big dog somebody skinned at the side of the road.

That's bad.

Snakebites arrived. Next thing Suzy and I were at Charlie's. Had another round. Disco dance floor streamed with colored light. Suzy did her snake dance. Glanced at me from time to time. Unloosened her hair so it spilled down her back. Around us pairings of every gender played out their fantasies. When A Man Loves A Woman came on. She put her arms around me. Pulled me to her. Her strong thighs probed mine. I felt the white glow. Up on the mountain blocks shifted. Larval squeechy creatures cut loose from their moorings. Drifted downstream. May and damsel flies flew toward the moon. We buzzed with night's drumbeat. At her door she turned. Parted my shirt with her hands. Bit my left nipple. Got the door unlocked and shut. I started to pull at her buttons but she slipped away. Pushed me down on the sofa. Unbuttoned me. Opened my shirt. Raked my chest with her fingernails. Climbed onto me. I was looking at her when I entered. Saw her face melt. Eyes close. Then she was looking down but didn't see me. The corners of her mouth turned down. Eyes distant. Whispered hoarsely.

I want you in my life.

What did you say?

I want a knife.

Her fingernail traced the nipple.

I drew up. Turned her under me. She fought but I was stronger. Stayed inside her until I felt it come. Then slowed. Made it deep and slow. Her head fell back. She put her heels around my back. Eyes half open. Glazed red. Gave a little cry. Our bodies welded with perfume. I tried to kiss her. Her eyes dilated like she saw me for the first time. Pushed me away. Picked up her panties. The bathroom door lock clicked.

Outside the moon fell toward the mountains. Illuminated clouds. Cold front coming. I walked toward the lighted Star atop the Hospital. Scout still had snow bones. I felt cold and lonely. It wasn't so bad that Suzy wanted to mark me. It was a small price to pay but I was unprepared. I found the truck parked at Caldwell Park.

Circe prepped Odysseus in order negotiate the terrain he would encounter. Terms had to be known in advance because they had to be agreed to without hesitation. Bells gonged from the Methodist, Presbyterian and First Christian Church. The Mormon Stake House was quiet. Didn't like bells. Spirits hid in them. Whether it was the sound or the bell I didn't know but as a theory it wasn't bad. Girls in pretty dresses walked to church. Boys held their Book of Mormon. The sun shone through the trees. The moon and the Snakebites left me with a bitter taste. Time to get out of town.

THIRTY FIVE

The sun backlit the Tetons. They looked like huge hulking spirits.
Blackfeet called it Land of Spiral Forces. Nobody knew the
Shoshone name. Meadowlarks sang. The towers of Radiation
Ranch fronted the whipsawed Lost River Range. At Howe the café
had New Owners. Best Homemade Pie in the World. It was. The
girl who brought it was pretty. Payoff for trout streams turned to
alfalfa. I looked past the fields at the eleven thousand foot Lemhis.
Aunt Ada and Uncle Gene worked for Little Sheep Company. She
cooked. He irrigated. It was the Depression. Each made a dollar a
day. The guy atop the haystack made twenty.

Twenty dollars?

Snakes everywhere in that country. When the boom of that
hayrick swung over it could rain rattlesnakes! Little Sheep
Company of course paid by the week.

I got a sixpack from the cooler. The girl slid it across the
scanner but it didn't read. She shrugged.

How about $6.99?

I tossed a twenty.

You should be in management.

The lady cook leaned at the kitchen window.

You could set her up in one of those. Looks like you got
money.

People have thought that about me. Ever since I was in
college. Maybe it was because I was always such a jerk.

They laughed. I walked onto the porch. Smelled sweet
water. Behind the café clear ditch water ran under cottonwoods.
Heard the whiffle of a long wing. Prairie falcon flew with deep
scything wing beats over the field, the Mormon Stake House, the
highway to Dubois. The sun rolled atop the eleven thousand
footers. At the end of the fields the road turned to gravel. Open
range. I crossed the pass into the Pahsimeroi. Big Fish Water.

Ranches at the mouth of every canyon. Streams tumbling out didn't make it past them. Nobody passed me until a herd of pronghorns ran along the truck. Heads high, white rumps flashing. Reappeared on the playa above. Borah and Leatherneck beyond. Say it so you will remember it.

Pahsimeroi.

I got out. Wind sweet and cold. Blue black clouds. Flashes of lightning banging the ridges. Heraclites whispered, War is the father of all things. Black clouds hurried in. I sprinkled corn in the cage. The pigeons fed. Dark clouds shrouded the peaks. Boom! Boom! Kyrie scanned the storm. Vast cliffs groaning with release from a billion year imprisonment. She rang up avidly. Worked her way through the seams of the storm. I watched her staggering flight as she dealt with its violence. Was going to fly right over the top! I slipped the pigeon. Kyrie had a mile to go. Slipped into a downdraft. Did it in seconds! No one would know how fast she descended.

I waded the Pahsimeroi. High, dark thunderclouds came on. The willows waved. I carried her back to the truck. We huddled in the camper as she fed. It got dark. The rain came. Wind rocked the truck. A boom made her look up. Blast waves rocketed back from Flatiron Mountain. Lightning bolts split shards of rock. Then it passed. Thunder became distant. Blue sky. The wind sweet as a lover's kiss. Chatterers, whistlers, chirpers in the willows. I wanted to spend the day on the Pahsimeroi. Drive up toward Mount Borah. Should've.

Drove the lower valley where ranchers lived year round. Turned west on 93. The Salmon River came sparkling in long, rolling riffles. I eased the truck up to forty. Sparkle trees stood along the gravel bars. I swung around a bend. Three shadows atop the spars. Bald eagles.

I loved bald eagles. They were the only birds that didn't fly when I tried to look at them.

I passed the Last Chance Saloon at Challis, the Buffalo Jump Cliffs, then mile high volcanic skree yellow, black and red. The highway climbed into Doug Fir. The river turned whitewater. Tumbled among white boulders. Fisher people stood on them waving wands. At Sunbeam Dam the river knifed through a gap. I saw wisps of steam. The hot spring spilled into a wagon box, brimmed over the rim, descended riverward. I soaked with beer in hand. An osprey kited. Could fly that way forever because it was as much the wind as its flowing. Evergreen moss draped the cliff on the other side. I heard thin crying. Saw wings flap atop a spar. Babies squeaking. I felt that hunger. But if Daddy up there in the wind had any anxiety he didn't show it. The river flowed clear. Fish hid but would show.

I drove. Saw the sign for Stanley. Bent a corner. The Sawtooths pierced the sky. Steel blades arrayed upward. Blue gray ridges. White avalanche chutes. I drove with elbows over the wheel. They changed with cloud and light. Peaks and secondary peaks. You couldn't see one without losing track of the others. Peaks you thought you saw were mirrors. Rock and ice hid lakes. You could never see the Sawtooths. They shifted from afar and when you were amid them were overwhelming.

I turned into their shadow. Wildflowers burned amid the aspen. Smoke drifted from campfires. I saw two Government pickups. Caleb knelt with a hand axe splitting wood.

You made it.

Beautiful drive.

Which way did you go?

Pahsimeroi.

He squatted with knees out. Held the log upright with one hand. Dropped the axe with the other. The edge flashed within a millimeter of his fingertips.

See any goats?

Pronghorns? Yeah. Ran along the truck for awhile.

They're like dogs. Like to watch for cars coming up the road. Run out to meet them.

He split a few more shards by rotating the log. The kindling fell away.

See you got your woman with you.

Me'whe buhni at'si.

He laughed. Held axe in mid air.

Buhni at'si gand'ho! Noo'ya bia'i chi!

Translate, Caleb.

Skunks have big balls.

He grabbed another log.

I'm going to look at fish in awhile. If you want to come.

I'd be obliged, Caleb.

Set up your tent.

I did. Remembered Mickey Angel telling me, Trust Caleb with your life. Just don't go climbing with him. He climbed into his rig. Tossed out wet suits, flippers, goggles. A government truck rolled up. Tall gangly guy got out. Long-billed fishing hat, dark glasses, waders wet from the river. The legendary Snorkel Bob. Could drop a fly into a bucket from thirty yards with side wind. Hated to be called Snorkel Bob. A tech for twenty years because the boys knew he couldn't fire a zombie. Spend the summer thinking about it. Olds 88 with narrow gauge piston and long stroke. Forty miles to the gallon and two hundred thousand without a refit that nobody bought. I guessed it was because they called it the 88. Lot of World War Two guys still around. Caleb nodded.

Bob, this be Errol. He's going to be riding with you.

Snorkel Bob put out his hand.

It's an honor.

How's that?

He looked at me through the shades. Pink flesh flaking off his nose from dancing with the Sun Goddess.

You're the dude that wouldn't sign off on the Lieutenant Governor's diversion dam, right?

Governor now.

Right. Then don't fuck with me.

You got it.

Caleb gave him a jab.

How'd you do?

Three fat ones!

I got the kindling ready. Wait 'til we get back.

We drove down Iron Creek. The Salmon rolled in long rolling waves past cross-buck fences and black cows. Then entered the canyon and scampered among big white boulders. I thought about Snorkel Bob. His gentility had thrown me off.

Hope Bob's not mad at me.

Snorkel Bob? No. He's different though. I was fishing the Teton with him once. Not his day. Was making long pretty casts.

Couldn't hit the money hole. Muttering to himself. I hollered.

Hey, Robert! Looks like your elbow's flying out a little too far.

He ducked his head the way he does.

Really? Which one?

Snorkel Bob. He's something.

Caleb pulled off the road. The river crashed and shuddered on the rocks. Willows bobbed in the wind. It was twilight. Wasn't a big river but big enough. Caleb pulled on the wet suit. Gave me his big smile.

You've done this before, right?

Nothing this big.

Stay by the bank. That's where the fish are. If you get in trouble just put your feet downstream.

Right.

Caleb saw fear like a traffic signal. Laughed. We climbed over the boulders. The river tongued through a chute then circled to descend the next. I saw the reversal. The skeleton of a fir bobbed in the current. Broken, jagged limbs underwater. Why they called them strainers. What would happen if I got swept against it. I felt the shadow at the bottom of the river. A pine twisted atop a cliff. Dike the river cut through. Caleb whooped. Was picking up energy. Pulled on the flippers. Stood with goggles at his forehead. Black hair streaming.

Use those size fourteens. What they say about big feet true?

I use them as advertisement.

Haw! When you've slipped through the glide hang on! Alright?

You're just trying to get rid of another white man, Caleb.

He threw back his head and laughed.

Scream if you need anything!

The river swept him away. I saw his flippers when he went through the chute and into the plunge pool. Then his arm went up. Grabbed a boulder. He grinned. Raised his fist as the water rocked him. I climbed backwards into the current. It swept me away. Just a dull gray roar. Slim silvery shapes scattered. I kicked. Jackknifed. Grabbed a rock and climbed. It was sweet and quiet. Just the sound of the waves. Caleb grinned with his arm around a boulder.

You ready?

He went underwater. I adjusted the snorkel. Put my head underwater. Crawled handhold by handhold. The boulders were granite. Had good purchase. Set up back whirls that helped. My forehead froze. Trout shimmered. Were looking the other way for insects to come down. Winnowing tail fins. A big brown with smaller rainbow and cutthroat on the flanks. Caleb pushed off. With a flick of flippers swept into the current. I thought about that strainer. Grabbed the boulder with both hands. Pulled off the goggles. Tried to see trout but couldn't. Caleb climbed from below. I already had a beer in the hot pool when he arrived. Stripped off the wet suit.

You missed fine ride, Errol.

Next time.

He cocked his head.

Don't always get that.

THIRTY SIX

The sun set off flares on the peaks. Grandad told me that on the rails at night when the conductor swung the lantern he heard music. I heard it now. The creek showed white among the aspen. Campfires flickered. Snorkel Bob hovered over the embers. I handed him an IPA. He looked at the label.

We don't get beer like this up here!

Can't beat Bridgeport. You throw the fish heads somewhere?

He glanced at Caleb laying kindling on the fire.

Not even an Indian eats fish heads.

Oh we have, Bob. Got to know the back door of the slaughterhouse too. No. He's got a bird with him. Doesn't want anybody to know.

What kind?

I said, Peregrine.

I've never seen one fly. Always wanted to.

We'll do that. I was thinking of flying her. Wouldn't mind if you had the entrails too.

They were full of hatch. I plated them. Served Kyrie. Went back to the fire. Saw her shadow. How her wings flared as she fed. Caleb lay filets in a bowl. Poured olive oil. Rolled them in corn meal. Cooked them by holding the grill above the embers. A small wiry guy came out of the tent. Took the beer I offered but didn't say a word all night. Another main chance guy.

So you don't catch and release, Bob?

Don't believe in it. Others might and I don't deny their right to. But I don't.

Why?

It's a blood thing. Using the soul of something for sport.

Better to kill it?

Way the world is made.

So if you wanted to fish the Madison or one of those trophy streams you'd have to draw?

A lot of streams you wouldn't be able to fish for years. The shape they're in.

No money in that, Bob.

No. And that's what it's about. But it's fishing pressure too. If you rehabilitated the streams of Idaho you'd have a million places to fish.

Long as the Idaho Cattleman's Association has the Legislature that's not going to happen.

Is the Legislature!

What about streams with remnant cutthroat populations that you want to bring back?

Once browns are in a stream nothing is going to bring them back. Short of going in periodically and taking them out.

You hook a cutthroat today?

I can't disclose that. You got another one of those Bridgeports handy?

I hadn't looked at the fishheads. Caleb wiped his eyes with his sleeve. Reached for a beer.

Think about it, Errol. You're in your living room watching the Bears play Green Bay. Just put a potato chip in your mouth and realize it's got a barb! It's hooked your upper lip! You're being dragged out the front door! If you had time to think about it? Were using your rational mind? You'd take the buck knife and cut your lip off. But you don't. You've panicked. A giant towers over you. Lifts the line to increase the pain of the hook on your mouth. Now you're fighting like hell but it's too late. He nets you. Big grin on his face. Reaches for a pair of pliers and pries the hook out. Gives you a pat on the back.

Have a nice day!

I laughed. These guys were crazy. And that fish was good. Right out of the cold creek. We sat around the fire and ate. Trucks drove past raising dust. I heard the whup-a-whuppa of a Harley. The biker rode past. Blue flame shooting out the pipes.

Looks like it needs tuning.

Snorkel Bob shook his head.

No. I'm guessing he had the cam work done at S& S Speed in St. Louis. That engine commences to purr at ninety.

Caleb reached for his beer.

I get a rash just hearing one come up the road.

Snorkel Bob ate sedately with legs crossed.

I've always loved bikes. Was in a barber shop in Rego Park. 1978. Remember it as well as anything. Heard a Harley approach. Got up to look. Old guy sitting in the chair.

He said, Every time I hear a Harley come down the street my heart starts to hurt.

Why is that?

My wife ran off with a guy on a Harley in 1962. Every time I hear that low shudder? I think he's bringing her back!

Hah!

Flames twisted through the kindling. I liked Harley's because they had ISU colors. Orange and black. Like Halloween. Strange to think of Halloween in July among the green pines and wildflowers. Caleb grinned. Black eyes gleamed in the firelight.

What you thinking about, Errol? Suzy? She likes you. Told me so.

Nice gal.

She said she might come visit.

I stared at the flames.

So Caleb. What was it like falling off Vulcan's Anvil?

Not much chance though. Big fire on Loon Creek. Getting bigger. Vulcan's Anvil? I was screaming like a little bitch, what do you think?

I laughed.

So what's on schedule tomorrow?

You and Bob are going to throw some hoops out East Fork.

Hoops?

It's a very strange and mysterious procedure.

Hooping cranes?

Bob does look like a hooping crane when he's on the river.

I didn't get the feeling Bob thought that was funny. He put his plate down.

Hooping measures the depth cobbles are embedded. How much silt there is. You toss it where you think Mama might dig her redd. Some say it's the head of a pool. From what I've seen it's the tail. Don't like the method myself. Compared to coring. I've seen salmon move gravel to a depth of two feet. That's a lot of rock. You see her burrowing in the gravel. The bones sticking out of her flesh.

He wore shades at night. Tipped his beer back.

Pretty awe inspiring. What they do. Anyway. Coring gives you the quality of gravel at depth.

I went to the cooler for more beer. Stars blazed. A breeze flowed cold from the upper lakes. Snorkel Bob settled into his chair.

The more I'm in rivers the more I see them as arteries. When they're healthy the country thrives. The animals feed on the salmon. The plants thrive on the elk and bear shit. You tie off the streams the land dies. It looks beautiful but it's empty. Without salmon you can't bring back the grizzly or the wolf. But Bonneville Power keeps cutting our checks.

And we keep cashing them.

Nothing going to change until they take those dams out.

Caleb poked the fire with a stick so it flared.

Even ten years ago you felt it. I was camped on Little Salmon when something woke me. The river rumbling. I'm thinking, Flash flood? Been a thunderstorm I didn't hear? I stood on the bank. Stars shining on the salmon in the river. Hatchery fish but doing their job. Roiling around to move the cobbles with their bodies. The sound like a deep moaning. I'm telling you. It was almost too much for your boy Caleb.

Snorkel Bob nodded.

The other thing about streams? When they're healthy the water boils through the gravels. The embryonic fish breathe oxygenated water. If you beat down the banks or clear cut? The alveoli clog up. The country dies.

Don't look that bad up here.

No. From what I've seen they're pretty clean. If the salmon came back the system would be ready for them.

So you haven't worked in vain.

Nice to think so.

Caleb grinned.

Your insurance paid up, Errol? You're taking him out Boulder Creek aren't you, Bob? Think he should take out some insurance?

Bob tossed kindling into the fire so it sprayed sparks.

It's a thought.

I said, Why is that?

The caretaker of the Livingston mill has a few screws loose. Might be the owner, I don't know. It's under foreign registration. Confederate flag flaps in the wind. He pulled a shotgun on some hikers going into the White Clouds. Said the parking lot was his land. He was charging toll. Smoky Bear boys went and had a talk with him.

Caleb stood up.

You felt bad for them having to do that. A shotgun does make for a mean and oozy corpse. Good night, boys.

THIRTY SEVEN

In the morning Caleb had the fire going. Figures moved at the campsites. Bang of toilet door. Wildflowers sent up incense. I leashed Kyrie. By the time I got coffee she gaped. Threw a cast. Shat simultaneously. Marvelous display of efficiency. Started putting her coverts in order. Snorkel Bob came over.

She's a beauty. Didn't know peregrines got that big.

She's got some Gyr in her. Her dad's a Prairie from the

Wapi. She's happy now. But the best of times? Wild little bitch.

She ignored us. Raised a foot to comb deck feathers. Had to brake at two hundred miles an hour. Bob looked on admiringly.

Is she good?

Climbs like a homesick angel. Hits with both feet. Isn't that right, Angel?

She looked at us with her implacable black eyes. Returned to combing the thousand tiny barbules. After breakfast I installed her in the tent. Snorkel Bob and I drove out Iron Creek. At Highway 75 I turned. Stainless steel daggers gleamed in the sun.

Drive down the road would you, Bob? I wouldn't mind looking at them awhile.

He did. They unfolded spires en echelon. More stunning than the Tetons. He drove with forearms draped.

Sometimes I don't even see them. Around them too much I guess. But out East Fork? You never see those cliffs the same.

We drove to Redfish Lake. Doubled back. I looked at the land drawn and quartered along the river. Mist drifting up. Black cows with their calves. I liked cows. Just didn't want them in the creeks. Bob nodded.

That's Bangerback Ranch. Cut off the flow from the upper Salmon last year.

How could they do that?

Show they could.

Self ennobling phonies. As if they could measure up.

You see coyotes along here in the morning.

The river dropped into the canyon. Ran jade green. Fisher people stood on the boulders. Men and women with tattooed arms. A silver haired couple left their scooter at roadside. All waved long poles over the river sparkling with diamonds.

It's a cold, violent, hungry environment for mama to lay her eggs in. She packs big eggs with lots of yolk to give them a chance to make it. Doesn't lay a lot. Digs a pan in the gravel to protect them. Right now she'll be lying up in a deep pool. Resting up before she starts digging.

The males don't help?

They're waiting. Made the thousand miles of falls and rapids. Fishermen. Eagles. They can wait. Everybody's waiting now. The river is a narrative of glides, pools and riffles. Down there it's mostly deep glides and plunge pools. Farther down it widens into big, gliding riffles. That's where we might see redds.

I pointed at the sign: Basin Creek Campground ½ Mile.

I could work better if I started with a good soak, Bob.

I'll show you a better one.

After a mile the road undercut granite. Hot water gushed from an outcrop into a series of steaming pools. Bob lay on his back, the hot water up to his goaty beard.

When I first came out here Cernera sent me out East Fork. I think he did it on purpose. Break me in. Couple of Sho Bans came along. Parked above East Fork. No sign or fence. We just walked down through the sagebrush. Went maybe twenty yards when a truck came roaring at us. Junior Heston. Screaming before he got out of the cab.

What you doing on my land! Who give you permission to cross my land!

His face three inches from mine. I'm staying calm.

I'm sorry, sir. If I'd known this was your land I'd never set foot on it.

He screamed at me. Used every obscenity known to man. Telling me what he was going to do to us. Was going to shoot us. Blow up the truck. No. That's not right. He was going to shoot us. Stuff us in the truck. Then blow it up. I apologized some more. We walked back to the truck. Since then they bought all the land along on East Fork. No access for twelve miles.

The sun shone through the mist on the river. It rolled past in big rolling waves. You heard a deep booming. Fronded firs on the far cliff swayed in the wind. A memory came back. I was a young blood up Bear Valley Creek. Waded barefoot on the bedded gravel. The current icy cold against my chest. Huge, bullet shaped salmon appeared. Slipped past on their way to the upper pools. I'd seen the last wild salmon enter the Sawtooths.

Never thought that possible. For a few thousand kilowatts and a hundred miles of barge water.

At Sunbeam Dam the river swept like a knife through a breach an unknown hero blew in 1934. Two kayakers side-slipped. Getting courage. In my mind saw how it used to look. Flat water.

Hillsides clear cut. Yankee Fork twenty miles of tailings. Gold wasn't even used for war! Warren Angus Ferris on the Craters of the Moon, 1830. Men with tongues swollen stumbling to their knees. Crested a ridge. Saw the sparkling curve of Lava Creek.

Oh! The cupidity of man! To think anything more beautiful than a clean, sparkling river!

Snorkel Bob slowed.

Start looking for redds. They're round, shallow depressions paler than the surrounding gravel.

I did but didn't. We passed the Highway Mile Marker for Spawning Salmon.

There aren't anadromous fish in the Main Salmon anymore. You knew that. Those that are are hatchery fish. See any? It's a little early yet.

Remember when the Salmon shone as much with the red backs of fish as with light.

Think you'll keep doing it, Bob?

He chewed his lip.

I've done the field work. I know how the system works. Kind of feel it's time to go back to the desk. Put it all together.

I hope you do, Bob.

Doug fir that occupied the hills now just stood in ravines. The river undercut the mountainsides. Vast fields of boulder skree tumbled into it. Big grey trees fell from the cliffs. East Fork tumbled into the Salmon. We crossed the bridge. Saw alfalfa fields. Big, gable-roofed log houses with satellite dishes, cross-buck fences.

A Missourian bought that a few years ago. Seems like a reasonable guy. Challis Land Stewardship Association elected him President. Maybe he'll help.

I said, Maybe the old guys are letting up. You know how politicians like to watch their right wing. Can say, This new guy did it.

Always a chance.

The road slanted up an ancient dike that intruded across the valley. East Fork cut a canyon through it

That's Ziegler's Hole. Big fish in there. We do a count every spring. It's deep and it's dark and fast. If there's a lot of water like this spring? It'll just blow you out.

What's your technique?

Enter downstream. Pull yourself through the pool. Keep your eyes moving. Guesstimate species and number as they scatter. Gives me a hell of a headache.

He drove on.

Heston's land starts here. For the next twelve miles they own it all. The most beautiful ranch you'll ever see.

It was. Cottonwoods spangled in the sun. Lush hay on both sides of the river. Mown so it looked like the fairway of a golf course. Stark pastel ridges. On my right the White Clouds showed up canyon.

Bob said, Imagine what the developers would do. I'm sure the Heston's been offered millions for it. Wouldn't doubt it.

He pointed at a two story white frame house with lilac bushes and fruit trees.

That's the house.

Then the V of a canyon across the river.

That's Herd Creek.

It tumbled white out of the narrow, brindle canyon.

I was telling you about Herd Creek. Nothing but native Chinook up there. Probably the only one left in the country. Last year Junior put a diversion dam across it. Completely blocked it.

Why would he do that?

For irrigation, he said. But I think he did it out of spite. To show he could. Some people wouldn't say that but I would. We went to him with hats in hand. Got him to reconstruct it so the fish could maneuver around it. If they got this far.

As we drove you saw the ownership. Old log cabins snug in mullein and thistle. Birthing sheds. Corrals no longer in use. In the way of the operation but held value as reference points. Graves of kin gave blood title. Bob nodded at tall trees in the sloughs.

I've got to hand it to them. They do a nice job. Could've cut those trees. Left lots of nice cover. It's a beautiful operation really.

He turned up a canyon toward the White Clouds. Big Boulder Creek came dashing in falls and plunge pools. A slurry line trestle crossed the skree. Splintered sections slipped with rock-fall. Breached dam half hidden by birch.

Heston's don't want it taken down. Say it would hurt the cutthroat fishery. Which is nonsense.

Salmon come up here?

I've talked to oldtimers. They say there weren't in Big Boulder. I'm not so sure. No reason why they wouldn't. Salmon spawned in every creek of the Columbia Basin.

They didn't concern themselves with the Big Boulder run because it wasn't big enough. The East Fork rippled with redfish. They harvested them with pitchforks. Used hand cranked telephones to spit electric shock. And the Mormon spyglass. Twelve inch pipe with glass at one end. Two man sport. One held the open end at her snout while the other grabbed her tail. Then the fun began.

We drove toward the White Clouds. Doug fir on the north facing side of the creek. Rainbow hoodoos on the right. Bob was right. They were something. At the end of the road loomed a three story corrugated steel building. The Livingston Mill. The windows suppurated rust. Aspen sparkled. A wind devil rose from the parking lot. Yellow ochre it danced past the mill and into the trees. Bob cursed.

Right by the trailhead! I can't believe the Forest Service allows it!

Forest Circus.

Gives me a headache to work around here.

What's in it?

The Periodic Table. Selenium. Arsenic. Phosphates. What's in rock before you grind it. See those cottonwoods? That's where the settling ponds are. When the creek blew it washed the sediment here. Nothing can grow on it. So they made a parking lot! Brilliant!

The White Cloud Trail was at our left. The mill loomed with its suppurating windows to our right. It had taken a lot of money to put up. When the price of gold went up would run again. I wondered about the machinery.

What do you say we look around?

You got a gun?

Back in my truck.

What do you pack?

45 Colt.

Well, Errol. That's a long way from me having it.

THIRTY EIGHT

He lifted Sadie out. She scampered. Sniffed fence and wildflowers. You could tell from her crafty eyes how fast her mind worked. Had the scene down from the last rain. Maybe before.

Nice dog.

Lab-border collie.

Good blend.

Got her at the pound. Her mama probably had her nose in the garbage when she got it.

Sadie scampered. Worked out the stiffness in her legs. Followed as we bushwhacked. Channel of dry river stones. Ghost of water. Then Boulder Creek came brawling. Cut a ten foot bank in the hillside. Doug fir taking the fall.

How much sediment has stayed in the creek?

Not that much that I can tell. It's in East Fork or the Main by now.

Birds sang.

Wheep! Wheep! Jooby-jooby-jooobee! Wheep! Wheep!

We bushwhacked. Found the creek again. Had lunch. Coyote willow waved. Breeze coming down from the White Clouds. A water dipper dove into a swirling pool. Came out to shake water from its stubby wings. I heard a song I didn't know. A warble that accelerated as it rose. Ended in two long whistles. The transcription of flight.

What's that song, Bob?

Never heard it. But I heard that the better the song the more sex they get. I bet that guy really gets it.

Where you from, Bob?

New York City.

Really.

New York had a fine fishery in my Dad's time. Caught flounder across the bay from Ellis Island. And Long Island? Paradise for fishing. No more.

He poured the last of his soup on a rock. Sadie lapped it avidly.

Nice to be out where you have a chance.

I looked at Boulder Creek.

This must be the original stream.

Right. He did it farther down.

When we got to the parking lot horse trailers had pulled in. A cowboy drew a gelding Morgan backwards down the ramp. Beautiful horse. When he put hooves to gravel reared. Then was on his side flailing. The cowboy held the bridle with one hand. Whipped the Morgan's genitals with the other. Snorkel Bob rolled down the window.

Wish you had a cock like that, cowboy? That your problem. You got a horse fly dick?

The cowboy glared but had his hands full. The Morgan twisted away from the whip. The bit cut his mouth.

Drive the truck, Bob.

He popped the clutch. Backed. Two cowboys came around the trailer. I made eye contact. Bob's hands white on the steering wheel.

I'm sorry, Bob.

Don't worry about it.

The little valley widened. Fir shelved the hillside. The creek wended its way through clumps of red willow. We didn't talk. He slowed.

You see any yellow ribbons? Let me know. They'll be along the road or on willows along the creek.

I watched but didn't. After a mile he consulted the log book. I looked over his shoulder. Sketches of pools, riffles, glides.

You haven't been to these sites?

Cernera plotted them a few years ago. Caleb retagged them. Cernera's gone and Caleb's on his way. That's how it goes.

He peered at Big Boulder then at the drawings.

Got to be down there somewhere.

He got out. Lifted Sadie out of the camper. Put on hip waders and long brimmed hat. Sat on the tail gate adjusting straps.

The bit that guy was using? The kind that locks around the back of the tongue. Try it sometime.

I said I was sorry.

No. We got work to do. That's what we're here for.

He packed the steel hoop, measuring stick and mayo bucket down to the creek. Followed a cattle trail through the willows.

Pushed aside branches. Arrived at a long riffle.

This is it!

Big Boulder darkened as it cut under a stand of aspen. Swung back with over-folding arpeggios. He stood knee deep at the top of the pool. Tossed the hoop.

First number I call out is depth the stone is embedded. Second, length. Third, width. Left to right across the top of the page. Make it legible.

Mosquitoes landed on my hands like little dark strange attractors. I slapped one.

I'm going back to the truck. Be right back.

Mosquitoes aren't bad here! At Grays Lake they carry you back to the swamp!

I climbed the embankment. When I got back he'd changed his mind. Tossed the hoop at the top of the riffle. Sat on the bucket. Plucked cobblestones. Called out numbers.

Point eight! Six point four! Three point seven!

Tossed the stone with an elegant motion. The creek went past willow and yellow potentilla. I held the booklet so I could keep my eye on the hoodoos. Yellow welded tephra. Water erodes down. Wind up. They stood upright like grotesques. The creek ran harmonically toward East Fork. Snorkel Bob stood up.

That's it!

Stretched his back. Waded toward me. I shook my head.

Pretty tedious, Bob.

Just don't tell anybody in Pocatello this is what I do.

We climbed the embankment. He pointed out grasses and forbs gone to seed.

The range is in pretty good shape. You can tell by the variety. Indian rice grass. Blue bunch wheat grass. Wildflowers have died back but in the spring they're really something.

The whole range like this?

For the most part. Except Road Creek. Go up there you want to see range that's been pounded.

What outfit?

Spanish Hook out of Challis.

He let Sadie out of the truck. I stared at the hoodoo ridge. Red, orange, grey blue. He looked up at them.

I'd like to walk that ridge. Maybe this fall. Start above the mine and take my time.

Foreshortening gave no idea the miles to the north shoulder of the White Clouds. Ginny thought it would be grand. My knees ached just looking at it.

Looks snaky, Bob.

We drove. Stately, grotesque hoodoos stood above the road. What do you do in the fall?

Drive around. Count redds. The salmon that made it are dead or dying. Kind of a bittersweet time. We do a body count before the bear and eagle get to them.

I saw fall come. Snow on the ridge. Mist rising from streams. The vast multitudes of invertebrates dying back into the mud. Yellow leaves fluttering in the wind. Ranchers riding pack horses into the canyons. The blue smoke of their campfires on the benches.

Think there going to be any salmon this year?

Caleb says there are. Caleb got the ju-ju. If they do he'll know where they are.

He parked. I pointed where the creek almost bent back toward us.

He consulted the log book.

No. But it's got to be down there somewhere.

We waded around until he found it. The creek ran under a cutbank held in place by moss and potentilla. From there it dashed through a talus chute. Standing waves. Back eddies where the current exceeded the polar moment of inertia. He established himself on his bucket. A cutthroat flashed past toward the shelter of the cutbank. I wanted to follow him. Beard and leaf moss winnowing. Small cobbles tumbling. Snorkel Bob tossed the last cobblestone. Appraised my tabulations.

Hope you can stand constructive criticism. You could write a lot clearer.

I can read them.

I've got to enter a lot of these when I get back!

Boulder Creek entered the canyon. The road skidded high above it. Jagged boulders down to whitewater. He peered past me.

See any?

You drive, Bob! I'll watch for ribbons!

Caleb said to watch for cattle trails.

Watch the goddamn road, Bob!

He grinned.

You're right. Got to assume Caleb is going to show discretion.

I thought of Caleb climbing Vulcan's Anvil in a pair of sandals.

You think?

Big Boulder plunged from rock to timber fall. On the far side we saw cattle trails. Bob pointed out grasses.

What's that?

Chinese rice.

Indian rice grass. That?

Tufted blue grass.

Blue bunch wheat grass. But nice try.

The creek swept against the cutbank. Cattle trampled. Bob pointed at it.

That would be the perfect example of an undercut pool. Depth of current. Shade. You bring that up at a meeting and the ranchers go berserk.

Would they have to fence the whole stream?

No. But it's more work no matter what you say.

The current pulled at our legs. Snorkel Bob with his long billed hat, shades and beard like some benevolent god of the stream. The site intact. Cows grazed above but it had a strong overhang lip. The creek ran trout colored. Bob plucked. Measured. Tossed. Clouds passed over the hoodoos. He picked up the hoop. I saw the depression at the head of the riffle.

You've kept to your hypothesis, Bob.

He looked back.

Give them some encouragement.

We climbed back to the truck. He lifted his leg to fart. Two doves flew from the road.

You're frightening the wildlife, Bob!

Bear the shame or bear the pain.

Lifted Sadie out of the truck. She frisked along the roadside. Lifted her nose to sniff. Looked back at us from time to time. Fun to know what she knew. We followed East Fork to the Salmon. At Clayton saw Caleb in the parking lot talking to Fish and Game.

Action down the road, boys! Wolves took down an elk in some guy's pasture!

Where?

Challis Creek. Some kind of circus. That DJ that dresses like Johnny Cash? Got a rifle and a six gun. Says he don't care if they put him in jail! Somebody got to take a stand for the Idaho rancher!

You going over?

Nope. Got reports to do. If I want to climb tomorrow--and I do--I can't be getting tangled up with that.

They haven't driven them off?

Those wolves are hungry!

Bob looked at me.

You want to go?

I had that chance. Turned to Caleb.

Check on Kyrie for me would you, Caleb?

THIRTY NINE

The Salmon swung along the north abutment of Lost River Range. Trophy houses. I chewed my lip.

You know where we're going?

He nodded. Bald Mountain rose up on the left. Pahsmeroi's pale blue in the distance. We turned west on a gravel road. Horses stood in pastures swishing their tails. Black Angus cows. Trucks and cars jammed along the road. Sheriff's rig with flashing lights. Women wearing hiking shorts had glasses up. A man in black stomped around swinging a rifle.

Not against the law to carry a gun.

Bob used the glasses. Handed them to me. I saw the downed elk through heat waves. The way it moved when the wolves tore at it. Black bitch and two pups. At the wood line Big Silver preened. Watched the scene.

Wow.

Man in black approached the women. Black hat with silver braid. Black shirt open at the front showed gray hair and paunch. High heeled black boots. Southern drawl but graduated from Idaho Falls High School. The women turned their backs.

You women turn my stomach! Come up here to watch butchery. Simple butchery. And the hard working folk just trying to make a living. You deserve a whipping! You really do. But I aint' going to do it!

Oh you'd like to!

I knew that voice. That red hair. Man in black pursed his mouth like an Old Testament Prophet.

Go back where you come from! Go back where you liberals come from! Shoo!

Roxie turned. Eyes narrowed.

Oh fuck off!

He stepped back. Eyes open wide. His voice took on the sanctimony of an old woman.

Well I never! Never thought I'd hear a woman talk like that! Around these parts no way!

Stomped off to talk to the sheriff. Waved his arms. Sheriff hitched up his belt. Walked over.

Ma'am? Our women don't talk like that around here.

Roxie gaped. Eyes slitted. Shrieked.

Our women!

Her breast heaved. She gathered breath. Wouldn't be speechless long. I walked over.

Sheriff? Let's walk over here a minute.

Turned and walked. A game warden taught me. They feel funny standing there so they follow. He had the sun at his back. Cowboy hat pulled low. Big guy.

What you got to say?

I leaned against the truck. Looked at the sky.

You're doing a good job, Sheriff. Got everything under control. Be a shame if you got in a pissing match with a doctor lady from Pocatello.

She a doctor?

She is. Get in fight with her? Right or wrong you're going to look bad.

You think.

I know.

He turned to look. Roxie and her friends were getting in the Subaru. Squeak of rack and pin as she cranked the wheel. He turned back to me.

Tell her to behave next time she in Custer County.

He went back to his rig. The DJ went under the fence. Waved the rifle as he climbed toward the elk. Wolves pivoted and loped to the wood line. The sun backlit dark, twisting clouds.

Looks like weather, Bob.

He kept the glasses up.

Four of them. Taking turns. Maybe more in the woods.

Trucks pulled up. The DJ had an audience. Maybe a national contract. We drove over the rise. Saw the river through the trees. Bob shook his head.

Sheriff's a piece of work.

Man in black made him look good though.

We drove. I watched the fields for birds. Saw one kiting at roadside.

Slow down, Bob.

A red tail kited with wing spread. Her eyes widened in anticipation. Pulled in wings. Dropped with talons flared. As we passed she spread her wings. Red tails had sand. Worked highways. Traffic a blind. Kept the sun behind her prey so they didn't see her shadow. Snorkel Bob grinned.

It's a good life.

At the outskirts of Challis pulled in at the Last Chance Saloon. Mexican Food. Steroid Ortiz swung the bat above the bar. Couple of ranch hands at a table with their legs stretched out. The barmaid set schooners on the bar. Bob told her to keep the change. That got a smile.

What brings y'all here?

Salmon Recovery.

Who you work for?

The Tribes.

Those Indians! Why don't they go away! They're a conquered people!

We have a treaty with them. Fort Bridger, 1863. They have

to be able to hunt and fish the Columbia Basin.

You ought to see how they act up here! Take the only fish in the river!

There's blame to go around. I agree with you, Ma'am.

We ordered another round. Bob set it down with a grin.

How do they make it so good and so cheap!

Cowboys came in. Ordered a pitcher. Racked. Their blocky bodies threw shadows across the room. Kept their hats on. Cowboys were like women. Always on. Bob turned to me.

Shoshones seem to be looked down on even by the other tribes. You heard that?

It's more like they're seen as being under a cloud. First small pox. Then the Oregon Trail. One day you're by the river fishing. Hear thunder but there's no clouds. Dust in the sky but the wind is wrong. Then a hundred thousand cattle are on top of you.

Didn't help they always sided with us.

No.

He nodded at the pretty bottles on shelves in front of the mirror.

You want a lick of the snake? I'm buying.

I need something to eat, Bob.

They got food here. Shot of Bushmills would do you good.

I looked at the menu. Old style Californio. Prices high. I didn't smell cooking. Glanced in the kitchen. Kid watching TV. Microwave operation. A Mexican wouldn't do that to you. Snorkel Bob had a shot of Bushmills. Cowboy came over. Five nine but six in boots.

Y'all with the wolf project?

No sir. We work with fish.

That's good. Don't want no wolf lovers around here.

Why is that?

They take all the elk. You go in for miles. Way past where you used to. None when you get there!

Snorkel Bob ducked his head.

They're wilder now. No question. But they did a study up the Selway? Showed the average kill by a wolf was sixteen years. The average by a licensed hunter was four and a half. That means we're taking the prime breeders.

I heard it before. Y'all make up whatever you want!

It's Science.

The cowboy pursed his mouth.

I'd like to take you outside!

Bob looked at him. Head wagged slightly.

Why? You want to fuck me?

Oh no! I almost fell off my chair! Cowboy turned red. Before he could move I leaned.

Listen, pal. You want trouble you found it. We're leaving shortly.

Your shot, Stan.

The cowboy at the table grey at the temples. Forearms of a stevedore. Hundred pound bales. I didn't want him at close range.

Spent a lot of money getting rid of wolves in this country.

I nodded. Our cowboy turned like it was the hardest thing he ever done. Snorkel Bob looked up innocently at the TV.

Let's go, Bob. I need something to eat.

They got food here.

Not what I want. You coming?

He looked the game with eyes narrowed.

Always been a Red Sox fan. Dad and I'd drive up I-95 to see them.

He alive?

No. Down the river. Like everything.

Come on, Bob.

He jerked his forearm away.

Going to watch the game.

Alright.

The sun had set. Clouds shot scarlet and pink. You smelled poplars and the river. A pick-up with trailer pulled up. Dust swirled. It didn't register. I went up to the Gold Dust. Had a hamburger at the counter. Night fell. When I went out saw blue and amber lights flashing at the bottom of Main. Sheriff's rig blocked the parking lot to the Last Chance. EMT's crouched by a man with his head at the foot of the steps. Sadie wailed. Sheriff stood with his thumbs in his belt.

I said, What happened!

I can't tell you. Life Flight will pick him up at the Carlson

Ranch.

Where they out of?

Pocatello.

Snorkel Bob lay with a tube in his mouth, hands limp at his side. EMT kept track of his pulse. The other pressed his side and hands. Spoke low.

Didn't get his hands up.

Happens.

Bob's eyes weren't seeing anything. I felt my knees buckle. Went over to the truck. Leaned against the hood. Sadie wailed. EMT stood up to make the call. I went over.

He going to make it?

I don't know.

You got his keys?

Sheriff's got them.

I went over to the Sheriff.

I need the keys. His dog's in there.

He handed them.

You can sign for them tomorrow.

Sadie leaped against the leash. I tried to walk her down the highway but she fought. I sat on the tailgate. Held her. They got Snorkel Bob into the ambulance. Turned on the siren. I went into the bar. The cowboys gone. An old guy bent over his drink at the end of the bar. Barmaid wiped down the counter.

Bar's closed.

Did you see it?

No. Bar's closed.

I went over to the old man.

What happened?

Your friend ran into the wrong person.

Who followed him?

Didn't see. But y'all ought to consider going elsewhere. You don't belong here.

Oh I do, old man.

Sadie cried all the way along the winding river. The camp quiet and dark. Stars blazed. Caleb came out of his tent.

Where's Bob?

I told him. He turned away. Came back at me with face

white. Eyes red. Hit me with both fists on the chest. I staggered. Got my heels under me. He howled.

Why did you leave him! Why didn't you stay with him!

He wouldn't go.

He picked up a camp chair. Threw it. The cooler. Tossed it. Cans, bottles scattering in all directions. Sean came out. Stayed out of the way.

Where'd they take him?

Pocatello.

Goddamn it! Goddamn it! Goddamn it!

He started taking gear out of his tent. Throwing it in the truck. His hair wild. Tears streaked his face. Turned to Sean.

Don't leave. Stay in camp.

He jumped in the cab. I grabbed the door frame.

Hold on, Caleb.

Got Sadie out of the truck. Put her beside him. He nodded without looking at me. Put the truck in gear. I held the door open.

I'm going to Challis tomorrow. Look around.

Do that, White Boy. Best keep in mind though. They did a renovation of that jail a few years back? Found a blind cell nobody knew about. Must've had some use for it. Drunk Indians and the like. You dig?

He looked back. Popped the clutch. Spun gravel. The headlights flashed through the trees.

I lay on my back. Drifted off. Saw Bob's smiling face. I'd wake. Or his face crushed on one side. I'd wake. An owl hooted. I remembered the road the Shoshone took to the Land of the Dead. One fork led to people that were kind and generous like home. The other to people that abused children. Lied. Used poison arrows. You had no way of knowing which to take. It didn't matter if you were a child or a noble woman you would have to live among those people. Had to have a guide. I thought about the blind cell in Challis. The stories nobody talked about.

FORTY

I made breakfast. Drove to Challis. Almost hit a big horn that leapt from pasture to road. I'd been watching the cliff. Sheriff had his boots on the desk. I saw the white angel chaps between cuff and boot. He looked at me with his meaty forearms across his chest. George W. Bush beamed on the wall. I told him what happened at the trailhead.

It was the same rig that came up to the saloon.

You sure of that?

Yes sir.

He drew his chin up so the corners of his mouth turned down. Pulled a notepad over.

License plate number?

I didn't get it.

No license plate number?

No. But you could find out who registered at the trailhead.

I could. What's your phone number, son?

I gave him Mickey Angel's.

He nodded. Put a toothpick in his mouth. Set his boots back on the desk.

Let me tell you a story, son. Was an old guy here when I come on. Sheriff in the old days. I cultivated him so to speak. Took him for coffee. Things like that. He was sheriff here twenty years if that tell you something.

When did your folks come here?

He looked surprised. Then away.

Granddad come here in the twenties to work the Blue Jacket Mine. When it played out he told Grandma they was moving on. She kind of set anchor on him. Been across this country twice and back again. Left a couple of kids along the way. So they got hold of some land on Challis Creek. Had not a pot to piss in nor window to throw it out of. One cutting of hay. A little hunting. A garden the deer would eat.

He looked up at me.

But I was telling you about Sheriff Wright. Got a call someone stole horses up Jackson Hole. To keep an eye out. Was north of town when he seen a rider come out of Joe's Canyon with a string. They called it Joe's Canyon on account Joe Wilson would go in there with a couple of mules and log it. Even though there weren't nothing in there but rocks and rattlesnakes. Sheriff Wright saw it was George Parley. Now George was rumored to be in the employ of the big outfits in the event they needed a claims adjustor. Just a rumor of course. But the outfits had a lot of play back then.

Still do.

Still do. George waved in a friendly fashion. Sheriff Wright rode over. Noticed the 44 George was holding behind the pommel.

What's on your mind, Sheriff?

Somebody stole some horses out of Jackson Hole, George. I seen these horse come out of the canyon. Thought I'd give a look.

George Parley smiled.

These are my horses, Sheriff. But you're welcome to check out my string anytime. Any time at all, Sheriff.

He was smiling. But Sheriff Wright noticed his eyes looked sad.

Oh that's alright, George. I don't have to look at your horses. I know you're good for them.

Sheriff smiled. Put his arms behind his head.

Old Sheriff Wright. Loved to tell stories on hisself. Another time a kid come in. Asked if he could have a word in private. Sheriff Wright could tell the kid'd been crying. Tears streaked his face. He was a Ord and Ords never got too close to the washbasin.

Done a bad thing, Sheriff.

Was at the still when a federal man come out of the brush. They made the best shine in the country up here. Don't know if it were the water or the technique but that shine got moved from Rock Springs to San Francisco. Give you an idea? A runner checked into the Hotel Utah with a twenty case consignment. Went to dinner. When he come back it was gone. Got the Chief of Police on the line.

I'd like that consignment back by noon, Chief. Or there'll be no more shipments to Salt Lake City.

Those twenty cases were in his room by noon. Give you an idea how good it was. So the federal man come with a gun. But you know? What I learned in Vietnam? You got a gun you best use it. The kid crying.

All I could see was my daddy slung across that revenuer's mule like a busted up deer! And I shot him. I shot him, Sheriff.

Right betwixt the eyes. And the look he gave me when he saw it coming? I see it ever time I close my eyes! Night and day! 'Bout to go crazy, Sheriff Wright!

You go in the washroom and clean up, son. Then we'll take a drive. That be alright with you?

Sheriff Wright was a courteous man. Everybody said so. They took the County car to where the river makes that big sweep under the cliff. Sheriff Wright walked him out past the gravel bars to the deep current. Took him by his skinny shoulders. Shoved him face down into the cold, cold water. Held him there.

Once for those that love you!

Twice for your sins!

Thrice for you eternal soul! And be at Church on Sunday.

The Sheriff closed his eyes. Raised his arms.

Verily I say to you, Brethren! I washed him clean in the River of the Spirit! And he shall have Eternal Life! Amen.

Dropped his big palms on the desk. Stared wide eyed at me. I leaned against the door frame.

No salmon in that river anymore, Sheriff.

He drew some papers toward him.

No. Hear you can get it frozen at the Challis Mercantile though.

I turned to go.

Son? he said. You're welcome here anytime in Custer County. Keep that in mind.

Outside I looked back at the Courthouse. Blind columns. Gabled roof above the balcony where old guys made proclamations. I drove up Main. Store fronts boarded up. An espresso shop and an antique shop closed. Road turned to gravel. Creek pounded. Cows higher up. Saw the A-frame in the stand of aspen. No Trespassing. Toyota Land Cruisers in the wildflowers. Japanese Imperial Army. Family models of the Seventies. Built for jungle but liked the Rockies. Dogs howled. Sauntered toward me looking sideways at each other. Deer bones draped along the roof. Harvey Gresham came out from the back tying his tie. Kept the front door locked.

Errol! What the hell!

How you doing, Harvey.

Terrible, man! Got a plane to catch! But make yourself at home!

Hadn't changed. Grey at the temples but moved like a cat. High compression. High rpms. Packed a 45 with the business suit. White silk shirt. Faded levis. Lizard skin boots.

You're looking good, Harvey. But the deer bones on the roof might indicate you been in Challis too long.

Got to, Errol. Dogs bring them in. You find them under the bed or in the closet. Women hate that.

In the kitchen graffiti covered the cabinets, door frames, refrigerator.

The history of the world, my sweet?
Who gets eaten. Who gets to eat!
B. Hogan
In warfare come like wind
Go like lightning.
Chuang Tzu
Hide and watch.
Captain Jesus

You must have great parties, Harvey.

You run hot you need heavy coolant. You know that.

The living room had a lodge pole in the center. Wood floor polished to high shine. Objets d'art on the walls. A bowl woven with native stems. Spider web of willow wands with a polished scapula and fluorescent shells. Cradle board with beaded sunrise at the head. Eagle feather duster with buckskin handle. Harvey had brief case in hand. Grabbed his keys.

Make yourself at home. I mean that.

Don't want to hold you up, Harvey. But Snorkel Bob got beat up last night. Thought you could give me an idea who it was.

He stood looking out the window.

Could be anybody.

He opened the suitcase. Checked it. Slammed it shut.

In any case, Errol? Operational for you to keep in mind. Everybody is related to everybody in this country. One way or another.

I said, So how you feeling?

Better all the time.

Ever tell Zuniland what happened?

They laughed. The Zuni? Evil. Like to play with snakes.

And they reach out.

They do.

How'd you get through it?

Sat my butt down. Realized Mother Earth was trying to destroy me cell by cell. Had to come to terms with that. Didn't matter if I were in Hell's Canyon or the Mayo Clinic! Had good marijuana too.

He decided he needed another shirt. When he took it off the rack I saw the long, black wool coat. Looked good when he ran up the steps of Federal Court. Picked up the 45. Spun the cylinder. Began inserting hollow points.

Like this country. You come to terms with it.

That's a lot of gun.

It's not whether you hit somebody, Errol. It's whether they stay down. Learned that in Vietnam.

They let you take that on the plane?

It'll get me out of Custer County.

I saw the blackboard covered with hieroglyphics. Energy. Function. Interplaning scalar systems.

I know you're in a hurry, Harvey. But what's this?

He looked at it top to bottom as if checking numbers.

That equation, Errol? Describes the total energy flow of the Columbia Basin. In American dollars of course.

You being an economist.

Yes sir. Fish money. Federal money. Indian money. Payment in kind money.

He snapped the cylinder shut. Winked at me.

How I make my money. Nice to see you, Errol. Lock up when you leave.

I went to the gallery. No chairs. Just the polished floor. Sacred symbols painted on the elk skin drum. When the maker drummed it the symbols went out into the universe.

I drove past the beat up creek, the boarded store fronts. Headed up 75. Crown of Thorn strainers left high and dry. Talus slopes red and yellow. All new rock if you reckoned a hundred million years new. Volcanoes. The emplacement of their disasters

quiet now. Trout colored. When the sun exploded would drift
elsewhere. New rivers. New women. New hawks. Whether it
created another Idaho I didn't know. Or the woman I loved. The
river came dancing. Fishermen's lines curved over shine and
sparkle. Up Iron Creek Sean wrote reports at the picnic table. I got
a beer.

You want to go to town? I'll stay in camp.

Thanks, Errol.

I unhooded Kyrie. Had another beer. When I woke it was
Sean's truck. I went to the creek to bathe.

Casanova Jack's in Stanley was lodge pole log with a plank
boardwalk. Platinum Escalade parked at the hitching post. Inside it
was quiet and dark. Just the barkeep and a woman shooting pool. I
put two quarters on the rail. Our eyes met. She was pretty. Had
stayed alive at 55. Pearly white blouse and tight jeans. Turquoise at
her throat and wrist set in silver.

Rack them.

You don't want to finish your game?

She had a million dollar smile.

I've already won.

You mind three ball?

I don't know it.

Seven balls remained on the table. I rolled one to the far
bank to check drift. Set three in triad. Sequestered the rest under
the table.

Nobody plays it anymore. My brother taught me it. I like it
because you shoot until the balls are down. Nobody takes your
mistakes. Best score is one. Don't see that very often. The worst is
the losing one. And the bonus? If you scratch or don't make point
you have balls for the next game.

She took a sip of her shot glass.

You go first.

Good play. What's the wager?

Mine's expensive.

I chalked. Sent the cue ball with top spin to give it torque.
After three caroms a solid went down.

The other thing? With three balls there's always an open
shot.

She watched. Eyes, jewelry glittering.

You must like control.

I do.

I missed a rail shot but made four. Racked them tight. She was pretty as she leaned over the table. Her silver bracelets and rings. Missed the tying shot. We sat by the window.

What happens if you tie?

Double up. With a few players you can get money in the game.

How much?

I didn't like to play for money. But once in Vegas my brother got me in a game with several hundred dollars on the rail. It was all we had. But Billy was a player. Could beat me one handed.

You're kidding?

No. He'd bounce the stick in his right hand. 'Til he got it sighted? Then draw the cue ball the length of the table. He made two. You heard the sigh. My turn. Gave it a whack. Made two on the break. Point two a cut shot in the corner. I chalked up. Took my time.

You missed.

It wasn't like we acted like we didn't know each other.

Always a price isn't there?

That sliding scale.

How did you effect your exit?

When Billy leaned over to tie his boots they might have glimpsed the 38 strapped to his ankle.

I had a price. My husband went on long business trips. I asked him to bring me flowers when he came home. When he stopped I didn't ask again. The price of a few flowers cost him twenty million dollars.

And you.

And me. Give me your hand.

She turned my hand palm up. Traced the lines with a lacquered nail. Eyes dimmed.

This is your Lifeline. See the fork? Death awaits you there. You'll have to decide whether to go on. It will be hard. If you do you'll live long.

When will that be?

She looked at my eyes.

Ten years.

I raised the beer glass with my left hand.

Ne swete forswelgan. Ne saer gefelan. He hond onhreran.

What's that?

Nor mead to swallow. Nor sorrow to feel. Nor hand to raise. The Seafarer.

The bartender brought two single malts. She took a sip.

This is your Loveline. It's very strong! You love hard and you love deep. But you're stubborn and selfish.

She looked at me bemusedly.

And you don't forgive.

It's hard for me.

It always is for those who need it most. But it will cause you much pain.

She stroked my hand as she looked at me. Then returned to my hand. Traced the sidereal lines.

You'll love two women deeply. I'm not sure you'll marry either one. Are you with someone now?

No.

I didn't think so. You look like you haven't slept in a clean bed for awhile.

True again.

Without releasing my hand she took a drink.

I don't think I should drive.

I looked away. The street had turned deep indigo. She released my hand. Stood up.

Well! Thanks for the game.

I'm sorry. Just things I got to take care of.

She cocked her head.

Another time then.

She strutted elegantly to the bar. I ate the salad. Wrapped half the steak in a napkin. Finished the single malt. When I went up to pay it was taken care of. The bartender slipped the receipt toward me.

Along Iron Creek birds sang midsummer songs. One had a tri partita trill he used over and over again. Iron Creek tumbled whitely at the boundary of darkness.

The river pushed cold against my thighs. At the far bank Snorkel Bob made looping casts. I let the hook float down a long deep roller. Steelhead took it. Bright red curve of her belly as she leapt. I damped the line. She was so big it screamed through the rings! Bob looked at me with goaty grin. I gave her line. Damped. Let go. When there was none left felt the tug. Knew the line would snap. It didn't. Worked her back against the current. She ran at me slim and silver. Looked me in the eye. Juked. Twisted in a triple roll. The hook flew. Gleamed. Steelhead Lady looked back as she shot down river. I felt white with loss. Snorkel Bob laughed. Turned and made another long, looping cast. Night came on. I limped on all fours along endless highways. Broken glass cut my pads. Trucks rushed past. I ran into barbed wire. Finally saw the house. Ran up on the porch. The sheriff came to the door. A wild screeching on the roof. I looked up. Billy crouched like a gargoyle. Grinned at me like when he was a little kid. Had hawk wings with slotted tips. Lifted them to fly. The sheriff raised his shotgun. I howled. Woke howling. A new dream arrived. My wife went to the door as if to leave but turned. Looked at me with that look of love that is more arousing than anything. Love flooded through me. When I put my arms around her she turned her face away. When she looked again it was white with hate.

FORTY ONE

Light came over the mountains. I sat by the fire with the mug in my hands. Stared at the flames. Clouds floated over. I fried eggs and potatoes. That brought Sean out. He poured coffee.

You see the paper? Nothing about Bob.

Didn't guess there would, I said. What you going to do?

Wait 'til Caleb comes back. You?

Headed out.

Might be a job for you, Errol. Keep the outfit together.

Caleb won't forgive me.

It wasn't your fault.

It was.

The Good Book says the highest of all virtues is charity.

That would include yourself.

    I'll keep that in mind.

    I walked past tents to the pump. Filled water bottles. Visited the toilet. Walked through wildflowers to the creek. Stripped. Let Iron Creek wash away my sins. Put on clean clothes. Packed the truck so I wouldn't come back. Crags came into view as the road turned left or right. Signed the register at the Trailhead. Cinched the pack. With Kyrie on the glove climbed through the lodge poles. The creek showed now and then. Giant granite boulders along the trail. Hoodoos shimmered above. Across the canyon a waterfall spilled down a two thousand foot wall. At the head Iron Creek cascaded from the nave. Ancient, gnarled pines attended like priests.

    I climbed switchbacks lee of the sun. Wildflowers shone among the deadfall. At the ridge I saw Alpine Lake. Breezes rippled Technicolor green across cobalt blue. Sub alpine fir stood like awls on a spit of granite that jutted into it. Looked like a grand arena for flying. A ground squirrel stared at me. I thought she was pregnant her belly hung so low. She took the crust I tossed. Nibbled it brazenly. Realized she had the concession where two hundred people a day stopped to look at Alpine Lake. It glittered like the most precious jewel on earth. Like the stained glass at Chartres it changed as the sun moved overhead or went behind a cloud.

    Krawk! Krawk!

    Four Clark's nutcrackers flew across the lake. I searched the rockslides. Saw white bark pines. Kyrie raised her wings. Ground squirrel dove.

    The trail edged up the wall. No cliff bands in the Sawtooths. Just wall and talus. The switchbacks so tight I had to turn my boots out. Hikers below. Perfect for mountain lions. She'd just roll down the cliff with you. I saw a lion take a mule deer on Kinney Creek. Took its head in her paws and licked its face. Her love for it so strong I heard the purring from across the canyon.

    I passed lightning scarred pines. Dropped along a brook garlanded with gentian and monkey flowers. Then stood at Sawtooth Lake. Knife peaks soared on all sides. Kyrie set her head at crazy angles. Scanned the peaks. Called out. The echo came with ripples on the water. Waves rolled in. Folded back on the ones following. That's how quiet that morning was. Rings bloomed on the water. Horseflies swarmed. I got line and number six hook. Waited 'til one settled on my hand. Watched me. Would have to commit in order to dip its cutter. Hunger won out. It angled its body and fed. When it turned red I whacked it. Slipped the hook. Tossed it on the water. Small fry approached but I kept it moving. Then an eight incher hit. Fought against the hook. I lay it on the rock. Watched its colors fade. Trout have few weakness but can't resist a blood-filled horse fly.

I remembered the meat packing plant on Kraft Road. Honcho told us to let him know when we got the carcass on the hook. Arrived with butcher knife and beer glass. Butchers know anatomy. Nicked the femoral. The beer glass filled with blood. He drained it in one draught! Grinned at us with blood running down his jowls.

Best cure for a hangover there is!

Terrorized the crew but left me alone. My dad was Ben Husky.

I tied the trout to a stone in the cold water. Watched the breeze bring diamonds. Kyrie's gun metal shoulders shone. Had never flown in such an arena. You felt the charge between her and Mount Regan.

Hoo! Hoo! Hawk!

She flew lazily. Clockwise over the white barks where bear used to feed. Nutcrackers silent. Everything silent under her wings. Swung past the gap. Past Mount Regan. Came back along the ridge. Turned to go higher when a dart fell out of the clouds. She turned hooks up. Fell backwards. The falcon swung up. Kyrie flew hard. Hooked wind. Kited for altitude. But the falcon stayed in command. Taunted her. I watched them circle. Was it a dance of love or death? Then Kyrie winged over. Went into a stoop with the falcon following. It made the cliffs ring. Just above the water she braked. Bow waves rippled. She flew for the rocks. The falcon hovered an instant. Slipped over the ridge.

My heart started again. I looked at the quarter mile of talus boulders big as cars. No lack of daylight though. Retrieved the trout. Pulled on the pack. Jumped from rock to rock. The sun banging down now. Sweat stinging my eyes. She was hot too. Gaped and fanned. Feathers care worn. Turned her back. Hobbled among the rocks. I saw her anger and humiliation. She had every reason. I sliced a filet. Held it out to her.

Eat now, Kyrie. Eat.

She did. I carried her to the water. Splashed it on her face. She liked it. Forgot her humiliation. We passed lightning alley. Followed the trail over the ridge. Looked for chalk on the cliff. Hadn't brought glasses. Always a mistake. A young woman with a pony tail ascended the trail. Something about the way she swung the walking stick. Forest service shoulder patch and shorts. Long, tanned legs flashed. I leaned against the cliff. Nowhere to hide. She'd seen my name on the register. Heat flashed. At the switchback Ginny looked up. Gave that Fourth of July smile.

Hi, Errol!

How you doing, Ginny.

She stood close so I smelled her lotion. How she stroked it on her flanks when we went to bed. Her brown eyes piercing. A silver ring in her left narine.

I'm Ok. They got me on the Disneyland tour as you can see.

Peered at me with serious brown eyes. Strands of black brown hair haloing her cheeks.

Last summer they had my digging water holes in the Pahsimeroi. Can you believe it? I said, There's no water here!

The cowboy said, I got to have me a seep! I'm paying for it, aint' I?

No lack of water in the Pahsimeroi.

Not where Orrin had his lease.

Married the wrong girl.

You guessed that.

She was brown as an Indian. Had her left leg cocked near mine. I felt the lust. The scent of her lotion was in my soul. Delicate dark fur. Her willingness to clasp herself to me. She narrowed her eyes.

You doing Ok?

She reached out her hand to stroke Kyrie but withdrew it.

How's she doing?

Had a wild flight up there. Don't know why I didn't think

there'd be peregrines.

They have an eyrie farther down. So you're doing Ok?

The concern in her voice. Like she were asking about a puppy or a foal.

I'm getting by.

Rosalie Sorrels is playing at Casanova Jack's tonight. If you wanted to meet there?

I would Ginny but--

She looked at me.

Alright, Errol. I'll be on my way.

Glanced at my hand. Saw the welt.

See you're up to your old tricks!

I shrugged.

You're crazy, Errol. If you were a little less crazy.

I know.

You don't know. You'll never.

She dug the climbing stick into the sand.

You could have stayed with me.

They would've made it that much harder.

She looked at the cliffs and the clouds.

So I had that one chance? Alright then.

She went up the trail. Rocks overhung. Wildflowers so exposed they faded long ago. I kept my eyes on the trail. Heart seethed. Keep going, Errol. Picture Rosalie. That long red dress and old guitar. Her hand across the strings like a branch in the wind. Would sing a verse then laugh. Her Irish dad descending the stairs buck-naked singing When A Bonny Meets A Bonny! That was her art. Made you feel you shared the memory as if by chance. Her rich laughter. The friends that stopped by. Teachers, engineers at Boeing that lost their jobs to the Blacklist. Didn't matter if they carried a BAR onto the sands of Tarawa! Outcasts. Sat around the table until late. Late gleam of gold.

My! Could they smoke!

You were with her around the table in 1955. It was an honor. Then she'd pick up the song again. I Remember Loving You. Howl like a dance hall maven then slip to a soft wail. And I think you loved me too. I tripped. Kyrie's talons cut the glove.

Sorry, Kyrie. Sorry.

I leaned against a scarred trunk. Thought about Ginny up on the mountain. What you can hold. What you can't take back. Almost turned around. Sunlight shot through the branches. Was enough heartache to go around. I drove past camp. Along river and rock fall. The cliff where the bighorns came down. Sat by the window in the Gold Dust Café. Waitress took my order. Big man wearing a red hunting hat sat at the counter.

Coffee, Len?

If you got it.

Oh we got it.

She poured the coffee. Stood by the kitchen. Nobody in the café. The old man stirred his coffee.

Little excitement the other night?

I barely turned my head but the waitress caught it.

Yep.

I heard the sirens.

Don't want to talk about it, Len.

How'd it start?

I told you, Len. I weren't there and I don't know what it was.

It was so quiet you heard the old man pour a second packet into his coffee.

Junior's like a dog that come up behind when you're not looking.

The waitress went into the kitchen. Old man didn't care.

One day somebody's going to put him down. Daddy won't be able to help him.

I looked out the window. The Sheriff's black and gold rig cruised up the street. Radio came on loud. Cowboy clone with a nasal twang. The waitress shoved a Styrofoam box with the check in front of me.

I didn't order it to go, Ma'am.

She was breathing hard. Deep lines warpaint couldn't hide. Weren't many dances left in her life if in fact there were any. I handed her the card.

Take care of this would you? Ketchup and Tabasco?

She took the card. Her hand shook when she dropped the slip on the table. I opened the Styrofoam box. poured on red stuff.

Who might Junior's daddy be?

The old man turned. Was a bear. With gray hair wasn't somebody you'd want to tangle with.

Our fine sheriff.

The bacon was half way to my mouth. I chewed it.

Looks like Junior strayed from the Church.

That's a way of putting it.

The front door swung open. A young couple wearing T-shirts and shorts came in with their kids. The waitress gave them a big smile.

Howdy, folks! Sit anywhere you want!

It was a friendly place. The old man turned back to his coffee. I looked at the hash browns. Charred bacon. Eggs already cold. Decided I'd take it to go. The black and gold pickup had tinted windshields so I couldn't see who was driving. Put the 45 beside my on the seat where it wasn't concealed. Drove up a block. Turned onto a side street. Ended at a pasture above Garden Creek. I looked at the mountain that surrendered zinc and lead. No trout in the creek. Sheriff's SUV followed me when I returned to Main. Left me at the bridge headed south on 93.

I drove until Mount Borah jutted into the sky. Pulled onto a cow road. Looked at the half billion year old brindle ridge. How the wind tried to sweep me off it. Slithered on my belly. At Mackay pulled in at the pump. My old friend Dwayne the clerk. Little good for nothing Dwayne. Shouldn't say that. He was good for killing. Killed his elk and killed his deer. Pronghorn and bear. When the window opened for trapping permits was first in line. First to fill. Tributaries of the Big Lost trapped out. One night in the Silver Dollar cried in his beer. No more varmints in East Fork because Fish and Game wouldn't let him kill the lions. Otherwise had his way. The ranchers didn't invite him to dinner but liked his kind around. Kept order. Looked at me under graying eyebrows. The hero of the country. I was getting my fill of it. Didn't stop at the Silver Dollar with the hand carved mahogany bar shipped in in 1902.

Volcanoes showed beyond the V of the Big Lost. Plumes of smoke here and there across the plain. It was late afternoon when I approached Pocatello. Wild fires seethed atop the Bannock Range.

At the Office Eichorn gave me a big grin.

Don't look like you'll be crawling into your hole up Mink Creek, Bird Man. Fire is general up there.

They close the road?

Can't tell you.

I'll wait 'til dark.

I did. Flames licked the darkness. Wind warm and smoky. Not the cold sweetness of the Sawtooths. But even with the hills going up in flames I was glad to be back. A two engine bomber went overhead.

FORTY TWO

The buildings of Old Town just shadows. Skate board Goths
slouched at Bernardo's. I ordered a mocha. Pulled the newspaper
toward me.

BANKER SHOT DEAD!
Constantine Papalos who arranged financing
For the Gate City, Northwood and Village Road
Malls was found dead with a gunshot wound
To the head. Police Spokesman Dan Carlson
Said the 81 year old Papalos was found early
Sunday morning by his grand nephew Gustavo
Demetrius who is visiting from Greece.

Carlson said the young man is "very
distraught."

"Nothing has been ruled out and we are
Actively searching for a suspect," he added.

Source close to the investigation said
Papalos installed a phone at the gate of his house
In exclusive Sagewood Estates. There was no sign
Of forced entry.

Papalos who was affectionately known as
Connie arrived in Pocatello in 1949. He was active
In the Greek Orthodox Church, Pocatello Chiefs
and the Chamber of Commerce. As a member of the
State Board of Education he worked closely with
Several administrations at ISU. A Bengal Gold Card
Booster he was a fixture at ISU Football games.

"It's a shock," said Clark Smith of the
Greater Pocatello Chamber of Commerce. "He
always gave back to the community."

A funeral is planned for Sunday at the
Church of the Assumption.

WILDFIRE RAGES. Color photo of a
Silvery two prop spilling orange red retardant.
SEARCH GOES ON. Matthew Stirling
last seen diving from Rattlesnake Rock.
PRESIDENT UP BEAT. In speech in Akron
President Bush tells Americans, "Buy that car. Take
that vacation. Let the troops do their job."

At the Meat Market Stan the Handyman tested the Ph in the
hot tub.

You getting out this weekend, Stan?

I was. A guy that works for the City said they clamped the
flow off at the dam. The channel below is pretty well defined. You
walk along bank pulling out twenty four inchers with a fly rod!

Better get out!

No. Don't like the idea of that kid down there. Be just my
luck to snag him. I'll wait 'til they find him.

They might never.

They mightn't.

He went into the pump room. Came back.

I said, What's your best river story, Stan?

My best story? Most folks don't know when the water's
low there's a big whirlpool before it goes through the turbines.
Always big fish waiting there. You seen that re-bar sticking out of
the old dam? Jack and I decided we'd hitch the boat to that. Just
ride the rim of that whirlpool. He got a hit right away. Big rainbow.
Saw that pink belly as she breached. Jack got a little excited. Stood
up. Of course the boat low sided. He went headfirst.

Oh no.

Was going by the second time when I got him by the hair. It
was the seventies so he had a lot of it.

He'd of been fish food.

You got it. Another time we were drifting toward Eagle
Rock jump shooting geese. It was winter. Big shelves of ice above
the current. Came around the bend and saw a flock standing with
their black feet on the ice. Tossed a few in the boat. Were
congratulating ourselves when we heard the roar at Rattlesnake
Rock. Was fast approaching. Realized at low water there was a
drop off. Had just time to grab our guns and jump. Stripped to our

skivvies. Got the boat and whatever gear was still floating around and went our merry way.

How old were you?

Twenty five.

That's a good age. I heard the Museum in Boise has the muzzleloaders Hunt left at Caldron Lyn.

Where'd they find them?

Caldron Lyn.

I darecn't say it was Colonel Hunt. Could've been any low-life trapper got surprised by the Falls. I don't see Hunt making it through Milner Mile.

It was October. They tried the river once more after they lost Clappine. They say it was his guns.

People say a lot of things. But you're right. A big river can do funny things.

Better get out, Stan. Summer's on the fly.

It is. You know when they rebuilt the dam they shut off the river at Palisades. Guys went and hooked fish out of the holes. There's a picture of them standing above a string of fish. A lot of them over three feet long. Can you imagine!

How do you fish the Rez, Stan?

I take the boat to where the sloughs come in. Late in the year there'll be beds of floating algae. The fish like to hang out under there because it's cool. I'll lay out a string with Velveeta cheese on number twelve hooks. Sit back and have a beer. Reservoir fish can not resist Velveeta cheese.

It's the aging process. You use a float?

Oh sure. Line of bobbers. It's like Sunday buffet at the Holiday Inn for those trout.

I went into the steam room. The old soldier hunched in meditation. I picked up the hose. Waited for it to turn cold then drank.

So Larry. What was the cavalry unit stationed here?

I don't know. But there was a lot of labor unrest here. From the eighties on.

116th. Fifty Second Brigade.

If that's the case they're still here.

Why didn't they use infantry?

Cavalry can have a salutatory effect on men in the street. Where were the barracks?

Out where FBI Headquarters is now. A guy whose grand-dad was stable master said he traded horse manure to a Chinaman for fresh vegetables.

Now that I think about it it was the same unit that came to Fort Hall in the sixties.

Fort Hall on Lincoln Creek. If you didn't need them for the railroaders you could use them on the Indians.

No. The Indians would've been wiped out without the 116th.

Probably right.

I am. At Little Rock in 1957 I was privileged to observe the effect a few well-trained troops had on several hundred rednecks.

What outfit?

101st. Eisenhower sent us in.

Because he had to. Even though it jeopardized his reception at Augusta National.

It's good to be President. As a bonus I saw what you can do with the butt of an M-1. We were guarding the route of the kids arriving at school. A huge redneck was berating a scrawny little trooper standing at attention. Called him no end of nasty things. Oh my yes. Was chewing tobacco so the spittle spattered the trooper's face. He turned to the CO.

Request permission to respond, Sir!

Do it.

When the butt of the M1 hit that redneck's face the blood flew. Blood, snot and teeth. It was very educational.

He didn't say, Use judicious force?

He said, Do it.

Federal power is a funny thing.

It is.

I went to the showers. Stood in the hot spray thinking about the 101st at Little Rock. Then Caldron Lyn. It's the southernmost point of the Snake. Takes a big swing left. The cliffs vertical, dark, foreboding but the river very smooth. As it turns back right the event horizon gives no information. Within thirty feet the Snake is a howling cascade. If you stand above it you feel the joints tremble.

Huge columnar blocks getting ready to fall.

The Hunt Party was lucky they hit the Milner Mile. If everything were against you? If you were in the middle of the current and the wind were from the east? If your wife were in the prow holding a crying baby. Dark was falling and camp was far? It would be possible to attempt a run of Caldron Lyn.

The smoke lifted over town. The ravines at the top of the alley dark blue. Two discarded men sat on the wall by the parking lot. Pigeon feathers drifted in the door of Michael Angelo's. He had his feet up.

Hard shift huh?

I said, You heard anything?

He shook his head.

I said, I'll be going to see him in awhile.

That'd be good.

Don't guess Caleb will forgive me.

Can't tell you, Errol.

I turned spinner racks.

You seen Gerald?

No.

When'd you last see him?

You were there.

I chose a Kirk Anderson color photo of Boulder Creek.

I was hoping I could put Kyrie back in the loft if you didn't mind.

Don't worry about it.

I tossed a five on the desk.

So I'll see you tomorrow. If you're going be around.

I'll be around. Unfortunately.

Don't take such a dim view of it. You got a lot of nice books. Could move to a place like Bozeman or Boise where they buy books. Find a girl to tend the till for you with the money you'd make.

He opened his book: Landscape and Memory.

Can't leave Pocatello, Errol. Too many enemies here.

The hospital stood on the bench. An office tower connected it to the University neighborhood. I didn't use elevators on principle. Looked for stairs when I saw Roxane Lovak's nameplate. She was reading a report. Looked up. Eyes dilated for an instant. Stood. Put red fingertips to the desk. White lab smock open at front. Short black skirt. Eyes narrowed when mine returned.

Sorry. Your name?

Errol. Errol Husky.

And?

I came to see a friend. Bob Leffland. Saw your name on the door.

The fish biologist.

Right. Just stopped to say hi.

She looked down for a moment then straight in my eyes.

Thank you.

De nada, Senora. Did you stay up there?

I'd had enough of Custer County. We drove straight back.

Takes getting used to.

I'm not sure I want to.

Did you come back through the Big Lost?

That's Mackay?

Right.

They shot a collared wolf there yesterday.

People have to have something to hate, Roxie. Other than themselves.

First time I used her name. We took a breath. She crossed her arms.

Look. I have a report to finish. But if you want to come back? Say an hour?

I will.

At the top of the stairs a concourse with big windows looked out at the mountains. ICU at the end of the hall. The nurse looked at her chart.

No visitors. I'm sorry.

Can I see it? Could you read it to me?

She drew the folder toward her. Nice bosom. Big sparkler on left hand.

Forty seven years old. Concussion. Fracture of left maxilla. Hairline fracture third cervical vertebra. Compound fracture of third and fourth rib left side. Compound fracture left clavicle.

She pushed the folder aside. Looked up at me.

What do you think?

Much obliged, ma'am.

Life Flight waited like a giant black wasp. Girls jogged along Memorial Boulevard. I climbed the lawn to the Mini Dome. A suite of huge boulders emplaced along the north wall. Calc silicate schist with staurite crystals in the calc zones. Blood garnets like drops of Dragon's blood. Taken from billion year old rock a mile beneath Wallace. The wealth taken to San Francisco and New York. Wallace and Wardner whores you tossed a few greenbacks. Political pimps with their names on buildings in Boise. Butte ruined for a few dollars less. Had to hand it to Brigham. Kept the cash in town. Or East Fork Loon Creek. Looked so pretty. Drew from tilted rock with a cyanide pond. Skull and Cross Bones. Don't Drink the Water. You wondered if there were grant money available. Teach those bear, deer, elk how to read that sign. Roxie was cinching up her smock.

I'm sorry. I need a rain check.

I could help. I've got a degree.

She shrugged. We went down the hall. A gurney rolled out of the Autopsy ward trailing the stink of death. I thought we were going to play with microscopes. The body lay under a white sheet. Roxie tossed me a white smock and gloves. Pulled a plastic cap over her hair. Glanced at me.

You want to button that up. They spurt.

The body under the sheet was a woman. Her grey hair slipped from under it. Tall like my mother. As Roxie reached for the sheet I had the conviction my mother died while I was in the mountains. My heart stopped. Saw my mother's face. Then the sad, gray face of an old woman replaced it. One eye half open. Roxie closed it. Read the report. Boom! Boom! I felt hot but my hands were cold. Cold sweat ran down my neck. Roxie moved in slow motion as she drew the sheet all the way off. The old woman lay with arms flung out palms up. Roxie ran her hands along torso and limbs.

Help me turn her over.

I did. She checked for bed sores. We turned her face up. Roxie took the scalpel from the side table. Laid it at the fourth chakra. Stroked a deep cut all the way to the pubis. Cold flesh parted. I saw the blue grey abdominal sac. With shears she cut through the sternum to complete the Y. Clamped it open. Snipped the pleural sac. The heart lies obliquely in the human body. Roxie's mask covered all but her green eyes. Glanced up at me.

You Ok?

Sure.

You don't look that great.

Valium would be nice.

She turned the heart side to side in her hands. Slit it with the scalpel to see the four chambers. Incised the coronaries. Pressed tip to yellow crust.

It's easy enough to see.

Returned the heart to its placement. Talked into the recorder. Took up the scalpel and slit the abdominal sac. The coiled intestines glistened. The stink spilled into the room. She reeled them to check for lesions. Lifted out the liver. Sectioned the breast. Data banked. Got the chainsaw.

Hold her tight. They jump.

I held the woman's naked shoulders. The chain saw buried its teeth across her forehead. Steam and smoking bone. The scream of the saw. Strong woman. Swung the cut past both ears.

Turn her over.

She completed the girdling of the skull. The chainsaw smoked with burned bone, shreds of flesh and hair. She tapped at the seam with a chisel and hammer. Pried back the skull to reveal the brain. The woman had a sad, resigned expression. The air conditioning hummed. Blew hard against my forehead. I sat down against the wall. Roxie looked at me.

You alright?

I gave her my best smile.

I thought we were going to play doctor.

She laughed. Snorted when she laughed. That made her laugh harder. Put her forearm across her eyes to stop but when she peeked at me started again. Her laugh went high and sweet as if she were crying.

You've got to get out of here! They don't like it when--

You're ruining my makeup!

I did. Descended to the old neighborhood. Lay back against a fence under the trees. It was Professor Lind's house. He taught that Indians husbanded wild plants. The service berry orchards of Gibson Jack. Peyote in the Pahsimeroi. Bamboo in a spring by City of Rocks. The fence gate opened next door. A terrier bent the corner. Ran at me with claws scraping pavement.

Come back, Ricky! He's not there!

Ricky kept coming.

He's not there, Ricky! They took him to the hospital for observation. He'll be there at least three days.

Ricky looked at the hospital. Then the dark window of Lind's house. Dropped his head. Returned to his mistress. I went back to the lab. Roxie set the microtome. Gave me a smile.

Thanks for the help.

Right.

No. It's hard the first time.

She scribbled her number on a sheet.

Call me.

When?

Sometime.

Tonight?

Not tonight.

I thought you said, Sometime.

Sometime is not anytime, Darling.

I'd heard Roxie was faithful within time zones. Might have been overstating. Keep that in mind, Errol. Her beautiful face. Breasts uncovered. Scalpels in both hands. Something like that. Smoke billowed on the ridge. It was hot. I thought about Snorkel Bob. Hoped he was up on the Madison. Wind flickering the trees. Dreams were usually bad when you were hurt but it was something to hope for.

FORTY THREE

Mickey Angel had floor lamps turned off. A slim guy in khakis and work boots talked to him.

Dark in here, Mickey Angel.

Trying to keep the heat down. Errol? This is Clay.

Clay shook my hand. Had a BLM patch on his shoulder.

Clay's the new range specialist for the South Desert.

Congratulations.

I told him, Just a job, Clay. Keep your mouth shut. Your heart closed. He's not listening.

Clay twitched.

Kind of hard to watch professional range managers take it up the ass out here.

I winced.

How long you been on shift?

Two months. Says in the contract you get fifty percent of the grass on an allotment. Sign on the dotted line. Most places I've been it's eighty to ninety if not a hundred.

Rent don't buy.

I got other news for you boys. FTC is packing up. Deep Creek Mine they wanted so bad? We Ok'd the permit and they just walked.

Oh no.

Big market for electricity contracts. The Ronny Raygun legacy. A company called Enron has driven up the price. FTC has contracts for ten years. Going to take the cash.

What's Smoky going to do?

Oh there'll be enough hurt to go around. Be seeing you boys.

Keep your chin up.

Clay nodded. Put on his cap and left. Handsome guy but had the look of a buck on the run. Cover burned off. Bubbleheads with automatic rifles. Or the guy whose wife is fucking his boss. Take your pick.

Guess they didn't tell him a few things when he signed on.

No.

Think it's true about FTC?

Not a good company. Had twenty years to put scrubbers on those stacks.

FTC separated phosphorus with electric arcs between graphite rods sixteen inches thick. Smoky ran a bulldozer on the slag heap. At night it smoked. I turned spinner racks.

Thought I'd let you know. Might be seeing Roxie.

His head fell.

Don't say that, Errol!

It was a little melodramatic. I looked at Ansel's photo of Angel Falls with the manzanita bush in blossom.

Laugh! He said bitterly.

It was a miracle how Ansel did it. How when you looked at the photo you heard the falls.

I said, I knew a photographer that worked with Ansel.

Listen to me, Errol!

You know the one? The Mission Church with white crosses in the foreground?

He said, Moonrise, Hernandez, New Mexico.

Right. I looked at it for years! Never wondered why with the moon behind the Church the crosses lit up. He said Ansel used a styptic pencil and solvent on the negative. Made the graveyard glow! How it is, Mickey Angel. You never see anything until somebody tells you. Got that card?

I should.

I said, Think digital will replace the dark room?

He looked sullen.

Digital gives you high contrast. But analog gets you information at the molecular level.

That's how he did it, Mickey Angel. Where Ansel was hanging out. Thank you.

He tossed the bills on his grandfather's desk. Looped his arm over the back of the chair. Looked out the window.

I said, Thank you.

He said, Don't take this wrong, Errol. You're a stand up guy. But the feeling I get? Things turn you just walk!

I did. Into the heat. The sun blazed on the window of Scott's Sports. Swirling like it was painted. Analog all the way. I went the back way into the loft. Drove Barton Road. Gate open so I kept going. Parked by an ISU van. Climbed with Kyrie on the glove. Men stood at a road cut. The tall one stooped. Rock pick in hand.

That you, Errol?

How you doing, Zach.

He grinned.

Didn't know Huns were in season.

Will be. What you up to?

These boys came all the way from Australia to find zircon. It's in the greenstone around here.

What do you do with zircon?

They're working on a theory the earth formed in the first million years after the dust commenced spinning. Zircon is the marker. I don't have the math myself.

The Australian said, You need deep rock. Zircon is the marker because uranium will take the place of zirconium in the metallic order. When the rock crystallizes the clock starts to tick. Zircon is a silicate isocahedron. Virtually indestructible.

How do you read it?

Zap it with an ion microprobe. That liberates the lead. The ratio of lead to uranium gives you the date it crystallized.

The greenstone here is six hundred million years old. Zach taught me that.

Greenstone comes from deep. Five billion year old cores of Archaeon zircon could be emplaced in it. If you found one? You'd see the outside melted at six hundred million.

What are you hoping to learn?

The age of the earth. How long it took to form.

That all?

Showalter said, Aussie's are used to thinking in terms of deep time. They have the oldest rocks on earth down there.

He swept his hand toward the Gunsight.

The greenstone erupted over there. Flowed this way. It's sitting on top because the Overthrust Sequence turned Chink's Peak upside down. Haven't found any though.

We stood at the edge. Volcanoes out on the Plain just babes in the river of time. The Wolf Jaw Mountains floated.

You taking them north?

Don't have time.

The Aussie's looked that way.

How far is it?

Eighty miles to the mountains. Call them Lost River. Another hundred to the Salmon. But it's a fast road.

We fly out tomorrow.

Cancel.

Zach ambled up to a road cut. I watched him trace the strata with his hand. It was too bad they didn't go north. Might calibrate the earth but wouldn't see the Sawtooths. I crossed an ancient stream terrace. Climbed the ravine. A hut of quartzite boulders stood beside an old mine. A big-toothed maple twisted between charred roof beams. I sat on the stoop. The ravine plunged toward I-84. Cars like multicolored beetles. I spritzed Kyrie's face. She hitched her shoulders to make herself available. Heard Huns on the hillside but this wasn't the day. The story was true. If anybody asked what the mountain was called the old guys said, That's the Chink's Peak.

I got a six pack of Bridgeport as a peace offering. A girl wearing shorts and a bra was talking to Mickey Angel. Had one leg on the arm of the chair so you could see the down of her inner thigh. When she leaned forward to shake my hand her breasts pooled. A lot of suspense there. Gave me a sly smile. I handed Mickey Angel a beer. Glanced at the girl. He shook his head. She frowned petulantly.

How old are you, Chantelle?

Nineteen.

That's a good age.

She's a dancer.

Chantelle smiled.

Most girls are taught to think of their body as a temple. Mine is an amusement park.

It gave you a flutter. I went on the roof. Set the trap. Smelled smoke. Fire season. When I came back Chantelle had gone. Too bad. Not many girls undressed like that in Pocatello.

She likes you, Mickey Angel.

She does.

He walked along the wall the beer in hand pushing back books. This was work to him. He took pleasure in it.

Trains move the books off the shelves.

Good thing you're on top of it.

The door frame rattled. Freight on the Main Line.

Chantelle's a pretty girl.

She is.

And of age.

He sat down. Put his feet up. Twirled the beer bottle.

Might be a reason she likes older men, Errol. You thought about that?

You're a good looking guy, Mickey Angel.

Might not be a reason you want to think about.

Right.

I swung my boots onto Jane Austen's shelf. Ed Abbey's higher. Desert Solitaire. Down The River. Ed Abbey playing his flute.

Ran into Showalter up on Chink's. Had a couple of Aussies with him looking for zircon. I heard they want to change the name to China Peak. What do you think?

I was against it. Then a Japanese American kid came in. Asked if there were a run near ISU. I said, Sure. And even as I told him I knew I could have thought of somewhere else.

Those Chinamen were tough though. Hauling water up that mountain.

Had mules. Got water from springs on the other side.

Still.

I was thinking about how land raised. Streams went elsewhere. Leonard rushed in.

You have sympathy cards don't you, Michael? I'm sorry I'm in a rush. The funeral for Constantine Papalos is tomorrow.

Were you friends?

No. He was a benefactor of the Church.

Card racks squeaked. I read the label on the bottle. A generous blend of Amarillo hops with hint of apple. 7.5 %.

What have you heard, Leonard?

Only that it was someone who used the pistol quite well. The heirs are not happy. The possibility of a long investigation. It's very hard to marry into Greek money.

The funeral is tomorrow?

Yes. You wait four days. The Orthodox believe the soul remains in the vicinity for that time in order to visit loved ones.

Or enemies.

If that is the case. Yes. This will do. This will do nicely.

He counted coins out of a leather change purse.

It was very professional. Very professional indeed. The nephew had gone out for the night. No sign of forced entry. Why he opened the door is the mystery.

You don't give Pocatello's Finest much of a chance?

No motive.

A lot of people at ISU had one.

That happened long before I came to Pocatello. Those people are gone. That's the way it is at the University.

He turned to go. Put his hand to his heart.

Oh My God!

What, Leonard?

Who's that man across the street?

We got up. Peered out the window. A tall elderly man passed the Round Up Room.

That's Carl Wagner. On his way to check his investments.

Thank God! I thought it was Constantine Papalos. Gave me quite a start!

Mickey Angel laughed. Eyes shut, dimples slotting his cheeks. Leonard peered out the window.

You're right. It's not him.

You two must have been quite close.

I meet a lot of people, Michael.

Mickey Angel and I discussed how difficult it was being Leonard. To know thirty languages. The façade you developed for when railroaders told you they wanted to learn Greek. Wagner poked his head in.

What's this on the sidewalk?

We went out. The pink, naked body of a baby pigeon lay on the sidewalk. I looked at the cornice from which it had wandered.

Squab, Carl.

That's squab?

You got it.

He followed us inside. Picked up a book with big, gnarled hands that had dealt a lot of losing cards. Wasn't the cards that were bad though. Was the way they were played.

Had a girlfriend in Vegas that turned green at the gills whenever she saw squab on the menu.

What did she do?

Anything she could get her hands on.

What did she do, Carl.

She was a dancer. Big brown eyes. Beautiful but crazy.

That's redundant, Carl.

No. She was really crazy. Worked in the kitchen at Drovny when she was little. Cooked a lot of squab there.

Where's Drovny?

It was in Poland but it's gone now. In 1945 it was a concentration camp. When I took her to the Tropicana or wherever I just hoped squab wasn't on the menu. Called ahead.

How did she survive?

It's quite a story really. Her father was a violinist. Could really play. When the SS found out they got him a violin. He played for their parties. That's how she got a job in the kitchen. He was indispensable. Winters were long in Poland even for the SS. The other prisoners hated them. He had no choice. He had brought her into the world.

Did you meet him?

No. The summer of 45 she heard officers shouting. The Russians were over the next hill. She hid in the oven. Just like in the Fairy Tale.

Mickey Angel's looked ill. His jaw tensed. Wagner opened his book. History of Firearms.

She was in the chorus line at the Desert Inn when I met her.

You didn't stay together?

No. It's hard for some people to come to terms with the fact there will always be people who want to kill you. Maybe she had Survivor's Guilt. I don't know. I just know when she got a couple of drinks in her and whatever pharmaceutical she could get her hands on you had to pay attention. That a horse coming down the street?

Skate board.

Wagner's smile was a mask.

You've heard the proverb? When you've known Hell Paradise is not enough?

He got slowly to his feet.

I've heard sound waves made on this earth travel forever

through space. If that's true the music of that violin floating over
the snow of a Christmas night in Poland is still out there. If you
went to the right place you could hear it. What it sounded like.

FORTY FOUR

Birds sang on Gibson Jack. Chickadee in the Doug Fir. Goldfinch
and towhee in the chokecherries. On Gibson Jack Ridge curl leaf
mahogany lit up. The cottony inflorescence became hook shaped
pods the wind nailed to the rock. I hiked a draw along a brook that
descended through cow parsnip with white parasols. Fed on
thimble and service berry. The path entered Doug Fir.
    Gobble-Gobble-Gobble!
    I searched the tree tops. Saw ravens at intervals.
    Honk! Honk!
    Heard the rolling drill of a woodpecker. Then whiffle of
broad wings. Saw the goshawk fly to his nest. Just big birds in the
Doug Fir. I climbed to the ridge. Saw Bannock Peak across the
valley. Remembered Sun Dance. Two old overweight squaws
danced in the heat in their buckskin bodices and long skirts. One
went down. A shadow passed over. Vulture sailed. Skimmed the
Doug fir below without a flap. Others sailed at different heights
joined to the same vortex. I ate an apple. Watched with head bent
back.
    Fox asked Vulture why he looked for dead on the ridge
when there was so much available on the roads! Vulture sailed on.
    Wind is better here.
    Ravens left the Doug Fir to harass the vulture. Had to flap
to keep up. The vulture imperturbable. Kept sailing. Raven gave it
up. But for general flying there was nothing like a raven. Winter
day. Snow banners fluttering from Scout. I skied blind. Just the
howling of wind and creaking of aspen. My forehead froze. Feared
for my penis. But when I crossed the creek would be in Doug Fir.
Did. Across it snow swirled like rapids. I heard a crazy cackling.
Jock skiers? No. Three ravens coming up low into the wind. Not
flying hard. Just slipping into vortex clusters. In a moment they
were out of sight.

Now as I descended they talked. Glided with wings spread.
Gobble-Gobble-Gobble!

I guessed they had fledglings. When I descended far enough
they stopped talking about me. In town it was a hundred degrees.
Sun banged. Heat waves shimmered. Building shadows invited.
Tank Top Timmy swayed at the bar. Red suspenders. Big, floppy
bear slippers with big brown eyes. Toothy mouths that flopped
open when he walked. He put his arm out.

What? No big hello?

Long shift, Tim?

Very. Buy you a beer. Buy you two beers. Buy you dinner.
Barkeep!

Max drew the beer. Nodded as he slid it across the bar top.
Tim tossed a five onto a pile of bills.

They need to send him to Happy School.

Happy School?

It's where they send you when they want you to be happy.
Like last year. Joey and I are working on a guy across the street.
Wasn't breathing. Joey having a hard time getting the tube in. A
drunk leaned over his shoulder.

That's my buddy, dude! Get your act together!

Joey scooped a pool of vomit and tossed it in his face. We
had to send him to Happy School.

He clapped me on the shoulder.

Thought you'd be gone by now!

Never leave Idaho in the summer, Timmy. You know that.
One of the Rules. Like, Leave a message on a girl's machine you
don't know that well.

Buy a used car after dark.

Right. What are others?

We could think of more if we had another round.

We did but couldn't. I downed the coaster. Should of
ordered a bottle because it slowed me down. I needed to slow
down.

So anything new and exciting?

I just thought of another. Ask a girl if she's pregnant.

Take that to the bank.

I got off a good one the other night. We got a call from Fort

Hall at four in the morning. Moon going down. Something about the moon at Fort Hall. A guy put a shotgun to his head but didn't figure the flash and bang. Papered the cottonwood overhead with his face. I loaded the needle double gauge. Nick the pilot wandered over.

Go back to your machine, Nick.

What?

Turn around and go back to your machine. Right now.

He did. Intubation was easy. The guy's trachea wasn't hard to find if you know what I mean. When we got back to Portneuf Regional Nick came over for that look he wanted so bad. Got it. Looked at the sky and keeled over.

Wouldn't of been good at Fort Hall.

No.

Tim drained his glass.

The big guys were waiting. Thorson. Bennett. Top drawer with sphincters to match. They took one look and just froze. You got to understand. All frames of reference in terms of treatment were gone.

He gave me his clownish grin.

So I said to them, Guess he couldn't face another day!

Jesus, Tim!

It woke them up. They went to work.

You always the hero?

Works out that way sometimes.

You honed that line all the way to Pocatello.

I did. But you got to understand, Errol. The reason I told you that story? The outcome has no meaning. None at all. You did your job. That's all. When you lay your ass down at night that's what you think about.

He hitched his thumbs into his suspenders. Wandered to the rest room. Stopped to boo-ga-loo with a blonde. She laughed at him. He vanished into the crowd. Ike watched the cooking channel.

Mind if I change the channel, Ike? There's a game on.

You do and I'll break your arm.

Just kidding, Ike. How's the work going?

It's done.

You get along with the dogs?

Those dogs, man. Everywhere I went there were dogs growling.

Maybe if you took them a treat.

Nobody feeds her dogs! They eat better than I do. Raw chicken breast. Yogurt. Once a week they get a cow knee she pays three bucks a piece for. Don't want to be getting in the way when they hunker down on those. Or when Big Dog decides the bitch has the one he wants.

What's his name?

Galileo.

How'd you get past him?

She has the doors gated. Opens a route. Don't want to be lingering under the deck though.

I heard that!

You did huh?

He turned back to the TV.

He's a big dog, man. He'll take you down.

I went next door for dinner. The Shanghai had red brocade drapes. Juke box from 1942. The waitress's warpaint and tunic looked made from that brocade. Scowled.

No check! No card! Cash only!

I sat at a lacquered wooden table with red cloth napkins. Nobody else around. It was quiet except for pans banging in the kitchen. Cook and waitress argued. Old story. Ike and the dogs. Funny they didn't like him.

I walked under the tracks. Turned down Main. The sun gilded the flanks of the Volcano. At Scotts people looked at bikes. In the parking lot by the High School kids in baggy pants glided on skate boards. Big kids arrived on little bikes with twelve inch wheels. I didn't know why they had them but now I did. They jumped them onto the low concrete wall and spun on the back wheel. Flew off. Landed with legs folded as shock absorbers. Skate boarders glided. Wheels chattered at the sidewalk seams. Nobody jiving. Just athletes intent on their work. Then I saw her. The Skate Board Queen with her red bandanna and combat boots. Flowed up the sidewalk using her arms and hips as calmly and rhythmically as water flowing. Her body had the muscular sequencing of a snake. Used the slant of the sidewalk to the gutter as energy. Maybe the moon. Pocatello drew them. Had water grade sidewalks and the trains. A freight highballed past the Oasis. Red double stacks slipped past. Clunketa-clunketa! Skate boards clattered. Merlin Lady shrieked. A half naked kid with back muscles like ropes jumped his bike onto the chain across the entrance. Set both wheels and swung. Hollered to his friend. Bikers and skateboarders circled looking for turns. Wheel rims gleamed. Skate Board Queen came around the corner pulled by the moon. It was rising.

I doubled the rope from thumb to elbow. Slung it. The girl at Scott's didn't give me a glance. Talked to a good looking guy with her toe curved around her calf. Skis stacked at the wall. Scalloped telemark skis in name only. Employees Only barred the stairs. The door at the top locked with a spring lever. Slipped easy. Light sifted in windows. Looked like I was in morgue. Sheet covered tables. I drew one back.

Oh my Lord!

James Dean with his pompadour. A red head with her arms around him riding a Vincent Black Lightning. Route 66. The Great American Dream. Chrome bumpers lit when you hit them. Albuquerque. Las Vegas. Pasadena. I dug in my pocket. Had a quarter. Swept the sheet off the next machine. Music of the Spheres. Flash Gordon veered toward the planets. Neptune and Pluto bonus points. Tally panel read 47,000. Lever down at the left corner guarded the Black Hole. Tally zero. The Planets glowed blue, purple, red, green as sweet electricity flowed. Chrome ball dropped. I sent it flying. The Planets piped Pythagorean intervals. I kept it drumming between the bumpers to jazz the tally. Overlay of tones returned dissonantly from the Irrational Universe. Hah! The gnomic music flowed into my hands. Up on the mountain Roxie reclined with her dogs on the couch. Picked up strange polychromatic frequencies! I nudged the frame with my hips to keep the ball in Outer Limits. Tally panel flashed fifty thousand. The ball took a crazy carom. Slipped past the Guardian Flipper.

The Black Hole of Doom!

I searched for a quarter. Had none. No way to jimmy a machine. The Universe ruled by Money. I pulled the plug. The Pinball Machine sighed. Colored lights faded. Went dark.

Trap door led to the roof. I was now surrounded by real

planets. The Moon. Mars above the Gunsight coppery red. Jupiter. Venus like a jewel. Bikes gleamed in the streetlight as they whirled. I made a sling. Tied bowline to chimney. Backed off. Pigeons flew from the cornice. Not like Kyrie's grandmother when I descended Pillar Butte. A fat, naked squab raised its stubby arms. Pecked at my glove. I slipped it into the ziplock. Its sister backed into the corner. The rope cutting into the back of my thighs. I was sweating. Got her zip locked too.

The moon rolled along Chink's Ridge. Lit up Slate Mountain so its quartzite forehead gleamed. I was buzzing. Parked at the trailhead. Hooves padded. Crashed through the brush. The antlered one with his harem. I ascended through the juniper. Smelled Doug fir and buck brush. Cool winds at the ravines. Why hummers nested on the faces. Then was on the ridge among juniper again. They lay prostrate to the wind. Twisted trunks bone white in the moonlight. Climbed toward the Scorpion with her tail down. A red eyed creature hissed. Grandpa Rattlesnake glared at me at eye level. The hissing his rattles. The writhing of scales on rock. Eyes like red carbuncles. Now I heard buzzing all around. And a booming. My heart. Hopped onto a rock. Shadows writhed. Real rattlers with rattles twitched. Felt my heat. My tell tale heart. Fangsters close by buzzed then ceased. Those farther away answered. A ceaseless undulating chorus under the stars. A rattlesnake lovefest. After the hunger of winter, the late cold spring, the gophers and mice spilled their babies. The snakes fed and were happy. Bellies full they gathered to make love. I stepped back into the trail. Fangster nearby ceased buzzing.

Don't look at shadows, Errol.

FORTY FIVE

Smoke shrouded Slate Mountain. I bathed in the creek. Scared up a green head and his mate. Shaved. Slicked my hair. Put on my best shirt. Took Fifth past Mount Moriah Cemetery. American flags flapped at all the car dealers. The twin crosses of the Church of the Assumption gleamed. People packed the pews. The cantor wailed. Slipped in grace notes. The parishioners murmured. Should have listened. Papalos lay with hands crossed in his coffin in front of the Iconostasis. The panel for Saint Veronica swung open. The Priest descended. Answered the cantor's ululation with a bass monotone. Swung the censer with his right hand. Rang the bell with his left. Turned his back. Returned through the Iconostasis to circle the altar. The bells detached me from where I was. Took me to the desert when I flew falcons with bells. The Priest raised his arms and prayed. The panel of Saint Paul swung open. Four boys in satin robes descended. Carried The Lantern, The Sun Disk with the Face of Christ, and The Book. Circled the pews. Returned behind the Iconostasis. The cantor wailed. The Priest's incantation was a low rumble. Begged for our souls. Begged forgiveness lest we be thrown to the Fires of Hell!

Have mercy!

Don't take them there, O Lord!

I scanned the purple haired old women. The young mothers with raven black hair. The old, grey, sparse-haired men with bird's eyes and hooked noses. A man with close cropped grey hair turned and looked at me.

Gerald!

The view became unreal. The incense. The bell. The ululation. Pretty girls with black hair pulled tight whispered to each other. The Priest turned his back. Ascended to the altar. Swept the altar with the censer. Fluttered a satin cloth above it while he chanted. Seraphim smiled down. Had white wings. Swords that carried the venom of God.

Be with us O Lord!

Have Mercy on our souls!

It was getting hot. Heavy doors closed against the traffic. Women fanned. Babies started to cry. The cantor raised his voice with renewed supplication. The Priest's drone like the implacable and inconsolable river.

We have sinned O Lord!

The congregation stood.

Yes. Forgive us O Lord. Through you we will have eternal life.

Because You came down and allowed your body to be broken!

For this our sins are washed away.

Forgive them, Lord! Forgive them! Forgive them!

The altar boys took the sacred furniture behind the Iconostasis. The congregation took their seats. The priest glanced at the coffin. Enumerated the good works of Constantine Papalos. Gerald, head bowed in grief, wore white silk shirt. The jacket folded at his wrist. I looked at the stained glass windows. Green trees. Golden fields of barley. The women fanned themselves. I remembered the bullfight at Guanajuato. The matador slim like a lily with the cape at his side. As he turned the bull imprinted it with his horn. Afterwards I accompanied the old priest to a sidewalk café.

His command was perfect, Ludo.

Ludo sipped his beer. Admired the scrollwork of the Church of Maria Infanta. As a young priest he had been tortured by the Germans. When the Russians arrived they did too.

The Veronica was finely done. But did you notice his thighs trembled at the Adorno? Out a little late with the ladies perhaps.

Why do they call it the Veronica?

Your religious education is rather shallow, Errol.

It is.

Christ was in the street with the Cross on His back. Veronica reached out to cool his face with a handkerchief. Of course the Image remained on it.

Ludo raised his glass to two pretty Guanajuata in white on their way to Mass. Iron bells gonged in the stone streets built with whips.

They say things do not become real to a Spaniard until he sees it bleed. Women. Bulls. Men. The bull is Christ. We are the bull.

But the bull doesn't know what's coming, Ludo.

Ludo raised his eyes to the stone minarets.

Do you think, Errol?

The Priest raised his caped arms.

Have mercy on him O Lord!

The congregation rose.

Because he believed in You he will be saved from the Fires of Hell!

He will be in a place of Light where there is neither suffering or pain.

Because of Your Mercy O Lord! Because You died for us!

He will live in Your Grace forever and ever beyond Time.

Intercede for him, Blessed Mary! Have mercy on him! Forgive his sins! Forgive him! Amen!

Constantine Papalos could be admitted into that Place of Light beyond all Time. Because of the forgiveness of Christ and the Blood He shed. The altar boys descended with the Book, the Lantern, and the Gold Disk. Passed the illuminated windows as the congregation turned to them. Gerald crossed himself. The angels returned to the Iconostasis. The Priest held communion. The congregation returned to their seats. People went up. Received blessing. A violet haired woman turned to me.

You too! Go! Have bread with us!

Thank you. But no.

You can! It's not consecrated!

I turned to look for Gerald. In the moment the woman spoke to me he was gone.

FORTY SIX

Stan the Handyman leaned against the counter with his mug of coffee. An old Chinese woman knitted as she waited for her husband.

How is your garden, Stan?

The tomatoes and onions have done alright. But the lettuce never came up. Got maybe ten percent of what I planted.

Why is that?

Squirrels were watching. Got to it as soon as I went inside.

Or waited 'til dark?

Owls discourage that behavior. No. They sit in the trees and watch me lay out lettuce seed for them. Somebody told me you could keep them out with moth balls. So this year I did. I think those squirrels were out there playing bocci ball!

Hah!

The picture of squirrels rolling moth balls down the rows

was funny.

I said, They've been here a long time. Native to North America. Got their game down.

Stan shook his head.

I guess.

Fox squirrels were everywhere now. Guide books from the Fifties showed none west of the Mississippi. When they fanned out they plugged nesting holes. It wasn't personal. It was Business. They were tough, relentless and cowardly. I watched a starling back one off a telephone pole. When he hit ground I thought he'd make a stand. Glanced at me as he ran.

What do you expect? I'm a squirrel!

In the mix for survival the lack of moral courage was essential. I curled twenty pound weight behind my neck. Watched the Iraq Report. A reporter gushed about the progress of the war. Had his camouflage hat and jacket. Was embedded. I thought how rare moral courage was. How deadly it was to have. The women of Munich snarling at Jewish mothers with babies in their arms! Mickey Angel said there was a big fire on Indian land. Would I mind tending the till?

You got it, Mickey Angel.

I put my feet up. Opened the Bounty by Caroline Alexander. A pretty girl in black Lycra slipped past. Purple sash around her hips. Spinner racks squeaked. When she came up to pay I noticed beads of sweat on her forehead.

How are you, Ma'am?

Pretty good today.

You've been sick?

I have Parkinson's.

Oh no! You're too young to have Parkinson's.

The doctor's told me I have a virulent and advanced form.

You seem to be managing it.

She shifted dancer-like. With her slight physique and palsy was dignified.

They told me there was no cure. The drugs they prescribed would only moderate the symptoms. I would get progressively worse until I was in a wheelchair.

I wouldn't have known you had Parkinson's.

She tilted her head back with her hand on her hip.

I didn't mind the death sentence. But the humiliation would be more than I could bear.

She turned her head. Looked out the window.

I searched for someone to help me. Heard about a Ninja sect in Pennsylvania that were into advanced healing. They didn't have a phone so I just went there. Took a bus. Walked for miles through the hills. It was November so I could see cabins through the trees. I just walked up to the door.

Were they Japanese?

They were monks. They shaved their heads and dressed in black robes. There were no chairs. The rooms had wooden floors. You slept on bamboo mats. The mornings were spent in meditation and in the afternoon we worked in the garden. In most cases they said they would have had to turn me away. But because I was an actress they thought I had a chance.

Why?

In acting you suspend your ego in order to enter the character. Like Blanche in Streetcar Named Desire? How does one enter the soul of someone so overtaken by delusion?

Meditation.

She beamed at me.

So they took me in. Fed me. Gave me baths and massages. Taught me rituals that would promote the regeneration of my body.

Like what?

The Sword Passage. At sunset a sword wrapped in velvet was laid at my feet. A candle on a gold candlestick was lit. The sword was four hundred years old. It had killed many warriors and bore the spirit of the Samurai who wielded it. For three days I fasted. Drunk only bitter teas. They warned me not to sleep. To use all my powers to draw the flame through the sword and into my body. Sometime in the early morning I saw the flame flow into the sword! When I touched the handle it was like a hundred thousand volts! The pain so exquisite! I held as long as I could and then I passed out.

How many times did you do that?

Thrice. The sword was brought at the new moon. I did the Sword Passage for a fortnight. I was using the spirit of the Samurai to rearrange the molecules of my body. Little by little I got stronger. With the waning moon they cared for me. And then in the late spring they told me I had to go. There was nothing more they could do for me. How I cried! I loved them so much!

You look wonderful.

Thank you.

She paid for the cards. Slipped out the door. The trees in the breezeway by Bernardo's whipped back and forth.

> Up rose Odin the ancient Goth
> And he on Sleipnir the saddle laid.
> Rode he to misty Hel.
> Met a whelp who came from Hel.
> That one so bloody about the chest.
> At the Father of Charms barked he long.
> Forth rode Odin. The Earthway roared
> Til he came to the high house of Hel.

Wildfires ran in the hills. A frail old man came in leaning on a cane. Wheezed.

Got any westerns?

I showed him. Pulled a chair over. Saw the gold braid on his cap. World War II.

So what planes are they flying at those fires. They got an old bomber don't they?

You bet. Martin Marauder. Sitting at the airport if you want to look at it.

World War II?

Yes sir. Two radial engines with 2600 horses. Ironing boards for wings. One a day in Tampa Bay.

He slid his hand palm down then flipped it.

Like that.

You flew?

The old man's hands fluttered as he reached for a book.

Held it firmly in his lap.

Forty six missions.

What did you fly?

P-51.

That was a hot plane.

You had to be strong. They were just bringing them in

when I hit Bristol. Refitted with the Rolls Royce Merlin. Brits had the Spitfire. That was some plane.

How old were you?

Twenty one. Went to the field that morning. Saw the P-51's in echelon. Pretty to look at. Had that updraft cowling. Wing CO standing there. I asked if I could fly one.

Right-O. Take that one there.

I don't need papers?

Laddy? The odds are you'll be dead before the ink is dry.

A pretty nurse stood by smoking a cigarette.

I've been dying to ride one of those since they came in!

The CO shrugged.

Put her in behind you. She can put her legs around the radio. Keep you company.

She did. I couldn't believe the power of that plane! We're at ten thousand right now! Clouds below. I was looking at the panel trying to figure out where everything was when I noticed puffs of smoke around us. Shock waves. Realized at four hundred miles an hour it doesn't take long to cross the English Channel. Banked as flak hit the wing. Hard to see with oil bleeding across the windshield but I made my way back. The nurse chattering away the whole time. We were taxiing down the runway when the engine froze. We did a spin. As I helped her out she smelled the smoke. Saw the ripped underbelly.

My! You do know how to show a girl a good time!

The old man laughed.

Always wondered what my little wife back in Preston would of thought.

I heard take-off was the most dangerous. Worse than having your wife mad at you.

He held his hands in his lap. Head had a sideways palsy.

You took off in darkness. Fog and darkness. Always fog. Took off in formation because it was faster. The guys leaned out with their orange flags. You started rolling. Had a wing tip on each side of you. Bent the throttle. Now you were really moving! Bang a wingtip? Ball of flame.

Immaculate trajectory, I said.

That's what you wanted. Didn't always get it though. There

were wings that lost half their cadets! Had a buddy was an instructor. Was shooting down the runway when the kid froze. He slammed his hand on the throttle. Felt it go soft. Realized when they were airborne he'd crushed the kid's hand.

Must've been hard on you.

Didn't get the shakes 'til I got home. When I was there it was to kill Germans. That's all there was to it.

He looked at me. Wasn't smiling anymore. Death in those eyes. Looked down at his paperback.

But I was a puppy at killing. There was a Pole that really had it. When the Germans broke through the Polish Army collapsed. You seen the pictures. How the Luftwaffe strafed women and children fleeing the Front. The kind of people they were. He stole a car. Headed south. When it ran out of gas stole another. Might have killed for it. I don't know. Crossed Rumania into Turkey. Got on a freighter. Ended up in that Canadian town on the West Coast I forget the name of.

Vancouver.

Right. Rode the rails to RAF Headquarters in Ottawa. They found out right away the man knew how to fly. Gave him a Hellcat. Hellcat had the first radar. He turned into a kind of rogue. Flew all night looking for German convoys.

How long could he fly?

Hellcat had fuel for a thousand miles at two hundred miles an hour. I think he used it sparingly. The panel had a red light that flashed when you dropped below a hundred feet. He was a red light dancer. When he picked up a convoy cut the engine. Glided in. Brought the news with his six Fifties.

Six Fifties?

Fifty caliber Browning Machine Gun. Hellcat had six. You got the slugs right there.

He pointed at a box of slugs Mickey Angel used for a bookend.

Didn't want to get hit by one of those. Went through quarter inch steel plate.

Stepan! You're going to kill yourself flying that way!

He'd grin.

But if you want to kill Germans it's the very best way!

And it was. With the blind of the hill they never knew he was there. Where'd you pick up the Fifties?

Out on the Lava Flows.

By American Falls?

Right.

They trained P-47s out there. And B-17s. There's a B-17 at the bottom of the Reservoir. Search and Rescue see it from time to time. Ghost plane.

Did Enola Gay ever land there? I heard it was in play in the event Wendover was socked in.

I never heard that. 'Course they wouldn't tell you. Why they built the runway so long. Those bombs were heavy. Good for a Marauder. Need a long runway. I'll take these.

He paid. His hands shaking. Shook as he went out the door. The cane shaking.

> A skilled warrior is at the helm
> A fine chariot warrior
> A wild hawk hurrying his horses southward.
> Surely it is Cuchulain's
> Chariot horses coming.
> Who says he's not coming to our defeat?
> I had a dream last year
> Whoever at the appointed time
> Opposed the Hound on the slope
> Let him beware.
> The Hound of Emain Macha
> In all his different shapes.
> The Hound of plunder and of battle
> I hear him and he hears.

FORTY SEVEN

Guttural rumble of twin prop rattled the rooftops. Had a high muzzle and tail fin. Flashed as it droned through the sky. Wind hurried the flames over the hills. Juniper ignited in balls of flame. Mickey Angel wandered in. I slipped the book on the shelf.

Where's the fire?

Working its way up the ridge. Burned a lot of nice juniper.

That'll make the ranchers happy.

He pulled a beer out of the pack. Handed it to me.

To the Wildland Boys.

Amen.

Hotter than a rattlesnake's bung hole out there.

Hotter than two field mice humping in a wool sock. Where'd you go?

Bannock Creek. Interesting how it would shoot out then work its way back.

Lost a couple of guys in the Owhyee that way. Waiting around in a water truck.

Ninja girl posed in front of the Round Up Room.

You know her?

He turned.

Elizabeth? Nice gal. Like to have the medication she's on.

Hard trade for Parkinson's.

What are you talking about, Errol? She's a little young for Parkinson's don't you think?

That's what she told me.

No. Just went around the bend. They thought they'd get her back but didn't.

What happened?

She fell for a guy in the theatre department. Then left for San Francisco. Big repertory company she said. Came back. The cops got a call from the airport at four in the morning. She was riding down the runways with the pedal to the metal. Was receiving messages from Polaris. Would be able to access another universe at that trajectory.

It's aimed there.

It is.

Pretty old message though.

Not at the wave length she was receiving it. Hand me another would you, Errol?

The paper cranes danced because the fan was going full blast. Misko tossed his cigarette. Threw back his shoulders. Bright red t-shirt with Che's face stenciled. Misko always let you know he was in the vicinity.

What a pair to draw to!

What's up, Misko.

Back from the Green. You'd of liked it, Bird Man. We were coming through the cliffs when a falcon dive bombed us. Screaming like a Banshee.

Peregrine or prairie?

You tell me.

Peregrines have gun metal shoulders.

I can't tell you, Bird Man. He was moving too fast. Had to hand it to him though. Twelve ounce bird challenging a ten thousand ton freight.

Where was it?

He got the Wyoming Gazetteer. Tracked the route with his big paw. Took the old recliner.

Next time we go out I'll give you a call.

I'd be obliged.

Mickey Angel looked away from me.

What plane they using?

Widowmaker. B-26.

Why they call it that?

The Baltimore Whore. No visible means of support. Ironing boards for wings. Big. Fast. Hard to handle.

Why the short wings?

Misko looked at him like was an idiot.

No drag, I said.

Misko pointed his finger at me. Snapped the thumb.

No lift. No drag. No errors. Nothing the Germans had could touch them. The Pacific was too big though.

That's what's up there?

You can hear a Marauder for miles. Eighteen pistons on a wing. Let's go. Bird Man can watch the store.

Mickey Angel shook his head.

I already been.

I nodded at the door.

You drive. I'll buy.

You're on, Bird Man.

We rolled down Main. Got a twelve pack at Midley's. Took City Creek Road to the ridge. The wind hot and hard. We leaned against the hood. Saw the blackened ridges where the fire had been. The tall flames where it was now. Whirlwinds of smoke billowed into the sky. Trucks with flashing yellow lights made a stand on Elk Meadows Road. Misko raised his beer.

Here comes one now.

The Marauder flashed in the sun as it came up the valley. The throaty drone, the whap-whap of prop turbulence hammering steel plate.

Blowing pretty hard for that plane. He's going to have to watch it.

You been in a fire, Misko?

Glacier Wall. 1977.

You were in school?

Played linebacker until my knee went out. Coach had a bar. Let us work off our tab. Owed him so much I got a second job. Found out firefighting wasn't my forte. You heard about Glacier Wall? Started the same night as the Sundance. Burned upwards toward Going To The Sun Highway. Got a nice updraft going. The crew standing on the Highway saw hundred foot fir trees torn up by the roots whirling like matchsticks!

The B-26 passed. A silver trout slipping over the blackened uplands.

Watch him. With that tailwind? When he banks across the ridge to come back? That's where the Dragon is. He'll make a big high bank.

He did. Beautifully and ponderously the plane did a wing over high above the ridge. Came back low and into the wind over the fire front. Orange sheets of retardant spilled from its belly. Pistons roared. Turned snout up and ascended. Misko pumped a fist. Opened another beer.

Nothing better than watching somebody else fight a fire. He treated the lee of the ridge with a certain respect, didn't he?

Once was enough for you?

You got it, Bird Man. You're on a mountain you never been on. Don't know where the fire is. Then it's all around you. Had a buddy got in like that. Couldn't see for the smoke but could feel the heat. Called in the chopper. Realized he'd waited too long. The fire too hot and the smoke too thick. He was just endangering the guy's crew. Cancelled the call. Were pulling the shake and bakes over their heads when they heard the Whap! Whap! of the copter. The pilot giving them the thumps up.

Thank God for Vietnam Vets.

Misko finished his beer. Reached for another.

No, Bird Man. Seeing flame broiled Misko on the menu was never high on my list. Too big for the work anyway. You look at those Wildland guys? All little guys like Mickey Angel. Or lean and rangy. How far does this road go?

It turns to ATV on the next ridge.

Wonder how Roxie is holding out.

Where does she live?

Mink Creek.

She might be getting a little ash fall.

Not happy I'll bet. All those animals.

What does she have?

Dogs. Horses. Cats. Parrots. You name it.

Heard she's quite the babe.

Got an ass like a thoroughbred mare.

We could drive there. Make sure she's Ok.

We could.

My feet crumpled beer cans. As we drove atop the ridge saw the Reservoir to the north like a shining sword. Misko was quiet. I didn't like big guys to be quiet.

So where're the Miskos from?

Jewish woodcutters. My mother was Irish. Learys from Galway. Said we were descended from kings. Every Irishman will tell you that. Know why Irish mothers think their boy is Christ? Doesn't leave home until he's thirty. Likes to hang out with the boys. Thinks his mother is a virgin.

Too bad those Irish kings had so many kids. You wouldn't be parking box cars all night.

Wasn't too many kids, Bird Man! Was too many fucking English!

We descended past the maples of City Creek. Poplars lower down. At Lewis and Main he turned left. Parked.

I said, I thought we were going to see Roxie.

You know the poem, Bird Man. The snow goes so far up

the side of the barn. Goes no farther. The woman that used to get up to give you a kiss at the door? Says Hi from the couch.

I didn't know you knew poetry.

I know a lot of things, Bird Man.

Thanks for the ride, Misko.

A freight high-balled past Lewis. Up on the ridge smoke billowed. Snakes coming down wouldn't make Johanna happy. I remembered driving truck for Blazer Oil. Ranches on the benches. Creeks and roads had the same names. Wouldn't take you to the same place. Finally saw the white gable roof canyoned behind. Heard the rattle when I stepped on the porch. Big one coiled in the corner. Head swaying. Rattle just a blur. I got the shovel out of the truck. Ghost appeared behind the screen door.

What you doing, son?

You got a rattler, sir! Right here on your porch!

The rattler getting angrier. Would charge if he had a mind. Read mine.

Thought I'd take care of him for you.

Don't want to do that, son. She's one of my mousers. Got a couple inside if you want to take a look.

I'll pass, sir. But thank you.

They're better than cats. And don't take sick on you.

Right.

I side stepped down the steps.

I'll be filling the tank now, sir.

Leave the bill on the swing if you want.

I'll do that.

Lot of cover around that oil tank. Old boards. Tumbleweeds. Rusted wheel rims. Just a little too much of lonely.

Black Max pawed at the window. Dad stared at the TV. Roadside bombs in Iraq. You saw troops in desert camouflage walking along a road then Boom! The image turned upside down. You didn't know if it was the concussion or the altered state of the cameraman. Arabs knew how to make bombs. Directional detonations they focused on the target. Mr. Newsman didn't tell you that. Dad leaned forward with hands clenched. Mom took the casserole out of the oven.

Magda taught me to make it! Come to the table, Ben!

The god of war was in his eyes but nothing could deter her pleasure. The casserole bloomed fragrance. Tasted of sour cream and cheese. She gave us hot rolls with tomato preserves spiced with cloves.

This is wonderful, Mama.

She beamed.

It's kafa. Magda taught me to make it. Buckwheat. Mushrooms. Onions. Cream. A little bacon. Magda told me that after the war buckwheat saved Poland. There would have been no children. It would have been a stillborn country.

Stillborn. Years the jet stream dipped. Frigid wind swept down in February. Cows dropped stillborn calves. Still couldn't get the cowmen to allow willows on the creeks.

How do you make it, Mama?

Slow cook the buckwheat in water. Saute the mushrooms and onion in bacon fat. Stir that into the buckwheat and bake. Magda told me the Polish woman baked it in a clay bowl. Poured milk on top. Put it under the bed wrapped in her Grandmother's shawl for when the man came home. You sliced it with a knife. It was all you needed.

And Grandmother's blanket.

Of course!

You had horses growing up didn't you, Mama?

Dad always kept horses. We rode Green Canyon Road to school. But by the time Ben and I came back he was old. The time of horses was gone. But you knew a horse determined the fate of our family?

I did.

No.

You wouldn't be here. None of us would. Dad was working at Raft River when War was declared. Packed saddle bags and rode Hondo all the way to Fort Reno. Down the California Trail and all the way along the Humboldt. Big and raw boned like you. Had that long-barreled Colt 45 Vera got when he died. Curse her! They showed him to the barracks.

Where do I board my horse?

The stable man down the street will give you good money for him.

I can't take my horse?

No.

Then I'm not signing up.

He rode all the way back. Stopped to see Mother at the teaching school at Albion.

My father looked up.

That war was hotter than people know. Forty thousand dead. The Spanish fought like tigers. Knew the terrain.

They bought the trading post at Strevell. Indians would come up the road. The man riding and the women walking. Mother would be cooking. Look out the window and see Indians peering in. Scared the dickens out of her. What they loved was the cast iron stove. When she wasn't looking they'd pick lice out of their hair. Set them on the stove to watch them dance! One day Carlton Pete came down the road without Mary. The wife she liked best.

Where's Mary?

She took sick. We left her down the road a ways.

Dad was in the hills hunting. She couldn't leave the girls. That was the end of the Strevell Trading Post.

Clocks ticked on the walls. The dead looked from the photographs.

I'll do the dishes, Mama.

No. Stay and talk to your father.

Could we have a couple of cigarettes?

She glared at me.

Dad and I watched Chink's Peak turn red in the sunset.

You realize, Dad. If Grandpa had gone to the Philippines we'd of had three generations in the Pacific?

The old man took the cigarette out of his mouth. Tapped the ash into his palm. Looked at it. Put it in his pants pocket.

Billy didn't have to go. I did everything I could.

He looked down the sixteenth fairway. Looked for cranes.

FORTY EIGHT

Dark blue front blocked out the moon. I felt the chill. Wind howled. Firefighters resting on their shake and bakes heard the

rumble. Flashes lit up Deep Creek Range. The rain came. A real
gully washer. The truck rocked. I slept fitfully. Dreamed I was a
ranger again. Rode the White Cloud Ridge. Looked down at the
scree on both sides. In the morning saw the stream had come down
the road. Braided strips of sand from larger rocks. Balanced them
harmonically. The wind was cold. My shoulders and thighs felt hot.
I wanted to howl. Did. At the Meat Market Stan pushed the
sweeper.

    Not a night to be out, Stan.

    No. I remember one August up Palisade Creek. Spent two
hours under an overhang. Lightning banging.

    Splitting rocks?

    You got it. Were hiking in the shadow of the mountain.
Didn't see it coming.

    Tetons got to be the lightning rod of the continent.

    You see a lot of storms at Raft River too. If you drive that
way.

    Cross draw from Salt Lake?

    No. Big systems just pile up there. Talking heavy action.
Station wagon rocking and rolling!

    In my mind I saw the Plain curve its horn up toward the
Great Divide.

    Makes sense.

    I shadow boxed with ten pound weights. Hit the steam
room. When I went outside a freight screeched. Thought it was
Merlin Lady. Was a freight with locked brakes. The brake pads the
bow, the wheels the string. Sound box: hundred ton box car.
Merlin Lady answered. Skreek! Skreek! The Poky High drum
corps beat kettle and snare. Boom! Ka-pow-pow! Boom! A fifteen
year old clarinetist played a jazz line. At Bernardo's the Goths in
black rags and combat boots lounged in the breezeway. I ordered a
latte.

    Use the phone, Bernardo?

    Roxie answered.

    Hello?

    What're you doing?

    Who's this.

    Errol Husky.

Clink of glass instruments.

You really want to know? I'm making a slide of some poor guy's prostate. It's rotten.

Jesus!

You wanted to know.

Make something up next time!

I don't have to tell him. Why I became a pathologist. Don't have to hurt anybody.

Right. Listen, Roxie. I was hoping you'd want to go out with me. See Kyrie fly.

Clink of instruments.

I have to be back by evening.

Easy. I'll be out of town for a couple of days but I'll call when I get back.

Alright. Call me.

The Journal featured a Marauder on the front page. Left hand corner an Indian dancer in full regalia. Like the Arabs and Jews the Shoshones got together at the full moon. Clatter of skate boards at the door. Goth kids came in with greasy trousers rolled up mid calf. Hair standing or hennaed in corns. Happy because the Skate Board Queen with her red bandanna and combat boots accompanied. Lay her board against the wall.

I'm going to take a dump.

That was important information. They laughed. Lounged in the sofas. An old guy with ice blue eyes and leather face tossed the paper down. Wore a wide brim oil cloth hat tied under his chin. I knew him.

You been in the field?

On a pipeline out in Wyoming.

Find anything?

A femur and acetabulum.

That's fantastic. Even if it's from the nineteenth century it's data.

I'm a paleontologist, Errol. The bones are fifty million years old.

Reptile or mammal?

Dinosaurs died out sixty five million years ago.

Not that big a margin. How you know?

Your vertebrate anatomy needs brushing up. Reptile bones are laced with Hamplonian vesicles because they grow so fast. Keep growing. Add vertebrae. A mouse and an elephant have the same number. You got it?

Thank you, Ian. So what brings you to town?

Needed a break. Wyoming gets old. You seen that license plate? That's a warning.

Skate Board Queen flounced into a chair. A goth kid with chain hanging from his pants presented her with a cup of coffee. I went outside. Another kid held the leash of a pit bull with a red bandanna around his neck. Clouds piled up over Michael Angelo's. I got the squab out of the fridge. Kyrie acted like she didn't see me.

Come on, Sweetheart. Eat something.

She hectored. Sent a jet of chalk against the wall. I made her bath. Flicked drops of water at her. She nipped. Stepped into the tray. Flew to the ledge. Finally to the glove. After she fed I loaded the truck. Thunderclouds rang up. Big Southern swung past. I stopped at Pickles in Arco. A guy at the next table talked about the Mackay-Arco game twenty years before.

Coach Lund sat Larry until it was too late. Had a pissing match the day before. But he never liked Larry. And you know Larry. If he didn't like you he told you to your face.

The grey haired couple nodded.

That's how they lost the game. Larry was expecting that scholarship to ISU. Kind of went off track after that.

Clink of coffee cups set down.

Never should of lost that game!

The couple shook their heads. Silence. Heard the story twice a week. South of town the Big Lost channel bone dry. Used to run through town and twenty miles east. Irrigators took it all. Had the whip hand. I thought of the guy back at the café. Passion run out of him like the Big Lost. At the bridge hand painted sign by an abandoned house.

This Is Not The River That Was Our Legacy!

I passed Big Cinder then the road to Fish Creek Reservoir. It clicked. Fish Creek Pass. What the cowboy was talking about. They were killing wolves up there. Picked up maps and phone at Headquarters. Wes was a big guy. Had a picture of three bucks stepping through the snow in front of Fremont Peak. Put his hands behind his head.

Don't give it a thought, Errol. I got thirty years and a G-8 in the bank. You want pulled out of there just give us a call.

I don't foresee it.

It's big lonely in there. Just critters and mosquitoes. And if weather comes in? Hard to negotiate where you are.

I'll be fine.

Very good. Do me a favor though would you? You see too many sheep? Or the fact the Little Lost looks a little ragged? Let it go. I wouldn't ask but he's a big guy around here. Wife does a weekly broadcast for NPR. Plight of the rancher so to speak.

Don't miss a trick do they?

No. But they work with us.

I headed east on Muldoon Road. Crossed the Little Wood. Big sign: Lone Star Security. Aerial Surveillance Twenty Four Hours A Day. Kept the bubbleheads out. At the top of the canyon the twelve thousand footers joined arms. I left the truck at Mormon Hill. Went over the ridge into the Little Lost. For six days never saw a human being. Looked for goshawk. Photographed cheat grass. It established under pines where deer and elk had lain. At night I listened to the Little Wood. Woke scared. Thought a bear was rolling boulders around. It was the Little Wood mumbling over the stones. From time to time saw red eyes. Wes was right. It was lonely out there. The fourth day I slunk along the river. Heard the cry of a wind cat. The goshawk flew. Settled on an overhang. Looked at me. I slipped the pack. Tried to offer him a bite. He raised wings barred cream and gold and flew. I guessed he was lonely too.

Never found his nest. Heard later they sent in a chopper with crew to find it. Didn't. When you left the Pioneers you saw blue mountains at the rim of the desert. The Pocatello Mountains the boundary of the Spanish Possessions. That night the cold arrived. It was only the twentieth of August but the clock had turned. Trees rattled. Crickets chirped a little louder. In a fortnight Swainson's gathered.

FORTY NINE

Pigeon down floated over the faded carpet. Mickey Angel looked up.

How was the shift?

Little more than I needed.

Good deal.

How'd you and Kyrie get along?

He raised his right hand with fore and middle fingers bandaged. Merlin bitch screamed from the tracks. Kyrie answered. Two Indian women came in.

You got any Indian books?

Along that wall.

I showed them. Mickey Angel had a hundred feet of Indian books where the light slanted from the street. Mama had long glossy hair. Wore a cobalt blue velvet tunic with beaded arabesques at the shoulders. You didn't buy those. Kyrie hectored me. Mama turned.

What you got back there?

Falcon.

She don't sound too happy.

No. Taking her out tomorrow though.

The daughter had shining, black eyes. Black shining hair. White blouse with turquoise choker. Tight blue jeans. Appraised me out the corner of her eye. I tucked a book square to the shelf.

Where you from?

Lapwai.

Nez Perce?

I'm Flathead.

She jerked her chin toward her daughter.

Her daddy's Nez Perce.

Mama and daughter looked like they were having a disagreement Pow Wow Time.

Her great, great grandfather was Joseph.

Nice.

Not nice. He was a son of a bitch. When white photographers came by he made his wives get him all prettied up. Wouldn't let them get their pictures taken though. Always ready for a picture himself. Long as they paid him. Never gave nothing to his wives. Kept it for himself.

Princess shrugged.

They hated him. His wives. He was stingy and he beat them. Kept them away from the white historians too. So they couldn't tell stories on him.

She crossed her palm with her index finger. Stones sparkled. Pulled a book out and lay it open. History of the Crow. Interview over. Poor Joseph. Condemned to hear women talk about what a bastard he was. Indians had long memories. Told Liljenblad about seeing the Wapi erupt. I turned away. Wild Bill looked at me with sad eyes. Every mother's son with his blue eyes and long blonde hair. Handle bar mustaches like the pearl grips of his Colt 45's. Didn't smile for nobody no more. I turned to Mickey Angel.

How about a shot in honor of Wild Bill?

Little early for me.

You need a pain killer, Mickey Angel. Catholic or Presbyterian?

I passed the brick buildings hemmed against each other. Terra cotta buckles of the Central Building. Headlines in the newspaper box.

Fires Contained. BLM Spokesman Clint Peterson said, It just burned juniper and sagebrush.

Got a pint of Jameson's. Found shot glasses in the back room.

I was thinking of going to the Pow Wow if you want to ride along. Look at the girls in their finery.

Got to pass. Going on the river with Misko. Got to rest up.

Where you going?

Tilden Bridge to the Rez. I asked Misko what he wanted me to bring. He said. Beer. I said, How about a case of Bud? He said, What are you going to drink?

Take your life jacket.

Don't worry about that.

What does he run?

Old Town eighteen footer.

Big whirlies out there. Don't want to be going into one of those.

It's all gravel bar river out there.

No. Big whirlpools. I saw a twenty foot skiff with an Evinrude go in one. Just went round and round.

How'd they get out?

We slipped to the low side. Tossed them a rope. They'd still be there. I had a friend took a depth finder out there. Holes a hundred twenty feet deep. Big fish too.

I'll be looking at birds.

Makes you wonder though. How long it took the Snake to cut those holes with rocks going round and round.

Not long if you look at it.

Big rocks. Always something to think about when you go on the Snake. You been upstream of Massacre Rocks? Beautiful. Red and black cliffs. Sequential eruptions. And now there's sturgeon.

You think there were before?

I always thought Shoshone Falls was the barrier to anadromous fish. That doesn't mean sturgeon weren't there before.

Mickey Angel cursed. Threw the book down. Went among the bookshelves. I picked up the book he was reading.

> Bulldozer scraping and landfill remove
> The religious aspect of the land.

That was a hard sell. He came back with Rocks, Rails and Trails.

Upper Snake River Uplift. Sixteen million years.

And before that? I asked. Before the big lava flows?

Nobody knows.

Acceripensiformes, I said. Three hundred million years. That old enough? Sturgeon tastes like halibut except better. Indians came down the Coast from north and south to fish the Columbia for sturgeon. That was the real deal. Salmon was for trade and to get through the winter. That's what Idaho had. A billion dollar sturgeon fishery.

Mickey Angel had me refill his shot glass

I read a story off the AP once. A redneck put onto the Sacramento on a Sunday lined for sturgeon. Hooked one. Guys tell me nothing fights like a sturgeon. They're so big and go so deep. It fought. Ran. Fought and ran. He held on 'til his arms were shot.

Knotted line to gunwale. Let it take him. It did. Headed for the sea.

The Big Mama.

Trees along the Sacramento passed. The towns too. Cars went by. The sun fell to the horizon which was where he was going. Went down. The moon came up. Somewhere in the early morning he saw the estuary. The sun went up in the sky. White birds flew from the reeds. It was getting hot. He was out of water. Hangover hitting hard. About five in the afternoon the line went slack. When he pulled her up she was as long as the boat. She pulled a half ton of boat and redneck three hundred miles. He got on the phone. His boss said, You're fired. Then it came out in the papers and he got his job back.

He get the wife, the dog and the truck back too?

Mickey Angel twirled the shot glass.

If she hadn't gotten disoriented in the diversion dams she would have won. Would have taken him under the Golden Gate to the sea. He'd of looked at those rollers coming at him and cut line.

You read it in the paper or talked to a guy that read it?

It doesn't matter, Errol. You know that.

I held the bottle up but he shook his head. Went back to his book. Merlin Lady screeched. I looked at Poky High with its ribs you could climb. Wondered if she wintered. How the fledglings survived when she drove them out. I parked under the maples on Lincoln Street. Dusk came early this side of town. Schindler told me she wasn't a merlin because they didn't like people.

Did you go and look at her?

No.

I thought about Snorkel Bob. It would have been nice to make the run with him through the trap rock of the Snake. Watch the ospreys. The great wheeling undercurrents that would sweep you two hundred yards to the other side before you knew it. I missed Snorkel Bob. We both felt the same way about the world. We felt like the Egyptians that when you died your soul was judged by the animals.

FIFTY

Lincoln Street fell into shadow. Women stood at the front steps calling their kids. Out over the plain the sun glared like a dragon. Combines kicked up pillars of dust. Dust curled up from the dancing grounds. I parked. Heard the drums and wail.

Kee-yee-yee-aiee!

Red tail looked down at me from high voltage wires. Flew to the next pole. Red tails perched among the transformers. Scattered across the field. Indians stood at cooking fires under poplar branch awnings. Mothers fed children. Dancers in full regalia cooked at propane stoves. Loudspeaker blared. Prairie Smoke! A high keening wavered. Drums commenced. People everywhere. Dust rising from their feet. The sun set feather bonnets ablaze. Bloods strutted in white t-shirts, tight levis and boots. Red glare in their eyes. Dancers glided. Young and old with gauntlets flaring with feathers. Sundance bustles of orange and yellow. Beaded breastplates. Eagle claws. Eagle feather dusters. Girls flitted past wearing buckskin dresses shimmering with bangles. The tobacco can bangles chimed with the swing of their hips. Meat smoked on grills under poplar branch arcades. Indian bread sizzled in deep fat fryers. Tacos and chilies handed out. Navaho silversmiths plied their hammers. Leatherworkers turned buckskin with hooked knives. The flute maker played his wooden flute.

Errol!

Willy Jack stood in the shadows between stalls. Waved me over. A gringo with him. Flat leather hat and wispy beard.

You got a drink, Old Man?

I do.

We got mixer at the Coca Cola stand. Returned to the shadows. Watched the pageant. Drums beat. The lines wove in and out in long, wild counter beat loops. Five-four. Seven-five. Fourteen-twelve. Somber with a wild, dark leanness. Willy Jack nudged his friend.

Show him, Newt.

Newton drew a leather pouch from his jacket. Obsidian spearhead glittered the length of his hand. Like the blade the Aztec priest used when he opened the chest of a naked girl atop the

Pyramid of the Sun. In five days, wrote Bernal Diaz, they slaughtered four thousand captives. The blood ran smoking down the steps. Volcanic Son et Lumiere.

That's Clovis.

No shit, Sherlock.

Where'd you find it?

We were digging a water line by City Creek. I looked down. Went, Oh my God!

Is it real?

Real as the world. See that caliche? You can't fake that. It was up on the bench. Mazama ash overlays this whole country. When the Flood dropped the valley floor it got carried it to where I found it. Pocatello, Idaho. 2003 AD.

The water line was by the creek?

No. City Creek is the other side of the playa now.

The spear point gleamed. Had the fluted middle where the shaft fit. Dancers promenaded in their finery. Rivers and blood flowing to this moment.

So it was here before the Flood.

Had to be.

That isn't going to make the anthropologists happy.

Got that right!

You ought to show it to somebody at the Museum. Somebody you trusted.

People I know been run out of town. Ain't going to change anybody's mind anyway.

He was right. It didn't fit dogma. A doctoral student at ISU found shards in the Pahsimeroi he dated at twelve thousand. Published. Letters arrived. The guy was incompetent. If ISU hooded him they'd lose accreditation. So they cut him. Then twenty years later dated shards at Hagerman at thirteen thousand. It was just a career. I turned the spear point in my hand. Saw the bison with eight foot rack they found in the cliffs above American Falls. Latrons latrons. The people camped along the Snake when the Flood arrived. Three hundred foot standing wave at Gunsight. I handed the spearhead back. Drums beat harder. Slim deer women ran toward the arena. Loudspeaker blared. General Tribal! Steep Canyon. Walla Walla, Washington!

Seven drummers at the kettle drum hit the first beat like a clap of thunder. Wailed. Dancers streamed into the arena. Turned counterclockwise. A great wheel of rainbow color. Old men with grey hair coiled in buns wore feather headdresses and Sundance bustles. Crouched, stamped, shook eagle feather dusters. Jingle dancers whirled with arms out. Fancy dancers wearing plumed headdress leapt like sand hill cranes. Lithe limbed soarers. Wings flashed. The old women stepped straight backed. Kept the double beat with back steps. Girls with outstretched arms trailed rainbows. Did cross steps and whirled. The jingle dress shimmered. Dancers swept out of sight then returned. High leapers and rainbow whirlers. Dust snaked upwards. A fancy dancer flew like a solar flare. Hung there an instant then returned to earth hidden amid the swirling flash of color. An old man stalked. Black eyes darted this way and that. Looked me in the eye. Raised the eagle claw. Shook it at me. The wheel kept turning. Two girls came cross stepping in their jingle skirts and beaded, calf-high moccasins. Came a wail. The drum thunder clapped. The girls did an extra cross step or two. Returned to their seats laughing.

I walked Willy Jack and Newt to the parking lot. Came back. Young bloods glared at me. Came to strut and fight. Necked with wild girls in the shadows of the arcades. An old Navaho woman hammered silver chains on her railroad track anvil. I had no one to buy for. Trays glittered with turquoise and silver. Hierarchic woven blankets. Beaded Shoshone hand bags and moccasins beyond compare. Jagged lightning on a hand-polished bowl.

White boy!

I turned.

Suzy wearing a white T shirt, turquoise necklace, tight blue jeans. Arm in arm with an old white haired woman. Oh my Lord. My crotch bloomed. She smirked. Gave me a hug.

Errol. This is my Mom. Porfira.

Porfira wore a purple shawl and levis like her daughter. White hair in a bun. Gave me her hand. Didn't smile. I saw the dim grey of cataracts in her eyes.

It's a pleasure.

She nodded kindly. Knew the pain and humiliation of age

would one day visit me. I turned to Suzy.

Thought you'd be on a fire.

The rains stopped everything. Now I have to think what I want to do.

You could stay here.

She don't like Fort Hall.

Where do you like?

Seattle.

There was a time every kid in Southern Idaho wanted to go to Seattle. Why they didn't say Portland I didn't know. The announcer summoned the jingle dancers. I walked them to the car. Mothers put children to bed under the poplar awnings. The moon lit up the field.

You weren't a dancer, Suzy?

She was always out in the Bottoms. Spearing fish.

Suzy laughed. Took her mother's elbow to guide her among the cars. Glanced back.

Call me.

I don't have your number.

It's Blue Horse. In the phone book. Only listing.

I walked back. A man scolded his kids. Little boys with mullets and pony tails.

You kids behave. Or I'll take you out in the Bottoms and drown you!

They laughed. Tried to kick him in the shins. Drums throbbed. Men around the kettle drum wailed. Out in the arena the girls whirled. Wore red, green, blue and gold capes. Held out their arms like birds of prey. As they high stepped the jingle bangles swayed. They whirled and spun like hundreds of butterflies. The sheet-like jingling of the tins rang with the boom of the drum. When they could dance no longer the lead drummer shouted.

Hunh!

The drummers held their sticks high. Then hit the beat extra hard. The jingle dancers started whirling again. Girls that had faded spun higher. Kept spinning. Beat new tattoos of cross steps across the arena. Capes gilded with silver and gold flashed. A wave of wings and wavelike glitter. Then the drum struck once.

Boom!

It was over. The dancers stood still. Let their heads fall back. Then stood straight again. Walked back with dignity toward the crowd. Everybody cheered. I clapped until my hands were sore. Walked back to the truck. The moon high and white. Slept by the river. Those jingle dancers dancing before my eyes.

FIFTY ONE

Stan Handyman pushed the carpet sweeper.

What's new, Stan.

I see the Gov's gearing up for re-election. Says he'll tell Fish and Game to look the other way if anybody shoots a wolf.

He'll say he was misquoted.

I'd been that road. We blocked a developer that wanted to bury Daniels Creek. A bag man named Goothie introduced a bill to the Legislature. I presented the case. Storm water abatement. Wildlife. Seventeen species of neo tropical birds. The Honorable James Durley stood up.

Creek! Vroom! Creek! Hell! That creek is so puny I can near piss across it!

Speaker banged his gavel.

Representative, you're out of order!

Damn right I'm out of order. If everything was working I could piss clean across it!

He fell over his chair when he sat down. Everybody laughed. Voted the destruction of Daniels Creek into to law 147 to 32.

I took Kyrie out. Heard distant keening. Saw a flight of gulls so high they glittered like a diamond bracelet. Got a bottle at the Grapevine and cow joints at Albertson's. The sun shone a beam over the Gap. The horses escorted the truck. Snorted and pranced. Huge dogs jumped with their paws at the railing and barked. Roxie came out and waved. The dogs put their heads between the railing. Big brown eyes, small velvet ears, black muzzles. Barked so hard their jowls sprayed. Roxie wore a cotton print blouse and shorts. Shushed them. They leaped against the gate with their paws atop it. Socks caught my eye. Jerked her chin back.

Come closer!

Roxie held the gate so I could slip through. Big dog barked at me. Knocked me off balance with his shoulder. His head like an alligator! Bumped me again. Roxie tugged at his leash.

Galileo! Down!

The two bitches jostled. Galileo circled. Looked up menacingly. Roxie had him by the collar so he couldn't stand on his hind legs.

They don't usually act this bad!

Right.

I got the gate locked. Held out the cow bones.

What do you think, Galileo?

He looked confused. His forehead wrinkled. Sat back on his haunches. The bitches sat like good girls. Out of the corner of my eye Roxie looked on. Nodded reluctantly. The knee joint weighed five pounds. Galileo took it in his mouth. Settled right there. The bitches took theirs and disappeared around the corner. Parrots whistled. Big parrots in cages. A long haired cat jumped to the fireplace mantel. Another jumped to the kitchen counter. Licked her paws. Another flew into the bedroom. I heard hoof beats. The horses ran in the pasture with tails flying. I sat on the sofa. Doggy door flapped. Socks came in. Climbed up beside me with her bone. Wedged her butt against me so I couldn't move. Roxie came out of the kitchen with the sandwiches and a bottle of wine.

She likes the pressure.

It's two of my best qualities, Roxanne. I smell interesting and I don't move.

Any others?

I'll eat anything.

I looked at Roxie with her hair tied behind but frizzy. The light gold of hair on her forearms and thighs. Didn't want to see those legs covered up.

You'll want to put on jeans, Darling. We'll be bushwhacking.

She came back wearing levis. Shirt tails tied in front so I could see her tummy. Dogs didn't realize we were going until we were out the gate. Galileo woofed. Crashed against it. Socks cried piteously. Roxie comforted them. Parrots whistled. I took Gunsight

Road to access I-25. Passed the faux two story red blockhouse the trappers called Mosquito Springs where my mother used to go ice skating when it was Merrydell Park. The freeway climbed the corner of the hill past the hotels at Pocatello Creek. Saw the plain flat beyond. Passed the Episcopal Cemetery at Fort Hall where Mary American Horse lay. Wore a white buckskin dress covered with elk teeth and Sundance bead trim. Beaded gauntlets and moccasins. Gringo collectors wept. We crossed the Snake at Tilden Bridge where the old folks tried the crossing. Arrived about now when water was low. Always had a coil in it though. Horses, oxen, people swept away. We drove toward Big Southern Butte. What looked like a strip of land from Pocatello Creek was all around now. Scabs of low ridges. Steel towers like Zuni Gods marched out of the south. A shadow hulked.

　　Golden Eagle.

　　That's a sign!

　　A sign she won't be in the air when we loose Kyrie.

　　I thought falcons were fastest.

　　It's not how fast you fly but how you dive. The eagle comes from much higher. I talked to a hang glider once who was at ten thousand when a golden came down at him. Grabbed the struts and screamed. Those talons can crush a forearm! Let alone the aluminum frame of a glider. A falcon doesn't stand a chance.

　　Do they eat them?

　　I think they do it out of spite. You train a bird for years. When you send her up? No guarantee she'll come back. Anders lost a bird last year that killed herself hitting a sage hen in mid air. In her prime. Five years old.

　　How old is Kyrie?

　　Seven.

　　She thought about that.

　　How many have you lost?

　　Three. Had Jezebel south of Boise. She was ringing up. Big spirals. When I served her she didn't descend. Got the telemeter. Nothing. The sun went down.

　　I crossed my forearms on the wheel. Looked at the desert. Bad form to cry on the first date. Had an advisor my fifth year. Big South Carolinian who'd been with the Big Red One in France.

Wispy grey hair, gentle southern voice. Invited me to lunch. Talked about the coastal rivers of the Carolinas with their great trees. Parrots. Fish. Lumber companies went first. Then developers with front end loaders. Took it all. He began to weep. A large man weeping in a busy upscale restaurant at noon was ludicrous. He saw I was embarrassed. Gave me a look I thought was forlorn but knew now was pity.

You found her?

A few miles away. Her neck twisted back. One wing torn off. Like she'd been broken and thrown away.

I'm sorry.

Falconry is fraught with tragedy. So I let fly. High as she wants.

The bells jingle jangled.

Billy got me those in Pakistan. I was proud of them. Have a music like no other. I heard of a Brit that had a set assayed. They found alloys they had no knowledge of! Can you imagine? The blood that stained them? Or the way a pretty girl wore them at her throat?

Why'd you give them up?

I was flying Greta out on the Bottoms. She saw a dove or maybe a magpie. I stayed all night. Knew I'd find her in the morning. Did. Or what was left of her. She'd slipped into a tree where she thought she was safe. But to a great horned owl those bells chimed like dinner bells.

The desert was gold with yellow topped rabbit brush. Scab ridges appeared. We crossed one then another. Men atop them became cairns. Weeds winnowed in the clefts. I turned up a little valley that still had sagebrush. Turned off the engine. Big Volcano loomed. That was an illusion.

This be the place.

How do you know?

This is the sagebrush they like. Not too tall. Tufts of new growth to eat. They're in here. I can feel it.

We sat in the cab. Looked at the last stand of sagebrush in this neck of the desert anyway.

Dad told me when he came back from the War he went with Grandad south of Twin. Didn't remember where it was. Just drove into the hills. It was like pictures you see of the Serengeti. Grouse rose and covered the sky. Flew from one side of the valley to the other. They could have killed a hundred just with passing shots.

Where'd they go?

Farms. Ranches. Always in need of more land. What they couldn't farm they grazed. Just this year the BLM authorized an increase in AUM's.

Why are you hunting them then?

No justification.

Tell me.

Sure. Was a time you'd see an anvil cloud five miles high. A tiny dart streak down its face. I want to see that again. And maybe? I'm just one of those guys have to get blood on their hands once in awhile. Shut the door softly would you, Darling?

I let the tail gate down. Wind whispered. Engine block ticked.

Stand back a little. She doesn't like being crowded.

Roxie found a rock. I spoke to Kyrie as I loosed the jesses. Her eyes flashed into the light. Raised her shoulders and shivered. Bit at the jesses.

She's beautiful, she said.

She's my sweetheart. Step up, Kyrie.

She did. Ruffled shoulder feathers. Looked around. Her long wings flashed. Roxie stood with excitement in her eyes. Kyrie flew off the glove at her. Roxie stumbled back with her hands up. I got her back on the glove.

She's a little jealous.

Roxie's eyes flashed. They took each other's measure. I walked Kyrie down the road. Came back. Roxie sat on the rock with her chin in her fist. I clipped the transmitter. Checked receiver.

The wind is into us so they can't hear us. You've got a hike ahead. Cut to the left right away. Fade back along the ridge. Keep me in sight. When I see you I'll let her go. When I wave start toward me.

She got up. Dusted her pants.

Think you two might be a little enmeshed?

I looked around. The flows had come out of the north past Big Southern.

It's a possibility. Keep the truck in sight. Easy to get lost out here. You want the glasses?

How do you know she'll come back?

Kyrie nipped at the glove. Hungry for sky.

I don't. But I'll serve her no matter what. She knows that.

Roxie departed through the brush. I leaned against the truck. Nuzzled her nape.

Wouldn't be so bad if you left, Kyrie. I'd get over it. The mind is a decent thing but it passes. Out of the furnace of the galaxies you will return.

Clouds circled. Always did on the Big Desert. High magnetic polarity. Kyrie rolled her shoulders. Looked around. After awhile I saw Roxie on the horizon. I slipped the jesses. Free on the glove Kyrie stretched. Flapped twice then leaned out. Raised her wrists high and flew.

FIFTY TWO

Flew lazily in the wind. Banked. Let it lift her higher. The sun shone through her wings. Swept into the upper sky. Was gone. I waved to Roxie. Purple fleabane and Russian thistle in the road. Tumbleweed purple with hard little flowers. Sagebrush feathery with seed tops. Whispered. The ridge became rock. I saw Roxie's floppy hat. The shadows of her breasts. She walked toward me swinging her arms. The ridge like crusts of black bread. The road went through it. I cut into the sagebrush. She veered toward me. The sage fragrantly brushed my legs. Roxie smiling as she looked down. Then jumped. A sage hen elevated in that moment. Gathered herself. Clucked as she flew over the ridge. I searched the sky. It was quiet again. I took a step. Now big birds exploded into flight all around me. The air turbulent as they wheeled. Then the sizzle of wing shear at distance. Roxie turned. Saw the dart. Kyrie with wings faired rippling light waves. Sizzle became scream. I ran. At the ridge saw the desert silent beyond. Roxie came up.

Where is she?

I don't know! Did you see her?

Yes!

You saw the hit?

I saw her flare. Then she was under the ridge.

What a descent! She knew what it would take!

We looked over the desert. It was as if nothing had happened. Just the whisper of the wind. Even the song birds had fallen silent. I handed her the glasses.

Scan them around. She's got to be close.

Roxie's eyes dilated. Eye shadow smudged. Red yellow hair half-undone wisped in the wind.

Right.

I went back toward the truck. Was she alright? Had I flown her for the wrong reasons? The grouse outweighed her nine to one. Had steel spurs. I ran. Drove the truck to the crest of the ridge. Roxie off to the south. Strange how views changed. I got a signal. Hollered. Started walking down slope. Saw everything now. Dead branches. Tephra. Kyrie glared at me. Her obsidian hooks sunk in the grouse under her. Her hooked beak dripping gore. It had been a fight. She panted. Her long wings spread lacked a primary. Roxie came through the brush. Kyrie flashed challenge. Returned to the feast. The feathers of battle all around.

It was a clean strike. No way she could have finished.

Roxie picked up a primary. Leaned against me. We looked at this Pieta. Embrace of blood. I got a bottle of dark wine out of the truck. Roxie stood. The flight feather in her hatband. Brushed the dust from her hands.

Make the toast!

You. You brought us luck.

To Kyrie then.

I offered wine to the Four Directions. As I drank the first mouthful caught Roxie's eye. A flash I saw in Kyrie's. We drank. Watched her feed. She was happy. The flesh smoked on her tongue. Her long feathers already glistening. Roxie's teeth were red.

I thought you took it away.

No.

Isn't that what you do?

Some do.

What if you wanted to fly her again?

I let her eat.

Why?

Because she's a pig.

No. Why?

I turned to Roxie. Noticed the freckles across the ridge of her nose.

I want her to love me. Know I won't cheat her.

Roxie held out her cup for more wine.

You just don't want her mad at you.

You got it.

Won't she eat too much?

She will. She's a gluttony bitch. Aren't you Kyrie?

Kyrie's crop bulged. She shifted talons. Looked up at me with eyes glowing. We were happy. This moment would not come again. Maybe in some paradise we would drink forever in the Big Desert while our falcon fed. But there was no place beyond time.

How does she kill a bird so big?

Strikes with her heel at a hundred miles an hour. Think about it. Tries for head or neck. If she hits shoulder or spine she'll break a foot. Knows that. And she reads the flight. Maybe this one was a little slow.

But she fought.

She did.

We drank. She fed. Then the comedy began. When I tried to get her on the glove she took grouse in beak. Hopped away under the brush. I showed plumber's crack as I crawled after her. Got my right hand under. Lifted them. Dug out the heart. It still smoked. She had to step to the glove to get it. Presented the hen to Roxie. She swaggered. Had the bottle in one hand and the grouse in the other.

I wouldn't have given my prize so easily either!

We went back to the truck. Lay the hen on the hood. Spread the wings.

First year female. See? New feathers replace old from the trailing edge forward.

I got the buck knife. Cut off head and feet. Tossed them to

the varmints. Pulled the wing to expose wrist joint. Tossed the wings. Started the ventral cut.

She said, I thought you shucked skin and feathers so they came off together.

No. Leave it 'til you decide how to cook it.

How are you going to?

I thought you would, Darling.

How would you?

The Sho-Bans cut off strips and fry them in corn batter. It doesn't matter. It'll be good no matter what you do.

Down stuck to my bloody hands. Roxie leaned against the truck with one foot on the front tire. Held the bottle for me to drink. I did. Slipped knife from sternum to vent. Got hold of the ventral sac. Strong smell of sage boiled up with the blue grey entrails. She looked away. I was full of bravado.

Too close to the chop shop?

She shook her head. Looked away.

I turned her face with my bloody hand.

I'm sorry.

Kissed her mouth. Tasted wine. Felt the stirring come up. Made my heart beat. She let her tongue touch mine. I stood with knife in hand, my left around her waist. Leaned her against the truck. When I opened my eyes hers did. Blood on her cheek. I licked it. Returned to cutting. Slipped the entrails out. Scraped the ribs clean of lung fragments. Iced it. Roxie leaned against the hood with glass in hand. Looked over the vast silence of the desert. I stepped between her legs. She stood willingly to me. I gave her wine in sips from my mouth. She put her arms around my neck. Wildfires start small. I put my hand down her back. Slipped it around to her vent. She didn't pull away.

Not now.

We kept kissing but slower. Gave me a smile.

Got to get back to the dogs.

A lot of desert out there. A lot farther going back than coming in. She slid against me. Lay her head in my lap and snored. At the Dam Fish and Game trucks parked on the mud flats. Figures carried garbage bags. Birds littered the shore. Roxie felt the truck slow. Opened her eyes. I smoothed her hair.

All forensics, isn't it?

Yes.

On the south shore the foundations of the old townsite rose from the mud. It looked like an ancient ruin. Roxie slept all the way to Mink Creek. Twilight. The dogs paced on the porch. Their eyes shone like big red lamps. The horses galloped. Roxie sat up. Rubbed her eyes.

I must look a wreck.

You look wonderful.

I got the meat out of the cooler. She climbed the stairs. Talked to the dogs. Had already forgotten about me. They leapt against the railing and barked. I thought it strange there were no myths that earthquakes were caused by the Dogs of Hell leaping at their chains.

FIFTY THREE

Should have slipped into my berth at Kinney Creek but didn't. Decided to put Kyrie to block. Then I wanted a drink. Box cars slipped down the track. I counted to seven before the crash and repercussion. Little Thunder Town. The Office door open but I crossed to the Lizard. The bartender faced the door. The drinkers with their backs to it. Light dim. Baseball on TV. Cubs and Phillies. Cubs had a big kid whose forkball dove at the plate. Big guys biting that steamy night in Philly. Crowd restless. A guy wearing a Vietnam campaign hat watched with both hands around his drink. I sat down.

Looks like the Cubs have a pitcher!

Screw the Cubs.

Everybody likes the Cubs!

The vet kept his eyes on the TV, grey hair curling under his hat.

I hate them. North Side Republican jerks. Had a friend from Chicago roomed with three Cub fans. They were from the North side and all jerks. He was from the South Side. White Sox fan and a Democrat. Screw the Cubs.

I turned to look at him. A little guy maybe a wrestler or a

safety in High School. Hunched over a shot and a beer. Denim jacket dirty and torn at the shoulder. He lit a cigarette.

So how you been, Errol?

I turned. Saw in the beat, blue eyes the kid Billy brought by after tree climbing or rock throwing.

Gary!

Put a paw on his shoulder.

How you been!

Oh I been alright.

Man it's good to see you!

He smiled mockingly, showed missing teeth.

Didn't recognize me, huh?

I wasn't looking. Where you been?

Little bit of everywhere. You?

Back for awhile. Seeing the folks.

How they doing?

Hanging in there.

He lit a cigarette. Coughed.

Your old man. He was something. When Billy and him went at it you'd thought there'd be blood on the floor. Billy so mad he's crying.

It's their country, Dad!

You don't have it, Billy. Think you can have what you want without getting blood on your hands.

Fuck you!

We'd run. Hit the Quik Stop. He'd slip a quart of Thunderbird under his coat while I bought a pack of gum. Go up City Creek and swing from the rope that hung from the big cottonwood. Swing over that creek and drink and howl.

He took a long hit.

Then we'd go to my house. Watch Midnight Nightmare 'til he fell asleep. Couldn't sleep without a TV. I'd wait 'til it got light then wake him. We'd sneak back. Your Dad waiting for him. Had to run then. Didn't want to listen to it.

Gary squinted through the smoke.

But you were savvy, Errol. I admired that. Knew when to make tracks.

I got a cigarette out of his pack.

I did what he said.

You underestimate yourself, Errol! The idea to play Annie, Annie Over with bows and arrows? That was yours.

He leaned back, cigarette at lips, mimed pulling a bow. I remembered the old house on South Johnson. The rotting rafters. Gold leaves floating. Pulled back his collar. Saw the white scar where the arrow missed his larynx. He grinned at me sardonically.

You forgot to yell.

We must of drove your mother crazy.

It was a short trip, Errol. You know that.

We played war. Jumped from the garage. Set plastic cars afire to roll them down the ramp.

Oh! It's the end for our hero! How will he escape the inferno!

Then his mother wasn't there anymore. His dad worked in the shop. Whine of table saw. Didn't talk anymore. Just another vet the sea tossed back.

Your Dad still alive?

No.

He tapped the glass on the bar.

Or the time you decided to plant a smoke bomb in Mary Kamisa's house. Always the young scientist you were. Waited behind the hedge while Billy and I slipped in. Bad timing. Mary's little brother in bed with chicken pox!

Gary laughed. Coughed smoke.

But your Dad? Was a player. When Billy got back? Every hare brained scheme he had your Dad'd tell him it wouldn't fly. Then give him the money. Had that smile though. Billy didn't see it. But I did. I missed the old days! Y'all'd have me over for dinner. The old man pounding the table.

Every young man needs a war under his belt!

Your mother wringing her hands.

Not at dinner, Ben! Please!

I didn't want to be on that ship off Okinawa either! But I went!

Billy tossed the napkin. I'd find him standing under a tree smoking a cigarette. Hands shaking.

How do you remember this, Gary?

How do I remember?

He looked at his gnarled dirty hands with long uncut fingernails.

You kill me, Errol. You really do. Your pretty mom always dressed up. Big nice house. Chandelier over the table. Your mother treating me like I was part of something fine.

He looked at me through a veil of smoke.

And Billy was my brother.

Tapped the shot glass on the counter.

Barkeep! So we got that apartment on Third behind the Odyssey. Parties every night. Babes coming over. Billy never lacked women. You know that. I'd be asleep. Hear this terrible scream. Billy crying. His eyes staring but not seeing anything.

I'm here, Billy! It's Ok! Go back to sleep!

Finally he'd look at me. Turn over and go back to sleep.

I said, I thought that happened when he came back.

No. Before. Babes learned not to sleep over. Didn't bring their toothbrush.

Did he say what it was?

He said it was something invisible and indefinable. Would come down the hall. He would feel its presence. Something vague and indefinable like a light. But he knew its intent.

It's alright, Billy. I'm here!

But there was no protection for him. He knew it. And then he just up and enlisted. Oh my Lord! Ended up at Quang Tri! Come back that Christmas with that look in his eyes! I tried to get him to smoke weed but he wouldn't. And your old man? Had a different look too. Billy standing beside him like he don't exist. Because you know, Errol? Nobody knows what they love in this world or how hard 'til it up and kicks them in the gut! They look at the sky. Say, What? What's this? But you know, Errol? Sitting here right now I'm not totally sure what your Dad was so scared of.

He loved Billy.

You think?

More than anybody.

Bartender set a shot and a beer on the bar. Gary tossed a wad of bills. Jerked his thumb at me.

Hit him too.

He raised the shot glass. Tossed it down. Grinned at me sardonically.

Always admired you Errol. How you did what you wanted. How you wanted. And in your time!

Vietnam like the back surge of a river when it's breached the levee. Billy backing me against the wall. What I wouldn't forgive. What Gary couldn't forgive. Because I'd withheld what he had not to give. I stood.

And I'll keep on.

What, Errol? Somebody stick a Kotex up your butt and light the fuse?

He tapped the cigarette pack on the bar. Looked at the TV. Hands shook. Hadn't expected to run into me anymore than I him. Change of pitchers. Relief man with jacket over his shoulders. Gary coughed. Stubbed out the cigarette.

Don't sweat it, man. You didn't kill your brother. Just turned your back on him.

I wasn't in the country.

No. You weren't.

He got off the stool like an old man.

See you later, Errol.

I said, How long you in town for?

Just passing through.

He started to walk out. Rolled on a bad hip. Fuzzy hair sticking out under his campaign hat. I remembered his baseball cap and big smile. Chipped front tooth. Always nicer than he had to be. Let me tag along. If the fishing was no good we'd climb the hillside. Talk and throw rocks. He and Billy climbed trees. I'd watch them scramble in the upper branches. Whoop and pound their chests. Days in early spring he'd show up with mitt and bat. We made the rounds.

Can Larry come out and play? No? We're sorry, Mrs. Larkin. We'll let him play First!

Larry came out reluctantly holding his pride and his mitt. If we picked up Nate we'd have five. Always a kid or two at the trailer court. With five you had pitcher, catcher and two in the outfield. Though the wind blew raw we made a lot of noise! I got older. Kids fell back to where kids without money go. Money the presence when you talked about where you were going that night. Gary turned.

Didn't think it funny, Errol? Billy killing himself the day after Father's Day?

I watched myself in the mirror. Tossed the shot down. Went out into the street.

Gary!

The name echoed. Box cars clashed atop Center Street. Warning bells clanged. Moon above Kinport. White and cold as a ghost but one that had pull. I took Second Street past the Black cliffs. Turned into the lot for Scabland Trail. Trains approached Cheyenne Crossing crying like heartache.

I woke in the afternoon. It had snowed. Fire maples red in the ravines. The hills white like white women with blood flowing between their legs. Driving onto the Plain saw the rapids where the Snake divided around Eagle Rock. Got the shotgun out. Descended to the river. Cottonwoods stood yellow on black against the sun. Wind scattered leaves. Bitter musk of dead leaves and carp. Heard whistling. Mallard and teal flying with the wind. The sun slanted red through the trees. A figure hunched in a heavy coat, shotgun at his side. Billy turned and grinned.

Where you been, Errol? I been waiting all day!

I knew he had. Hadn't taken a shot. He cocked his head.

Bring anything?

I pulled the flask out of my game pocket. He grinned.

One thing I could always depend on you for!

We sat on the spit of land. The wind roughened river red. Ducks flashed out of the sun wings whistling. We watched. Guns boomed upriver. The Snake acted angry as it coiled against the wind. Waves slapped against the bank. Billy nudged me. Nodded upriver. Five bluebills swerved into the wind. Looked for harbor. We had it. They cupped wingtips and dropped. Billy gave me that big grin. We crept through the brush. Roar of wind and trees covered our approach. Stepped together onto the bank. The bluebills fanned for purchase. I swung the barrel along the lead male as he righted himself for flight. Two fell. Billy popped the smoking cartridges. Slapped me on the back. We got in the skiff. Billy rowed. Ducks flew overhead in successive flights. It was as if all the birds of the river decided to fly that evening. Geese barked. Flew in perfect formation into the sun. It didn't seem to be falling anymore. Held transfixed above the blood red river. Everything drenched in red light. Trees, cliffs on the far side of the river, the bellies of the geese as they flew. Herons. Pelicans rising and dipping in unison. Great shoals of wings and voices. Eagles with slotted wing tips circled high above. And the sun went down. The cliffs loomed dark. Low dark clouds approached with flashes of lightning.

Billy! Where we going?

When he turned he was old and beat. His eyes grim.

It was like this, Errol. Just this time of day. We were coming back late. Intelligence said Charlie not in the vicinity. But he was. With Kalishnikovs. The boat splintered before I heard the fire. What it was doing to the men. They weren't standing. Just keeled over. You know what a slug that size does to a man?

I know.

Billy's mouth turned bitter. Eyes feral.

You don't, Errol! Why do you say it?

His face distorted with hate.

Why don't you just say you're sorry!

Sorry!

The word echoed against the cliffs. He lowered the shotgun at me, tears streaming. I whipped my arms. They had become wings. Swept me upwards. High in the wind. I was looking down. He raised the shotgun at me. Then knelt in the prow of the skiff as if in prayer.

Billy!

The name wailed in the wind. Ten thousand ton rail car came out of the Gap. Crying for Cheyenne Crossing. Reverberation rumbled. Shook the cliffs. I crawled out. Sat on the tailgate. The freight passed. The sun threw Chink's shadow across the valley. Red wings quarreled in the willows. The signal light at Cheyenne Crossing jingle jangled.

FIFTY FOUR

Mickey Angel with his feet up like some bad angel.

What do you know, Errol?

Not enough.

Look like something the cat drug in.

Easy now. What you reading?

Eternal Frontier. Says there were cheetah in the Pahsimeroi. The reason prairie goats got so fast.

I sat down.

People talk about bringing them back.

Not too cold?

Cats tolerate cold but are predictable. Like you Mickey Angel. Show up at the door every day at eleven. I watched a lion in the Owyhees use the same trail every evening on the minute! Cheetahs in Africa are in trouble for the same reason. Have a behavioral loop that turns them to inbreeding. Mountain lions don't. They found lions in North Dakota had been tagged in Idaho.

Mickey Angel put his hands behind his head.

Daddy's going to kill them.

You got it.

He said, They did a study Down County. Tracked honcho day and night. So were on the ridge at dawn when Elder Anderson made the rounds in the tin can compound below. Crazy. Families intermarrying down there for a hundred and fifty years.

I said, Good for the smart boys at the University of Utah.

Right. Sexual politics is interesting though. Leaf nosed bats are polygamous. Control of the harem linked to roosting sites. What the boys fight over. We found males with chipped teeth and scars that held the same roost for five years! After the young were weaned the females took off.

Vegas? Palm Beach?

Highlands to the north. Males stay at the roost. The females go into estrous twice a year so come back knocked up. The home boys smell it but we observed no spousal abuse or infanticide. Know why? Didn't matter who they'd shacked up with the year before. They fluttered around like they just couldn't make up their minds! Were all like that. Had solidarity. Then they'd pick a mate

and settle in. Males that were aggressive to females drifted out of
the gene pool. That's how we saved the Highlands. Showed it
essential to the gene pool. Same with the Yellowstone bears.

You might not know it, Mickey Angel. Before you got
here? They went and culled the adult males indiscriminately.

When was that?

Mid seventies.

I drifted through the stacks. Under Metaphysical a woman
read with her legs folded under her. Beautiful women always
lurking at Mickey Angel's. The white skin of her lower back
showed. I got a squirrel out of the freezer. Warmed it in hot water.
Gave it. When I went to the front of the store she handed Mickey
Angel a stack of books.

Have you heard about a haunted pond by Inkom?

No.

I stopped at the Red Pony on my way from Salt Lake. Have
you been there?

On my way back from the Rock.

The Rock?

The ski hill.

She roused her shoulders sensuously.

A railroader was at the bar. He told me of a haunted pond
along the tracks. When a train goes by you can see the headlights
shining from the depths. He said it's a ghost train.

A lot of those.

The woman pointed with her red fingernail.

That's what this book is about. Psychic events trapped by
bodies of water. It could happen don't you think? Holographs work
that way. If there were enough emotional energy--if the ghosts had
no other place to go--they would be trapped in that water.

A train?

The woman raised her chin. Shook her long, glossy black
hair. Narrowed her wolf grey eyes.

The train was in the mind of the spirits! Don't you see?
They were on a journey!

I turned the spinner rack.

You've heard about the water babies?

I just moved here. Finding my way around.

On the Reservation is a place called the Bottoms. Has springs and creeks that flow into the Snake. The Indians don't build there because it's sacred. To an Indian that means something. Best fishing and hunting in the country. But if you stay too late and get lost? You might hear water babies.

I want to go there!

It'll cost you. The Trespass Permit is seventy five a day. And it's arbitrary which is worse. Water babies or the Tribal Police.

She shone her eyes on me. I'd seen that look before. Joan of Arc before the castle of the Black Prince.

You know your way around?

Mickey Angel tallied the books.

He worked for Fish and Game. Give him your number.

I said, We could take a canoe. Slip up one of those creeks. If you didn't mind being on the Snake after dark.

She gave me her number.

I saw Blackfoot Reservation on the map. Are they different than the Shoshone?

That's the Blackfoot Reservoir. It's confusing. People say they were out on the Rez. You don't know what they're talking about.

The dark lady left with her package. Mickey Angel looked ruefully at the out of town check.

Thanks for the assist, Mickey Angel.

A canoe on the Snake, Errol? Take out some insurance.

I will. What do you say we go for a hike this afternoon? Close up early.

Misko asked me to come by. He's bending iron for a fence. Fun to watch if you want to come along.

I might.

Crossed the tracks at Benton Street. Looked at the ribbons of steel shining to the Gap. The long ridges Billy and I used to climb. The time we saw two sand hills doing the pas de deux. Gazing into each other's eyes. Saw us and lifted. Sailed without a wing beat over the town and Chink's Peak! Leonard with his white hair and white T-shirt read Thucydides in the shadow of the porch. In the library I read Robert Stuart's account of his return along the

Snake. Found Reznor, Hoback and Miller naked as the Indians
fishing at Salmon Falls.

> The fish began to jump soon after sunrise
> When the Indians in great number with their spears
> Swim in to near the center of the Falls;
> Where some placing themselves on the rocks
> And others to their middles in the water
> Dart on all sides--assail the salmon
> Who struggling to ascend and perhaps exhausted
> With repeated efforts become easy prey.
> And Miller said that they stopped here
> On the way down--it was in the afternoon
> By far the best spearing time
> When to his utter astonishment the Indians
> In a few hours killed some thousands of fish;
> And one salmon in particular leaped
> In the presence of himself and others
> From the commencement of the foam
> At the foot of the pitch
> Clear over all the waterfalls
> Which in my opinion
> Must have been over thirty feet!

I dreamed. When my wife and I first married we camped in
the Jarbidge. Narrow canyons with little creeks tumbling out. As
we made camp a truck parked on the road. Redneck came over
carrying a five foot rattlesnake. That was the strange thing about
the Jarbidge. The diamondbacks. After the climb we went into
town. A big Indian with long braids lay in the shade of the
cottonwoods in the park. Gave us the big hello. He was dressed in
high Shoshone style. Long sleeve shirt with braided leather
gauntlets. Black vest and turquoise choker. Hid the bottle behind
the tree. Followed us into the saloon. Bartender gave him the evil
eye. Had grizzled eyebrows and cold blue eyes. Just moose and
bear stared from the walls. I ordered gin and tonic before he could
think about it too long. Joseph liked it very much. His breath
scourged juniper bark. My wife moved to the other side of me.

I said, When did salmon last come up the Bruneau?

When I was a little kid.

When was that?

1955. I went with my Uncle 'cause nobody else would go.

Shimmer fish are gone, old man!

We'd go up Salmon Falls Creek. Less Indians there. So we headed north then east then south. Lot of fires that year. Fires all over the desert. Got our poles out and walked down to the river. No shimmer fish. Stayed several days until we ran out of food. My uncle could not believe they had not come back. Then we ran out of food. The people laughed at us.

Ain't no fish no more, old man! They put in a dam on the Snake. There ain't no shimmer fish in Salmon Falls Creek!

Joseph nursed his gin and tonic.

Every summer my uncle asked me if I wanted to go catch big fish. Like it was an honor. I would tell him how high that dam was. That fish could not jump over it. He didn't believe me. It was impossible to him they wouldn't come back. Every summer he'd come to me.

Time to catch big fish!

We'd load the truck and head north. Then east. When we got to Salmon Falls Creek we camped and waited for the shimmer fish to arrive.

Joseph laughed.

And you know? They never did!

I ordered another round. Joseph wanted music.

You like Georgie Possum?

I do.

He put quarters in the juke box. Georgie sang, Today I Started Loving You Again. Joseph put his hands out to my wife. I shook my head.

I get first dance, Joseph.

We dance across the plank floor with the sparkle trees out the window. The bartender looked on morosely. Joseph swayed on the barstool and clapped. All in all it was a good party.

When I arrived at the store Mickey Angel was high-grading books. A Pioneer League ticket stub drifted to the floor.

How hot is it out there?

Getting frost out. Thinking of a cold one. You want one?

It's a little early.

Not by much.

Your liver might like the respite.

There's a side effect to not drinking they don't talk about, Mickey Angel. Sobriety.

I picked up the stub. Great Falls Electrics vs. Pocatello Braves. July 3rd 1965. The click when the ball skipped the bat. Fly balls arcing through the field lights. If you got one you held on.

You heard about Swedes didn't you? What they do with them when they die?

Mickey Angel shook his head. Filed the fore edge of a paperback with an emery board. Blew puffs of dust.

They wait five years to dig them up. Shoot the liver to make sure it's dead.

He grinned that crooked grin.

Still, Errol. You look a little off color.

It's the heat, Mickey Angel.

You don't know heat.

Elroy came from behind the stacks in his coveralls and red handkerchief.

Feeding a fire box up a long grade in the Rockies on a summer day gave you a feeling for heat.

Didn't know you were a fireman, Elroy.

Started out. You'd be shoveling coal. Fire box blazing. Sun banging on the iron. If you forgot the leather apron that morning when you kissed the wife the new levis she bought you would be cinders by evening.

He leaned against a shelf.

Or neglect the heavy gloves when you went to pick up a crow bar you'd left on the track just a moment before. Blisters made a coal shovel difficult to handle. Or grab hold of the railing on the sun side.

The UP had to keep rolling.

It did. But turned a lot of hard drinking railroad men to religion.

How's that?

Got an idea how hot it could get. How much you want for this fine book, Michael.

The Romany Rye by George Borrow.

Six bucks with your intellectual discount.

What's that?

Twenty per cent.

Gracious! That all I get? But you were talking about drinking. Now Alcohol Bronson. There was a man who liked to drink! Was at Tarawa. You kind of wanted to go the other way if you saw him in the bar. He'd put his big paw on your shoulder if he was out of money. Then you'd see him prowling the alleys with the whips and the jingles. Then you didn't see him at all.

You seen Alcohol?

No.

Diesel Steens wiped down engines. We called him Diesel because of the kerosene he smelled of. He'd walk into the Wyoming, order a drink, start to light a cigarette? Boys dove for cover! So they dried out a boiler. Told Diesel to go in and wipe it down. Win Perkins was standing on the siding when he heard the scream. Swore Diesel exited the boiler and established footing fifteen feet below without having touched metal at any time!

Elroy slapped his thigh with the paperback.

Alcohol was sitting in the corner of the boiler. They figure he made six round trips to Ogden duty free.

Must not of looked too good.

No. But he found a place unavailable to whatever was looking for him.

A ravaged face looked in the window. Carl Wagner checking to see who was in place. Came in.

Hot out there! I thought it was fall!

You must have had some hot rides back from Vegas, Carl.

One. Had acquired controlling interest in a mine outside Tonopah.

How was that?

All it took was a pair. Told the guy I'd take it if he showed me where it was. He had the map. I drove. Last point of reference I remember was the Paiute Reservation. Blue mountains got closer then farther away. I like the desert but you're looking at a landscape where things have been dying of thirst for a hundred million years.

He looked at the map. Then a blue ridgeline in the distance.

That was the road back there.

We doubled back. Heat waves. The road ahead gone. I hit the brakes. Walked to the edge of a crater.

This on your map?

Walked the Caddy down the escarpment and up the other side. Came to a dry valley then another. At Highway 93 saw the Skull and Crossbones for the road we'd just traveled. My skin crawled all the way to Ely! But after a drink and a steak I felt better. Traded it in when I got to Twin Falls.

Jesus, Carl!

It was a brand new DeVille!

So you ran a game in Vegas?

Just played the tables.

Black Jack?

Poker. Had a friend who was dealing at a club off the Strip. Told me he'd kick some cards my way.

What was it called.

The Flame.

Jesus, Carl. You were clipping the Mob?

No. This guy was good. You got to understand. There are three classes of dealers in Nevada. In the event you decide to play there. The first can do anything with the cards at any time. The second can do that for any amount of money no matter who is watching.

Carl got slowly to his feet.

The last does all the above and still sleeps at night.

FIFTY FIVE

Mickey Angel closed the blinds. We went into the street. The sun blazed on the mountains.

You sure I'm invited?

He said make sure I brought you.

We better get beer.

He said he had some.

It's a long drive, Mickey Angel.

We stopped at the Grapevine. Got Bass IPA which was

drunk by Eduard Manet. Drove Highway 91 to the Gunsight.
Misko's house was on the highway. Tall steel door swung apart to
reveal firebox with propane jets. Misko, naked to the waist, leather
gloved, lay the rods so they splayed like bandilleros.

What's up?

Thought you needed supervision.

Yeah right.

Or a beer.

Thanks, Bird Man.

The shop baked. The sun banged on the roof. The firebox
spit fire. Why he had chosen a hot afternoon to forge I didn't know.
Tilted his head back to drain the IPA. His sweat streaked torso
gleamed. Ropes in those forearms. Limped over to a tall machine
with a shaft three inches square. Flipped the switch. The mighty
engine built compression. Ka-whump! Ka-whump!

That come from the Naval Ordnance Plant?

Misko went to the firebox where the rods glowed white.

Ship hammer on the Sioux City. They'd be at sea a year.
Repairs had to be made. After the Sioux City was scrapped it sat
around the yard at Bremerton.

What'd it cost you?

The freight was two grand if that gives you an idea.

The rods glowed white. He grabbed one and carried it to the
Hammer. Set the tip on the anvil. Stepped on the pedal. The
hammer dropped in unison to the piston. Misko feathered its
descent so the rod flashed whiter hot as it flattened. Carried it to
the old-style anvil. His muscles rippled as he shaped it with a
twenty pound mallet. Checked length and shape against a stencil.
Carried it back to the Hammer. Heat was tremendous as he turned
rod into spear point. Ka-whump! Ka-whump! I went outside.
Ninety in the shade. Trees coughed shadows. The high ravines
turned red. The skree was steep. Deer criss-crossed it on paths ten
thousand years old. I listened to the bang of Odin's Hammer. High
wail of a freight came out of Inkom. Blared for Black Rock
Crossing. Freight cars thundered. Great Northern. Wisconsin
Central. Rio Grande and Santa Fe. Old iron. Old blood. Saw the
mountain again. North facing. I could cross track and pasture.
Climb Indian Peak. Hadn't brought water. Always a mistake.

Mickey Angel and Misko came out. Had a towel over his shoulders. Put his feet on a lawn chair. Pointed at the front of the yard.

The fence is going up across there. Spanish points for when the Militia comes.

I didn't know you handled iron.

My grandfather was a machinist.

In the blood.

You got it. But like he told me. You want to be on the rolling stock, son. They need you sooner than later.

What else he tell you?

Misko grunted.

When a sucker got luck? The player don't stand a chance.

You want to keep that in mind.

You do.

Two kids with fifty pound packs and a dog on a leash came down Highway 91. Heads down. Arms glistening with sweat. Looked over.

How far to town?

Ten miles.

The one looked at the other. Started walking. Mickey Angel stood up.

I'll give you a lift.

They looked at the jeep. He had straps with metal teeth that clamped when you pulled. Strapped the backpacks atop. They were big boys. Got in the back seat with knees pulled up. The dog leaned his snout out the window.

How'd you end up in Inkom?

Darren said, Man, look at those cliffs. So we jumped. Took us all day to find out it was posted.

The only access is Green Canyon on account of the ski hill.

Well it was a easy town to get into but hard to get out of.

Where you headed?

Montana.

That's tricky.

We passed the cross of the Church of the Assumption. Swung north on Yellowstone. Sign said Blackfoot-Idaho Falls. The main track to Montana ran a block west. Mickey parked at Lewis and Clark Park.

That's the Main Line. Trains have to take it slow because of
the crossing streets to Yellowstone. There's a warehouse district a
quarter mile up where you can hide out under the trees.

They shouldered the packs. Walked into the shade of the
park. The dog trotted behind them. We went west. Sign pointed
right for American Falls. The volcano showed its teeth.

I said, Could have told them about those cliffs.

They wanted to get to Montana.

We went to the store. I sat with my back against the
Adventure shelf. Books men wrote about rivers, mountains. Saw
the kids with their dog waiting along the track. Handed Mickey
Angel a Bass.

Seen Johanna lately?

No.

She loves you, Mickey Angel.

Don't want to talk about it.

Wish I had a woman love me like that.

We're alright at love, Errol. Better at fighting.

We just need guidance, Mickey Angel. Find somebody else
then! She'd cut bait.

He got up. Started pushing books trim to the shelving.

I don't want to hurt her. Already have enough.

I checked the black and white cards on the spinner rack.
The one by Ansel of boulders under the ridge.

You love her, Mickey Angel. You'll help two kids get to
Montana but you won't help yourself.

I heard the thump of fore edges hitting the back of the
shelves.

When she gets going, Errol? It's like I'm at Lunch Counter.
I'm going down and I'm not coming up.

I said, Social workers are like that.

He sat down. Tilted an IPA. Looked at the brick mortared
above the shelving.

Historical Preservation wants this building to last a
thousand years. Trains will take it down long before that.

A train moaned as it turned the corner at the Volcano. Past
the hobo jungle and the petroglyphs on Kraft Hill. Like an old horn

player using a mute. A few minutes later it blared twice as the hogger warned the yard men. Mickey Angel dropped his chin.

Seems to me you should worry more about yourself.

How's that?

Misko.

Misko doesn't bother me. I like him.

You don't know. Bridger told me about the time Reece Lindblad shunted a couple of cars on the snake in front of him.

What's a snake?

It crosses the yard with switches at the tracks so you can get from one side to the other. Misko hit the brakes. Went looking for him. Reece is a big guy. Jumped from the cab with a right cross. Misko just shook his head.

Got a bad knee though.

Mickey Angel stared at me. The horn blared. Not a thing of dream anymore. Ten thousand tons rumbling on eight hundred forged steel wheels. All the names of the American Empire that were no more. Wisconsin and Southern. Reading and Detroit. Great Northern. Now double stacked container cars coded Japan, Germany, China. The implacable rumble of money and fate rattled the door frame. The horn turned pretty again as it neared the Black Cliffs. It probably was the trains that rattled the books off the shelf. I twirled the empty bottle.

But you don't know, Mickey Angel. Might be the moon. Pulling the books off your shelves.

Next morning I went to the Meat Market. Red light at the steam room. Shadow in the corner. Salvatore Cruz.

You know, Cruz? You Mexicans are missing a trick with this cock fighting.

Yeah? How's that?

Could be selling lean, fight hardened fryers on the national market. Think of the advertising.

I remember the first cock fight I went to. Wore three pairs of pants.

How's that?

I thought they were going to make me fight with my cock! Always cock fighting at the labor camp. Worst beating Grandad gave me was when I killed his prize rooster. Forgot to take the gaffs off.

How'd you kill a rooster by not taking the gaffs off?

I killed him by putting him in the ring! Forgot to take them off when I threw him back with the hens. Would of worked too. Grandad would of thought he fucked himself to death. Don't know why he knew it was me. When he got through Grandma hit me a couple of licks.

You weren't born! You were kicked out of a stone wall by a donkey!

Might be true. When I got a dog I named him Spic. White dudes would see me on the street.

Hey Spic!

I'd turn to Spic.

You going to let them talk to you like that, Spic?

Cruz shook his head.

Every Sunday I go to St. Joe's. Get down on my knees. Thank the Lord for everything he gave me. Put another five in and beg forgiveness for what I had to do to get it. See you, Bro.

Old silverbacks entered the pool. Some waded at the shallow end. It looked like a painting by Goya. Death at the Spa. LaVon stayed in the Jacuzzi. He'd been a Hell's Angel over Germany. The Big Eighth had forty thousand killed in two years. The Ninety Sixth Bomber Group at Pocatello had the highest casualty rate in the Big Eighth the first six months of 1944. LaVon came back to become not a Hell's Angel but a Mormon carpenter. Lay back letting the water warm his legs. Foam popped at his gray, withered chest.

How you doing today?

I said, It's a beautiful day.

It is. But I got to mow the lawn.

Good for you to do a little work.

I always worked. When I was your age I worked hard every day. Came home and my wife cooked me a good dinner and I slept good. Now I cook for her.

What do you cook?

I make blueberry muffins. Maybe fry up some bacon.

Sounds like you cook pretty good.

A silver back paced in the pool.

Put a little ground pecan in there. That goes really good.

Just grind it up a little?

You bet.

LaVon turned back to me.

Basques make great muffins. And lamb of course. My uncle had eighty acres in sugar beets out in Tyhee. He'd let this Basquo pasture his sheep when he brought them out of the hills. They'd eat the sugar beet tops and what came out the other end was fertilizer. He had the best sugar beets in the country. One day I rode my horse out there. Basquo sitting at the stoop of his wagon.

Tie up your horse, boy! Stay for dinner!

I did. He went into the shade of the wagon. Cut a strip from a downer sheep that was lying there.

You going to eat that downer sheep?

We don't eat the live ones!

LaVon splashed water over his chest.

It was real good but I didn't go there for dinner again. Downer sheep. Didn't seem to hurt him though.

Didn't want to eat what you could sell.

No.

That was in the fall?

When they brought them out of the hills. Kept them until the price went up. That was what my uncle's pasture was for.

I remembered Mother telling me about when they lived in Shoshone. Stock cars rolled in from Camas Prairie. All night long bellowing and crying. Mamas looking for babies. Lambs and calves looking for their mamas. She couldn't sleep for it. Memorized her lessons. Taught herself math. That was the winter of the Asian Flu. The black draped Ford truck. The steam drill banging at the frozen ground of the graveyard.

I padded to the locker room. The old soldier stared at the foam in the Jacuzzi. USA Today on the bench. Military Mistakenly Recruits Gays! Had logged onto a website for young men. I showed it to the old soldier.

He said, Don't ask. Don't tell.

I heard the Gurkhas had a gay tradition.

I don't know about that. But there was a Gurkha regiment in Korea when I was there. They were really something.

I heard they scared even the Turks, I said. Something going back to World War I.

The Chinese weren't happy about it. The Gurkhas waited 'til night. Slipped into their barracks. Wouldn't kill them all. Just slit a few throats. Very bad for morale. Wake up to see your buddy with his throat cut.

And not a sound.

Well maybe the soft gurgling of blood bubbling up.

I walked back from the New Waitress-New Attitude Café. Looked at the blue ridge at the end of the Main. Remembered the Basque sheepherder that had been in those hills too long. When they 86'd him from the Wyoming he stood on the street bellowing like a bull. When the cops arrived he wrapped his arms around a lamppost. They called in a five hundred horse power back-hoe with tow chain. Remembered too the Basque picnic at Mountain Home. The men staggering from one end of the park to the other with hundred pound weights in each arm. Wore white shirts, red scarves and shiny black pants. Cottonwoods yellow against the blue sky. The women chattering as they turned strips of lamb marinated in red sauce on the huge grills. Men played cards under the trees. Slammed down winners or cursed their luck. I'd watched for hours in the sheep camps. Never got a clue what the rules were. Guessed the cases changed with the time of day, the season or the saint. I tried to charm one of the women.

What could I do to get the recipe?

You can't.

There must be some trial I could undergo!

It's impossible. Nobody knows what it is. Grandma makes it in a big pot. That's her over there.

Grandma sat under a tree with her white hair, her black shawl and her cane.

It's a lot of work for her but she won't let anybody help.

Grandma! We say. You don't have to work so hard! Tell us how to do it!

If I told you how to do it you wouldn't need me anymore. You'd leave me alone to die!

That's not true, Grandma!

But she won't. She is indomitable.

The woman had lustrous black hair. Wore a white blouse and gold crucifix at her throat. Brushed the fragrant marinade on the sizzling meat. I didn't think Grandma's stance unreasonable. She'd been beautiful once too. Had she revealed the recipe on her deathbed? I crossed the tracks at Benton Street. Dove went well with tomatoes and thyme but it took a lot to cover a grill. I liked watching them fly more than killing them. Went to the Library. Read Stearn's History of Westward Journeying Naturalists. My book would be an inventory of the animals in Southeast Idaho according to historical records. The petroglyphs on Marsh Creek would be included. I read and took notes. Returned past the houses built in the twenties. Prairie-style mansions with out-jutting roof beams. Colonials with green shutters. As I walked the Overpass saw a swirl of white by the Train Station. Gulls. Flew like swallows. All the way to the horizon that was the only place trees stood by the tracks. I guessed a huge swarm of flying insects were moving with the wind. They had rested up in the trees. The Franklin gulls caught them at the crossing. I turned south along the Greenway. A figure hobbled ahead. Campaign hat. Frayed denim jacket.

Gary!

I saw him cock his head but he kept walking. Disappeared around a stand of trees. I ran.

Gary! Talk to me!

Birds answered. The river flowed quietly. I peered into the coyote willow of the levee. Saw the culvert pipe above flood line. He was in there. Lying on his back with his eyes open. Waiting for me to go away.

FIFTY SIX

I got two bottles of Willamette Valley Zinfandel at the Grapevine. Crossed the tracks toward Gunsight. The road curved toward Slate Mountain with its sheer rock in shadow. Horses stood at the fence whisking their tails. Accompanied me. Big woofy dogs romped on the porch. Raised their black muzzles to bark. Roxie came out to scold. Wore her hair down with a printed shirt open at the throat. I

had the wine in one hand and the bones in the other. She opened
the gate using her butt to block the dogs. They circled. Looked at
me angrily. The bitch nuzzled my crotch. Snorted. I tore the
cellophane. Right away they had eyes for the sweet, white bones.
Galileo took the five pound bone and crouched at the corner. The
bitched took theirs and disappeared. The horses stamped and
whinnied, prancing with their long tails flying. Roxie gave me a
big smile. When she reached for the wine I gave it but moved
inside her hands. Held her hard but kissed soft. Reached up and
opened her blouse. She broke away. Stared at me with pale green
eyes.

 Whatever happens it doesn't mean anything, right?
 Right.
 I pulled her back. Imprisoned her arms as I pulled the
blouse off her shoulders. Kissed her throat. Her hair poured over
me.
 We have to go inside.
 Her bed viewed Slate Mountain. I glimpsed horses running.
Lifted her onto the bed. Kissed and nipped her breasts. Pulled her
pants down and whiffed her vent. She lay against the pillows like
women have been doing for ten thousand years. In tents and above
city streets. Her throat was fragrant with roses and horse manure.
Her eyes closed. I kept mine open. Went to that place where the sea
moves on the rocks, the waves coming from a long ways away.
They were getting higher. I tried to kiss her but she turned her head
and arched her back. I was vaguely conscious of howling. The gate
to the bedroom crashed. A hundred twenty pound dog leapt on the
bed. Her cold, bristly muzzle sniffing my butt. The others arrived.
The bed general with huge dogs, heavy paws, anxious yipping.
Roxie reached out both hands. Stroked and talked to them. They
lay on both sides. Had brought their bones. I heard the crunching of
bone on bone. The cold wet of a cow bone against my leg. We
started again. Roxie put her hands in my hair and smiled. After
awhile it arrived from a ways away. Quiet at first then bigger and
stronger. Rushed through the rocks. She set her heels and arched
her back. Her eyes glazed. The blood rushed to her face. She
opened her mouth and gave a cry. The dogs gnawed at their bones.
I snuggled my nose at the hollow where throat joined wishbone.

The bed moved as Galileo got up. Picked up the bone in his mouth and hopped to the floor. Out the window birds sang. The dogs left. Lay around the bedroom with their heads bent to the bones held in their forepaws. Roxie stroked my back with her fingernails.

They just needed information.

I guess they got it.

I pulled her against me. Smelled her perfume and the real smell of her body mixed with mine.

What do you think they found out?

She laughed.

You must be clean!

In the morning it was cool. The sun burned the mist from Scout. I got the bathing tray out of the truck. Roxie stood in her nightgown on the deck. Watched Kyrie bathe.

Call when you get back!

I will.

Pigeons swirled above Main. Divided and wheeled away. At the Meat Market a silver back and his son talked in the steam room.

Saw twenty nice bulls but it never worked out. Saw wolves too. Passed within twenty yards.

What'd they do?

Just looked at me and moved on.

See any bear?

No. Have in the past. Used to be a lot of bear in that country. Wolves must of took them out.

Wolves take out bear?

The only thing a bear can do against wolves is go up a tree.

Right. We used to watch coyotes in the Lamar. They're gone now. Well. This is too hot for me.

They left. I thought it a good thing they brought the wolf back. Like the Jew she could be blamed for everything. I got a six pack at Ridleys. Headed past the Reservoir. With Piilar Butte on the horizon she made a stunning descent. A hard strike. I released the second pigeon. She beat me back to Pocatello. Mickey Angel was talking to a silver hair. A tall kid came up with a paperback. Mickey Angel stood and shook his hand.

Peter! I didn't see you come in! How you doing?

Peter grinned. Looked behind him then back at Mickey
Angel.

Two weeks leave. Just seeing the folks. Then I go back.

Where?

Afghanistan. They're moving us around.

You getting to see any Ports of Call?

Peter checked behind him. The tall shelving. The door. I
moved into his line of vision so he could keep track of me too. He
laughed.

The Belfast cops weren't too happy about us packing heat
around town.

I wouldn't guess. Buy you a beer?

Peter brightened. Wasn't old enough to buy beer. Mickey
Angel went to the back. Peter fidgeted. Checked the door for
incoming. Didn't look like he was packing. Mickey Angel came
back with a Budweiser. Peter drank it quick. I don't remember
what he said. Just paid for his book and left. Silverhair nodded.

That was a good thing you did, Michael.

You never know though do you?

No.

Silverhair turned in his chair.

Well looky there.

The old gambler strolled past the Round Up Room.

See that guy? Carl Wagner. Smarter dead ten years than
most men alive. In the fifties he ran the biggest game in North
America.

Vegas?

West Yellowstone! You'd go up there middle of winter.
Snow piled on both sides of the road. Thirty below. When you got
there all the stores boarded up except the lodge. The only cars big
limousines with license plates from Illinois and Wisconsin. Big,
gloomy-eyed guys in long, black coats standing at the door. They
didn't want you there. Carl hasn't told you that?

No.

Funny thing.

I thought about Carl. How many blinds he kept track of in
that club off the Strip. How much you showed. What you kept

quiet. We were all like that. It was just where the payoff was. Whether you were able to get it. What you wanted. What you had to have.

Borrow your phone, Mickey Angel?

Take it outside.

I did. Across the intersection the old stone building where Billy had his aquarium. Got answering machine. Strolled along Union Pacific Avenue. A freight rolled in. Hogger hit the brakes. Box cars boomed like big guns. The old buildings shook. Billy walking out of the Oasis Bar. Jumped. Glanced to see if I'd noticed. Grinned and slapped me on the back.

Had to keep your eye on those guns, Errol. Sent a two hundred pound jacketed explosive twenty five miles!

I grinned. When you're young you think everything works out. It does. He walked past the freight entrances to the old buildings, hands in his pockets.

You could really reach out and touch somebody.

I drove out Bannock Highway. Indian Peak in the evening light. Stopped in front of the condo. The old man at the window with Black Max in his arms.

How you doing, Dad?

He looked at me with worry. Max barked and squirmed but the old man had him locked in.

Alright. How are things with you?

Just making rounds. Where's Mom?

Your mother?

Yes.

She's gone.

Where'd she go?

She left me.

What do you mean?

We had a fight. She's gone.

He turned to look out the window.

She's not coming back.

She's coming back, Dad. Just went to the store or something.

No. She's not.

I found the vodka. Poured a double.

What was the fight about?

Just a misunderstanding. One of those things that happen between a man and a woman.

She's coming back, Dad.

He shook his head. Held Black Max. Stared out the window. I stood beside him. Looked out. Felt sorry for him. Never thought that possible. Had wanted to ask what he said to Billy that Father's Day. Get some consciousness of what had been done. What I'd been accomplice to. But the old man was broke down and scared as a little kid. There would be no denouement.

She's coming back, Dad. Don't worry.

The clocks chimed near and distantly. After awhile headlights shone on the house. Mother's car turned into the driveway. I left. On Bannock Highway two saloons faced each other at the old bridge. The Blue Heeler had leather traces and rusting traps hanging on the walls. Through the pool table light I saw two cowboys at the bar. Rodeo on TV. They watched without talking. I ordered a Budweiser. A bull ride came on. I could tell by the way they watched it they were riders. Small men wearing crisp white shirts. Clean vests, pressed levis and good boots. The way their shoulders sloped showed they were strong as little bulls themselves. It came out of the chute. Commenced to high side. The rider reached for the rafters with his glove. One. Two. Three. He was airborne. Came down flat on his back with chaps flying. The bull stood on his front hooves. The clowns waved banners, flags, ladies' pink panties. It twisted quick as you please. Almost horned one. The clown dodged. Ran for the barrier. Nobody looked at the rider anymore as the clown flew over it. Shook as the bull hit. Commercial flashed on. Diesel 350's with lots of torque. John Mellencamp sang, This Is My Country! Rider next to me raised his glass. Let out a whoop.

He almost got him, didn't he?

Charlie Jensen, wasn't it?

If it was, Charlie might be losing a step.

Let's hope he got it back.

So this is a rerun? I said.

Oh yeah. You can tell by the boys wearing mustaches. Around here they grow one for the May drive. Whether they can or not. Shave it off when they come back.

Of cowboys I liked bull riders best. Their manners were impeccable.

So the bull knows Charlie, huh?

Oh yeah. And he don't like him.

You guys in town for the rodeo?

Yes sir.

I heard they're talking of making y'all wear a helmet like a bike rider wears.

They're talking.

Think they'll do it?

No sir.

Would it be safer?

It might. But you got to think about it. And if you do? You come to the conclusion that helmet would add three pounds to your head for the bull to use to twist it off.

Your head.

Yes sir.

What's more dangerous? A bull fight or a bull ride?

I can't tell you. I just know in a bull fight the bull has never seen a man with a cape. Or a lance. Don't know what they are. Got that one shot to figure out how to kill that man. Usually that don't happen 'til his throwing hump been sliced. Then he realizes it's the man in the funny outfit he wants to go after. But it's too late. You're through if you're the bull. In bull riding the bull has seen it all before. He's seen the rider and he's seen the clown and there ain't no killing him. If he's good and can put on a show? He's worth money. Big money.

How much?

Say fifty thousand dollars.

That's a lot of money.

A lot of money. Now a bull rider? Or a clown? He's expendable.

And the bull knows him.

Knows him. Wants to hurt him. And how to get it done.

The bull rider sipped his whiskey.

But like they say. You got to expose yourself to the money.

The TV flashed back to the rodeo. They returned their

attention to it. I liked them and respected them. So when I finished my beer and got up to leave I didn't wish them luck.

{The End}